W9-BKE-616

VEIL OF MIDNIGHT

MIDNIGHT RISING

MIDNIGHT AWAKENING

"This is one of the best paranormal series around. Compelling characters and good world-building make this a must-read series."
—Fresh Fiction

"One of the Top 10 Best Romance Novels of 2007."
—Selected by the Editors at Amazon.com

"Ms. Adrian's series just gets better and better.... *Midnight Awakening* was exactly what I hoped it would be then so much more.... I'm intrigued and without a doubt completely hooked."
—Romance Junkies

"Vengeance is the driving force behind this entry in the intense Midnight Breed series.... Things look bad for the characters, but for the readers it's nothing but net!"
—*Romantic Times*

KISS OF CRIMSON

"Vibrant writing heightens the suspense, and hidden secrets provide many twists. This dark and steamy tale ... is a winner and will have readers eager for the next Midnight Breed story."
—Romance Reviews Today

KISS OF MIDNIGHT

Also by Lara Adrian

Taken by Midnight

MIDNIGHT BREED SERIES
BOOK EIGHT

LARA ADRIAN

 A DELL BOOK • NEW YORK

Taken by Midnight is a work of fiction. Names, characters, places,
and incidents are the products of the author's imagination or are used
fictitiously. Any resemblance to actual events, locales, or persons,
living or dead, is entirely coincidental.

A Dell Mass Market Original

Copyright © 2010 by Lara Adrian, LLC
Excerpt of *Deeper Than Midnight* © 2010 by Lara Adrian, LLC

Published in the United States by Dell, an imprint of The Random House
Publishing Group, a division of Random House, Inc., New York.

DELL is a registered trademark of Random House, Inc., and the colophon
is a trademark of Random House, Inc.

This book contains an excerpt from the forthcoming book *Deeper Than
Midnight* by Lara Adrian. This excerpt has been set for this edition only
and may not reflect the final content of the forthcoming edition.

ISBN 978-0-440-24527-8
eBook ISBN 978-0-440-33968-7

Cover design: Jae Song

Printed in the United States of America

www.bantamdell.com

2 4 6 8 9 7 5 3 1

To Heather Rogers,
for being awesome

ACKNOWLEDGMENTS

With each book I write, I am reminded how fortunate I am to be working with so many talented, conscientious people who comprise my publishing and literary representation teams, both in the United States and abroad. Thank you very much for everything you do. It's a privilege to be working with all of you.

Special thanks to my home team for basic care and feeding, and for handling all the countless things that tend to slip while I'm happily immersed in my writing. I couldn't do this without your love and support.

And to my readers, a debt of gratitude for embracing my characters and for honoring me with the gift of your time and friendship whenever you sit down to read one of my books. I hope you continue to enjoy the ride!

Taken by
Midnight

CHAPTER
One

Life . . . or death?

The words drifted at her through the darkness. Detached syllables. The rough scrape of a flat, airless voice that reached into the heavy drowse of her mind and forced her to come awake, to listen. To make a choice.

Life?

Or death?

She groaned against the cold plank floor beneath her cheek, trying to bar the voice—and the relentless decision it demanded—from her mind. This wasn't the first time she'd heard these words, this question. Not the first time in the space of some endless hours that she'd peeled one heavy eyelid open in the frigid stillness of her cabin home and found herself looking into the terrible face of a monster.

Vampire.

"Choose," the creature whispered thinly, the word drawn out in a slow hiss. He crouched over her where she lay, curled and shivering on the floor near the cold fireplace. His fangs glistened in the moonlight, razor sharp, lethal. The tips of them were still stained with fresh blood—her blood, drawn from the bite he'd made in her throat only moments before.

She tried to get up, but couldn't rouse her weakened muscles to so much as flex in response. She tried to speak, managed only a rasping moan. Her throat felt as dry as ash, her tongue thick and listless in her mouth.

Outside, the Alaskan winter roared, bitter and unforgiving, filling her ears. No one to hear her screams, even if she'd tried.

This creature could kill her in an instant. She didn't know why he hadn't. She didn't know why he kept pressing her for the answer to a question she had been asking herself nearly every day of her life for the past four years.

Ever since the accident that had taken her husband and little girl.

How often had she wished she'd been killed along with them on that icy stretch of highway? Everything would have been so much easier, less painful, if she had.

She could feel a silent judgment in the unblinking, inhuman eyes that fixed on her in the dark now, searingly bright, pupils as thin as a cat's. Intricate skin markings tracked all over the creature's hairless head and immense body. The webbed pattern seemed to pulse with violent color as he watched her. Silence lengthened while he patiently examined her as he might an insect trapped inside a glass jar.

When he spoke again, this time his lips did not move. The words penetrated her skull like smoke and sank deeply into her mind.

The decision is yours, human. Tell me what it will be: life, or death?

She turned her head away and closed her eyes, refusing to look at the creature. Refusing to be part of the private, unspoken game he seemed to be playing with her. A predator toying with his prey, watching it squirm while he decided whether to spare it or not.

How it shall end depends on you. You will decide.

"Go to hell," she slurred, her voice thick and rusty.

Iron-strong fingers clamped onto her chin and wrenched her around to face him once more. The creature cocked his head, those catlike amber eyes emotionless as he drew in a rasping breath, then spoke through his bloodstained lips and fangs.

"Choose the course. There isn't much time now."

There was no impatience in the voice that growled so near her face, only a flat indifference. An apathy that seemed to say he truly didn't care one way or the other what answer she gave him.

Rage boiled up inside her. She wanted to tell him to fuck off, to kill her and get it over with, if that's what he meant to do. He wasn't going to make her beg, damn it. Defiance churned in her gut, pushing anger up her parched throat and onto the very tip of her tongue.

But the words wouldn't come.

She couldn't ask him for death. Not even when death might be the only escape from the terror that held her now. The only escape from the pain of having lost the two people she'd loved the most and the seemingly pointless existence that was all she had left since they'd been gone.

He released her from his hard grasp and watched with maddening calm as she sagged back down to the floor. Time stretched, impossibly long. She struggled to summon her voice, to speak the word that would either free her or condemn her. Crouched near her still, he rocked back on his heels and cocked his head in silent consideration.

Then, to her horror and confusion, he extended his left arm and sliced one talonlike fingernail deep into the flesh above his wrist. Blood spilled from the wound, dripping wetly, scarlet raindrops falling to the wood planks below him. He thrust his finger into the open cut, digging into the muscle and tendons of his arm.

"Oh, Jesus. What are you doing?" Revulsion squeezed her senses. Her instincts clamored with the warning that something awful was about to happen—maybe even more awful than the horror of her captivity with this nightmarish being who'd taken her prisoner hours ago to feed off her blood. "Oh, my God. Please, no. What the hell are you doing?"

He didn't reply. Didn't even look at her until he'd withdrawn something minuscule from within his flesh and now held it pinched between his bloodied thumb and finger. He blinked slowly, a brief shuttering of his eyes before they pinned her in a hypnotic beam of amber light.

"Life or death," the creature hissed, those ruthless eyes narrowing on her. He leaned toward her, blood still dripping from the self-inflicted wound in his forearm. "You must decide, right now."

No, she thought desperately. *No.*

A rushing surge of fury rolled up from somewhere

deep inside her. She couldn't hold it down. Couldn't bite back the burst of rage that climbed up her raw throat and exploded out of her mouth in a banshee scream.

"No!" She raised her fists and pounded on the hard, inhuman flesh of the creature's bare shoulders. She thrashed and raged, railing at him with every ounce of strength she could summon, relishing in the pain of impact every time her blows landed on his body. "Damn you, no! Get the hell away from me! Don't touch me!"

She beat her fists against him again, over and over. Still, he crept closer.

"Leave me alone, damn it! Get away!"

Her knuckles connected with his shoulders and the sides of his skull, blow after blow, even as a heavy darkness began to descend on her. It felt thick around her, a sodden shroud that made her movements sluggish, her thoughts muddled in her mind.

Her muscles slackened, refusing to cooperate. Yet still she pounded on the creature, striking slowly, as though she were throwing punches in the middle of a black, tar-filled ocean.

"No," she moaned, eyes closed to the darkness that surrounded her. She kept sinking deeper. Farther and farther into a soundless, weightless, endless void. "No...let me go. Damn you...let me go..."

Then, when it seemed as though the darkness that enveloped her might never release her, she felt something cool and moist pressed against her brow. Voices speaking in an indiscernible jumble somewhere over her head.

"No," she murmured. "No. Let me go..."

Summoning the last shred of strength and will she possessed, she threw another punch at the creature holding her down. Thick muscle absorbed the blow. She latched on to her captor then, grabbing at him, clawing at him. Startled, she felt the crush of soft fabric bunching in her hands. Warm, knit wool. Not the clammy, bare skin of the creature who'd broken into her cabin and held her prisoner.

Confusion fired a warning shot in her sluggish mind. "Who . . . no, don't touch me . . ."

"Jenna, can you hear me?" The deep, rolling baritone that sounded so near her face was somehow familiar to her. Oddly soothing.

It beckoned to something deep within her, gave her something to grab hold of when she had nothing but fathomless dark sea around her. She moaned, still lost, but feeling a slender thread of hope that she might survive.

The low voice she somehow needed desperately to hear came again. "Kade, Alex. Holy shit, she's coming out of it. I think she's finally waking up."

She sucked in a hard breath, gasping for air. "Let me go," she murmured, uncertain she could trust her feelings. Uncertain she could trust anything now. "Oh, God . . . please, no . . . don't touch me. Don't—"

"Jenna?" Somewhere nearby, a female voice took shape above her. Tender tones, sober concern. A friend. "Jenna, honey, it's me, Alex. You're all right now. Do you understand? You're safe, I promise."

The words registered slowly, bringing with them a sense of relief and comfort. A feeling of peace, despite the chill terror that was still washing through her veins.

With effort, she dragged her eyelids open and blinked away the daze that clung like a veil to her senses. Three forms hovered around her, two of them immense, unmistakably male, the other tall and slender, female. Her best friend from Alaska, Alexandra Maguire. "What...where am..."

"Shh," Alex soothed. "Hush now. It's all right. You're somewhere safe. You're going to be okay now."

Jenna blinked, worked to focus. Slowly, the shapes standing around her bedside became human. Half sitting up, she realized her fists were still full of the wool sweater worn by the larger of the two males. The immense, fierce-looking African American with the skull-trimmed hair and linebacker shoulders, whose deep voice had helped pull her out of the drowning terror of her nightmare.

The one she'd been pounding on relentlessly for God knew how long, mistaking him for the hellish creature who'd attacked her in Alaska.

"Hey," he murmured, his broad mouth curving gently. Dark brown, soul-searching eyes held her waking gaze. That warm smile quirked with unspoken acknowledgment as she loosened her death grip on him and settled back onto the bed. "Glad to see you decided to join the land of the living."

Jenna frowned at his light humor, reminded instead of the terrible choice that had been forced on her by her attacker. She exhaled a rasping sigh as she struggled to absorb her new, unfamiliar surroundings. She felt a bit like Dorothy waking up in Kansas after her trip to Oz.

Except the Oz in this scenario had been a seemingly endless torment. A horrifying trip to some kind of blood-soaked hell.

At least the horror of that ordeal had ended.

She glanced at Alex. "Where are we?"

Her friend came near and placed the cool, damp cloth to her forehead. "You're safe, Jenna. Nothing can hurt you in this place."

"Where?" Jenna demanded, feeling an odd panic beginning to rise. Although the bed she lay on was plush beneath her, abundant with fluffy pillows and blankets, she couldn't help but notice the clinical white walls, the fleet of medical monitors and digital readers assembled all around the room. "What is this, a hospital?"

"Not exactly," Alex replied. "We're in Boston, at a private facility. It was the safest place for you to be now. The safest place for all of us."

Boston? A private facility? The vague explanation hardly made her feel better. "Where's Zach? I need to see him. I have to talk to him."

Alex's expression paled a bit at the mention of Jenna's brother. She was silent for a long moment. Too long. She looked over her shoulder to the other man standing behind her. He was vaguely familiar to Jenna, with his spiky black hair, penetrating silver eyes, and razor sharp cheekbones. Alex said his name on a quiet whisper. "Kade..."

"I'll get Gideon," he said, offering her a tender caress as he spoke. This man—Kade—was obviously a friend of Alex's. An intimate one at that. He and Alex belonged together; even in Jenna's rattled state of consciousness, she could sense the deep love that crackled between the couple. As Kade stepped away from Alex, he shot a look at the other man in the room. "Brock, make sure things stay calm in here until I come back."

The dark head nodded once, grimly. Yet when Jenna glanced up at him, the big man called Brock met her gaze with the same gentling calm that had greeted her when she'd first opened her eyes in this strange place.

Jenna swallowed past a knot of dread that was climbing steadily into her throat. "Alex, tell me what's happening. I know I was...attacked. I was bitten. Oh, Jesus...

there was a . . . a *creature*. It somehow got into my cabin and it attacked me."

Alex's expression was heavy, her hand tender where it came to rest on Jenna's. "I know, honey. I know what you went through must have been awful. But you're here now. You survived, thank God."

Jenna closed her eyes as a raw sob choked her. "Alex, it . . . *it fed off me*."

Brock had moved closer to the bed without her notice. He stood directly beside her and reached out to stroke his fingertips along the side of her neck. His big hands were warm, and impossibly tender. It was the oddest sensation, the peace that emanated from his light caress.

Part of her wanted to reject his uninvited touch, but another part of her—a needy, vulnerable part that she hated to acknowledge, let alone indulge—could not refuse the comfort. Her banging pulse slowed under the gentle rhythm of his fingers as they traveled lightly up and down the length of her throat.

"Better?" he asked quietly as he drew his hand away from her.

She exhaled a slow sigh with her weak nod. "I really need to see my brother. Does Zach know I'm here?"

Alex's lips pressed together as an aching silence grew long in the room. "Jenna, honey, don't worry about anything or anybody else right now, okay? You've been through so much. For now, let's just focus on you and on making sure you're well. Zach would want that, too."

"Where is he, Alex?" Despite the fact that it had been years since Jenna wore the badge and uniform of an Alaska State Trooper, she knew when someone was sidestepping the facts. She knew when someone was trying to protect another person, trying to spare them from pain.

As Alex was doing with her this very moment. "What's happened to my brother? I need to see him. Something's wrong with him, Alex, I can see it in your face. I need to get out of here, right now."

Brock's big, broad hand came toward her again, but this time, Jenna swept it away. It had only been a slight flick of her wrist, but it knocked aside his hand as though she'd put all of her strength—and then some—into the motion.

"What the hell?" Brock's eyes narrowed, something bright and dangerous crackling in his dark gaze, there and gone before she could fully register what she was seeing.

And at that very moment, Kade returned to the room, two other men with him. One was tall and lean, athletically built, his disheveled crown of blond hair and rimless, pale blue sunglasses that rode low on the bridge of his nose giving him something of a geeky mad-scientist vibe. The other, dark haired and grim faced, strode inside the small room like a medieval king, his very presence commanding attention and seeming to suck all of the air out of the place.

Jenna swallowed. As former law enforcement, she'd been accustomed to facing down men twice her size without flinching. She'd never been easy to intimidate, but looking at the likely thousand-plus pounds of muscle and brute strength that now surrounded her in these four men—to say nothing of the distinctly lethal air they seemed to wear as casually as their own skin—she found it damned hard to hold the scrutinizing, almost suspicious, gazes that were locked onto her from each man in the room.

Wherever she'd been brought, whoever these men were whom Kade associated with, Jenna got the very distinct impression that the so-called private facility wasn't a hospital at all. It sure as hell wasn't a country club.

"She's been awake only for a few minutes?" asked the blond, his voice carrying just the barest hint of an English accent. At Brock and Alex's joint nods, he walked up to the bed. "Hello, Jenna. I'm Gideon. This is Lucan," he said, gesturing to his mountain of a companion, who now stood next to Brock on the other side of the room. Gideon frowned at her over the top of his shades. "How do you feel?"

She frowned back at him. "Like a bus ran me over. A bus that apparently dragged me from Alaska all the way to Boston."

"It was the only way," Lucan interjected, command palpable in his level, ask-no-permission tone. He was the leader here, no question about that. "You hold too much information, and you needed specialized care and observation."

She didn't like the sound of that at all. "What I need is to be back at home. Whatever that *monster* did to me, I survived it. I won't be needing any kind of care or observation because I'm fine."

"No," Lucan countered grimly. "You are not fine. Far from it, in fact."

Although it was said without cruelty or threat, an icy cold dread seeped through her. She looked to Alex and Brock—the two people who'd assured her just a few minutes ago that she was all right, that she was safe. The two people who'd actually managed to make her feel safe, after waking up from the nightmare that she could still taste on her tongue. Neither of them said a thing now.

She glanced away, stung and not a little afraid of what that silence might truly mean. "I have to get out of here. I want to go home."

When she started to swing her legs over the edge of the bed to get up, it wasn't Lucan or Brock or any of the other huge men who stopped her, but Alex. Jenna's best friend moved to block her, the sober look on her face more effective than any of the brute strength standing ready elsewhere in the room.

"Jen, you have to listen to me now. To all of us. There are things you need to understand . . . about what happened back in Alaska, and about the things we still need to figure out. Things only you may be able to answer."

Jenna shook her head. "I don't know what you're talking about. The only thing I know is that I was held captive and attacked—bitten and bled, for God's sake—by something worse than a nightmare. It could be out there still, back in Harmony. I can't sit here knowing that the monster that terrorized me might be doing the same hideous things to my brother or to anyone else back home."

"That won't happen," Alex said. "The creature who attacked you—the Ancient—is dead. No one in Harmony is in danger from him now. Kade and the others made sure of that."

Jenna felt only a ping of relief, because despite the good news that her attacker was dead, there was still something cold gnawing at her heart. "And Zach? Where is my brother?"

Alex glanced toward Kade and Brock, both of whom had moved closer to the side of the bed. Alex gave the faintest shake of her head, her brown eyes sad beneath the layered waves of her dark blond hair. "Oh, Jenna . . . I'm so sorry."

She absorbed her friend's words, reluctant to let the understanding sink in. Her brother—the last remaining family she had—was dead?

"No." She gulped the denial, sorrow rising up the back of her throat as Alex wrapped a comforting arm around her.

On the wave of her grief, memories roared to the surface, too: Alex's voice, calling to her from outside the cabin where the creature lurked over Jenna in the darkness. Zach's angry shouts, a current of deadly menace in every clipped syllable—but menace directed at whom? She hadn't been sure then. Now she wasn't sure it mattered at all.

There had been a gun blast outside the cabin, not even an instant before the creature leapt up and hurled itself through the weather-beaten wood panels of the front door and out to the snowy, forested yard. She remembered the sharp howl of her brother's screams. The pure terror that preceded a horrific silence.

Then . . . nothing.

Nothing but a deep, unnatural sleep and endless darkness.

She pulled out of Alex's embrace, sucking back her grief. She would not lose it like this, not in front of these grim-faced men who were all looking at her with a mix of pity and cautious, questioning interest.

"I'll be leaving now," she said, digging deep to find the don't-fuck-with-me cop tone that used to serve her so well as a trooper. She stood up, feeling only the slightest shakiness in her legs. When she listed faintly to the side, Brock reached out as if to steady her, but she righted her balance before he could offer the uninvited assist. She didn't need anyone coddling her, making her feel weak. "Alex can show me the way out."

Lucan pointedly cleared his throat.

"Ah, I'm afraid not," Gideon put in, politely British, yet unwavering. "Now that you're finally awake and lucid, we're going to need your help."

"My help?" She frowned. "My help with what?"

"We need to understand precisely what went on between you and the Ancient in the time he was with you. Specifically, if there were things he told you or information he somehow entrusted to you."

She scoffed. "Sorry. I already lived through the ordeal once. I have no interest in reliving it in all its horrible detail for all of you. Thanks, but no thanks. I'd just as soon put it out of my mind completely."

"There is something you need to see, Jenna." This time, it was Brock who spoke. His voice was low, more concerned than demanding. "Please, hear us out."

She paused, uncertain, and Gideon filled the silence of her indecision.

"We've been observing you since you arrived at the compound," he told her as he walked over to a control panel mounted on the wall. He typed something on the keyboard and a flat-screen monitor dropped down from the ceiling. The video image that blinked to life on the screen was an apparent recording of her, lying asleep in this very room. Nothing earth-shattering, just her, motionless on the bed. "Things start to get interesting around the forty-three-hour mark."

He typed a command that made the clip advance to the spot he mentioned. Jenna watched herself on-screen, feeling a sense of wariness as her video self began to shift and writhe, then thrash violently on the bed. She was murmuring something in her sleep, a string of sounds—words and sentences, she felt certain, even though she had no basis to understand them.

"I don't get it. What's going on?"

"We're hoping that you can tell us," Lucan said. "Do you recognize the language you're speaking there?"

"Language? It sounds like a bunch of jibberish to me."

"You're sure about that?" He didn't seem convinced. "Gideon, play the next video."

Another clip filled the monitor, images fast-forwarding to a further episode, this one even more unnerving than the first. Jenna watched, transfixed, as her body on-screen kicked and writhed, accompanied by the surreal soundtrack of her own voice speaking something that made absolutely no sense to her.

It took a lot to scare her, but this psych ward video footage was just about the last thing she needed to see on top of everything else she was dealing with.

"Turn it off," she murmured. "Please. I don't want to see any more right now."

"We have hours of footage like this," Lucan said as Gideon powered down the video. "We've had you on twenty-four-hour observation the whole time."

"The whole time," Jenna echoed. "Just how long have I been here?"

"Five days," Gideon answered. "At first we thought it was a coma brought on by trauma, but your vitals have been normal all this time. Your blood work is normal, too. From a medical diagnostic standpoint, you've merely been…" He seemed to search for the right word. "Asleep."

"For five days," she said, needing to be sure she understood. "Nobody just falls asleep for five days straight. There must be something else going on with me. Jesus, after all that's happened, I should see a doctor, go to a real hospital."

Lucan gave a grave shake of his head. "Gideon is more expert than anyone else you can see topside. This thing cannot be handled by your kind of doctors."

"My kind? What the hell does that mean?"

"Jenna," Alex said, taking her hand. "I know you must be confused and scared. I've been there myself very recently, although I can't imagine anyone going through what you have. But you need to be strong now. You need to trust us—trust *me*—that you are in the best hands possible. We're going to help you. We'll figure this out for you, I promise."

"Figure what out? Tell me. Damn it, I need to know what's really going on!"

"Let her see the X rays," Lucan murmured to Gideon, who typed a quick series of keys and brought the images up on the monitor.

"This first one was taken within minutes of your arrival at the compound," he explained, as a skull and upper spinal column lit up overhead. At the topmost point of her vertebrae, something small glowed fiercely bright, as tiny as a grain of rice.

Her voice, when she finally found it, held the barest tremor. "What is it?"

"We're not sure," Gideon replied gently. He brought up another X ray. "This one was taken twenty-four hours later. You can just make out the threadlike tendrils that have begun to spread outward from the object."

As Jenna looked, she felt Alex's fingers tighten around

her own. Another image came up on-screen, and in this one, the tendrils extending from the brightly glowing object appeared to lace into her spinal column.

"Oh, God," she whispered, reaching up with her free hand to feel the skin at her nape. She pressed hard and almost gagged to register the faint ridge of whatever it was embedded inside her. "He did this to me?"

Life . . . or death?

The choice is yours, Jenna Tucker-Darrow.

The creature's words came back to her now, along with the recollection of his self-inflicted wound, the nearly indiscernible object he'd plucked from within his own flesh.

Life, or death?

Choose.

"He put something inside me," she murmured.

The slight unsteadiness she'd felt a few moments ago came back with a vengeance. Her knees buckled, but before she ended up on the floor, Brock and Alex each had an arm, lending her their support. As terrible as it was, Jenna could not tear her eyes away from the X ray that filled the screen overhead.

"Oh, my God," she moaned. "What the hell did that monster do to me?"

Lucan stared at her. "That's what we intend to find out."

CHAPTER
Two

Standing in the corridor outside the infirmary room a couple of minutes later, Brock and the other warriors watched as Alex sat down on the edge of the bed and quietly comforted her friend. Jenna didn't break down or crumble. She let Alex wrap her in a tender embrace, but Jenna's hazel eyes remained dry, staring straight ahead, her expression unreadable, glazed with the stillness of shock.

Gideon cleared his throat, breaking the silence as he glanced away from the infirmary door's small window. "That went well. Considering."

Brock grunted. "Considering she just came out of a five-day Rip van Winkle to learn that her brother is dead, she's been leeched by the granddaddy of all bloodsuckers, brought here against her will—and oh, by the way, we've found something embedded in your spinal cord that probably didn't originate on this planet, so congratulations, on top of all that, there's a good chance you're part Borg now." He exhaled a dry curse. "Jesus, this is messed up."

"Yeah, it is," Lucan said. "But it would be a hell of a lot worse if we didn't have the situation contained. Right now, all we need to do is keep the female calm and under close observation until we gain a better understanding of the implant itself and what, if anything, it could mean to us. Not to mention the fact that the Ancient must have had a reason for placing the material inside her in the first place. That's a question that begs an answer. Sooner than later."

Brock nodded in agreement with the rest of his brethren. It was only a slight movement, yet the flexing of his neck muscles set off a fresh round of pain in his skull. He pressed his fingers into his temples, waiting for the knifelike agony to pass.

Beside him, Kade frowned, jet-black brows furrowing over his wolfy, silver eyes. "You okay?"

"Peachy," Brock muttered, irritated by the public show of concern, even though it was coming from the one warrior who was as tight as a brother to him. And even though the hard stab of Jenna's trauma was shredding him from the inside out, Brock merely shrugged. "No big thing, just par for the course."

"You've been eating that female's pain for almost a week straight," Lucan reminded him. "If you need a break—"

Brock hissed a low curse. "Nothing wrong with me that a few hours back out on patrols tonight won't cure."

His gaze strayed to the small panel of clear glass that looked in on the infirmary room. Like all of the Breed, Brock was gifted with an ability unique to himself. His talent for absorbing human pain and suffering had helped keep Jenna comfortable since her ordeal in Alaska, but his skills were just a Band-Aid at best.

Now that she was conscious and able to provide the Order with whatever information they needed about her time with the Ancient and the alien material embedded inside her, Jenna Darrow's problems were her own.

"There's something more you all need to know about the female," Brock said as he watched her carefully swing her bare legs over the edge of the bed and stand up. He tried not to notice how the white hospital gown rode halfway up her thighs in the instant before her feet touched the floor. Instead he focused on how readily she found her balance. After five days of lying flat on her back in an unnatural sleep, her muscles absorbed her weight with only the smallest tremor of instability. "She's stronger than she should be. She can walk without help, and a few minutes ago, when it was just Alex and me in the room with her, Jenna was getting agitated about wanting to see her brother. I went to touch her and calm her down, and she deflected my hand. Tossed me off like no big thing."

Kade's brows rose. "Forgetting the fact that you're Breed and have the reflexes to go along with it, you've also got about a hundred pounds on that female."

"My point exactly." Brock glanced back at Lucan and the others. "I don't think she realized the significance of what she'd done, but there's no mistaking the power she threw at me without really trying."

"Jesus," Lucan whispered tightly, his jaw rigid.

"Her pain is stronger now than it has been before, too," Brock added. "I don't know what's going on, but everything about her seems to be intensifying now that she's awake."

Lucan's scowl deepened as he glanced at Gideon. "We're certain she's human, and not a Breedmate?"

"Just your basic *Homo sapiens* stock," the Order's resident genius confirmed. "I asked Alexandra to conduct a visual scan of her friend's skin right after they arrived from Alaska. There was no teardrop-and-crescent-moon birthmark anywhere on Jenna's body. As for blood work and DNA, all of the samples I took came back clear, as well. In fact, I've been running tests every twenty-four hours, and there's been nothing notable. Everything about the woman to this point—aside from the presence of the implant—has been perfectly mundane."

Mundane? Brock barely refrained from scoffing at the inadequate word. Of course, neither Gideon nor any of the other warriors had been present for the head-to-toe body search performed on Jenna upon her arrival at the compound. She'd been racked with pain, drifting in and out of consciousness from the time Brock, Kade, Alex, and the rest of the team who'd joined them in Alaska had made the trip back home to Boston.

Given that he was the only one who could level her out, Brock had been drafted to stay at Jenna's side and keep the situation under control as best as it could be. His role was supposed to have been purely professional, clinical and detached. A specialized tool kept close at hand in case of an emergency.

Yet he'd had a startlingly unprofessional response to the sight of Jenna's unclothed body. It had been five days ago, but he remembered every exposed inch of her ivory skin as though he were looking at it again now, and his pulse kicked at the memory.

He recalled every smooth curve and sloping valley, every little mole, every scar—from the ghost of a c-section incision on her abdomen, to the smattering of healed puncture wounds and lacerations that peppered her torso and forearms, telling him she'd already come through hell and back at least once before.

And he'd been anything but clinical and detached when Jenna lapsed into a sudden convulsion of agony in the moments after Alex had finished searching in vain for a birthmark signifying that her friend was a Breedmate like the other women who lived at the Order's compound. He'd placed his hands on both sides of her neck and drawn the pain away from her, all too aware of how soft and delicate her skin was beneath his fingertips. He fisted his hands at the thought as it rose up on him now.

He didn't need to be thinking about the woman, naked or otherwise. Except now that he'd gone there, he could think of damned little else. And when she glanced up and caught his gaze through the glass of the little window in the door, an unbidden heat went through him like a flaming arrow.

Desire was bad enough, but it was the odd sense of protectiveness serving as a chaser that really threw him off kilter. The feeling had begun in Alaska, when he and the other warriors first found her. It hadn't faded in the days she'd been at the compound. If anything, the feeling had only gotten stronger, watching her fight and struggle through the strange sleep that had kept her unconscious since she'd come out of her ordeal with the Ancient in Alaska.

Her frank gaze still held his from across the infirmary:

cautious, almost suspicious. There was no weakness in her
eyes, nor in the slight tilt of her chin. Jenna Darrow was
clearly a strong female, despite all she'd been through,
and he found himself wishing she'd been a mess of tears
and hysteria instead of the cool, in-control woman whose
unflinching stare refused to let him go.

She was calm and stoic, as brave as she was beautiful,
and it sure as hell wasn't making her less intriguing to
him.

"When was the last time you ran blood work and
DNA?" Lucan asked, the grave, low-voiced question giving Brock something else to focus on.

Gideon pushed back his shirtsleeve to check his watch.
"I drew the last sample about seven hours ago."

Lucan grunted as he pivoted away from the infirmary
door. "Run everything again now. If the readings have
changed so much as an iota from the last sample, I want
to hear about it."

Gideon's blond head bobbed. "Given what Brock has
told us, I'd also like to take some strength and endurance
measurements. Any information we can gather from
studying Jenna could be crucial to figuring out what exactly we're dealing with here."

"Whatever you need," Lucan said grimly. "Just get it
done, and fast. This situation is important, but we also
can't afford to lose momentum on our other missions."

Brock inclined his head along with the other warriors,
knowing as well as any of them that a human in the compound was a complication the Order didn't need when
they still had an enemy on the loose—namely Dragos, a
corrupt Breed elder whom the Order had been pursuing
for the better part of a year.

Dragos had been working in secret for many decades,

under more than one assumed identity and within clandestine, powerful alliances. His operation had grown numerous and long-reaching tentacles, as the warriors were discovering, and every one of those grasping arms was working in concert toward a single objective: Dragos's complete and total domination over both the Breed and humankind alike.

The Order's primary goal was his destruction and the swift, permanent dismantling of his entire operation. The Order meant to take Dragos out at the roots. But there were complications to that goal. He had all but vanished recently, and there were, as always, layers of protection in front of him—secret allies within the Breed nation, maybe outside of it, too. Dragos also had an unnumbered army of skilled assassins at his command, every one of them born and bred specifically for killing. Deadly Breed males who were direct progeny of the otherworlder who, until his escape to Alaska a few weeks ago and subsequent death, had been under Dragos's command.

Brock glanced into the infirmary room where Jenna had begun to pace back and forth like a caged animal. To say the Order had their hands full at the moment was putting it mildly. Now that she was awake, at least his part was over. His talent had seen Jenna through the past week; where she went from here would be up to Gideon and Lucan to decide.

Inside the room, Alex pivoted away from her friend and approached the door. She opened it and stepped out to the corridor, her brown eyes soft with concern under the dark blond bangs that fringed her forehead.

"How's she doing?" Kade asked, moving toward his woman as though gravity pulled him there. They were a newly mated pair, having met during Kade's mission in

Alaska, but looking at the warrior and his pretty bush pilot Breedmate, it seemed impossible to Brock that they had only been together for a couple of weeks. "Does Jenna need anything, babe?"

"She's confused and upset, understandably," Alex said, moving into the shelter of Kade's body just as he had done with her. "I think she'll feel better after a long shower and some fresh clothes. She says she feels stir crazy in the room and wants to take a walk to stretch some of the tightness out of her legs. I told her I would ask if it was all right."

Alex looked to Lucan as she said it, directing the request to the Order's oldest member, its founder and leader.

"Jenna is not a prisoner here," he replied. "Of course she is free to wash and dress and walk around."

"Thank you," Alex said, gratitude brightening some of the uncertainty in her eyes. "I told her she wouldn't be kept here as a prisoner, but she didn't seem to believe me. After what she's been through, I guess that's not surprising. I'll go tell her what you said, Lucan."

As she turned to slip back into the infirmary, the Order's leader cleared his throat. Kade's mate slowed and swung a glance over her shoulder, some of the wind already leaving her sails as she met Lucan's stern look. "Jenna is free to walk about and do most anything she likes—so long as someone is with her, and so long as she doesn't try to leave the compound. See that she has whatever she needs. When she's ready for her walk around the compound, Brock will take her. I'm putting him in charge of her well-being. He'll make sure Jenna doesn't lose her way."

Brock had to work to bite back the curse that rose to his tongue.

Just frigging great, he thought, wanting like hell to reject the continued assignment that would keep him in close quarters with Jenna Darrow.

Instead he acknowledged Lucan's order with a nod.

CHAPTER
Three

Jenna's hands were fisted as she shoved them deep into the pockets of the belted, white terry robe that covered her thin hospital gown. Her feet swam in the new, but extra-large, man-size slippers Alex had retrieved out of a cabinet drawer in the infirmary room where Jenna had awakened less than an hour ago. She shuffled beside her friend, walking along a lighted, marble-white corridor that snaked and twisted in a seemingly endless maze of similar walkways.

Jenna felt oddly numb, not just from the shock of hearing that her brother was dead but from the fact that the nightmare she'd awakened from had not ended with her survival. The creature that had attacked her in her cabin might have been killed, as she'd been informed, but she wasn't free of its hold.

After what she saw in the X-ray images and on the video feed from the infirmary, she knew with a bone-deep dread that part of that fanged monster still held her in its ruthless grasp. She should be screaming in terror for that knowledge alone. Deep down, fear and grief roiled. She clamped a hard lid on her bubbling hysteria, refusing to show that kind of weakness, even to her best friend.

But there was a true calmness inside her, one that had been with her in the infirmary room—since the moment Brock had put his hands on her and promised she was safe. It was that reassurance as well as her own determination to soldier on that kept her from breaking down as she walked the labyrinth of corridors with Alex.

"We're almost there," Alex said as she led Jenna around another corner, toward another long stretch of gleaming hallway. "I thought you'd be more comfortable getting cleaned up and dressed in Kade's and my quarters rather than the infirmary."

Jenna managed a vague nod, although it was hard to imagine that she might be comfortable anywhere in this strange and unfamiliar place. She walked cautiously, her rusty cop instincts prickling as she passed unmarked room after unmarked room. There wasn't a single exterior window in the place, nothing to indicate where the facility was located, nor what might lie beyond its walls. No way to tell even whether it was day or night outside.

Above her head, tracking the length of this corridor like the others, small black domes concealed what she guessed must be surveillance cameras. It was all very state-of-the-art, very private, and very secure.

"What is this place, some kind of government building?"

she asked, voicing her suspicions out loud. "Definitely not civilian. Is it some kind of military facility?"

Alex slid her a hesitant, measuring glance. "It's more secure than any of those things. We're about thirty stories belowground, not far outside the city of Boston."

"A bunker, then," Jenna guessed, still trying to make sense of it all. "If it's not part of the government or military, what is it?"

Alex seemed to consider her reply for a moment longer than was needed. "The compound we're in, and the gated estate that sits above us on street level, belongs to the Order."

"The Order," Jenna repeated, finding that Alex's explanation was raising more questions about the place than it answered. She'd never been anywhere like this before. It was alien in its high-tech design, a far cry from anything she'd ever seen in rural Alaska or any of the places she'd been in the Lower Forty-eight.

Adding to the strangeness, beneath her slippered feet, the polished white marble was inlaid with glossy black stone that made a running pattern of odd symbols along the floor—arcing flourishes and complex geometric shapes that somewhat resembled tribal tattoos.

Dermaglyphs.

The word leapt into her thoughts out of nowhere, an answer to a question she didn't even know to ask. It was an unfamiliar word, as unfamiliar as everything about this place and the people who apparently lived here. And yet the certainty with which her mind supplied the term made it feel as though she must have thought or said it thousands of times.

Impossible.

"Jenna, are you all right?" Alex paused in the corridor

a couple of steps ahead of where Jenna's own feet had ceased moving. "Are you tired? We can rest for a minute, if you need to."

"No. I'm okay." She felt a frown creasing her forehead as she glanced up from the intricate design on the smooth floor. "I'm just . . . confused."

And that was due to more than just the peculiarity of where she found herself now. Everything felt different to her, even her own body. Some part of her intellect knew that after five days unconscious in a sickbed, she probably should be exhausted from even the short distance she'd just walked.

Muscles didn't naturally rebound from that kind of inactivity without a bit of pain and retraining. She knew that from her own personal experience, from the accident four years ago that had put her in the hospital ICU in Fairbanks. The same accident that had killed her husband and young daughter.

Jenna remembered all too well the weeks of hard rehabilitation it had taken to get her back on her feet and walking again. And yet now, after the ordeal she'd just awakened from, her limbs felt steady and nimble. Completely unaffected by the prolonged lack of use.

Her body felt oddly revived. Stronger, yet, somehow not quite her own.

"None of this makes sense to me," she murmured, as she and Alex continued their progress down the long corridor.

"Oh, Jen." Alex touched her shoulder with a gentle hand. "I know about the confusion you must be feeling right now. Believe me, I know. I wish none of this had happened to you. I wish there was some way to take back what you've gone through."

Jenna blinked slowly, registering the depth of her friend's regret. She had questions—so many questions—but as they walked deeper into the maze of corridors, the mingled sounds of voices carried out from a glass-walled room up ahead. She heard Brock's deep, rolling baritone and the lighter, quickly spoken, British-tinged syllables of the man named Gideon.

As she and Alex neared the meeting room, she saw that the one called Lucan was there, too, as were Kade and two others who only fortified the large-and-lethal vibe that these guys seemed to wear as casually as their black fatigues and well-stocked weapons belts.

"This is the tech lab," Alex explained to her. "All the computer equipment you see in there is Gideon's domain. Kade says he's some kind of genius when it comes to technology. Probably a genius when it comes to just about everything."

As they paused in the passageway, Kade glanced up and gave Alex a lingering look through the glass. Electricity crackled in his silver eyes, and Jenna would have to be unconscious in her sickbed not to feel the shared heat between Alex and her man.

Jenna got her own share of looks from the others gathered in the glass-enclosed room. Lucan and Gideon both turned her way, as did two other big men who were not familiar to her. One of them a severe-looking, golden-eyed blond whose stare felt as cold and unfeeling as a blade, the other an olive-skinned man with a thick crown of chocolate-brown waves that accentuated his long-lashed topaz eyes and an unfortunate mass of scars that riddled the left side of his otherwise flawless face. There was curiosity in the men's frank stares, maybe a bit of suspicion, too.

"That's Hunter and Rio," Alex said, indicating the

menacing blond and the scarred brunet respectively. "They're members of the Order, too."

Jenna gave a vague nod of acknowledgment, feeling as conspicuous in front of these men as she had her first day on the job with the Alaska State Troopers, a fresh-from-the-academy rookie and a female besides. But here, the feeling wasn't so much about gender discrimination or petty male insecurities. She'd known enough of that bull-shit during her tenure with the Staties to realize this was something different. Something a whole lot deeper.

Here, she felt that by virtue of her mere presence, she was treading on sacred ground. In some unspoken way, she got the sense from the five pairs of eyes studying her that in this place, among these people, she was somehow the ultimate outsider.

Even Brock's dark, absorbing gaze settled on her with a weighty appraisal that seemed to say he wasn't sure he liked seeing her there, regardless of the care and kindness he'd shown her back in the infirmary.

Jenna wouldn't have argued that point for a second. She tended to agree with the vibe she was getting through the glass walls of the tech lab. She didn't belong here. These were not her people.

No, something about each of the hard, unreadable faces fixed on her told her that they were not her kind at all. They were something else . . . something *other*.

But after what she'd been through in her cabin in Alaska—after what she'd seen of herself in the infirmary room—could she even be certain of what she was now?

The question chilled her to her bones.

She didn't want to think about it. Could hardly bear to accept that she'd been fed upon by something as monstrous and terrifying as the creature that had held her

prisoner in her own home all those hours. The same creature that had implanted the bit of foreign matter in her
body and turned her life—what little had been left of it—
inside out.

What was to become of her now?

How would she ever get back to the woman she was
before?

Jenna nearly sagged under the weight of more questions she wasn't ready to consider.

Making it worse, the sense of confusion that had followed her through the corridors of the compound rose up
on her again, stronger now. Everything seemed to amplify
around her, from the soft buzz of the fluorescent lights
over her head—lights that glared too bright for her sensitive eyes—to the accelerating drum of her heartbeat that
seemed to be heading for overdrive, pushing too much
blood through her veins. Her skin felt too tight, wrapped
around a body that was quickening with some strange
new awareness. She had felt its stirrings from the moment
she'd opened her eyes in the infirmary, and instead of lev-
eling out, it was getting worse.

Some strange new power seemed to be growing inside
her.

Stretching out, awakening . . .

"I'm feeling kind of weird," she said to Alex, as her
temples ticked with the pound of her pulse, her palms
going moist where they remained fisted deep inside the
pockets of her robe. "I think I need to get out of here, get
some air."

Alex reached out and brushed a strand of hair from
Jenna's face. "Kade's and my quarters are just up this way.
You're going to feel much better after a hot shower, I'm
sure."

"Okay," Jenna murmured, allowing herself to be guided away from the glass wall of the tech lab and the unnerving stares that followed her.

Several yards ahead in the curving hallway, a pair of elevator doors slid open. Three women walked out wearing snow-dusted winter parkas and wet boots. They were followed by a similarly bundled-up young girl who held a pair of dogs on leashes—a small, exuberant mutt terrier and Alex's regal gray-and-white wolfdog, Luna, which had apparently also made the recent move from Alaska to Boston.

As soon as Luna's sharp blue eyes lit on Alex and Jenna, she lunged forward. The girl who held the leash let out a little yelp, more giggle than anything, her parka hood falling back and freeing a mop of blond hair to bounce around her delicate face.

"Hi, Alex!" she said, laughing as Luna pulled her along the corridor in her wake. "We just got back from a walk outside. It's freezing up there!"

Reaching out to pet Luna's big head and neck, Alex gave the child a welcoming smile. "Thanks for taking her. I know she likes being with you, Mira."

The little girl bobbed her head enthusiastically. "I like Luna, too. So does Harvard."

Whether in protest or agreement, the scrappy-looking terrier barked once and danced frenetically around the larger dog's legs, stubby tail wagging about sixty miles an hour.

"Hello," said one of the three women. "I'm Gabrielle. It's good to see you up and around, Jenna."

"I'm sorry," Alex interjected, rising to make quick introductions. "Jenna, Gabrielle is Lucan's Breedmate."

"Hi." Jenna brought her hand out of her robe pocket

and extended it in greeting to the pretty auburn-haired young woman. Beside Gabrielle, a striking African-American woman offered a warm smile as she extended her hand in welcome.

"I'm Savannah," she said, her voice like velvet and cream, instantly making Jenna feel at home. "I'm sure you've already met Gideon, my mate."

Jenna nodded, feeling ill-equipped for pleasantries despite the warmth of the other women.

"And this is Tess," Alex added, indicating the last of the trio, a heavily pregnant blonde with tranquil, sea-green eyes that seemed wise beyond their years. "She and her mate, Dante, are expecting their son very soon."

"Just a few more weeks," Tess said as she briefly clasped Jenna's hand, her other coming to rest lightly on the large swell of her belly. "We've all been very concerned about you since you arrived here, Jenna. Do you need anything? If there's something we can do for you, I hope you'll let us know."

"Can you zap me back in time about a week?" Jenna asked, only half joking. "I'd really love to erase the past several days and go back to my life in Alaska. Can anyone here do that for me?"

An uneasy look passed between the women.

"I'm afraid that's not possible," Gabrielle said. Although regret softened her expression, Lucan's mate spoke with the serene confidence of a woman cognizant of her own authority but disinclined to abuse it. "What you've been through is terrible, Jenna, but the only way through it is forward. I am sorry."

"No sorrier than me," Jenna said quietly.

Alex murmured a few hushed words of good-bye to the other women. Then she scratched Luna behind the ears and gave the wolfdog a quick kiss on the snout before navigating Jenna back toward their trek up the passageway. Somewhere in the distance, Jenna picked up the harsh grate of metal striking metal, and the muffled sounds of laughter amid a spirited conversation—by the tone of it, a good, old-fashioned pissing contest—between at least one woman and no less than three men.

Jenna shuffled alongside Alex as they turned a corner in the corridor and the din of voices and weaponry faded away. "How many people live here?"

Alex cocked her head, considering. "The Order has ten members right now who live here at the compound. All but Brock, Hunter, and Chase are mated, so that makes seven of us Breedmates, plus Mira."

"Eighteen people in total," Jenna said, absently counting them off in her mind.

"Nineteen now," Alex corrected, as she slanted a gauging look over her shoulder.

"I'm temporary," Jenna said, walking along, up another length of marble hallway, then pausing behind Alex as she slowed in front of an unmarked door. "As soon as one of your new secret agent pals figures out how to get rid of the thing in my neck, I'll be leaving. I don't belong here, Alex. My life is in Alaska."

The way Alex's sympathetic smile wavered on her lips put a lurch in Jenna's pulse.

"Well, here we are." She opened the door to a private apartment and motioned Jenna inside. She walked ahead of her and turned on a table lamp, filling the spacious quarters with a muted glow. Alex seemed anxious somehow, walking through the place like a whirlwind and talking too fast. "I want you to make yourself at home, Jen. Relax for a minute in the living room, if you like. I'll get

you some fresh clothes and start the shower for you. Unless you'd rather close your eyes for a little while? I could
give you one of Kade's T-shirts to sleep in and turn down
the bed for you."

"Alex."

She disappeared into the adjacent bedroom, still talking a mile a minute. "Are you hungry? Would you like me
to fix you something to eat?"

Jenna walked over to the open doorway. "Tell me
what's going on here. I mean, what's *really* going on."

Finally, Alex paused.

She pivoted her head around and just stared for what
felt like a full minute of silence.

"I want to know," Jenna said. "Damn it, I *need* to know.
Please, Alex, as my friend. Tell me the truth."

Alex stared at her, let out a long exhalation as she
slowly shook her head. "Oh, Jen. There's so much you
don't know. Things I didn't know myself until just a couple of weeks ago, after Kade showed up in Harmony."

Jenna stood there, watching her normally frank and
forthright friend struggle for words. "Tell me, Alex. What
is this all about?"

"Vampires, Jen." The word was whispered, but Alex's
gaze didn't waver. "You know they're real now. You saw
that for yourself. But what you don't know is that they're
not like we've been taught to believe from movies and horror novels."

Jenna scoffed. "That thing that attacked me was pretty
horrific."

"I know," Alex continued, imploring now. "I can't excuse what the Ancient did to you. But hear me out. There
are others of his kind that are not so different from us, Jen.
On the surface, of course, we aren't quite the same. They

have different needs for survival, but deep down, there is a core of humanity inside them. They have families and friends. They are capable of incredible love and kindness and honor. Just like us, there is good and bad among them, too."

It wasn't that long ago—a mere week, in fact—that Jenna would have burst out laughing at hearing something so outlandish as what Alex was telling her now.

But everything had changed since then. A week ago felt like a century from where she was standing now. Jenna couldn't laugh, couldn't even muster a word of denial as Alex went on, explaining how the Breed, as they preferred to be called, had come to exist and then thrive for thousands of years in the shadows of the human world.

Jenna could only listen as Alex told her how the Order had been founded centuries ago by Lucan and a handful of others, most of whom were long dead. The men headquartered in this compound were all warriors, including Kade and Brock, even the charmingly geekish Gideon. They were Breed, preternatural and deadly. They were something *other*, just as Jenna's instincts had told her.

To a man, the Order's members, then as now, had pledged themselves to provide protection for both the human race and the Breed, their mission hunting down blood-addicted vampires called Rogues.

Jenna held her breath when Alex softly confessed that when she was a child in Florida, her mother and younger brother were attacked and killed by Rogues. Alex and her father had narrowly escaped with their lives. "The story we told everyone about my mom and Richie when we moved to Harmony was just that, Jen. A story. It was a lie we both wanted to believe. I think Dad eventually did, and then the Alzheimer's took care of the rest. I almost could have believed our lie, too, until the killings began up in Alaska. Then I knew. I couldn't run from the truth anymore. I had to face it."

Jenna closed her eyes, letting all of these incredible realizations settle on her shoulders like a heavy cloak. She could hardly dismiss what she'd been through, no more than she could dismiss the raw pain of her best friend's experience as a child. Alex's ordeal was in her past, thankfully. She had carried on. She had found happiness finally, perhaps ironically, with Kade.

Jenna hoped she might be able to move beyond the nightmare she'd endured, but she felt the cold touch of a shackle when she thought about the bit of unknown material floating beneath the base of her skull.

"What about me?" she heard herself murmur. Her voice rose with the spike of anxiety that flooded her bloodstream. "What about the thing that's inside me, Alex? What is it? How am I going to get rid of it?"

"We don't have those answers yet, Jenna." Alex moved closer, concern creasing her brow. "We don't know, but I promise you, we'll find a way to help you. Kade and the rest of the Order will do everything in their power to figure this out. In the meantime, they will protect you and make sure you're well cared for."

"No." Jenna wrapped her arms around herself. "All I need is to be back home. I want to go back to Harmony."

"Oh, Jen." Alex slowly shook her head. "The life you knew in Alaska is gone now. Everything in Harmony is changed. Precautions had to be taken."

She didn't like the sound of that at all. "What are you talking about? What precautions? What's changed?"

"The Order had to make sure that word of the Ancient and the strange happenings around town didn't leak out to the rest of the population." Alex's gaze stayed steady on hers. "Jenna, they scrubbed everyone's memories of the week surrounding the killings in the bush and the other deaths around Harmony. As far as anyone up there is concerned, you and I have both been gone from Harmony for months already. You can't go back and raise a lot of questions. It would all come crashing down around us if you do."

Jenna forced herself to hold it together as she processed everything she was hearing. Vampires and covert headquarters. An alternate world that had existed alongside her own reality for thousands of years. Her best friend of the past two decades having barely survived a vampire attack as a child.

And then the part that brought back a fresh wave of grief: the recent multiple homicides in Harmony, which apparently included her brother. "Tell me what happened to Zach."

Alex's face was full of regret. "He had secrets, Jen. A lot of them. Maybe it's better if you don't know everything—"

"Tell me," Jenna said, hating the gentle treatment she was getting, particularly from Alex. "We've never let bullshit stand between us, and I sure as hell don't want to start now."

Alex nodded. "Zach was dealing drugs and alcohol to the Native populations. He and Skeeter Arnold had been working together for some time. I didn't figure it out until just before Zach..." She exhaled softly. "When I confronted Zach about what I knew, he got violent, Jen. He pulled a gun on me."

Jenna closed her eyes, sick to think that her older

brother—the decorated cop she strived to emulate practically all her life—was, in fact, corrupt. Granted, they had never been truly close, siblings or not, and they'd been drifting apart more and more in recent years.

God, how many times had she pressed Zach to look into Skeeter Arnold's questionable activities around Harmony? Now Zach's reluctance to do so made a lot of sense. He didn't really care about what was going on in town. He was more concerned with protecting himself. How far would he have gone to protect his dirty little secret?

"Did he hurt you, Alex?"

"No," she said. "But he would have, Jen. I took off on my snowmachine, out to your place. He followed me. When we got there, he fired off a shot—to scare me, more than anything. Everything happened so fast after that. The next thing I knew, the Ancient had crashed out of your cabin and took him down. After the initial strike, it was over very quickly for him."

Jenna stared then, for a long moment, utterly at a loss for words. "Jesus Christ, Alex. Everything you're telling me here . . . it's all true? All of it?"

"Yes. You said you wanted to know. I couldn't withhold it from you, and I think it's better that you understand."

Jenna stepped backward, stumbling a bit. She was suddenly awash in confusion. Suddenly swamped in emotion that shortened her breath and put a tight squeeze on her chest. "I have to . . . need some time alone . . ."

Alex nodded. "I know how hard this must be for you, Jenna. Believe me, I know."

She drifted toward the adjoining bathroom, Alex moving across the floor with her, sticking close as though she thought Jenna might collapse. But Jenna's legs weren't about to give out on her. She was stunned and shaken by what she'd just heard, but her body and mind were far from weak.

Adrenaline coursed through her, flooding her senses and putting her fight-or-flight instinct on high alert. She forced a calmness into her expression as she looked at Alex now, while inside she felt anything but calm. "I think I'll take that shower now. I just . . . I want to be alone for a little while. I need to think . . ."

"All right," Alex agreed, ushering her inside the enormous bathroom. "Take whatever time you need. I'll get you some clothes and shoes, then I'll be right outside if you need me."

Jenna nodded, her eyes following Alex to the door and waiting for it to close behind her. Only then did the tears begin to fall. She wiped at them as they streamed down her cheeks, hot as acid, even while the rest of her felt chilled to the core.

She felt lost and scared, as desperate as an animal caught in a trap. She had to get out of this place, even if it meant chewing off her own limb to escape. Even if it meant using a friend.

Jenna cranked the hot water in the massive two-person shower. As the steam began to fill the room, she thought about the elevator that had carried the other women and the young girl down from the outside.

She thought about freedom, and what it might take for her to taste it.

"Still another two bloody hours to sundown," Brock said, glancing at the clock on the tech lab wall as if he could will the night to come. He pushed off the conference table he'd been leaning against, his legs antsy, his body needing to move. "The days may be short this time of year in New England, but damn, do they crawl sometimes."

He felt eyes on him as he began a tight prowl of the room. It was only himself, Kade, and Gideon in the tech lab now; Lucan had gone to find Gabrielle, and Hunter and Rio had both left to join Renata, Nikolai, and Tegan in the weapons room for a bit of sparring before the start of the night's patrols in the city. He should have gone with them. Instead he'd stayed behind in the lab, curious to see the results of Gideon's latest blood work on Jenna.

He paused behind the computer screen and watched a set of stats scroll on the display. "How much longer is it going to take, Gid?"

For a few seconds, the clatter of fingers racing over a keyboard was the only reply. "I'm just running one last DNA analysis, then we should have some data."

Brock grunted. Impatient, he crossed his arms over his chest and continued wearing a track in the floor.

"You feeling all right?"

When he pivoted his head, he met Kade's narrowed, assessing look. He scowled back at the warrior. "Yeah, why?"

Kade shrugged. "I don't know, man. I'm not used to seeing you so twitchy."

"Twitchy?" Brock repeated the word like it had been an insult. "Shit. I don't know what you mean. I'm not twitchy."

"You're twitchy," Gideon put in over the clickety-clack of his work at the computer. "In fact, you've been visibly distracted for the past few hours. Ever since Alex's human friend woke up today."

Brock felt his scowl deepen even as his pace across the

floor grew more agitated. Hell, maybe he was on edge, but only because he was eager for darkness to fall so he could hit the pavement on patrol and do what he'd been trained to do. That was all. It had nothing to do with any-thing—or *anyone*—else.

If he was distracted by Jenna Darrow, it was because her presence in the compound was a breach of Order rules. They had never permitted a human inside their headquarters. All of the warriors were acutely aware of that fact, a point made obvious when she and Alex had walked past the tech lab a short time ago. And that this human woman carried something alien inside her— something undetermined, which may or may not prove detrimental to the Order and its mission against Dra-gos—made her presence there all the more disturbing.

Jenna had everyone on edge to a certain degree. Brock was no different. At least, that's what he told himself as he paced one final time behind Gideon's workstation, then exhaled a rough curse.

"Fuck it, I'm outta here. If anything interesting comes in on that blood work before nightfall, I'll be in the weapons room."

He strode to the tech lab's door and paused as the wide glass panel slid open in front of him. No sooner had he stepped across the threshold than Alex came rushing toward the lab from the direction of her and Kade's quar-ters.

"She's gone," Alex blurted as she entered the room, clearly upset. "It's Jenna . . . she's gone!"

Brock didn't know why the news should hit his gut like a physical blow. "Where is she?"

"I don't know," Alex replied, misery in her eyes.

Kade was at his mate's side in less than half a second. "What happened?"

Alex shook her head. "She took a shower and got dressed. When she came out of the bathroom she said she was tired. She asked me if she could lie down for a while on the sofa. When I turned around to get her a pillow and spare blanket from the closet, she was just . . . gone. Our apartment door was wide open into the corridor, but there was no sign of Jenna. I've been looking for the last few minutes, but I can't find her anywhere. I'm worried about her. And I'm sorry, Kade. I should have been more careful. I should have—"

"It's okay," he said, gently stroking Alex's arm. "You didn't do anything wrong."

"Maybe I did. I told her about the Breed and about the Order. I told her everything about Zach, and about how we left things back in Harmony. She had so many questions, and I thought she had a right to know."

Brock stifled the curse that was riding at the tip of his tongue. He knew damn well that he would have been hard-pressed to lie to Jenna, too.

Kade nodded, sober as he dropped a kiss on Alex's brow. "It's okay. You did the right thing. It's better that she knows the truth up front."

"I'm just afraid that the truth has sent her into a panic."

"Ah, Christ," Gideon muttered from his position in front of the compound's computer banks. On one of the panels that monitored the estate's motion detectors, lights started blinking like a Christmas tree. "She's in the mansion at ground level. Or, rather, she was in the mansion. We've got a security breach on an exterior door."

"I thought all topside points of entry were locked as

procedure," Brock said, not meaning it to come out as the accusation it sounded like.

"Have a look for yourself," Gideon said, pivoting the monitor as he clipped on a hands-free headset and punched a speed-dial number. "Lucan, we have a situation."

While the Order's leader got a quick rundown, Brock stalked over to the computer command center, Kade and Alex following. On the security camera feed from the estate above the compound, one of the mansion's steel-reinforced lock bars was twisted off its mountings like a piece of taffy. The door was flung open to the daylight outside, the glare of solar rays on the snow-filled yard nearly blinding, even on-screen.

"Holy hell," Brock muttered.

Beside him, Alex gasped in disbelief. Kade was silent, his gaze as grim as it was stunned when his eyes slid to Brock. On the phone, Gideon was now giving urgent orders to one of the Order's more formidable females in residence, namely Renata, to head topside on the double and bring Jenna back in.

"I've got her location on camera now," he told Renata. "She's on the east side of the property, heading southeast on foot. If you take the south service door, you should be able to head her off before she reaches the perimeter fence."

"The perimeter fence," Brock murmured. "Jesus Christ, that thing is juiced with more than fourteen thousand volts of electricity."

Gideon kept talking, advising Renata of Jenna's progress and position.

"Cut the power," Brock said. "You have to cut the power to the fence."

Gideon swiveled a dubious look on him. "And let her waltz right off the property? No can do, my man."

Brock knew the warrior was right. He knew the smartest, best thing to do for the Order was to ensure that the human woman stayed contained within the compound. But the thought of Jenna coming into contact with a potentially lethal dose of electricity was too much. It was, in a word, unacceptable.

He glanced at the security camera feed and saw Jenna, clad in a white sweater and jeans, her loose brown hair flying behind her as she raced across the snowy yard at a blind clip toward the edge of the property. Straight for the ten-foot-tall fence that hemmed the estate in from all sides.

"Gideon," he growled, as Jenna's fleeing form grew smaller on the monitor. "Cut the goddamn power."

Brock didn't wait for the other warrior to comply. He stalked over and slammed his hand down on the control panel. Lights blinked on, and a persistent beeping kicked up in warning of the disabled power grid.

A long silence filled the room.

"I see her." Renata's voice came over the speaker in the lab. "I'm right behind her."

They watched on-screen as Nikolai's mate sped on foot in the direction of Jenna's trail in the snow. Moments ticked by as they waited for further word.

Finally, Renata spoke, but the curse she hissed into her mouthpiece wasn't what anyone in the room had hoped to hear. "God*damn* it. No . . ."

Brock's veins went cold with dread. "What's happened?"

"Talk to me," Gideon said. "What's going on, Renata?"

"Too late," she replied, her voice oddly wooden. "I was too late—she got away. She's gone."

Gideon leaned in, cocking his head toward Brock. "She climbed the bloody fence, didn't she?"

"Climbed it?" Renata's answering laugh was more of a sharp exhalation. "No, she didn't climb it. She . . . ah, shit. Believe it or not, I just watched her jump over it."

CHAPTER
Four

The road hummed beneath Jenna's jeans-clad backside and the soles of her snow-sodden shoes, the smell of smoked meat and male sweat wafting at her from all directions inside the unlit confines of the delivery van. She sat on the floor among stacked crates and cardboard cartons, jostling with every bump. Her stomach roiled, though whether from the adrenaline that was pouring through her or the cloying mix of processed meat and body odor that hammered her nostrils, she couldn't be sure.

How she'd managed to get off the compound's property was a blur. Her head was still swimming with the disturbing revelations of the past few hours, and her senses had been on overdrive from the moment she made the decision to attempt escape. Even now, sights and sounds and motion—every bit of sensory input—seemed to be flying at her in a chaotic blur.

Up in front of the van, the driver and his passenger chattered animatedly in a thick, Slavic-sounding foreign language. They had known enough English to agree to take her into the city when she'd flagged them down on the street outside the estate grounds, and at the moment that had been good enough for her. Except now that they had gone a few miles, she couldn't help but notice they had stopped smiling at her and trying to talk to her in broken English.

Now the driver cast furtive glances at her in the rearview mirror, and she didn't like the sound of the low-voiced, chuckling exchanges the two men shared as she bounced around in back of the darkened van.

"How far to downtown?" she asked, holding on to a crate of hard salami as the van took a left through a caution light. Her stomach pitched with the motion, her ears ringing, head pounding. She squinted through the windshield at the front of the vehicle as it headed toward the late-afternoon glow of the city in the distance. "The bus station, yes? That's where you said you'd take me. How far is it?"

For a second, she wondered if either of them could hear her over the loud rumble of the van's engine as the driver gave it more gas. The sound seemed deafening to her. But then the passenger pivoted around and said something to her in his own language.

Something that seemed to amuse his lead-footed friend behind the wheel.

A knot of dread formed in Jenna's gut. "You know

what? I've changed my mind. No bus station. Take me to the police. Po-lice," she said, dragging out the word so there could be no misunderstanding. She gestured to herself as the driver flicked a scowling glance at her in the mirror. "I'm a cop. I am police."

She spoke with the no-bullshit edge that came to her like second nature, even all these years since she'd been in uniform. But if the pair of jokers up front picked up on her tone or what she was telling them, they didn't seem moved to believe her.

"Police?" The driver chuckled as he looked over at his companion. *"Nassi, nuk duken si ajo e policisë për ju?"*

"No," the one apparently named Nassi replied, shaking his head, thin lips pulling back from crooked teeth. His thick-browed gaze traveled in a slow crawl over Jenna's body. *"Për mua, ajo duket si një copë e shijshme e gomarit."*

She looks like a tasty piece of ass to me.

Jenna thought the dark leer that Nassi sent her must have been enough to tell her what he'd said, but the words seemed so clear to her. Impossibly clear. She stared at the two men as they began a private conversation in their native tongue. She watched their lips, studied the sounds that should have been entirely foreign to her—words that she couldn't possibly understand yet, somehow, did.

"I don't know about you, Gresa, my friend, but I could do with a bit of prime American tail," Nassi added, so confident that his foreign speech would slip right past her, he had the balls to look Jenna square in the eye as he spoke. "Take this bitch back to the office and let's you and me have a little fun with her."

"Sounds good to me." Gresa laughed and dropped his foot down on the gas pedal, sending the delivery van speeding under a highway overpass and into the throng of busy traffic.

Oh, God.

Jenna's feeling of dread from a few minutes ago went as cold as ice in her belly now.

The sudden jolt of acceleration threw her back on her ass. She scrambled to hold on to the crates around her, knowing her chances of escaping the fast-moving vehicle were nil. If the fall out of the van didn't kill her, the roaring cars and trucks flying by on both lanes beside them certainly would.

Making everything worse, her head was beginning to spin with the barrage of lights and noise from outside the van. Automobile exhaust fumes, coupled with the stench inside the vehicle, formed a nauseating olfactory stew that had her stomach turning on itself, threatening to rise up on her. All of her surroundings seemed amplified and too intense, as though the world had somehow gotten more vivid, more choked with detail.

Was she losing her mind?

After all that she'd been through recently, after all she'd seen and heard, she shouldn't be surprised if she was cracking up.

And as she sat back, miserable against the crates and cartons, listening to the two men discuss their ideas for her in eager, violent detail, she got the feeling that her sanity wasn't the only thing at risk right now. Nassi and his friend Gresa had some rather nasty plans for her back at their office. Plans that included knives and chains and sound-proof walls so no one would hear her screams, if Jenna could trust her sudden newfound fluency in their language.

They were arguing over which of them would get to

enjoy her first, as they wheeled the van off the main road and into a ratty section of the city. The pavement narrowed, streetlights growing more sparse the deeper they traveled into what looked to be an industrial area. Warehouses and long, red-brick buildings crowded the street and alleyways.

The delivery van bounced over large potholes and uneven asphalt, the tires crunching in the iced-over brown slush that bunched on both sides of the pavement.

"Home sweet home," Nassi said, in English this time, grinning at her from around his passenger seat. "Ride is over. Time to collect our fare."

The two men laughed as the driver put the van in park and cut the engine. Nassi came out of his seat and started to head back inside the van. Jenna knew she would have only a few seconds to act—precious seconds to disable one or both of the men and bolt.

She inched into a stable position, preparing for the moment she knew was coming.

Nassi smiled broadly as he walked farther into the vehicle. "What do you have to offer us, hmm? Let me see."

"No," Jenna said, shaking her head and feigning the helpless female. "No, please."

He chuckled wolfishly. "I like a woman who will beg. A woman who knows her place."

"Please, don't," Jenna said as he stepped ever closer. The stink of him nearly made her retch, but she kept her eyes fixed on him. When he got within arm's length of her, she thrust out her left hand, palm forward, as though to physically hold him off.

She knew he would grab her.

She counted on it, and could barely contain the answering jolt of triumph that surged through her veins as he snatched her by the wrist and hauled her up off the floor of the van.

She put her weight into the movement, using his own brute force to launch herself at him. With the heel of her free hand, she smashed him hard under the nose, driving soft cartilage up into his septum with a bone-crunching *pop*.

"Aaghh!" Nassi howled in agony. "*Putanë!* Bitch, you will pay for that!"

Blood gushed from his face and onto her as he thrust his hands out and roared toward her. Jenna feinted left, dodging his grasp. Up in front of the van, she heard the other man scrambling around, moving out of the driver's seat to fumble with the console between the seats.

She didn't have time to worry about him right now. Nassi was furious, and in order to get out of the van, she'd have to get through him first.

Jenna locked her hands together and brought her elbows down on her attacker's spine. He shouted in pain, coughing as he made another sloppy grab for her. She eluded him again, dancing out of his reach as though he were standing still.

"*Puthje topa tuaj lamtumirë, ju copille shëmtuar!*" she whispered to him tightly, a threat she made good on when she then brought her knee up between his legs and nailed him with a sharp blow to the groin.

Nassi went down like a ton of bricks.

Jenna spun on a scream of her own, ready to do battle with his friend Gresa now.

She didn't see the gun in the other man's hand until the flare of the shot burned as bright as lightning. The sudden crack of the bullet as it exploded toward her was deafening.

She blinked, dazed and oddly detached, as the searing fire of its impact slammed into her.

"Have we got anything?"

Lucan strode into the tech lab where Brock, Kade, Alex, Renata, and Nikolai were all gathered around Gideon's workstation.

Brock had his hands braced on the desk, staring over Gideon's shoulder at the monitor. He gave Lucan a grim shake of his head. "Nothing solid yet. Still searching DMV records for possible matches."

Jenna had been gone more than an hour. Their best lead on where she might have fled was a couple seconds of surveillance footage captured by a mounted security camera on the south perimeter of the estate.

At roughly the same time that Renata saw Jenna leap the fence and disappear off the grounds, an unmarked white delivery van drove by on the street adjacent to the property. Gideon had only been able to get a partial reading on the van's Massachusetts commercial plates before it rounded a corner and disappeared out of range. In the time since, he'd hacked into the Boston DMV and had been running plate number combinations, trying to narrow down whom the van was registered to and where it might be found.

Brock was sure that if they located that van, Jenna couldn't be far behind.

"Whether we've got solid leads or not, as soon as the sun sets in the next hour and a half, we're gonna need patrols scouring the city," Lucan said. "We cannot afford to lose this woman before we understand what she might mean to our operations."

"And I can't afford to let anything happen to my dearest friend," Alex said, pointing out the emotional wrinkle in the whole situation with Jenna. "She's upset and hurting. What if something bad happens to her out there? She's a good person. She doesn't deserve any of this."

"We'll find her," Brock said firmly. "I promise you, we will."

Kade met his gaze and gave a solemn nod. After the stunning circumstances of Jenna's escape from the compound, finding the human woman with the bit of alien material inside her body was a mission none of the warriors would shirk. Jenna Darrow had to be retrieved, no matter what it took.

"Hang on, hang on," Gideon murmured. "This could prove interesting. I just got a couple of new hits on the latest sequence. One of them is registered to an auto garage in Quincy."

"The other one?" Brock asked, leaning in to get a closer look.

"Meat-packing plant in Southie," Gideon said. "Outfit called Butcher's Best. Says they specialize in personal cuts and catering."

"No shit," Renata said, her chin-length dark hair swinging as she pivoted her head to look at the others gathered in the lab. "The banking exec who lives a couple of miles up the road is hosting his Christmas house party next weekend. Makes sense that a catering van might be up this way."

"Yeah, it does," Lucan agreed. "Gideon, let's get an address for this place."

"Coming right up." He hit a few keys and both the street listing and a satellite map appeared on-screen. "There it is, down in the underbelly of Southie."

Brock's eyes fixed on the location, burning as hot as laser beams. He pivoted around and stalked out of the tech lab, determination in every hard clip of his boot heels on the marble floor.

Behind him, Kade dashed out of the lab into the corridor. "What the fuck, man? The sun won't be setting for a good while. Where are you going?"

Brock kept walking. "I'm gonna bring her back."

CHAPTER
Five

The sun was just beginning to dip below the tip of the Boston skyline as Brock swung one of the Order's SUVs onto a side street in Southie. Under his black leather duster, he was geared up in UV-protective black fatigues, gloves, and wraparound shades. At a decade or so past a century and several bloodlines removed from first-generation Breeds like Lucan, Brock's skin could withstand the sun's rays for a short period of time, but there wasn't a member of his kind alive who didn't treat the daylight with a healthy dose of respect.

He had no intention of frying his own bacon, but the thought of sitting at the compound waiting on twilight while an innocent woman was wandering the city, alone and upset, had been too much for him to stand. His decision was made all the more sound when he spotted the nondescript white delivery van sitting outside the address Gideon had traced. Even before Brock got out of the Rover, the odor of fresh-spilled human blood reached his nose.

"Fuck," he muttered under his breath, stalking through the frozen slush and street grime toward the vehicle.

He peeked inside the passenger window and his gaze snagged on a spent bullet casing on the floor between the seats. The coppery smell of hemoglobin was stronger here, nearly overpowering.

Being Breed, he couldn't control his body's reaction to the presence of fresh blood. Saliva surged into his mouth, his canine teeth ripping farther out of his gums until the fangs pressed into the flesh of his tongue.

Instinctively, he dragged the scent into his nostrils, trying to determine if the blood was Jenna's. But she wasn't a Breedmate; her blood scent did not carry its own unique stamp as did Alex's or that of the other females at the compound.

A Breed male could track the scent of a Breedmate for miles, no matter how faint. Jenna could be bleeding sight unseen right under Brock's nose, and there would be no way for him to tell if it was her or any other *Homo sapiens*.

"Damn it," he growled, swinging his head in the direction of the meat-packaging plant nearby. The fact that someone had recently bled inside the delivery van was all the proof he needed that Jenna was likely in danger.

His rage simmered toward boiling in anticipation of what he would find inside the squat red-brick building. From the street as he approached the place, he could hear men's voices and the hum of a ventilation system compressor droning on the roof.

Brock crept around to a side door and peered inside its small wire-reinforced window. Nothing but packing crates and boxes of wrapping material. He grasped the metal knob and twisted it off in his fist. Tossing it into a pile of filthy snow by the stoop, he slipped inside the building.

His combat boots were silent on the concrete floor as he moved through the storage and cleanup area, toward the center of the small plant. The rumble of conversation grew louder as he progressed, at least four distinct voices, all of them male, all of them edged with the coarse syllables of an Eastern European language.

Something had them agitated. One of the men was shouting and upset, coughing wetly and wheezing more than breathing.

Brock followed the long, grated drain that ran down the center of the room. His nostrils filled with the chemical stench of cleaning products and the sickly sweet odor of old animal blood and spices.

The open doorway ahead of him was curtained with several vertical strips of plastic. As he got within a few feet of it, a man speaking Albanian over his shoulder came in from the other room. He wore a blood-smeared apron, his bald head covered in an elasticized plastic cap, a large cleaver clutched in his hand.

"Hey!" he exclaimed as he pivoted his head and saw Brock standing there. "What you do in here, asshole? Private property! Get the fuck out!"

Brock took a menacing step toward him. "Where is the woman?"

"Eh?" The guy seemed caught off guard for a second

before he regrouped and brandished his cleaver in front of Brock's face. "No woman here. Get lost!"

Brock moved fast, knocking the blade out of the man's hand and crushing his throat in his fist before the son of a bitch had a chance to scream. Stepping around the silenced corpse, Brock parted the plastic curtain and walked into the main processing area of the building.

The presence of spilled human blood was stronger in here, still fresh. Brock spotted a man seated alone on a stool inside a windowed office, a bunched-up, red-soaked cloth held under his nose. In this area of the building, sides of beef and pork hung suspended on large hooks. The room was chilly, ripe with the stink of blood and death.

Brock's boots chewed up the distance as he stalked to the office and threw open the door. "Where is she?"

"W-what the fuck?" The man scrambled up off the stool. His heavily accented voice was clumsy with an unnatural lisp, nasal from the severe break in his nose. "What is going on? I don't know what you're talking about."

"Like hell you don't." Brock reached out and grabbed a fistful of the guy's blood-splattered shirt. He lifted him off the ground, letting his feet dangle four inches from the concrete. "You picked up a woman outside the city. Tell me what you've done with her."

"Who are you?" the man croaked, the whites of his eyes growing wider as he struggled—and failed—to get loose. "Please, let me go."

"Tell me where she is, and maybe I won't kill you."

"Please!" the man wailed. "Please, don't hurt me!"

Brock chuckled darkly, then his acute hearing picked up the sound of rushing footsteps, moving stealthily behind the butcher tables and equipment in the adjacent room. He glanced up . . . just in time to see the glint of a steel pistol barrel trained on him.

The shot erupted, shattering the office window and ripping into the flesh of his shoulder.

Brock roared, not from pain but fury.

He swung his gaze on the bastard who shot him, pinning the human with the fiery amber light of his eyes, which had transformed from their normal dark brown to the molten color of his other, more lethal nature. Brock curled his lips back off his teeth and fangs and bellowed in rage.

There was a high-pitched shriek as the man holding the gun turned tail and ran.

"Oh, Christ!" wailed the wheezing human whom Brock still held fast by the throat. "I do nothing to her— I swear! Bitch broke my nose, but I didn't touch her. G-Gresa," he sputtered, lifting his hand to point in the direction his buddy had fled. "He shot her, not me."

At that unwelcome newsflash, Brock's fingers tightened around the fragile human windpipe. "She's been shot? Tell me where the fuck she is. Now!"

"T-the chiller," he gasped. "Oh, shit. Please don't kill me!"

Brock squeezed punishingly harder, then tossed the blubbering son of a bitch against the far wall. The human cried out in pain, then dropped in a sniveling heap on the concrete floor. "You'd better pray she's all right," Brock said, "or you're gonna wish I had killed you just now."

Jenna huddled on the floor of the large walk-in refrigerator, her teeth chattering, body shivering in the cold.

Outside the sealed steel door, loud noises sounded. Heavy crashes, men shouting...the abrupt *crack* of gunfire and the bright clatter of breaking glass. Then a roar so intense and deadly, it jerked her head upright just as it was starting to become too weighty to keep lifted, her eyelids growing too difficult to hold open.

She listened, hearing only silence lengthening now.

Someone neared the cold cell that held her. She didn't need to hear the thud of approaching footsteps to know that someone was there. As chill as it was inside, the blast of icy air coming from the other side of the locked door was arctic.

The latch gave a *snick* of protest in the instant before the entire steel panel was ripped from its hinges on a deafening metallic squeal. Steam poured out of the opening, shrouding a massive, black-clad mountain of a man.

No, not a man, she realized in dazed astonishment.

A vampire.

Brock.

His lean face was so stark, she hardly recognized him. Huge fangs gleamed white behind the broad mouth that was drawn grim and furious. His breath sawed in and out between his lips, and behind a dark pair of wraparound sunglasses, twin coals blazed with a heat Jenna felt as surely as a touch when he scanned the fogged space and found her slumped and shivering in the corner.

Jenna didn't want to feel the rush of relief that swamped her as he strode inside and dropped down onto his haunches beside her. She didn't want to trust the feeling that said he was a friend, someone to help her. Someone she needed, in that moment. Maybe the only person who could help her.

She started to tell him she was okay, but her voice was

thready and weak. His ember-bright eyes seared her through the veil of his dark shades. He glanced down and hissed when he saw her wounded thigh and the blood that had soaked the leg of her jeans and formed a small pool beneath her.

"Don't talk," he said, stripping off his black leather gloves and pressing his fingers against both sides of her neck. His touch was light but comforting, seeming to warm her from the inside out. The chill drifted away from her, taking the pain of her gunshot wound with it. "You're going to be all right now, Jenna. I'm gonna get you out of here."

He stripped off his black duster and wrapped it around her shoulders. Jenna sighed as the heat from his body and the scent of him—leather and spice and strong, deadly male—enveloped her. As he leaned back, she noticed that a bullet hole had torn through the beefy round of his shoulder.

"You're bleeding, too," she murmured, more alarmed by his injury than by the thought that her rescuer was a vampire.

He shrugged off her concern. "Don't worry about me. I'll live. It takes more than that to slow down one of my kind. You, however . . ."

The way he said it, the grave look that ran across his face as his shaded eyes drifted to her bleeding thigh, seemed almost accusatory.

"Come on," he said, reaching out to gently scoop her into his arms. "I've got you now."

He carried her out of the refrigerated room like she was nothing but feathers in his arms. At five foot eight and fit, a tomboy from the time she took her first steps, Jenna had never been the type to be toted around like some kind of fragile fairy princess. As a former cop, she'd never expected that from a man, nor wanted it.

She had always been the protector, the first one into danger. She hated that she was so vulnerable now, but Brock's solid arms felt so good underneath her, she couldn't muster the will to be offended. She held on tight as he strode through the small plant, past the grisly meat hangers and more than one broken, lifeless person lying on the floor.

Jenna turned her head away and buried her face in Brock's muscular chest as they cleared the last room of the plant and exited to the outside. It was dusk on the street, the snow-packed alleyway and crouching buildings bathed in the darkening blue of evening.

As Brock stepped off the stoop, a sleek black SUV rolled up from a cross street. It came to a stop at the curb and Kade jumped out of the backseat.

"Ah, fuck," Alex's mate growled. "I smell blood."

"She's been shot," Brock said, his deep voice grave.

Kade stepped closer. "You okay?" he asked her, his light gray eyes taking on a faint yellow light in the gathering darkness. Jenna nodded her reply, watching as the points of his lengthening fangs glinted behind his upper lip. "Niko and Renata are with me," he told Brock. "What's the situation inside?"

Brock grunted, dark humor beneath the dangerous tone of his voice. "Messy."

"Figures," Kade said, quirking a wry look at him. "You don't look so good yourself, my man. Nice hit to the shoulder. We need to get Jenna back to the compound before she loses any more blood. Renata's behind the wheel of the Rover. She can take her in while the rest of us clean up inside."

"The human is my responsibility," Brock said, his chest vibrating against Jenna's ear. "She stays with me. I will bring her to the compound."

Jenna caught the look of curiosity that flashed across Kade's face at Brock's statement. He narrowed his eyes but said nothing as Brock strode past him to the idling SUV, Jenna carried lightly in his arms.

CHAPTER
Six

How we doing?" Renata asked Brock from behind the wheel of the black Rover as the vehicle sped out of South Boston on a course for the Order's compound. Her green eyes flicked to the rearview mirror, slender dark brows knit in a frown. "Our ETA's about fifteen minutes out. Everything okay back there?"

"Yeah," Brock replied, glancing down to where Jenna lay, resting quietly across his lap in the backseat. He had sliced off one of the seatbelts and tied it around her thigh as a tourniquet, hoping it would help stanch the blood loss. "She's hanging in."

Her eyes were closed, her lips slightly parted and tinged with blue from the cold she'd been subjected to inside the meat chiller. Her body still trembled under the cover of his leather duster, though he guessed her shuddering was more in reaction to shock than any amount of discomfort. His Breed talent was making sure of that. With one palm cupped around her nape, the other stroking her temple, he drew Jenna's pain into himself.

Renata cleared her throat pointedly as she watched him in the mirror. "What about you, big guy? Hell of a lot of blood back there. You sure you wouldn't rather drive and I'll look after her until we get to the compound? Say the word and I'll pull over. Won't take but a minute."

"Keep driving. Situation's under control back here," Brock said, although he wondered if Niko's shrewd Breed-mate would buy it, given that his growled reply was spoken through gritted teeth and fully extended fangs.

It had been hard to contain his reaction to Jenna bleeding when he first found her inside the building. Now that he was trapped in close confines with her, feeling the heat of her spilling blood through the leather of his duster, smelling its coppery fragrance, and hearing the low thud of each heartbeat that pushed still more blood from her wound, Brock was living a private hell in the back of the SUV.

He was Breed, and there was none among his kind who could resist the pull of fresh human blood. It didn't help him any that the last time he'd fed had been . . . hell, he wasn't even sure. Probably pushing a week, which would have been bad even in the best of circumstances. And these were hardly the best of circumstances.

Brock focused all his effort on pulling Jenna's pain. Easier to keep his mind off his hunger that way. It also helped keep him from noticing how soft her skin was, and how the curves of her body fit so nicely against him.

The absorbed pain of her injury—and the slighter irritation of his own—was the only thing that kept his body from having yet another sort of reaction to her, as well. Even then, he couldn't totally ignore the uncomfortable tightness of his fatigues, or the way the light flutter of her pulse against his fingertips where they rested against her nape made him yearn to put his mouth against her instead.

To taste her, in all the ways a man could crave a woman.

It took a great deal of effort to shake the thought from his mind. Jenna was a mission, that's all. And she was human, with the fragility and short shelf life to go along with it. Although if he was being honest with himself, he'd be the first to admit that he had long preferred mortal females over their sisters who were born Breedmates.

When it came to romantic entanglements, he tried to keep things casual. Nothing too permanent. Nothing that might last long enough for him to let down a woman who had grown to trust him.

Yeah, he'd already been there, done that. And he damn well had the guilt and self-loathing to prove it. No desire to go down that particular stretch of road ever again.

Before his memories could drag him toward the shadows of his past failings, Brock glanced up and saw the gated entrance of the Order's compound looming ahead. Renata announced their arrival to Gideon on her hands-free headset, and as the Rover rolled to a stop at the tall iron gate, it unlocked and swung open to welcome them inside.

"Gideon says the infirmary is prepped and waiting for us," she said as she drove to the fleet garage in back.

Brock grunted in response, hardly able to speak now for the crowding presence of his fangs. The whole back section of the Rover was bathed in amber, the glow of his transformed eyes throwing off light like a bonfire even from behind the dark lenses of his shades.

Renata parked the vehicle inside the large hangar, then jogged around to help him get Jenna out of the backseat and into the elevator that would take them down from street level to the compound headquarters belowground. Jenna roused as the doors closed and the hiss of the hydraulics went into action.

"Put me down," she mumbled, struggling a bit in Brock's arms as though she was annoyed with the assistance. "I'm not in pain. I can stand up by myself. I can walk—"

"No, you can't," he said, cutting her off, his words terse and rasping. "Your body is in shock. Your leg needs tending. You won't be walking anywhere."

Through the daze of her lingering shock, Jenna glowered at him, but kept her arms linked around his neck as the elevator came to a stop at the compound below. Brock stepped out, walking briskly. Renata followed, the lugsoles of her combat boots thudding in counterpoint to the soft, wet patter of blood that dripped to the floor from Jenna's wound.

As they rounded a curve in the corridor that would take them to the infirmary, Lucan met them in the passageway. He stopped dead in his tracks, feet braced apart, hands fisting at his sides. Brock could just make out the subtle flaring of the Gen One's nostrils as the scent of fresh blood traveled the corridor.

Lucan's eyes zeroed in on the bleeding human, their

gray color flashing with sparks of light, pupils narrowing swiftly to catlike slivers. "Holy hell."

"Yeah," Brock drawled. "Gunshot wound to the right thigh, .45-caliber round with no sign of exit. We tied it off, but she's lost a damned lot of blood between here and the place in Southie where I found her."

"No shit," Lucan said, his fangs clearly visible now, twin points gleaming as he spoke. He grated out a harsh curse. "Go on, then. They're waiting for her in the infirmary."

Brock gave the Order's leader a grim nod as he continued past him. In the infirmary, Gideon and Tess had prepared an operating table for Jenna. Gideon's face went a bit pale at the sight of her, and when he clamped his jaws together, a muscle jerked in his lean cheek.

"Set her down right here," Tess said from beside the surgery table, jumping in when Gideon, the otherwise calm and collected Breed male who'd stitched up his fair share of combat wounds for the other warriors, seemed at a loss now that the patient in question was human and leaking red cells like a faucet.

"Fuck me," Gideon said after a long moment, his British accent coming on stronger than normal. "That's a lot of blood. Tess, can you—"

"Yes," she put in quickly. "I can handle it on my own."

"Okay," he said, visibly affected. "I'll, ah . . . I think I'm gonna wait outside."

As Gideon made his exit, Brock placed Jenna on the stainless steel table. When he didn't move away, Tess glanced up at him in question. "You're injured, too?"

He shrugged his good shoulder. "It's nothing."

She pursed her lips, not entirely convinced. "Maybe Gideon ought to make sure of that."

"It is nothing," Brock repeated, impatient. He took off his shades and hooked them into the collar of his black shirt. "What about Jenna? How bad is she?"

Tess glanced down at her and gave a faint wince. "Let me have a look. It's a shame my talent is suppressed because of the baby, or I could heal her in a few seconds, instead of the hour or more it's likely going to take to get the worst of the bleeding under control."

Tess had been a skilled and caring veterinarian before she moved in to the Order's compound and became Dante's mate. She'd since taken on a vital role as Gideon's right hand in the infirmary, tending to much larger—and, no doubt, more disagreeable—clientele than she'd dealt with in her former clinic in the city.

As a Breedmate, she also possessed an extraordinary talent—one that was unique to her and which would be passed down to the son she would bear, as Brock's mother had passed her own down to him. Tess had a healing touch, as well, only her ability went even further than his. Where Brock's talent gave him the power to absorb human pain, the effect was only temporary. Tess could actually restore health, even restore life, in any living creature.

Or, rather, she had been able to, before pregnancy had stifled her power.

But she was still a damned good physician, and Jenna could not be in more capable hands. Still, Brock found it difficult to step back from the operating table, in spite of the bloodthirst that was twisting his gut and wringing him out from the inside.

He stood there, stock-still, as Tess scrubbed her hands, removed the makeshift tourniquet, then did a cursory visual examination of the wound. She asked Renata to stay nearby and assist her, then spoke reassuringly to Jenna, explaining what she had to do to extract the bullet and tend the wound.

"The good news is, there's no bone damage and, from what I can tell, it will be a fairly simple procedure to remove the bullet and repair the artery it nicked." She paused. "The bad news is, we're not really equipped down here for this type of injury—meaning a human injury. In fact, you're the first non-Breed patient that's ever been in the compound's infirmary."

Jenna's gaze slid to Brock as if to confirm what she was hearing. "Lucky me, stuck in a vampire hospital."

Tess smiled sympathetically. "We'll take care of you, I promise. Unfortunately, we don't have a need for things like anesthesia. The warriors don't require it when they come in with injuries, and those of us who are mated have the blood bond to aid with healing. But I can give you a local—"

"Let me help," Brock interrupted, already moving around the table to stand at Jenna's side. He held Tess's questioning look. "I don't care about the blood. I'll deal. Let me help her."

"All right," Tess replied softly. "Let's get started."

Brock stared unblinking as Tess picked up a pair of scissors from the instrument tray and proceeded to cut away Jenna's ruined clothing. Inch by inch, from the ankle of her right leg to her hip, the blood-soaked denim fell aside. In scant minutes, all that covered Jenna's lower body was a skimpy pair of white cotton bikini panties.

Brock swallowed, his throat working audibly at the combined one-two punch of seeing so much soft feminine skin while his senses were drenched with the coppery siren's call of Jenna's blood.

He must have growled his hunger out loud, because in that same instant, Jenna's eyelids lifted, startled. No doubt he was a scary sight, looming over the operating table, his gaze rooted on her, every muscle and tendon in his body strung as tight as piano wire. But fearful or not, Jenna didn't look away. She stared him down, unblinking, and he saw in her courageous hazel eyes a bit of the frontier cop he'd heard she used to be.

"Renata," Tess said. "Will you help me move Jenna just a bit so we can get rid of these clothes?"

The two Breedmates worked in tandem, removing the bloodied jeans and his ruined duster while Brock could only stand there, immobilized by thirst and something else that ran even deeper.

"Okay," Tess prompted, catching his heated gaze with a knowing look. She had scrubbed and dried her hands and was pulling on a pair of surgical gloves from a box on the rollaway tray. "I'll begin whenever you're ready, Brock."

He reached out to Jenna and laid the palm of his hand against the side of her neck. She flinched at first, that uncertain gaze flicking up to meet his as if she might jerk away from his touch.

"Close your eyes," he told her, an effort just to keep the hungered rasp from his voice. "It will be over in just a few minutes."

Her chest rose and fell in rapid movement, her eyes locked on his, not quite trusting.

And why should she? He was born of the same stock as the creature that had terrorized her in Alaska. The way he looked right now, Brock figured it was a small wonder she didn't leap up from the table and try to fend him off with one of Tess's neatly arranged scalpels.

But as he gazed down at her, Jenna blew out a soft breath. Her eyes drifted closed. He felt the strong pound of her pulse beneath his thumb... then the first piercing jolt of pain as Tess began cleaning and tending Jenna's wound.

Brock concentrated all his focus on keeping her comfortable, wrapping his talent around the acid burn of antiseptics and sharp, probing surgical instruments. He swallowed Jenna's pain, idly aware of Tess's efficient work as she retrieved the bullet from deep within the muscle of Jenna's thigh.

"Got it," Tess murmured. The chunk of lead clattered into the basin of a stainless steel bowl. "That was the worst part. The rest of the procedure will be a piece of cake."

Brock grunted. He could bear the pain easily enough. Hell, a gunshot wound and patch-up was standard issue just about every night for one or more of the warriors coming off patrol. But Jenna hadn't signed on for this shit, ex-cop or not. She hadn't asked to be part of the Order's battles, though why that should matter to him, he didn't know.

He was feeling a lot of things he had no goddamned right to feel.

Hunger still stirred in him like a tempest, rising up from two powerful, equally demanding sources. Giving in to either one would be a mistake, especially now. Especially because the object of his twin desires was a woman the Order needed to keep safe. To keep on their side, at least until they could determine what she might mean to their war with Dragos.

And yet he wanted her.

He felt protective of her, even though he knew he was

unsuitable for the job, and even though she seemed to balk at the idea of needing help from anyone. Lucan had made her his responsibility, but Brock could hardly deny that she'd become his personal mission even earlier than that. From the moment he first laid eyes on her in Alaska, after the Ancient had tormented her for days in her own home, he'd been emotionally invested in keeping her safe.

Not good, he chided himself. Bad fucking idea, letting himself get personally involved where his business was concerned.

Hadn't he learned that lesson the hard way back in Detroit?

Getting personally invested in any mission was the fast lane to failure.

Minutes must have passed as he contemplated the years that stood between that dark chapter of his life and the place he stood now. He was dimly aware of Tess operating in attentive silence, Renata standing by with the needed instruments and supplies as they were requested. It wasn't until the final suture was in place and Tess had walked to the sink to scrub up that Brock realized he was still touching Jenna, still caressing the line of her carotid with the pad of his thumb.

He cleared his throat and pulled his hand away. When he spoke, his voice was a raw scrape of sound. "Are we finished here yet, Doc?"

Tess paused at the sink, turning to look over her shoulder at him. "What about your injury?"

"I'm good," he said. He had no intention of sticking around any longer than necessary, and besides, his Breed genetics would heal him in no time.

Tess gave him a faint shrug. "Then, we're finished."

On the table beside him, Jenna's gaze found his and

held, steady and strong. Her lips, still pale and bluish from shock and cold, parted on an expelled little puff of air. Her throat worked as she swallowed and tried again. "Brock...thank—"

"I'm out of here," he snarled, knowingly harsh. He took a step back from the table, then, with a self-directed curse, he pivoted on his heel and stalked out of the infirmary.

CHAPTER
Seven

Brock swung the black Rover out of the Order's estate and headed into the night alone. Normally the warriors ran their patrols in teams, but, frankly, he was feeling like piss-poor company—even for himself.

His veins were throbbing with aggression, and the hunger that had sunk its claws into him in the infirmary with Jenna wasn't doing anything for his attitude, either. He needed to feel the pavement under his boots and a weapon in his hand. Hell, at the rate his night had been going thus far, he'd even welcome the nut-freezing chill of the early December wind that he normally despised.

Anything to distract him from the need that was raking him raw.

To help on that score, he pulled his cell phone from the pocket of his fatigues and speed-dialed Kade.

"Sunshine Cleaning," the warrior answered wryly. "How are things back at the ranch?"

Brock could only growl.

Kade chuckled. "That good, huh? When's the last time someone brought a bleeding human into the compound? Or any human, for that matter."

"Things were a bit tense for a while," Brock admitted. "Fortunately, Tess stepped in and patched Jenna up. She's going to be okay."

"Glad to hear that. Alex would never forgive us if we let anything happen to her best friend."

Brock really didn't want to discuss Jenna, or the responsibility of keeping her safe. He scowled as he headed deeper into the city, his gaze scanning the streets and alleyways, on the lookout for thugs or assholes—any excuse to pull over and engage in a little hand-to-hand. Human or Breed, he could give a shit, so long as they put up a decent fight.

"What's the status of the location in Southie?" he asked Kade.

"Like it never happened, my man. Niko and I got rid of the bodies, the broken glass, and all the blood. The meat chiller where they held Jenna looked like it had been used for a fucking slaughterhouse."

Brock's jaw went tight as he relived the moment he'd found her in a flash of vivid recollection. His temper flared even hotter when he thought about the two bastards who'd harmed her.

"What about the witnesses?" In the long half second of silence that answered him, Brock ground out a curse. "The two guys who picked Jenna up outside the compound and brought her out there—I left one of them semiconscious in an office outside the meat chiller, the other hightailed it after he shot me and caught a glimpse of my fangs."

"Ah, fuck," Kade said. "There was no one in the building except the corpses we disappeared. We didn't know about witnesses, man."

Yeah, right. Because in the heat of the moment, with Jenna bleeding and shivering in his arms, Brock neglected to mention that fact.

"God*damn* it," he ground out, slamming his fist against the dashboard of the Rover. "It's my fault. I fucked up. I should have told you there were live ones that needed to be contained."

"Don't sweat it," Kade said. "We're not that far away. I'll tell Niko to head back. We can have another look around the place, chase down your two runners, and scrub their memories of the whole thing."

"Not necessary. I'm already on it." Brock hung a sharp left at the nearest intersection and gunned it for Boston's South End. "I'll report in once I have the situation contained."

"You sure?" Kade asked. "If you want some backup—"

"I'll call in when it's handled."

Before his brother-in-arms could comment about the lethal tone of Brock's voice, he clapped the phone closed and shoved it back into his pocket as the Rover barreled into the underbelly of the city.

By the time he reached the neighborhood of the meatpacking plant, his pulse was hammering with the need for violence. He parked the vehicle on a side alley and trekked through the snowy lots so that he came up behind the building. Lights burned inside, and through the brick and mortar of the place, he could hear the muffled rumble of raised male voices, both of them heavily accented and one of them verging on hysteria.

Brock leapt silently onto the roof of the old building and made his way over to a snow-crusted skylight that looked down into the plant below. The two assholes he wanted to see were roaming back and forth among the hanging sides of beef, sharing a fifth of cheap vodka and smoking cigarettes held in shaking fingers.

"I'm telling you, Gresa," shouted the one with the broken nose. "We need to call the cops!"

The shooter—Gresa, evidently—took a long swig from the bottle, then gave a stern shake of his head. "Tell them what, Nassi? Look around you! Do you see any evidence of what we think we saw in here tonight? I say, nothing happened. No cops."

"I know what I saw," Nassi insisted, his voice still climbing. "We need to tell someone!"

Gresa strode over and shoved the vodka at him. While Nassi drank, his friend gestured to the quiet plant. "There is no blood, no sign of trouble. No sign of Koli or Majko, either."

"They're dead!" Nassi wailed. He lapsed into a few words in his native tongue before continuing again in broken English. "I saw their bodies, so did you! They were here when we ran out of the building. I know you saw them, Gresa! What if that man—that . . . *whatever* he was— took them away? What if he comes back for us now, too?"

Jenna's shooter reached around to the small of his back and pulled out his pistol. He wagged it in front of him like a prize. "If he comes back, I have this. I shot him once, I can shoot him again. Next time, I will kill him."

Nassi put the bottle to his mouth once more and

gulped down what was left. He dropped the empty to the floor at his feet. "You are a fool, Gresa. Soon, I think you will be a dead fool. But not me. I'm leaving. I quit this stinking job, and I am going home."

He stormed out of Brock's line of vision, his companion hard on his heels.

By the time the two men stepped out of the building to the dark street outside, Brock was waiting. He dropped down off the roof and now stood there in front of the door, blocking their path.

"Going somewhere?" he asked them pleasantly, giving them a good flash of fang. "Maybe you need a lift."

They both screamed—bone-scraping cries of pure human terror that were music to Brock's ears.

He leapt on the man in front, the one with the broken nose. Ripping into the vulnerable throat, Brock didn't drink, but killed instead. He cast the limp body to the snow, then cocked his head toward the one who'd put the bullet in Jenna's thigh.

Gresa screamed again, the gun in his hand trembling violently. Had Brock been human, or had he been distracted as he had been earlier in the plant, when his fury at Nassi had made him miss the fact that a pistol was trained on him from across the room, Gresa might have been able to shoot him again now.

He fired a shot, but it was clumsy and ill-aimed.

And Brock moved as fast as lightning, lunging into a dive that knocked Gresa off his feet and sent his errant bullet veering off into the dark.

With a twist of his arm, he snapped the shooter's wrist and straddled him on the ground. "Your death will be slower," he snarled, curling his lips off his teeth and fangs and pinning Jenna's assailant with a blast of amber light from his transformed eyes.

Gresa whimpered and sobbed, then howled in terror as Brock bent down and sank his jaws around the artery pounding wildly in the human's neck. He dragged the alcohol-tinged blood into his mouth, feeding in a frenzy of rage and thirst.

He drank, and drank some more.

The blood nourished him, but it was the fury—the vengeance for what these men had done to an innocent female, to Jenna—that truly satisfied him.

Brock drew back and roared his triumph up to the night sky, blood trickling down his chin in a hot trail. He fed some more, and then he grasped the human's skull between his hands and gave a savage jerk, breaking the neck.

When it was over, when the last of his rage and thirst had begun to ebb, and all that remained was the expedient disposal of the dead, Brock cast a clearer eye on the carnage he'd wrought. It was total and savage.

A complete annihilation.

"Jesus Christ," he hissed, dropping down onto his haunches and raking his hand over the top of his head.

So much for keeping things business when it came to Jenna Darrow.

If this had been a test, he figured he'd just failed it with flying colors.

CHAPTER
Eight

I hope everyone's hungry," Alex said, emerging from the swinging door of the estate's mansion kitchen, a large bowl of fresh-cut fruit in one hand, a basket of steaming, aromatic herbed biscuits in the other.

She placed both on the dining room table in front of Jenna and Tess, who'd been instructed by Alex and the other women of the compound to sit back and allow themselves to be served breakfast.

"How are you doing, Jen?" Alex asked. "Do you need anything? If you need to prop up your leg, I can bring in an ottoman from the other room."

Jenna shook her head. "I'm fine." Her leg was feeling much better since her surgery last night, and she wasn't in any great deal of pain. It was only at Tess's insistence that she was using a cane to get around. "There's really no need to fuss over me."

"That's my best friend the bush cop for you," Alex said, directing a wry eye-roll toward Tess and giving a dismissive wave of her hand. "Just a little gunshot wound, no need for concern."

Jenna scoffed lightly. "Compared to the week I've had already, a bullet hole in my thigh is probably the least of my worries."

She wasn't looking for sympathy, just stating a fact.

Tess's hand came down gently on her wrist, startling Jenna with its warmth and the genuine caring that shone in the young woman's eyes. "None of us can even pretend to know what you've been through, Jenna, but I hope you understand that we are here for you now. You're among friends—all of us."

Jenna resisted the pull of comfort that Tess's words had on her. She didn't want to feel relaxed in this place, among Alex and these seemingly kind strangers.

Nor with Brock.

Least of all with him.

Her mind was still reeling from his unexpected rescue of her in the city. It had been a mistake to take off as she had, ill-prepared and emotionally unhinged. She hadn't been so long resigned from police work that she didn't remember the surest way to get one's ass caught in a sling was to run off half cocked into unfamiliar territory. All she'd known in that split second before she'd bolted from the compound was a desperation to escape her dark new reality.

She'd made a classic rookie error in judgment, fueled by pure emotion, and ended up needing backup to drag her ass to safety. That her backup had come in the form of a formidable, scary-as-hell vampire was something she wasn't sure she'd ever be able to wrap her brain around.

Deep down, she knew Brock had saved her life last night. Part of her wished he hadn't done it. She didn't want to owe him anything. She didn't like being indebted to anyone, and most certainly not to a man who couldn't even be classified as human.

God, what a messed-up turn her life had taken.

Her thoughts growing progressively darker, Jenna drew her hand away from Tess's light grasp and settled back into her chair.

Tess didn't push her to talk, simply leaned over the table and breathed in some of the drifting steam from the biscuits.

"Mmm," she moaned, her slender arm cradling the swell of her large baby bump. "Is this Dylan's basil and cheddar recipe?"

"By popular request," Alex replied brightly. "There's more where this came from, including Savannah's incredible crème brûlée French toast. Speaking of which, I'd better go fetch some more of the feast."

As Alex pivoted around and disappeared back into the kitchen, Tess cast Jenna a sly look. "You haven't lived until you've had Dylan's biscuits and Savannah's French toast. Trust me, absolute heaven."

Jenna offered a polite smile. "Sounds good. I was never much of a cook. My biggest claim to fame in the kitchen was a smoked moose-meat omelet with Swiss cheese, spinach, and redskin potatoes."

"Moose meat?" Tess laughed. "Well, I can guarantee you none of us have ever had anything like that. Maybe you can make it for us sometime."

"Maybe," Jenna said noncommittally, lifting her shoulder in a slight shrug.

If not for the disturbing bit of foreign material embedded in her upper spine, and, now, the gunshot wound that had grounded her for God only knew how long, she'd be gone from this place already. She wasn't sure how much longer she would be made to stay, but as soon as she was able to walk out of there again, she'd be history. Never mind what the Order thought they needed from her; she had no interest in sticking around to be their guinea pig.

It was still beyond strange to think she was actually sitting there—in a secret, military-grade headquarters populated by a team of vampire warriors and the seemingly sane, perfectly likable women who appeared to be happy and comfortably at home among them.

The surrealism of the whole thing got even stronger when Alex and the rest of the Order's females—five youthful, stunningly beautiful women and the blond little girl named Mira—filed out of the kitchen with the rest of breakfast. They chatted companionably, as relaxed among one another as if they'd been together all their lives.

They were a family—Alex included, even though she'd just arrived a week ago, along with Jenna.

An easy rhythm settled over the dining room as gold-rimmed plates were passed around and heaped with all manner of delicious things. Crystal juice glasses were filled to their sparkling brims, and delicate, bone china cups soon steamed with fragrant dark roast coffee.

Jenna watched in studious silence as the meal got under way. Warm maple syrup and soft pads of butter made the rounds of the table, stopping for the longest time with little Mira, who soaked her French toast in sticky sweetness and globbed butter onto her biscuit as though it were frosting. Mira wolfed down the biscuit in two big bites, then attacked the rest of her meal with the same unbridled gusto.

Jenna smiled in spite of herself at the child's ravenous appetite, feeling a pang of melancholy, if not guilt, when she thought about her own daughter. Libby had been such a cautious little girl, self-disciplined and serious, even as a toddler.

God, what she wouldn't give now to be able to watch Libby enjoying something as simple as breakfast across the table from her.

With sugar-coated fingers, Mira reached for her glass of orange juice and took a big gulp. She sighed contentedly as she set the glass back down with a soft thump. "May I have some whipped cream for my peaches?" she asked, pinning Jenna with her uncanny violet eyes.

For a moment, Jenna felt trapped in that gaze. She shook off the sensation and reached for the china bowl that sat halfway between her own plate and Mira's across the table.

"May I *please* have some whipped cream," Renata corrected from her seat to the right of the little girl. The tough-looking brunette gave Mira a decidedly maternal, affectionate wink as she reached out to intercept the bowl that Jenna passed her.

"May I please," Mira amended, looking anything but chided.

Jenna sliced into the decadent French toast and popped a bite into her mouth. It was just as Tess had promised—heavenly. She could hardly keep from moaning out loud as she savored the creamy, vanilla taste of it.

"You like?" asked Savannah, who was seated at one end of the long dining room table.

"It's delicious," Jenna murmured, her taste buds still vibrating with bliss. She sent a brief, encompassing glance around to everyone gathered there. "Thank you for letting me share all of this with you. I've never seen so much food in my life."

"Did you think we were going to make you starve?" Gabrielle asked from the opposite end of the table. Her smile was friendly, inviting.

"I'm not sure what I thought," Jenna answered truthfully. "To be honest, I don't know how to process any of this just yet."

Gabrielle inclined her head in a slow nod, looking sage and regally serene, even though she was no doubt a few years younger than Jenna's age of thirty-three. "That's understandable. You've been through a lot, and your situation is unique to us all."

"My situation," Jenna said, idly pushing a piece of syrup-soaked bread around her plate. "Meaning the unidentified object that's lodged at the base of my skull?"

"Yes, that," Gabrielle acknowledged, a gentle note to her voice. "And the fact that you were fortunate enough to escape the Ancient with your life. The fact that he fed from you and let you live is—"

"Unheard of," piped in another of the women from her seat next to Gabrielle. She had a mane of fiery red hair, her pretty face dotted with peachy freckles. "If you knew what he was capable of—if you had any idea what's happened to so many others..." Her voice trailed off, a small shudder making her fingers tremble around the fork she held. "It's nothing short of a miracle that you're still alive, Jenna."

"Dylan's right," Tess agreed. "Since roughly a year ago, when the Order first discovered the Ancient had been awakened, we've been trying to locate him and Dragos, the son of a bitch responsible for bringing that kind of dangerous being back into the world."

"I'm not sure which of them is the worse evil," Renata interjected. "The Ancient has claimed a lot of innocent lives, but it's Dragos, the Ancient's sadistic grandson, who's been pulling all the strings."

"You mean to tell me that creature has offspring?" Jenna asked, unable to contain her revulsion.

Gabrielle took a sip of her coffee, then carefully set the cup down in its saucer. "That creature and several others like him fathered the entire Breed race on Earth."

"On Earth?" Jenna barked out a disbelieving laugh. "Are you talking about aliens now? That vampire who attacked me—"

"Was not from this world," Savannah finished for her. "It's true. No harder to believe than the existence of vampires themselves, if you ask me, but it's the God's honest truth. The Ancients raped and conquered after crashlanding here some thousands of years ago. Over time, a few of their victims became pregnant with what would become the first generation of the Breed."

"This actually makes sense to all of you?" Jenna asked, still incredulous. She glanced over at Alex beside her. "You believe this, too?"

Alex nodded. "Having come to know Kade and everyone else here at the compound, how could I not believe it? I also saw the Ancient with my own eyes, in the moments before he was killed on a cliff outside Harmony."

"And what about this other person—Dragos?" Jenna asked, unwillingly curious to make all of the pieces of this astonishing puzzle fit together somehow. "Where does he come in?"

Dylan was the first to answer. "As it turns out, Dragos woke the Ancient much earlier than we had guessed. Decades earlier, in fact. He held him in secret, and used him for creating a whole new generation of Gen Ones— the strongest members of the Breed, being that they are directly descended from the Ancient's bloodline and not genetically diluted, as the later generations are."

"Dragos has been breeding a personal army of the most powerful, most deadly members of the race," Renata added. "They are raised under his watch, trained to be ruthless killers. Dragos's private assassins whom he can call out at any time to do his bidding."

Gabrielle nodded. "And in order to create those first-generation offspring, Dragos also needed a stock of fertile women on which to breed the Ancient."

"Breedmates," Alex said.

Jenna glanced at her. "And what are they?"

"Women who are born with unique DNA and blood properties that make them capable of sharing a life bond with members of the Breed and bearing their young," Tess said, her hand idly roaming over the top of her pregnant belly. "Women like all of us gathered around this table right now."

Shock and horror clenched Jenna's gut. "Are you saying that I—"

"No," Tess said, shaking her head. "You're mortal, not a Breedmate. Your blood work is normal, and you don't have the mark that the rest of us do."

At her frown, Tess held out her right hand, which bore a small red mark between her thumb and forefinger. It was a tiny crescent moon with what looked to be a teardrop, falling into its center. "All of you have this same tattoo?"

"It's not a tattoo," Alex said. "It's a birthmark, Jenna. All Breedmates are born with one somewhere on their bodies. Mine is on my hip."

"There aren't a lot of us in the world," Savannah said. "The Breed considers all Breedmates to be sacred, but not Dragos. He's been collecting women for years, holding them captive, we assume for the sole purpose of birthing his Gen One assassins. A lot of them have been killed, either by Dragos himself or the Ancient."

"How do you know that?" Jenna asked, horrified by what she was hearing.

Down the table from her, Dylan cleared her throat. "I've seen them. The dead, that is."

The cop part of Jenna perked to full attention. "If you've got dead bodies, you've got hard evidence, and probable cause to turn this asshole, Dragos, in to the authorities."

Dylan was shaking her head. "I haven't seen the bodies. I've seen the dead. They . . . appear to me sometimes. Sometimes they speak to me."

Jenna didn't know whether to burst out laughing or hang her head in defeat. "You see dead people?"

"Every Breedmate has a particular talent or ability that makes her unique from any other," Tess explained. "For Dylan, that ability is a connection to other Breedmates who have died."

Renata leaned in, bracing her forearms on the edge of the table. "Through Dylan's talent, we know for certain that Dragos is responsible for numerous Breedmate deaths. And through another friend of the Order, Claire Reichen, whose talent led us to actually locate Dragos's base of operation a couple months ago, we know that he is holding many more Breedmates prisoner. Since then, Dragos's operation has gone to ground. Now the Order's primary mission—aside from taking the bastard out ASAP—is to find his new headquarters and bring his victims to safety."

"We've been helping wherever we can, but it's hard to nail a moving target," Dylan said. "We can search missing persons reports online, looking for faces I recognize. And we run day missions to women's shelters, orphanages, flophouses... anywhere we might get a lead on vanished young women."

Renata nodded. "Particularly those with possible ESP skills or other unusual capabilities that might hint at a potential Breedmate."

"We do what we can," Gabrielle said. "But we haven't caught a real break yet. It's like we're missing the key that will unlock the whole thing, and until we find that, all we're doing is chasing our own tails."

"Well, hang in there," Jenna said, that rusty old cop side of her sympathizing with the frustration of following go-nowhere leads. "Persistence is often a detective's greatest ally."

"At least we don't have to worry about the Ancient anymore," Savannah said. "That's one less battle to be fought."

Around the breakfast gathering, a chorus of agreeing voices answered the statement.

"Why *did* the Ancient let you live, Jenna?"

The question came from Elise, the petite short-haired blonde on the other side of Tess. The reticent one of the group who looked like a fragile flower but had the frank, unwavering gaze of a warrior. She probably needed that inner steel, considering the company she and the other women in the compound were keeping.

Jenna glanced down at her plate and considered her answer. It took her a long moment to form the words. "He made me choose."

"What do you mean?" Savannah asked, her brow furrowing in question.

What will it be, Jenna Tucker-Darrow?

Life . . . or death?

Jenna felt every pair of eyes rooted on her in the quiet. Forcing herself to meet the unspoken questions that hung like a weight in the air, she looked up. She squared her chin matter-of-factly and spoke the words succinctly, if quickly. "I wanted to die. It's what I would have preferred—at that moment, especially. He knew that, I'm certain of it. But for some reason, he seemed to want to toy with me, so he made me decide whether or not he would kill me that night."

"Oh, Jen, that's awful." Alex's voice hitched a little. Her arm came around Jenna's shoulders in a sheltering embrace. "That cruel son of a bitch."

"So," Elise prompted, "you told the Ancient to let you live and he did—just like that?"

Recalling the moment with harsh clarity now, Jenna gave a deliberate shake of her head. "I told him I wanted to live, and the last thing I remember is him slicing open his arm and removing that thing—that tiny bit of God-knows-what—that's now embedded inside of me."

She felt, rather than saw, the subtly exchanged glances that traveled around the table.

"Do you think that might be significant?" she asked, directing the question to the group as one. She tried to tamp down the sudden twinge of fear that was suddenly reverberating in her chest. "Do you think him placing that object inside me has something to do with whether I live or die?"

Alex took her hand in a reassuring grasp, but it was Tess who spoke before anyone else. "Maybe Gideon can run a few more tests and help us figure that out."

Jenna swallowed, then nodded.

Her plate of food sat untouched for the duration of the meal.

In a shadowed corner of an expansive luxury hotel suite in Boston, heavy drapes securely closed to block even the slightest ray of morning sunshine, the Breed male called Dragos sat in a silk-upholstered chair and drummed his fingernails on the mahogany lamp table beside him. Tardiness made him impatient, and impatience made him deadly.

"If he doesn't arrive in the next sixty seconds, one of you needs to kill him," he said to the pair of Gen One assassins who flanked him like muscled, six-and-a-half-foot hellhounds.

No sooner had he said it than, out in the foyer of the presidential suite, the private elevator gave a soft electronic chime, announcing an arriving guest. Dragos didn't move from his seat in the other room, waiting in irritated silence as another of his homegrown, personal guards escorted a civilian Breed male—a lieutenant in Dragos's secret operation—into the suite for his private audience.

The vampire had the good sense to bow his head the instant his gaze lit on Dragos. "Apologies for keeping you waiting, sire. The city is teeming with humans. Holiday shoppers and tourists," he said, disdain in every cultured syllable. He peeled off his black leather gloves and tucked them into the pocket of his cashmere coat. "My driver had to circle the hotel a dozen times before we were able to get close to the service doors below street level."

Dragos continued to drum his fingers on the table. "Something wrong with the lobby entrance?"

His lieutenant, born second-generation Breed like Dragos himself, blanched slightly. "It's the middle of the day, sire. In that much sunlight, I would burn to a crisp in minutes."

Dragos merely stared, unfazed. He wasn't happy with the inconvenience of their meeting location, either. He would much rather be enjoying the comfort and security of his own residence. But that wasn't possible anymore. Not since the Order had interfered in his operation and sent him scrambling for cover.

Out of fear of discovery, he no longer permitted any of his civilian associates to know where his new headquarters was located. As a further precaution, none of them knew the locations of his other sites and personnel, either. He couldn't run the risk that any of his lieutenants might fall into the Order's hands and end up compromising Dragos in the hopes of sparing themselves from Lucan's wrath.

Just the thought of Lucan Thorne and his self-styled warrior knights put a bitter taste in Dragos's mouth. Everything he'd been working toward—his vision of a future he could hardly wait to catch in his ready hands— had been spoiled by the actions of the Order. They'd forced him to turn tail and run. Forced him to destroy the very nerve center of his operation—a scientific research super-laboratory, which had cost him hundreds of millions of dollars and several decades of effort to perfect.

All of it gone now, nothing but cinder and shrapnel in the middle of a thick Connecticut forest.

Now the power and privilege that Dragos had been accustomed to for centuries had been replaced by skulking in the shadows and constantly watching over his shoulder to make certain his enemies weren't closing in on him. The Order had made him flee and cower like a rabbit desperate to evade the hunter's snare, and he liked it not one damned bit.

The latest irritation had taken place in Alaska, with the escape of the Ancient, Dragos's most valuable, irreplaceable tool in his quest for ultimate domination. Bad enough that the Ancient had broken free during transport to his new holding tank. But the disaster was made all the worse when the Order somehow managed to find not only the Alaskan lab but the fugitive otherworlder, as well.

Dragos had lost both of those important pieces to the warriors. He wasn't about to forfeit another damned thing to them.

"I want to hear good news," he told his lieutenant, glaring up at the male from under the furrow of his scowl. "How are you progressing with your assigned task?"

"Everything is in place, sire. The target and his immediate family members have just returned to the States this week from holiday abroad."

Dragos grunted in acknowledgment. The target in question was a Breed elder, nearly a thousand years old— Gen One, in fact—which was precisely why Dragos had him in his sights. In addition to wanting Lucan Thorne and his band of warriors put out of business, Dragos had also returned to one of his initial mission objectives: the systematic and total extinction of every Gen One Breed on the planet.

That Lucan himself and another of the Order's founding members, Tegan, were both Gen Ones only made that goal all the sweeter. And all the more imperative. By removing all of the Gen Ones—save the crop of assassins bred and trained to serve him unquestioningly—Dragos and the other second-generation members of the race would become, by default, the most powerful vampires in existence.

And if, or, rather, when Dragos tired of sharing the future he alone had envisioned and ensured was brought to fruition, then he would call upon his personal army of assassins to remove every second-generation contemporary, as well.

He sat in contemplative, if bored, silence as his lieutenant rushed to review the finer points of the plan that Dragos himself had masterminded just a few days earlier. Step by step, tactic by tactic, the other Breed male laid everything out, assuring him that nothing had been left to chance.

"The Gen One and his family have been under our surveillance round the clock since their arrival back home," the lieutenant said. "We are ready to pull the trigger on the operation on your command, sire."

Dragos inclined his head in a vague nod. "Make it happen."

"Yes, sire."

The lieutenant's deep bow and scraping retreat was almost as pleasing to Dragos as the notion that this pending offensive strike would make it clear to the Order that he might be down, but he was far from out.

In fact, his presence at the swank Boston hotel—and one of several important introductory meetings that had taken weeks to arrange between him and a hand-picked group of influential humans—would solidify Dragos's position on the ladder toward his ultimate glory. He could practically taste success already.

"Oh, one more thing," Dragos called out to his departing associate.

"Yes, sire?"

"If you fail me in this," he said pleasantly, "be prepared for me to feed you your own heart."

The male's face bleached as white as the carpet that blanketed the floor like snow. "I will not fail you, sire."

Dragos smiled, baring both teeth and fangs. "See that you don't."

CHAPTER
Nine

After the death-soaked mess of his night's work in the city, Brock considered it a personal triumph that he'd managed to avoid Jenna for most of the day that he'd been back at the compound. With the two men's bodies dumped in the frigid backwaters of the Mystic River, he had stayed out alone until near dawn, trying to shake off the fury that seemed to follow him all night.

Even after he'd been back at the Order's headquarters for some hours that morning, the unwarranted—completely unwanted—sense of rage that gripped him when he thought of an innocent woman coming to harm made his muscles vibrate with the need for violence. A couple of sweaty hours of blade work in the weapons room had helped take off some of his edge. So had the scalding, forty-minute shower he'd punished himself with following the training.

He might have felt damned good, felt that his head was screwed on straight and tight again, if not for the one-two punch that Gideon had delivered not long afterward.

The first hit was the news that Jenna had come down from breakfast with the other women of the compound and had asked him to run another round of tissue testing and blood work. She had recalled something about the time she'd spent in the Ancient's company—something that Gideon had said left the stalwart female pretty shaken up.

The second blow had come almost immediately after the first samples were drawn and run through the analyzers.

Jenna's blood counts and DNA had changed significantly since the last time Gideon had run them.

Yesterday, her results were normal. Today, everything was off the charts.

"We can't jump to conclusions. No matter what these reports seem to indicate," Lucan finally said into the quiet, his deep voice grave.

"Maybe we should run another sample," said Tess, the only one of the females in the tech lab at the moment. She glanced up from the disturbing lab results to look at Lucan, Brock, and the rest of the Order who'd been summoned there to review Gideon's findings. "Shall I get Jenna and bring her back down to the infirmary for a second test?"

"You can," Gideon said, "but running another sample isn't going to change a thing." He took off his pale blue glasses and tossed them onto the acrylic workstation in front of him. Pinching the bridge of his nose, he slowly shook his head. "These kinds of DNA mutations and massive cellular replications simply don't occur. Human bodies aren't advanced enough to handle the demands that changes of this significance would place on their organs and arteries, to say nothing of the impact something like this would have on the central nervous system."

Arms crossed over his chest, Brock leaned against the wall next to Kade, Dante, and Rio. He said nothing, struggling to make sense of everything he was seeing and hearing. Lucan had advised that no one jump to conclusions, but it was damned hard not to assume that as of right now, Jenna's future well-being was severely in question.

"I don't get it," Nikolai said from the other side of the tech lab, where he sat at the large table along with Tegan and Hunter. "Why now? I mean, if everything was normal before, why the sudden flood of mutations to her blood and DNA?"

Gideon shrugged vaguely. "Could be the fact that until just yesterday she'd been in a deep sleep, almost a coma. We knew her muscle strength had increased once she had awakened. Brock saw that firsthand, and so did we, when Jenna fled the compound. The cellular changes we're seeing now could have been a delayed reaction to simply waking up. Being conscious and alert may have acted as some kind of switch inside her body."

"Last night she was shot," Brock added, biting back the angry snarl that was clogging the back of his throat. "Could that have anything to do with what we're seeing in her blood work now?"

"Maybe," Gideon said. "Anything is possible, I suppose. This isn't something that I, or anyone else in this room, have ever seen before."

"Yeah," Brock agreed. "And doesn't that just suck ass."

From the rear of the tech lab, his booted feet propped up on the conference table while he tipped back in his chair, Sterling Chase cleared his throat. "All things considered, maybe it's not such a good idea to give this woman so much freedom around the compound. She's too big of a question mark right now. For all we know, she could be some kind of goddamn walking time bomb."

For a long moment, no one said a thing. Brock hated the silence. Hated Chase for putting something out there that none of the warriors would want to consider.

"What would you suggest?" Lucan asked, shooting a sober look at the male who had spent decades as part of the Breed's bureaucratic Enforcement Agency before joining up with the Order.

Chase arched a blond brow. "If it were up to me, I'd remove her from the compound ASAP. Lock her away someplace tight and secure, as far away from our operation as she can get, at least until we have a chance to take Dragos down, once and for all."

Brock's growl erupted from his throat, dark with animosity. "Jenna stays here."

Gideon put his glasses back on and gave a nod in Brock's direction. "I agree. I would not be comfortable removing her now. I'd like to keep an eye on her, get a better understanding of what's happening to her on a cellular and neurological level, at a minimum."

"Suit yourselves," Chase drawled. "But it's gonna be all of our funerals if you're wrong."

"She stays," Brock said, aiming his narrowed gaze down the table to where it skewered the smirking ex-Agent.

"You've had a hard-on for this human since the second

you saw her," Chase remarked, his tone light but his expression dark with challenge. "You got something to prove, my man? What is it—you just one of those born suckers for a damsel in distress? The Patron Saint of Lost Causes. Is that your deal?"

Brock vaulted across the table in a single leap. He would have had his hands around Chase's throat, but the vampire saw him coming and moved just as fast. The chair toppled, and in half a second the two big males were eye to eye, jaw to jaw, locked in a simmering standoff neither one of them could win.

Brock felt strong hands peeling him away from the confrontation—Kade and Tegan, there before he could take the shot Chase deserved. And behind Chase were Lucan and Hunter, the two of them and the rest of the warriors ready to dial the situation down if either male thought to escalate it.

Glaring at Chase, Brock allowed himself to be guided away from his comrade, but only barely. For what wasn't the first time, he considered the antagonistic, aggressive nature of Sterling Chase, and he pondered what it was that drove the otherwise skilled—once upstanding—male to be so volatile.

If the Order had a time bomb to worry about in its midst, Brock wondered if he wasn't looking at the source of that danger right now.

"What the hell is taking them so long?"

Jenna hadn't realized she'd spoken her frustration out loud until Alex reached over and took her hand in a reassuring grasp. "Gideon said he wanted to run some extra tests on your samples. I'm sure we'll hear something soon."

Jenna huffed out a sharp sigh. Cane in hand, even though she felt only the smallest need to lean on it, she got up from the sofa she'd been sitting on and limped to the other side of the apartment's living room. She had been brought there by Alex and Tess following her blood draw in the infirmary a few hours ago, told she'd been granted use of the private quarters as her own for the duration of her stay at the compound.

The residential suite was a big improvement over her room at the infirmary. Spacious and comfortable, with oversize leather furniture and dark wood tables that were meticulously polished and free of clutter. Tall wooden bookcases were lined with a library's worth of classics, philosophy, politics, and history. Serious, thought-provoking books that seemed in contrast to the shelf full of neatly organized—good grief, *alphabetized*—popular commercial fiction that sat alongside it.

Jenna let her gaze wander the shelves of titles and authors, needing even the momentary distraction to keep herself from dwelling too long on what might be keeping her waiting all this time for answers from Gideon and the others.

"Tess has been down there for more than an hour," she pointed out, idly pulling a book about female jazz singers from its place in the history section. She flipped through a few pages, more to give her hands something to do than out of any real interest in the book.

As she thumbed past a section on 1920s-era nightclubs, a yellowed old photograph slipped out. Jenna caught it before it fell to the floor. The beaming face of a pretty young woman dressed in shimmering silk and glossy furs stared out of the image. With her large, almond-shaped eyes and porcelain-light skin that seemed to glow against her long jet-black hair, she was beautiful and exotic, particularly within the setting of the jazz club behind her.

With her own life spiraling into confusion and worry, Jenna was struck for a moment by the sheer jubilation in the young woman's smile. It was such a raw, honest joy, it almost hurt Jenna to look at it. She had known that kind of happiness herself once, hadn't she? God, how long had it been since she'd felt even half as alive as the young woman in that photograph?

Angered by her own self-pity, Jenna slid the picture back between the pages, then returned the book to its place on the shelf. "I can't take this not knowing. It's driving me crazy."

"I know, Jen, but—"

"Screw this. I'm not waiting here any longer," she said, pivoting to face her friend. The tip of her cane thumped on the rug-covered floor as she made her way to the door. "They must have some of the results back by now. I have to know what's going on. I'm going down there myself."

"Jenna, wait," Alex cautioned from behind her.

But she was already in the corridor, walking as fast as she could manage between the impediment of her cane and the twinge of pain that shot through her leg with every hasty step.

"Jenna!" Alex called, her own footfalls quickly gaining in the empty hallway.

Jenna kept going, around one curving length of polished white marble to another. Her leg was throbbing now, but she didn't care. Tossing away the cane that only slowed her down, she all but ran toward the muffled sounds of male voices coming from up ahead. She was panting as she reached the glass walls of the tech lab, a sheen of pain-induced sweat beading above her lips and across her forehead.

Her eyes found Brock before anyone else in the solemn-looking group. His face was taut, the tendons in his neck drawn tight as cables, his mouth flattened into a grim, almost menacing line. He stood in the back of the room, surrounded by several other warriors, all of them seeming tense and uneasy—all the more so now that she was there. Gideon and Tess were huddled near the bank of computer workstations at the front of the lab.

Everyone had paused what they'd been doing to stare at her.

Jenna felt the weight of their gazes like a physical thing. Her heart lurched. Obviously, they had the analysis of her blood work. Just how awful could the results be?

Their expressions were unreadable, everyone holding her in cautious, silent observation as her footsteps slowed and came to a stop in front of the tech lab's wide glass doors.

God, they looked at her now as though they'd never seen her before.

No, she realized as the group of them remained un-moving, simply watching her through the clear wall that stood between her and the sober meeting on the other side. They were looking at her as though they might have expected her to be dead already.

As though she were a ghost.

Dread settled cold and heavy in her stomach, but she wasn't about to back down now.

"Let me in," she demanded, pissed off and terrified. "Goddamn it, open this fucking door and tell me what's going on!"

She lifted her hand and fisted it, but before she had a chance to pound on the glass, it slid open on a soft hiss. She stormed inside, Alex following in on her heels.

"Tell me," Jenna said, her gaze traveling from one silent face to another. She lingered on Brock, the one person in the room aside from Alex for whom she felt a measure of trust. "Please . . . I need to know what you've found."

"There have been some changes in your blood," he said, his deep voice impossibly low. Too gentle. "In your DNA, as well."

"Changes." Jenna swallowed hard. "What kind of changes?"

"Anomalies," Gideon interjected. When she swung her head to look at him, she was struck by the concern in the warrior's eyes. He spoke carefully, looking and sounding far too much like a doctor doling out the worst kind of news to his patient. "We've found some odd cellular replications, Jenna. Mutations that are being passed into your DNA and multiplied at an excessive rate. These mutations were not present the last time we analyzed your samples."

She shook her head, as much in confusion as it was reflex to deny what she thought she was hearing. "I don't understand. Are you talking about some kind of disease? Did that creature infect me with something when he bit me?"

"Nothing like that," Gideon said. He shot an anxious look at Lucan. "Well, not exactly, that is."

"Then what *exactly*?" she demanded. The answer hit her not even a second later. "Oh, Jesus Christ. This thing in the back of my neck." She put her hand over the spot where the Ancient had inserted that granule-size bit of unidentified material. "This thing he put inside me is causing the changes. That's what you mean, isn't it?"

Gideon gave her a faint nod. "It's biotechnology of some kind—nothing the Breed or humankind has the capability to create. From the newest X rays we took today, it appears the implant is integrating into your spinal cord at a very accelerated rate, as well."

"Take it out."

A round of uneasy looks traveled the group of big males. Even Tess seemed awkwardly silent, unwilling to hold Jenna's gaze.

"It's not that simple," Gideon finally replied. "Perhaps you should see the X ray for yourself."

Before she could consider whether she wanted to see proof of anything she was being told, the image of her skull and spinal column blinked full-screen on a monitor mounted to the wall in front of her. In an instant, Jenna noted with sick familiarity the rice-size object that glowed brightly at the center of her uppermost vertebrae. The threadlike tendrils that had been present yesterday were more numerous in this newer slide.

Easily hundreds more, each thin strand weaving intricately—*inextricably*—through and around her spinal cord.

Gideon cleared his throat. "As I said, the object is apparently comprised of a combination of genetic material and advanced high technology. I've never seen anything like it, nor have I been able to find any human scientific research that even comes close to what this is. Given the biological transformation we're seeing in your DNA and blood work, it would seem the source of the genetic material was the Ancient himself."

Which meant part of that creature was inside her. Living there. Thriving.

Jenna's pulse hammered hard in her breast. She felt the pump and rush of her blood racing through her veins— mutated cells that she imagined were chomping their way through her body with each heartbeat, multiplying and growing, devouring her from within.

"Take it out of me," she said, her voice climbing in her distress. "Take the goddamned thing out of me right now, or I'll do it myself!"

She reached up with both hands and started clawing at her nape with her fingernails, desperation making her go a little crazy.

She didn't even see Brock move from his position on the other side of the tech lab, but in less than a moment, he was right beside her, his large hands wrapping around her fingers. His dark brown eyes found her gaze and didn't release her.

"Easy now," he said, a low whisper as he gently, but firmly, drew her hands away from her nape and held them in his warm grasp. "Breathe, Jenna."

Her lungs squeezed, then released on a hitching sob. "Let go of me. Please, leave me alone, all of you."

She pulled back and tried to walk away, but the heavy drumbeats of her pulse and a sudden ringing in her ears made the room around her pitch violently. A dark wave of nausea swept her, cloaking everything in a thick, dizzying fog.

"I've got you," Brock's soothing voice murmured somewhere close to her ear. She felt her feet leave the ground and for the second time in as many days she found herself caught up in the safety of his arms.

CHAPTER
Ten

He didn't make excuses for what he was doing or where he was taking her. Merely strode out of the tech lab and carried her back up the corridor she'd come from with Alex a few minutes before.

"Let go of me," Jenna demanded, her senses still muddled, ringing with each long stride of Brock's legs. She shifted in his arms, trying to ignore how even that small bit of movement made her head spin and her stomach twist. Her head fell back over his muscled forearm, a pained groan leaking out of her. "I said put me down, damn it."

He grunted but kept walking. "I heard you the first time."

She closed her eyes, only because it was too hard to keep them open and watch the ceiling of the corridor contort and swirl above her as Brock carried her deeper into the compound. He slowed after a moment, then turned sharply, and Jenna glanced up to see that he had brought her back to the apartment suite that was now her private quarters.

"Please, put me down," she murmured, her tongue thick, throat gone bone dry. The pounding behind her eyes had become a jackhammer throb, the ringing in her ears a deafening high-frequency whine that seemed to want to split her skull wide open. "Oh, God," she gasped, unable to hide her agony. "It hurts so much . . ."

"Okay," Brock said quietly. "Everything's gonna be okay now."

"No, it won't." She whimpered, humiliated by the sound of her own weakness, and the fact that Brock was seeing her like this. "What's happening to me? What did he do to me?"

"It doesn't matter right now," Brock whispered, his deep voice held too tight. Too carefully level to be believed. "Let's just get you through this first."

He crossed the room with her and knelt down to place her on the sofa. Jenna lay back and let him gently straighten her legs, not so far gone with discomfort and worry that she didn't recognize the tenderness of the strong hands that could probably crush the life from someone with little more than a twitch of this man's will.

"Relax," he said, and those strong, tender hands came up near her face. He leaned over her and lightly stroked her cheek, his dark eyes compelling her to hold his gaze. "Just relax and breathe now, Jenna. Can you do that for me?"

She'd calmed a bit already, easing into the sound of her name on his lips, the feathery warmth of his fingers as they skated slowly from her cheek to her jaw, then down, along the side of her neck. The short bursts of breath that sawed in and out of her lungs began to slow, to ease, as Brock cupped her nape in one hand and glided his other palm in an unrushed, soothing back-and-forth motion across the top of her chest.

"That's it," he murmured, his gaze still locked on hers, intense and yet so impossibly tender at the same time. "Let go of all the pain, and relax. You're safe, Jenna. You can trust me."

She didn't know why those words should affect her as much as they did. Maybe it was the pain that had weakened her. Maybe it was the fear of the unknown, the gaping abyss of uncertainty that had suddenly become her reality since that frigid, horrific night in Alaska.

And maybe it was just the simple fact that it had been a long time—four lonely years—since she'd felt the firm, warm caress of a man's touch, even if offered only in comfort.

Four empty years since she'd convinced herself she didn't need tender contact or intimacy. Four endless years since she'd remembered what it was to feel like a flesh-and-blood woman, like she was desired. Like she might one day be able to open her heart to something more.

Jenna closed her eyes as the prick of tears began to sting at them. She pushed aside the swell of emotion that rose up on her unexpectedly and focused instead on the soothing warmth of Brock's fingertips on her skin. She let his voice wash over her, feeling his words and his touch work in tandem to coax her through the anguish of the strange trauma that had seemed to be shredding her from the inside out.

"That's good, Jenna. Just breathe now."

She felt the vise of pain in her skull loosen as he spoke to her. Brock caressed her temples with his thumbs, his fingers splayed deeply into her hair, holding her head in a comforting grasp. The piercing ring in her ears began to fade away, until, at last, it was gone.

"You're doing great," Brock murmured, his voice darker than before, just above a growl. "Let it go, Jenna. Give the rest of it to me."

She exhaled a long, purging sigh, unable to keep it inside her as long as Brock was stroking her face and neck. She moaned, welcoming the pleasure that was slowly devouring her agony. "Feels nice," she whispered, helpless to resist the urge to nuzzle further into his touch. "The pain isn't so bad now."

"That's good, Jenna." He drew in a breath that sounded more like a sharp gasp, then exhaled a low groan. "Let it all go now."

Jenna felt a tremor vibrate through his fingertips as he spoke. Her eyelids snapped open and she gaped up at him, stricken by what she saw.

The tendons in his neck were strung tight, his jaw clamped down so hard it was a wonder his teeth didn't shatter. A muscle ticked wildly in his lean cheek. Beads of perspiration lined his forehead and upper lip.

He was in pain.

Staggering pain—just as she had been, not a few minutes before his touch had seemed to ease her agony away.

Realization dawned on her then.

He wasn't just calming her with his hands. He was

somehow pulling her pain out of her. He was siphoning it, willingly drawing her pain into himself.

Offended by the idea, but even more embarrassed that she had let herself lie there and imagine that his touch was something more than pity, Jenna flinched out of his reach and scuttled into a seated position on the sofa. She breathed hard with outrage as she stared into his dark eyes, which flashed with specks of amber light.

"What the hell do you think you're doing?" she gasped, leaping to her feet.

The muscle that had been ticking in his jaw gave a tight twitch as he stood up to face her. "Helping you."

Images crowded into her mind in an instant—a sudden vivid recollection of the aftermath of her captivity with the creature who'd invaded her cabin in Alaska.

She'd been in pain then, too. She'd been terrified and in shock, awash in so much confusion and horror, she thought she might die from it.

And she remembered the warm, caring hands that comforted her. The face of a grimly handsome stranger who'd come into her life like a dark angel and kept her safe, kept her sheltered and calm, when everything in her world had been thrown into chaos.

"You were there," she murmured, stunned to realize it only just now. "In Alaska, after the Ancient was gone. You stayed with me. You took away my pain then, too. And later, after I was brought here to the compound. My God... did you stay at my side all of the time I was in the infirmary?"

His eyes remained fixed on her, dark and unreadable. "I was the only one who could help you."

"Who asked you to?" she demanded, knowingly harsh,

but desperate to purge the heat that was still traveling through her, unbidden and unwanted.

Bad enough he'd thought it necessary to coddle her like some kind of child through her prolonged ordeal. All the worse when he seemed to think it was necessary to do so now, as well. She'd be damned before she let him think for one second that she had actually welcomed his touch.

His expression still pained from what he'd done for her a few moments ago, he shook his head and blew out a low curse. "For a woman who doesn't want anyone's help, you sure seem to need it a lot."

She barely resisted the temptation to tell him where he could shove that sentiment. "I can take care of myself."

"Like you did last night in the city?" he challenged. "Like you did just a few minutes ago in the tech lab, right before my arms were the only thing that came between your stubborn ass and the floor?"

Humiliation stung her cheeks like a slap. "You know what? Save us both some grief, and don't do me any more favors."

She spun away from him and started walking toward the door that was still open onto the corridor outside. Each miraculously painless step she took only heightened her anger at Brock. Made her all the more determined to put as much distance between them as possible.

Before she got within a yard of the threshold, he was standing in front of her. Blocking her path, even though she hadn't seen or heard him move.

She stopped short. Gaped at him, astonished by the preternatural speed he evidently had at his control.

"Get out of my way," she said, and tried to move past him.

He sidestepped her, putting his immense body directly

in front of her. The intensity of his gaze told her he wanted to say something more, but Jenna didn't want to hear it. She needed to be alone.

Needed space to think about everything that had happened to her . . . everything that was still happening, growing more terrifying all the time.

"Move aside," she said, hating the small hitch that crept into her voice.

Brock slowly lifted his hand and swept a tousled hank of hair off her brow. It was a tender gesture, kindness she craved so badly but was too afraid to accept. "You're in our world now, Jenna. And whether you want to admit it or not, you're in way over your head."

She watched his mouth as he spoke, wishing she didn't find herself so riveted to the movements of his full, sensual lips. He was still weathering her pain; she could tell by the slight flare of his nostrils as he drew in his breath and blew it out on a controlled exhale. The tension in his handsome face and strong neck hadn't abated, either.

Seeing him carrying a burden that belonged to her made her feel small and powerless.

All her life, she'd struggled to prove herself worthy— first to her father and her brother, Zach, both of whom let her know in no uncertain terms they doubted she'd had what it took to make it in law enforcement. Later on, she'd striven to be the perfect wife and mother. Her entire life had been structured on a foundation of strength, discipline, and capability.

Incredibly, as she stood there in front of Brock now, it wasn't the fact that he was something other than human— something dangerous and otherworldly—that made her want the floor to open up and swallow her whole. It was the dread that he could see through the hard shell of the anger she wore like body armor and that he might know her for the scared, lonely failure she truly was.

Brock gave another faint shake of his head in the long silence that hung between them. His eyes took her in slowly, drifting all over her face before coming back up to meet her gaze. "There are worse things than needing to lean on someone once in a while, Jenna."

"Damn it, I said get out of my way!" She shoved at him, her palms connecting with his broad chest as she pushed with all the anger and fear she had inside her.

Brock flew backward several paces, nearly crashing into the far wall of the corridor.

Jenna sucked in her breath, stunned and amazed at what she'd just done.

Horrified by it.

Brock was a towering force, six and a half feet tall and likely 250-plus pounds of muscle and strength. Something far more powerful than her. Something far more powerful than anything she'd ever known.

And she had just physically shoved him a couple of feet across the floor.

His brows lifted over his surprised gaze. "Jesus Christ," he muttered, more wonder in his voice than anger.

Jenna brought her hands out before her and stared at them as though they belonged to someone else. "Oh, my God. How did I . . . What just happened?"

"It's all right," he said, walking back toward her with that maddeningly calm ease of his.

"Brock, I'm sorry. I honestly didn't mean to—"

"I know," he said, nodding soberly. "No worries. You didn't hurt me."

A bubble of hysteria climbed up the back of her throat. First, the shocking news that the implant was somehow altering her DNA, and now this—a strength that couldn't possibly belong to her, yet somehow did. She thought back on her escape from the estate grounds and the bizarre language abilities that she'd seemed to have picked up since the Ancient had left a piece of himself embedded in her spinal cord.

"What the hell is happening to me, Brock? When will all of this finally stop?"

He took her trembling hands between his palms and held them steady. "Whatever is going on, you don't have to go through it alone. You need to understand that."

She didn't know if he was speaking for everyone in the compound or himself. She had no voice to ask him for clarification. She told herself it didn't matter what he meant, yet it didn't keep her heart from racing as she stared up at him. Under the heat of his fathomless brown eyes, she felt the worst of her fears melt away.

She felt warm and protected, things she wanted to deny but couldn't so long as Brock was holding her in his hands and in his gaze.

He frowned after a long moment and slowly released her hands, letting his palms skate down the length of her arms. It was a sensual caress, lingering too long to be mistaken for anything less than intimate. Jenna knew it, and she could see that he knew it, too.

His dark eyes seemed to grow even deeper, swallowing her up. They fell slowly to her mouth and stayed there as Jenna's breath rasped out of her on a shaky little sigh.

She knew she should step away from him now. There was no reason for them to remain this close, nothing but a few scant inches separating their bodies. Less than that amount of space between his mouth and hers. All it would take was a slight dip of his head or an upward tilt of hers and their lips would come together.

Jenna's pulse kicked at the thought of kissing Brock.

It had been the furthest thing from her mind when he'd carried her into this room. Nor even a few moments ago, when her fear and anger had her hissing and snarling like a wild animal caught in a hunter's trap.

But now, when he was standing so close she could feel the heat of his body radiating toward her, the spicy scent of his skin tempting her to put her head against him and breathe him in, kissing Brock was a secret urge that pulsed through her with every fluttering beat of her heart.

Maybe he knew what she was feeling.

Maybe he was feeling the same thing.

He ground out a harsh curse, then took a small step back from her, staring at her hard, scowling fiercely. "Ah, fuck . . . Jenna . . ."

When he reached up and tenderly caught her face in his big hands, all the air seemed to evaporate out of the room. Jenna's lungs froze in her chest, but her heart kept hammering, racing so fast she thought it might explode.

She waited, in terror and in hope, bewildered by the need she had to feel Brock's mouth on hers.

His tongue swept quickly over his lips, the movement giving her a glimpse of the sharp points of his fangs, glinting like diamonds. He cursed again, then withdrew to arm's length, leaving a chasm of cold air swimming in front of her where the heat of his body had been just a second before.

"I shouldn't be here right now," he murmured thickly. "And you need some rest. Make yourself comfortable. If there aren't enough blankets on the bed, you'll find more in my walk-in closet off the bathroom. Use whatever you like."

Jenna had to mentally shake herself back to conversation mode. "This, um . . . are these your quarters?"

He gave a faint nod, already stepping out to the hallway. "They were. Now they're yours."

"Wait a minute." Jenna drifted after him. "What about you? Do you have somewhere else to stay?"

"Don't worry about it," he said, pausing to look at her where she leaned against the doorjamb. "Get some rest, Jenna. I'll see you around."

Brock's blood was still coursing hotly in his veins a short while later, when he stood outside one of the last remaining residential suites and dropped his knuckles on the closed door.

"It is eleven minutes earlier than we agreed" came the deep, matter-of-fact voice of the Breed male on the other side.

The door swung open and Brock was skewered by a pair of unreadable bright gold eyes.

"Avon calling," Brock said by way of greeting as he lifted the black leather duffel bag that contained all the personal gear he'd taken from his quarters earlier that day. "And what do you mean, I'm not supposed to be here for eleven more minutes? Don't tell me you're going to be one of those uptight roomies who runs everything by the clock, my man. My choices were limited, seeing how you and Chase have the last two rooms left in the compound. And to tell you the truth, if Harvard and I had to share quarters, I'm not sure we'd both survive the week."

Hunter said nothing as Brock stepped past him and

strode inside the room. He followed along to the bunk area, as stealthy as a ghost. "I thought you were someone else," he remarked somewhat belatedly.

"Yeah?" Brock pivoted his head around to look at the stoic Gen One, genuinely curious about the Order's newest, most reclusive member. Not to mention the fact that he was eager to steer his mind away from overheated thoughts about Jenna Darrow. "Who were you expecting besides me?"

"It is not relevant," Hunter replied.

"Okay." Brock shrugged. "Just trying to make conversation, that's all."

The Gen One's expression remained impassive, utterly neutral. Not surprising, considering the way the male had been raised—one of Dragos's homegrown assassins. Hell, the guy didn't even have a proper name. Like the rest of the personal army Dragos had bred off the Ancient, the Gen One had been referred to simply by his chief purpose in life: Hunter.

He'd come to the Order a few months ago, after Brock, Nikolai, and some of the other warriors had led a raid on a gathering of Dragos and his lieutenants. Hunter had been freed during the skirmish and was now allied against his maker in the Order's efforts to bring Dragos down.

Brock paused in front of the pair of double beds that sat on either side of the modest barracks-style bunk room. Both of them were made up with military precision, tan blanket and white sheets tucked in without a single wrinkle, a sole pillow meticulously arranged at the head of each bunk.

"So, which one do you want me to take?"

"It makes no difference to me."

Brock glanced back at the impassive face and inscrutable

golden eyes. "Then tell me which one you usually sleep in, and I'll take the other."

Hunter's flat stare didn't change one iota. "They are furniture. I have no attachment to either one."

"No attachment," Brock muttered around a low curse. "You can say that again, man. Maybe you can give me some pointers on that don't-give-a-damn-about-anything attitude of yours. I'm thinking it would come in real fucking handy from time to time. Especially when it comes to women."

With a growl, he tossed his gear onto the bunk at his left, then scrubbed his palm over his face and the top of his head. The groan that leaked out of him was ripe with frustration and the pent-up lust he'd been stifling since he'd forced himself to walk away from Jenna and the temptation he sorely didn't need.

"Damn," he ground out, his body thrumming all over again from just the remembered image of her beautiful face, tipped up to look at him.

If he hadn't known better, he would have thought she'd been waiting for him to kiss her. Everything male inside him had been clamoring with that certainty at the time, but he knew it would be the last thing Jenna needed.

She was confused and vulnerable, and he supposed he was a better man than the one who might take advantage of that fact simply because his libido craved a taste of her. Of course, that didn't make him feel any better about the raging hard-on that was suddenly coming back to life again, honor be damned.

"Way to go, hero," he berated himself tightly. "Now you're gonna need to soak in a tub of ice water for a week to pay for being noble."

"Are you unwell?" Hunter asked, startling Brock to

realize the other male was still standing behind him in the room.

"Yeah," Brock said, giving a sardonic chuckle. "I am unwell, all right. If you want to know the truth, I've been unwell since the moment I laid eyes on her."

"The human female," Hunter replied with grim understanding. "It is apparent that she is a problem for you."

Brock blew out a humorless sigh. "You think?"

"Yes, I do." There was no judgment in the answer, only level statement of fact. He spoke like a machine: total precision, zero feeling. "I presume everyone in the tech lab reached the same conclusion today, when you allowed Chase to provoke your anger over his comments regarding your attachment to the woman. Your actions showed a weakness in your training, and worse, a lack of self-control. You reacted carelessly."

"Thanks for noticing," Brock replied, suspecting his sarcasm was wasted on the unsociable, unflappable Hunter. "Remind me to bust your balls from here to next week if you ever loosen up enough to let a woman get under your skin."

Hunter didn't react, merely stared at him without a speck of emotion. "That will not happen."

"Shit," Brock said, shaking his head at the rigid Gen One soldier who'd been raised on neglect and punishing discipline. "You obviously haven't been with the right woman if you can sound so sure of yourself."

Hunter's expression remained stoic. Distant and detached. In fact, the longer Brock looked at him, the more clearly he began to see the truth. "Holy hell. Have you *ever* been with a woman, Hunter? My God . . . you're a virgin, aren't you?"

The Gen One's golden eyes stayed fixed on Brock's

gaze as though he considered it a test of will that he not permit the revelation to affect him. And Brock had to hand it to the guy, not a single degree of emotion flickered in those uncanny eyes, nor in the perfectly schooled features of his face.

The only thing that made Hunter flinch was the soft shuffle of slippered feet that sounded from the corridor outside. A child's voice—Mira—called into the living room.

"Hunter, are you here?"

He turned without offering an excuse and went to meet the little girl. "Now is not a convenient time," Brock heard him tell her in that deep, level tone of his.

"But don't you want to know what happens when Harry puts on the invisibility cloak?" Mira asked, disappointment dimming her normally bright voice. "It's one of my favorite parts of the whole book. You have to hear this chapter. You're gonna love it."

"She's right, that is one of the best parts." Brock came out of the bunk room, not sure what made him grin more—the realization that the stone-cold, Gen One assassin was an untried virgin, or the newer, equally amusing idea that the appointment Brock had apparently interrupted by coming to drop off his gear was Hunter's reading hour with the compound's youngest resident.

He gave Mira a wink and a smile as she plopped herself onto the sofa and cracked open the book to the place she'd left off. "Relax," he told Hunter, who stood there, stiff as a statue. "I'm not going to tell anyone your secrets."

He didn't wait to check for a reaction, just strolled out to the corridor and left Hunter staring in his wake.

CHAPTER
Eleven

Cross your fingers, you guys, but I think we may have just gotten the lead we've been looking for." Dylan hung up the phone and spun her desk chair around to face Jenna, Alex, Renata, and Savannah, all of whom had been gathered in the Breedmates' meeting room for the past couple of hours.

Actually, to call it a meeting room hardly did it justice. No less than half a dozen computer workstations sat at the ready on a long table at the back of the room. Boxes of manila files were organized by location and housed in a tall bookcase for easy access. Nearly every inch of wall space was covered with highlighted, pin-dotted maps of New England and detailed investigation charts that would have put most police cold case units to shame. Among those maps and charts were several expertly hand-drawn sketches of young women—faces of a few of the missing, whom the Order and their diligent Breedmates were determined to find.

No, Jenna thought as she took in her surroundings, this was no mere meeting room.

This was a room devoted to strategy, mission, and war.

Jenna welcomed the energy of the place, especially after the disturbing news she'd gotten about her blood work. She had also needed a distraction from thinking about the unexpectedly heated moments she'd shared with Brock in his—or, rather, her—quarters in the compound. She had all but jumped at the chance to get out of there after he'd left. It had been Alex who came looking for her not long afterward, and it was Alex who brought Jenna with her to the Breedmates' war room for some companionship and conversation.

She hadn't wanted to get interested in the work the women of the Order were involved in, but as she sat there among them, it was next to impossible for the cop in her to ignore the scent of a good information chase. She sat up a bit straighter in her chair at the conference table as Dylan walked over to a laser printer and grabbed the sheet of paper that slid into the output tray.

"What've you got?" Savannah asked.

Dylan slapped the printed page down on the table in front of the gathered women. "Sister Margaret Mary Howland."

Jenna and the others leaned in to look at the scanned image. It was a group photograph of a dozen or so young women and girls. From the style of their clothes, it appeared to have been taken perhaps twenty years ago. The group was gathered on the lawn below the steps of a wide covered porch, the kind of organized pose that schoolkids were sometimes corralled into for an annual class picture. Except in this case, it wasn't a school behind them but a large, unassuming house proclaiming itself to be the St. John's Home for Young Women, Queensboro, New York.

A kindly faced, middle-aged woman wearing a cross pendant and a modest summer dress stood just to the side of the group assembled under the white eave that bore the painted sign. One of the youngest girls stood with the older woman, her thin shoulders held in a caring grasp, her little face upturned and beaming with affection.

"That's her," Dylan said, pointing to the woman with the maternal smile and sheltering arms. "Sister Margaret."

"And she is?" Jenna asked, unable to hold her curiosity in check.

Dylan glanced over at her. "Right now, assuming she's still alive, this woman is possibly our best bet for finding out more about the Breedmates who have gone missing or ended up dead at Dragos's hands."

Jenna gave a small shake of her head. "I'm not following."

"Some of the women he's killed—and probably many that he's still holding prisoner now—came from runaway shelters," Dylan said. "See, it's not unusual for Breedmates to feel confused and out of place in mortal society. Most of us have no idea just how different we are, let alone why. Besides our common birthmark and shared biology, we've all got some kind of unique extrasensory ability, too."

"Not the stuff you see on TV talk shows or commercials for psychic hotlines," Savannah interjected. "Real ESP talents are often the surest way to spot a Breedmate."

Dylan nodded. "Sometimes those talents are a blessing, but a lot of times they're a curse. My own talent was a curse for most of my life, but fortunately I had a mother who loved me. Because I had her, no matter how confused and scared I got, I always had the security of home."

"But not everyone is that fortunate," Renata added. "It was a string of Montreal orphanages for Mira and me. And, from time to time, we called the street home."

Jenna listened in silence, counting her own blessings that she had been born into a normal, relatively close-knit family, where her biggest childhood problem had been trying to compete with her brother for approval and affection. She couldn't imagine having the kinds of problems females born with the teardrop-and-crescent-moon birthmark had to bear. Her own issues, as incomprehensible as they were, seemed to diminish a bit as she considered the lives these other women had lived. To say nothing of the hell the ones who were dead or missing had been made to endure.

"So, you believe that Dragos is preying on young women who end up in these kinds of shelters?" she asked.

"We know he is," Dylan said. "My mom used to work at a runaway shelter in New York. It's a long story, one for another time, but basically it turned out that the shelter she worked at was being funded and directed by none other than Dragos himself."

"Oh, my God," Jenna breathed.

"He'd been hiding behind an alias, calling himself Gordon Fasso when he moved within human social circles, so no one had any idea who he truly was . . . until it was too late." Dylan drew in what seemed to be a fortifying breath.

"He killed my mom after he realized he'd been unmasked and the Order was closing in on him."

"I'm sorry," Jenna whispered, meaning it completely. "To have lost someone you love to that kind of evil..."

The words drifted off as something cold and fierce bubbled deep inside her. As a former police officer, she knew the bitter taste of injustice and the need to right the scales. But she tamped the feelings down, telling herself the Order's fight against their enemy, Dragos, didn't belong to her. She had battles of her own to face.

"I'm sure Dragos will get what's coming to him in the end," she said.

It was a lame sentiment, knowingly offered from an emotional arm's length. But she hoped she would be proved right. Sitting with these women now, having gotten to know them all a bit better in the short time she'd been at the compound, Jenna prayed for the Order's success against Dragos. The thought of someone as perverse as he being loose on the world was beyond unacceptable.

She picked up the image printout and glanced at the warm expression of the nun who stood like a good shepherd next to her vulnerable flock. "How do you expect this woman—Sister Margaret—might be able to help you?"

"Staff turnover is high at youth shelters," Dylan explained. "The one where my mom worked was no exception. A friend of hers who used to work with her there just gave me Sister Margaret's name and that photograph. She says the sister retired a few years ago, but she'd been volunteering in several New York shelters since around the 1970s, which is just the kind of person we need to talk to."

"Someone who's been around the shelters for a long

time and might be able to identify past residents from a basic sketch," Savannah said, gesturing to the hand-drawn faces tacked to the walls.

Jenna nodded. "Those sketches represent women who've been in area shelters?"

"Those sketches," Alex said from beside Jenna, "are Breedmates being held by Dragos as we speak."

"You mean they're still alive?"

"They were a couple of months ago." Renata's voice was grim. "A friend of the Order's, Claire Reichen, used her Breedmate talent for dreamwalking to locate Dragos's headquarters. She saw the captives—upward of twenty of them—locked in prison cells in his laboratory. Although Dragos relocated his operations before we could save them, Claire has been working with a sketch artist to document the faces she saw."

"In fact, that's where Claire is right now, she and Elise both," Alex said. "Elise has a lot of friends in the Breed civilian community here in Boston. She and Claire have been working on a couple of new sketches, based on what Claire saw that day in Dragos's lair."

"Once we have faces of the captives," Dylan said, "we can start looking for names and possible family members. Anything that can help bring us closer to who these women are."

"What about databases for missing persons?" Jenna asked. "Have you compared the sketches to profiles listed with groups like the National Center for Missing Persons?"

"We did, and we've come up empty everywhere," Dylan said. "A lot of these women and girls in the shelters are runaways and orphans. A lot of them are throwaways. Some of them are walkaways, who deliberately cut all ties with family and friends. The end result is the same: They have no one to look for them or miss them, so there were no reports filed."

Renata grunted softly in acknowledgment and seemed to speak from some experience. "When you have no one and nothing, you can vanish and it's like you never existed in the first place."

From her years in Alaska law enforcement, Jenna knew how true that could be. Folks could disappear without a trace in big cities or small interior communities alike. It happened every day, although she never would have imagined it happened for the reasons that Dylan, Savannah, Renata, and the other women were explaining to her now. "So, what's your plan once you have identified the missing Breedmates?"

"Once we have enough of a personal link to even one of them," Savannah said, "Claire can try to connect via dreamwalking and hopefully bring back some information about where the captives have been moved."

Jenna was used to quick digestion and comprehension of facts, but her head was starting to spin with everything she was hearing. And she couldn't stop her mind from searching for solutions to the problems being laid out before her. "Wait a second. If Claire's talent led her to Dragos's lair once, why can't she just do it again?"

"For her talent to work, she needs some kind of emotional or personal link to whomever she's attempting to find in the dream state," Dylan answered. "Her link before wasn't to Dragos but to someone else."

"Her former mate, Wilhelm Roth," Renata put in, all but spitting the name like a curse. "He was a vile individual, but next to Dragos, his cruelty was nothing. No way could we ever let Claire try to tap into Dragos personally. It would be suicide."

"Okay. So, where does that leave us?" Jenna asked, the word *us* slipping out of her mouth even before she realized she'd said it. But it was too late to take it back, and she was much too intrigued to pretend differently. "Where do you see things going from here?"

"Hopefully, we can find Sister Margaret and she can help us figure that out," Dylan said.

"Do we have any way to contact her?" Renata asked.

Dylan's excitement dimmed a bit. "Unfortunately, we can't even be sure she's still alive. My mom's friend said she would be in her eighties by now. The only good news for us is that the sister's convent was based in Boston, so there's a chance she could be local. All we have to go on right now is her social security number."

"Give it to Gideon," Savannah said. "I'm sure he can hack into a government computer somewhere and get whatever info we need on her."

"My thought exactly," Dylan replied with a grin.

Jenna considered offering her own help in locating the good sister. She still had friends in law enforcement and a few federal agencies. It would only take a phone call or an email to call in a few chips, ask for a confidential favor or two. But the women of the Order seemed to have everything under control.

And she was better off not letting herself get entangled in any of this, she reminded herself sternly, as Dylan picked up the phone next to her computer workstation and called the tech lab.

A few moments later, both Gideon and Rio arrived in the war room. The two warriors received a quick summary of what Dylan had uncovered. Before she'd even finished explaining, Gideon seated himself at the computer and got busy.

Jenna watched from her seat at the table as everyone else—Savannah, Renata, Alex, Rio, and Dylan—gathered around to watch Gideon work his magic. Savannah had been right; it didn't take him more than a few minutes to hack through a secured, U.S. government website firewall and start downloading the records they needed.

"Sister Margaret Mary Howland, alive and well, according to the Social Security Administration," he announced. "Collected last month's check for two hundred ninety-eight dollars and some change at an address in Gloucester. It's printing out now."

Dylan grinned. "Gideon, you're a geek god."

"I aim to please." He sprang out of the chair and grabbed Savannah into a fast, hard kiss. "Tell me you're dazzled, baby."

"I'm dazzled," she replied drolly, laughing even as she slapped playfully at his shoulder.

He grinned, shooting Jenna an arch look over the top of his pale blue shades. "She loves me," he said, pulling his beautiful mate into a tighter squeeze. "She's mad for me, really. Can't live without me. Probably wants to take me to bed immediately and have her wicked way with me."

"Hah! You wish," Savannah said, but there was a heated gleam in the gaze she turned on him.

"Too bad we're not having this same luck getting a bead on TerraGlobal," Rio said, his arm wrapping around Dylan's shoulders in what seemed to be an instinctively intimate move.

Renata frowned. "Still no luck there, eh?"

"Not much," Gideon interjected. He must have seen

Jenna's confused look. "TerraGlobal Partners is the name of a company we believe Dragos is using to front some of his secret operations."

Alex jumped in next. "You remember that mining company that opened shop outside Harmony a few months back—Coldstream Mining?" At Jenna's nod, she said, "It belonged to Dragos. We believe it was meant to be used as a holding facility for the Ancient once they'd transported him to Alaska. Unfortunately, we all know how that worked out."

"We were able to trace the mining company back to TerraGlobal," Rio added. "But that's about as far as we've been able to get. We know TerraGlobal has lots of layers. It's just taking too damn long for us to peel them away. Meanwhile, Dragos digs himself in deeper, every minute farther out of our reach."

"You'll get him," Jenna said. She tried to ignore the little kick in her heart rate that urged her to strap on a couple of weapons and lead the charge. "You have to get him, so you will."

"Yeah," Rio replied, his scarred face drawn tight with determination as he nodded in agreement and glanced down into Dylan's eyes. "One day, we *are* going to get that son of a bitch. He's going to pay for everything he's done."

Under his strong arm, Dylan smiled sadly. She burrowed into his embrace, trying unsuccessfully to stifle a yawn.

"Come on," he said, brushing some of her loose red waves out of her eyes. "You've been putting in a lot of hours on all of this. Now I'm taking you to bed."

"Not a bad idea," Renata said. "Nightfall is going to

come early, and I'll bet Niko is still testing out new rounds in the weapons room. Time to go collect my man."

As she said her good-byes and headed out, Dylan and Rio, then Savannah and Gideon did the same.

"You want to come hang out with Kade and me for a little while?" Alex asked.

Jenna gave a mild shake of her head. "Nah, I'm okay. I think I'll stay here for a few minutes, unwind a bit. Been a long, strange day."

Alex's smile was sympathetic. "If you need anything at all, you come find me. Deal?"

Jenna nodded. "I'm fine. But thanks."

She watched her friend slowly turn and disappear up the corridor. When there was nothing left in the room but quiet and solitude, Jenna stood up and walked over to the wall of maps and charts and sketches.

It was admirable, what the Order and their mates were trying to do. It was important work—more important than anything Jenna would ever have come in contact with in rural Alaska, or anywhere else for that matter.

If everything she'd learned the past couple of days was true, then what the Order was doing here was nothing short of saving the world.

"Jesus Christ," Jenna whispered, struck by the enormity of it all.

She wanted to help.

If she was able—even in some small way—she had to help.

Didn't she?

Jenna paced around the war room, a battle of her own waging inside her. She wasn't ready to be part of something like this. Not when she still had so much to figure out for herself. With her brother dead, she had no family left at all. Alaska had been her home her entire life, and now that was gone, as well, a part of her prior existence erased to help the Order preserve their secrets as they pursued their enemy.

As for her future, she couldn't even begin to guess. The alien matter embedded inside her was a problem she never could have imagined, and no amount of wishing was going to take it away. Not even Gideon's mental brilliance seemed capable of extricating her from that tangled complication.

And then there was Brock. Of all the things that had happened to her between the invasion of her cabin home by the Ancient and her current, unexpected—although not unbearable—embrace by everyone in the Order's headquarters, Brock was proving to be the one thing she was least prepared to deal with.

She was nowhere close to ready when it came to the feelings he aroused in her. Things she hadn't felt in years, and sure as hell didn't want to feel now.

Nothing in her life was certain anymore, and the last thing she needed was to involve herself any further in the problems facing the warriors and their mates.

Nevertheless, Jenna found herself drifting over to the computer workstation on the desk nearby. She sat down at the keyboard and brought up an Internet browser, then went to one of those free email sites and created an account.

She opened a new message and typed in the address of one of her friends with the Feds up in Anchorage. She asked a single question, an inquiry to be looked into confidentially as a personal favor.

She drew in her breath, then hit send.

CHAPTER
Twelve

In the showers adjacent to the weapons room, Brock reached around his back and cranked the temperature setting from hot to scalding. Hands braced on the teak door of the private shower stall, head bent low to his chest, he welcomed the searing pound of water that sluiced over his shoulders and down his naked back. Hot steam roiled up all around him, thick as fog, from his head to the tiled floor at his feet.

"Christ," Kade hissed from a couple of stalls down from him. "Two solid hours of hand-to-hand sparring wasn't enough punishment for you? Now you feel the need to boil yourself alive over there?"

Brock grunted, slicking his hand over his face as the

steam continued to gather and the heat continued to batter his too-tense muscles. He'd found Kade in the weapons room with Niko and Chase after he'd dropped his gear in his new shared quarters with Hunter. It seemed reasonable to expect that a hard few rounds of blade work and hand-to-hand training would be enough to exhaust some of his restlessness and distraction. It should have been, but it wasn't.

"What's going on with you, man?"

"I don't know what you mean," Brock muttered, pushing his head and shoulders farther under the scalding spray.

Kade's scoff echoed in the cavernous shower room. "Like hell, you don't know."

"Shit." Brock exhaled the curse into the mist that wreathed his head. "Why do I get the feeling you're gonna enlighten me?"

There was a hard squeak of a spigot handle, followed by the bang of Kade's shower door as he stepped out and walked into the connected dressing area. A few minutes later, Kade's voice sounded from the other room. "You ever going to tell me what happened last night down in Southie at that meat-packing plant?"

Brock closed his eyes and blew out something that sounded like a growl, even to his own ears. "Nothing to tell. There were loose ends. I cleaned them up."

"Yeah," Kade said. "That's what I guessed had happened."

When Brock lifted his head, he found the warrior standing across the way from him. Kade was fully dressed in a black shirt and jeans, leaning back against the opposite wall. His steely silver gaze narrowed, knowing.

Brock had too much respect for his friend to try to

deceive him. "Those humans were scum who thought nothing of harming an innocent woman. You expect that kind of brutality to be condoned?"

"No." Kade stared, then gave a sober nod. "If I found myself face-to-face with anyone who'd laid a finger on Alex, I'd have to kill the bastard. That's what you did, isn't it? You killed those men."

"They were hardly men," Brock ground out. "They were rabid dogs, and what they did to Jenna—what they thought they could get away with—probably wasn't the first time they'd hurt a woman. I doubt Jenna would have been the last. So, yeah, I put them down."

For a long time, Kade said nothing. He just watched him, even after Brock stuck his head back under the furious pound of the spray, feeling no need to explain any further. Not even to his closest friend in the Order, the warrior who was like kin to him.

"Damn," Kade murmured after a lengthy silence. "You care about her, don't you?"

Brock shook his head, as much in denial as it was to slick the water off his face. "Lucan gave me the responsibility of looking after her, of keeping her safe. I'm only doing what's expected of me. She's another mission, no different than any other."

"Oh, yeah. No doubt about that." Kade smirked. "I had a mission like that up in Alaska not too long ago. Maybe I mentioned it to you once or twice?"

"This is different," Brock grumbled. "What you and Alex have is . . . not the same at all. Alex is a Breedmate, for one thing. There's no threat of getting serious with Jenna. I'm not the long-term type, and she's human, besides."

Kade's dark brows knit into an intense frown. "I don't think any of us can be sure exactly what she is now."

Brock absorbed the truth of that statement with a renewed sense of concern, not only for Jenna, but for the Order and the rest of the Breed nation, as well. Whatever was happening to her, as of today, it appeared to be accelerating. He couldn't deny that the news of her blood work changes troubled him. To say nothing of the fact that the damned bit of alien matter was actively delving deeper into her body, infiltrating on a level not even Gideon seemed prepared to combat.

Brock blew out a low curse under the punishing deluge of the shower. "If you're trying to make me feel better about all of this, feel free to stop anytime."

Kade chuckled, clearly enjoying himself. "I don't expect you'll be having any heart-to-heart talks with your new roomie, so this is me, showing you I care."

"I'm touched," Brock muttered. "Now, get the fuck out of here and let me scald myself in peace."

"Gladly. All this talk of missions and women reminds me that I have important duties of my own that I've been neglecting back in my quarters."

Brock grunted. "Give Alex my best."

Kade merely grinned as he saluted him, then strolled toward the exit.

After he was gone, Brock lingered under the water only a few minutes longer. It was late in the day, but he was too wired for sleep. And Kade's reminder about Jenna and her changing biology had his mind churning.

He toweled off, then got dressed in a gray T-shirt and dark jeans. He stomped into his black leather boots, feeling the sudden urge to head back into the weapons room and blow off more steam until nightfall, when he could finally escape the compound again. But working up a sweat hadn't done him much good the first time; he doubted it would do anything for him now.

Uncertain what would take off his edge, Brock found himself stalking down the central corridor of the compound, toward the tech lab. The halls were quiet, deserted. Not surprising for the time of day, when the mated warriors would be in bed with their females and the rest of the headquarters' occupants would be getting some rest before patrols rolled out at sundown.

Brock probably should have been thinking about that, too, but he was more interested in knowing if Gideon had turned up anything more about Jenna's blood work results. As he entered the stretch of corridor that would take him to the lab, he heard movement in another of the compound's meeting rooms.

Following the sound of shuffling papers, he drew to a pause outside the open door of the Breedmates' mission command center.

Jenna was alone inside the room.

Seated at the conference table, several manila file folders fanned out before her and a couple more stacked neatly at her elbow, she was bent over a pad of paper, pen in hand and thoroughly engrossed in whatever she was writing. At first, he didn't think she knew he was there. But then her hand paused halfway down the page, her head lifting. The soft brown layers of her hair shifted like silk as she pivoted to see who was standing in the doorway.

That had been his cue to duck away fast, before she saw him. He was Breed; he could have been there and gone before her mortal eyes could register his presence. Instead, for some idiotic reason he had no interest in examining, he took a step inside and cleared his throat.

Jenna's hazel gaze went wider when she saw him.

"Hey," he said.

She gave him a brief smile, looking more than a little caught off-guard by him. And why shouldn't she be, after the way he'd left things with her the last time he saw her? She pulled one of the file folders over and set it on top of her notepad. "I thought everyone had gone to bed."

"They have." He walked farther into the room and made a quick visual scan of the information spread out on the table. "Looks like Dylan and the others have managed to recruit you already."

She shrugged, a weak denial. "I was just . . . looking at a few things. Comparing notes on some of the files, jotting down a couple of my thoughts."

Brock took a seat in the chair next to her. "They'll appreciate that," he said, impressed that she was lending a hand. He reached for the notes she'd been writing. "Can I have a look?"

"It's nothing much, really," she said. "Sometimes it just helps to have a fresh pair of eyes."

He glanced at her crisp, precise handwriting that filled most of the page. Her mind seemed to operate in the same organized manner, based on the logical flow of her notes and the list of suggestions she'd made for investigating the missing persons cases that Dylan and the other Breedmates had been pursuing for the past few months.

"This is good work," he said, not flattery, just fact. "I can tell you're a damned good cop."

Again the denying shrug. "I'm not a cop anymore. I've been out of it a long time."

He watched her speak, heard the regret that lingered in her voice. "Doesn't mean you're not still good at what you do."

"I stopped being good at it a while ago. Something happened, and I . . . I lost my edge." She looked over at him then, unflinching. "There was a car accident four years ago. My husband and my six-year-old daughter were both killed, but somehow I survived."

Brock nodded faintly. "I know. I'm sorry for your loss."

His sympathy seemed to fluster her somewhat, as though she wasn't quite sure what to do with it. Maybe it would have been easier for her to talk about the tragedy on her own terms, without the knowledge that he'd already been privy to the information. Now she looked at him uncertainly, as though she feared he would judge her in some way. "I . . . struggled to accept that Mitch and Libby were gone. For a long time—even now—it's hard to know how I'm supposed to move on."

"You live," Brock said. "That's all you can do."

She nodded, but there was a hauntedness to her eyes. "You make it sound easy."

"Not easy, necessary." He watched her pick idly at a broken staple on one of the reports. "Is that why you resigned from law enforcement, because you didn't know how to live after the accident?"

Staring at the cluttered table space in front of her, she frowned, silent for a long moment. "I quit because I couldn't perform my duties anymore. Every time I had to report for a traffic violation, even a fender bender or a blown tire, I would be shaking so badly by the time I reached the scene, I could hardly get out of my vehicle to offer help. And the truly awful calls, the serious accidents or the domestic disturbances that often ended in violence, left me sick to my stomach for days afterward. Everything I'd learned in training and on the job had been shattered when that tractor trailer full of timber crossed the icy highway and plowed into my life." She glanced over at him then, her green-brown gaze as tenacious and un-flinching as he'd ever seen it. "I quit being a cop because I knew I couldn't do my job the way it needed to be done. I didn't want anyone who relied on me to possibly pay for my negligence. So, I resigned."

Brock had respected Jenna's courage and resilience from the moment he first laid eyes on her. Now the meter on his opinion of her had just climbed up another notch or ten. "You cared about your work and the people who depended on you. That's not a sign of weakness. That's strength. And you obviously had a great deal of love for your job. I think you still do."

Why that simple observation should strike a nerve in her, he didn't know, but he'd have to be blind to miss the flare of defensiveness that sparked in her eyes. She glanced away as though realizing her slip, and when she spoke, there was no anger in her voice. Only a flat sort of resignation. "You know a lot about me, huh? I guess there isn't much that you and the Order don't know by now."

"Alex gave us the basics," he admitted. "After what happened in Alaska, there were things we needed to know."

She grunted. "You mean, after I started talking alien gibberish in my sleep and became the unwilling ward of the Order."

"Yeah," he said, remaining seated as she stood up and walked away from him, arms crossed over her breasts. He noticed she'd completely given up the cane Tess and Gideon had prescribed for her, and her injured leg put only a mild limp in her step. "I see your gunshot wound must be healing up all right."

"It's much better." She tossed him a vague nod over

her shoulder. "Actually, it didn't seem that serious to begin with."

Brock inclined his head as though he agreed, but he recalled all too clearly just how serious the gunshot had been. If she was healing at an accelerated rate, he guessed the DNA replications Gideon had discovered might have something to do with that. "I'm glad you're feeling better," he said, thinking she probably didn't need any reminders about the unknown matter that was integrating with her body.

Her gaze lingered on him, softening. "Thank you for what you did for me last night—coming to find me, and getting me out of that awful place. I think you saved my life. I know you did, Brock."

"No problem."

God, he hoped she would never learn the details of just how savagely he'd dealt with her assailants. She wouldn't be thanking him if she'd seen him in action that night, or if she'd witnessed the vicious way he'd slaked both his bloodthirst and his fury on the pair of lowlife humans. If Jenna knew what he was capable of, she'd no doubt view him in the same way she did the Ancient who'd attacked her.

He didn't know why that should bother him like it did. He didn't want her to equate him to a monster, at least not so long as he was tasked with watching over her for the Order. She needed to trust him, and as her assigned protector, he needed to make sure that she did. He had a job to do, and he wasn't about to lose sight of his responsibility.

But the issue with Jenna went deeper than that, and he knew it. He just didn't have any intention of dissecting it—now or anytime in the foreseeable future.

He watched her drift toward the wall of maps and charts that documented the Order's pursuit of the Breedmates whom Dragos was suspected to have taken captive. "It's amazing work they're doing," Jenna murmured. "Dylan, Savannah, Renata, Tess . . . all of the women I've met here are truly incredible."

"Yeah, they are," Brock agreed. He got up and moved to where Jenna now stood. "The Order has always been a force to be reckoned with, but in the year since I've come on board, I've watched our strength redouble because of the involvement of the females in this compound."

She gave him a look that he found difficult to read.

"What?" he asked.

"Nothing." A brief smile touched her lips as she gave a small shake of her head. "I'm just surprised to hear that, is all. Most of the men I've ever been around in the workplace—hell, even my own father and brother—would have rather eaten their badges than admit they were better off for teaming up with a woman."

"I don't carry a badge," he said, returning her smile. "And I'm not most men."

She laughed softly but didn't turn away from his gaze. "No, no, you're not. Yet you're one of the few here who doesn't have a Breedmate."

He considered the comment, more than a little intrigued that she was curious about him on a personal level. "Business is one thing. Taking a blood-bonded mate is something else. It's a forever kind of deal, and I'm allergic to long-term relationships."

Her intelligent eyes held him, assessing. "Why is that?"

It would have been easy to give her a charmingly meaningless reply, the kind of glib crap he was used to dealing out to Kade and the other guys whenever the subject of Breedmates and emotional entanglements came up. But he couldn't look at Jenna and be anything but honest, no matter how it might make him appear to her. "Long-term means too many chances for me to let someone down. So, I make an effort to steer clear."

She didn't say anything for a long minute or two. Just faced him in silence, her arms still wrapped around herself, a hundred unspoken emotions deepening the color of her eyes. "Yeah, I know what you mean," she said finally, her voice a bit raspy, hardly above a whisper. "I know all about letting people down."

"No way am I going to believe that." He couldn't see the capable, confident woman failing at anything she set out to do.

"Trust me," she said soberly, then pivoted away from him and walked to the other wall, where a handful of sketches had been posted alongside case notes and printed maps. When she spoke again, there was a casualness to her voice that seemed forced. "So, is this allergy to long-term relationships something new for you, or have you always avoided commitment?"

He got an instant mental image of sparkling dark eyes and a mischievous, musical laugh that he still heard sometimes, like a ghost hiding in the far corners of his memories. "There was someone once. Well . . . there could have been someone. She died a long time ago."

Jenna's expression went slack with remorse. "Brock, I'm sorry. I didn't mean to make light—"

He shrugged. "No apology necessary. It's ancient history. A hundred years ago." Almost literally, he realized, stunned by the fact that so much time had come and gone since his carelessness had cost the life of someone he was supposed to protect.

Jenna drifted back toward him then and seated herself on the edge of the long table near him. "What happened to her?"

"She was murdered. I was working as a bodyguard at the time for her family's Darkhaven in Detroit. It was my responsibility to keep her safe, but I screwed up. She vanished on my watch. Her body turned up months later, brutalized beyond recognition and thrown in a filthy stretch of river."

"Oh, my God." Jenna's voice was soft, her brow creased with sympathy. "That's awful."

"Yeah, it was," he said, recalling all too well the horror of what had been done to her, before and after she'd been killed. Three months in the water hadn't made what was left of her any easier to look at.

"I'm sorry," Jenna said again, and reached out to rest her palm against the bulk of his biceps.

He tried to ignore the sudden flare of awareness that blazed through him at the contact. But attempting to tune out his attraction to her was like telling fire to not be hot. Touch it, and you still got burned. As he was burning now, when he glanced down to where Jenna's pale hand lingered over his darker skin.

When he lifted his gaze back to hers, he could tell by her subtle, indrawn breath that his eyes were likely alive with sparks of amber light, their transformation betraying his desire for her. She swallowed but didn't look away.

God help him, she didn't remove her soft hand from him, either, not even when his low growl of male need curled up from the back of his throat.

Thoughts of what had happened with her just hours earlier in his quarters flooded back to him on a heated wave of recollection. There had been nothing but a few bare inches between them then, as now. Then he'd wondered if Jenna had wanted him to kiss her. He'd been uncertain about her feelings, about the possibility that she might be feeling anything close to the desire he had for her. Now he needed to know with a ferocity that staggered him.

To be sure he wasn't misreading things, for his own sanity if nothing else, he brought his free hand over and covered her fingers with his. He drew closer to her, coming around the front of her where she leaned her weight against the table.

She didn't flinch away. Not Jenna. She stared him square in the eyes, confronting him head-on, as he should have expected she would. "I really don't know how to deal with all of this," she said softly. "The things that have happened to me since that night in Alaska . . . all the questions that may never be answered. I can handle that. Somehow, I'll learn to handle all of that. But you . . . this . . ." She glanced down then, only briefly, staring at their connected hands, at their entwined fingers. "I'm not very good at this. My husband has been gone four years. There hasn't been anyone since. I've never been ready for that. I haven't wanted . . ."

"Jenna." Brock stroked the underside of her chin very gently, lifting her face up toward his. "Would it be all right if I kissed you?"

Her lips wobbled into a small smile that he could not resist tasting. He bent his head and kissed her slowly, easing her into it, despite the intensity of his own need.

Although she'd confessed to being out of practice, he would never have known it from the sensual feel of her lips against his. Her kiss, both soft and direct, giving and taking, set him aflame. He stepped in tighter until he was standing between her legs, needing to feel her body pressed to him as he swept his tongue along the velvety seam of her mouth. He ran his hands down her sides, helping her up onto the conference table when her injured thigh began to tremble beneath her.

The kiss had been a mistake on his part. He'd thought he could leave it at that—just a kiss—but now that he'd started with Jenna, he wasn't sure how he would find the strength to stop.

And from the feel of her in his arms, her pleasured mewls and broken sighs as their kiss ignited into something far more powerful, he was certain that she wanted more of him, too.

Apparently, he couldn't have been more wrong.

It wasn't until he felt moisture on his face that he realized she was crying.

"Ah, Jesus," he hissed, backing off at once and feeling like an ass when he saw her tearstained cheeks. "I'm sorry. If I was pushing you too fast..."

She shook her head, clearly miserable, but she wouldn't speak.

"Tell me I didn't hurt you, Jenna."

"Damn it." She sucked in a hitching sob. "I can't do this. I'm sorry, it's my fault. I never should have let you—"

The words broke off, and then she was pushing him away from her, scrambling out from under him and all but running for the corridor.

Brock stood there for a second, every part of him tight and aching, raw with need. He should let her go. Chalk this up to a disaster narrowly averted, and put the all-too-tempting Jenna Darrow out of his mind.

Yeah, that's exactly what he should do, and he damned well knew it.

But by the time the thought had formed, he was already halfway up the corridor, following the soft sounds of Jenna's weeping back to his former quarters.

CHAPTER
Thirteen

Jenna felt like the biggest coward—the biggest damned fraud—as she fled up the corridor, sucking back tears. She'd let Brock think she didn't want him. Probably made him believe he'd been forcing himself on her in some way with that kiss, when it had nearly melted her into a puddle on the conference room table. She had let him worry that he'd done something wrong, possibly even hurt her somehow, and that was the most unfair thing of all.

Yet she couldn't stop running, needing to put distance between them with a determination that bordered on desperate. He made her feel too much. Things she wasn't prepared for. Things she craved so deeply but didn't deserve.

And so she ran, as terrified as she'd ever been and hating the cowardice that pushed her each step of the way. By the time she reached her quarters, she was shaking and breathless, tears streaming in hot trails down her cheeks.

"Jenna."

The sound of his deep voice behind her was like a caress of warmth against her skin. She turned to face him, astonished by the speed and silence that had brought him there not even a second after she'd arrived. Then again, he wasn't human. Not really a man at all—a fact she had to remind herself of when he was standing so near, the sheer size of him, the raw intensity of his dark gaze, speaking to everything that was woman inside her.

Her mouth still smoldered from his kiss. Her pulse was still thrumming heavily, heat still kindling deep into the core of her body.

As if he knew this, Brock moved closer. He reached out to her, took her hand in his, saying nothing. There was no need for words. Despite her slowing tears and the tremble of her limbs, she couldn't hide the desire she felt for him.

She didn't resist as he drew her nearer, into the heat of his body. Into the comfort of his arms. "I'm scared," she whispered, words that didn't come easy to her, and never had.

His eyes locked on hers, he gently stroked the side of her face. "You don't have to be afraid of me. I won't hurt you, Jenna."

She believed him, even before he bent his head and brushed her lips in an achingly tender kiss. Incredibly, impossibly, she trusted this man who was no man. She wanted his hands on her. Wanted to feel this connection to someone again, even if she wasn't at all ready to think beyond the physical, yearning to touch and be touched.

"It's okay," he murmured against her mouth. "You're safe with me, I promise."

Jenna closed her eyes as his words sank into her, the same words he'd soothed her with in the shattered darkness of her Alaskan cabin, then again in the compound's infirmary. Brock had been her steady link to the living world after her ordeal with the Ancient. Her only lifeline during the endless nightmares that had followed in the days after she'd been brought to this strange place, changed in so many terrifying ways.

And now...?

Now she wasn't sure where he fit in the confusion that remained of her life. She wasn't ready to think about that. Nor was she at all certain she was ready to give in to the feelings he stirred in her.

She pulled back slightly, doubt and shame welling up from the part of her that was still in mourning, the open wound on her soul that she had long ago come to accept might never fully heal.

Pressing her forehead against the warm solidity of his chest, the soft cotton of his gray T-shirt laced with the exotic scent of him, Jenna drew in a fortifying breath. It leaked out of her as a quiet, broken sigh. "Did I love them enough? That's what I keep asking myself, ever since that night in my cabin..."

Brock's hands skated lightly over her back as he held her, strong and compassionate, the steady calm she needed in order to relive those torturous moments when the Ancient had pressed her to decide her own fate.

"He made me choose, Brock. That last night in my cabin, I thought he was going to kill me, but he didn't. I wouldn't have fought him if he had. He knew that, I think." She was sure of it, in fact. She had been in a bad place the night the Ancient invaded her cabin home. He'd seen the nearly empty bottle of whiskey on the floor beside her and the loaded pistol in her hand. The box of photographs she brought out every year around the anniversary of the accident that had robbed her of her family and left her to carry on alone. "He knew I was prepared to die, but instead of killing me, he forced me to speak the words out loud, to tell him what I wanted more—life, or death. It felt like torture, some kind of sick game he was making me play against my will."

Brock ground out something coarse under his breath, but his hands remained gentle against her back, a tender, soothing warmth.

"He made me choose," she said, recalling every unbearable minute of her ordeal.

But even worse than the endless hours of imprisonment and being fed upon, the horror of realizing her captor was a creature not of this earth, was the awful moment when she heard her own voice rasp the words that seemed torn from the deepest, most shameful pit of her soul.

I want to live.

Oh, God . . . please, let me live.

I don't want to die!

Jenna swallowed past the lump of anguish in her throat. "I keep thinking that I didn't love them enough," she whispered, miserable at the thought. "I keep thinking that if I really loved them, I would have died with them. That when the Ancient forced me to decide if I wanted to live or not, I would have made a different choice."

When a sob caught her breath, Brock's fingers brushed the underside of her chin. He lifted her face to meet his solemn gaze. "You survived," he said, his voice firm yet infinitely tender. "That's all you did. No one would blame you for that, especially them."

She closed her eyes, feeling the weight of her regret ease a bit with his soothing words. But the void in her heart was a cold, empty place. One that gaped even wider as Brock gathered her close, comforting her. His warmth and caring seeped inside her skin like a balm, adding deeper emotion to the desire that hadn't lessened for the nearness of his body to hers. She curled into the shelter of his arms, resting her cheek against the solid, unwavering strength of him.

"I can take it away, Jenna." She felt the warm press of his mouth, the riffle of his breath through her hair, as he kissed the top of her bowed head. "I can carry the grief for you, if you want me to."

There was a part of her that rebelled at the idea. The tough woman, the seasoned cop, the one who always charged to the front of any situation, recoiled at the notion that her grief could be too much for her to bear on her own. She had never needed a helping hand, nor would she be the one to ask—not ever. That kind of weakness would never do.

She drew back, denial sitting at the tip of her tongue. But when she parted her lips to speak, the words wouldn't come. She stared up into Brock's handsome face, into his penetrating dark eyes, which seemed to reach deep inside her.

"When was the last time you allowed yourself to be happy, Jenna?" He stroked her cheek so lightly, so reverently, she shivered under his touch. "When was the last time you felt pleasure?"

His large hand drifted down, along the side of her neck. Heat radiated from his broad palm and long fingers.

Her pulse kicked as he cupped her nape, his thumb caressing the sensitive skin below her ear.

He brought her toward him then, tilting her face up to meet his. He kissed her, slow and deep. The unhurried melding of his mouth against hers sent a current of liquid heat arrowing through her veins. The fire pooled in the center of her, the raw core filling with bright, fierce longing.

"If this isn't what you want," he murmured against her lips, "then all you have to do is tell me. At any time, I'll stop—"

"No." She shook her head as she reached up to touch his strong jaw. "I do want this. I want you—so much right now, it's scaring me half to death."

His smile spread lazily, those sensual lips parting to reveal the white flash of his teeth—and the growing length of his fangs. Jenna stared at his mouth, knowing that basic human survival instincts should be throwing off all sorts of alarms, warning her that getting too close to those sharp canines could be deadly.

But she felt no fear. Rather, her mind recognized his transformation with an inexplicable sense of acceptance. Excitement, even, as the absorbing brown of his eyes began to glitter with fiery amber light.

Above the crewneck collar of his gray T-shirt and beneath the short sleeves that clung to the knotted bulge of his smoothly muscled biceps, Brock's *dermaglyphs* pulsed with color. The Breed skin markings deepened from their usual dark bronze hue to shades of burgundy, gold, and deepest purple. Jenna ran her fingers along the swirling curves and tapered arches of his *glyphs*, marveling at their unearthly beauty.

"Everything I thought I knew is different now," she

mused aloud as she stood in the circle of his arms, idly tracing the pattern of the *glyphs* that tracked down his thick forearm. "It's all changed now. I'm changed—in ways I'm not sure will ever make sense to me." She glanced up at him. "I'm not looking for more confusion in my life. I don't think I could handle that on top of the rest of it."

He held her stare, no judgment in his eyes, only patience and an aura of unerring control. "Are you confused right now, when I'm touching you . . . or when I'm kissing you?"

"No," she said, astonished to realize it. "Not then."

"Good." He bent his head and claimed her mouth again, suckling her lower lip, catching it between his teeth as he stroked her back, then palmed his hands along the curve of her ass. He squeezed her possessively, hauling her electrified body up against the hard ridge of his groin. He nuzzled into the crook of her neck, his lips warm and wet on her skin. When he spoke again, his voice was thicker than before, edged with the same kind of need that was roaring through her. "Let yourself feel pleasure, Jenna. If you want it, then that's all this needs to be between us. No pressures, no strings. No promises neither one of us is ready to make."

Oh, God. It sounded so good, so tempting to give in to the desire that had been crackling between them ever since she woke up at the Order's compound. She wasn't ready to open her heart again—she might never be ready for that vulnerability again—but she didn't know if she was strong enough to resist the gift Brock was offering her.

He kissed the hollow at the base of her throat. "It's all right, Jenna. Give the rest to me for now. Let everything else go, except this."

"Yes," she sighed, unable to hold back her breathless gasp as his caress roamed her body. His strong, gifted hands sent tingles of energy through her veins, his preternatural talent drawing away the lingering weight of her sorrow and guilt and confusion. His hot, skilled mouth left only sensation and hunger in its wake.

He kissed a slow path up the length of her throat, then along her jawline, until his lips found hers once more. Jenna welcomed his passion, opening to him as his tongue swept the seam of her mouth. He groaned as she sucked him in deeper, growled with pure male approval as she wrapped her fingers around the back of his head and held him more firmly against her mouth.

God, she had no idea how badly she'd craved a man's touch. She'd gone so long without intimacy, willingly depriving herself of sexual contact and release. For four years, she had convinced herself she neither wanted it nor deserved it, just a further self-imposed punishment for the offense of having survived the accident that killed her loved ones.

She had believed herself immune to desire, yet now, with Brock, all those once-impenetrable barriers were crumbling, falling down around her like nothing more than dried, weightless leaves. She couldn't feel guilt for the pleasure he was giving her. Whether due to Brock's powerful ability to absorb her anguish, or the depth of her own repressed need, she couldn't be certain. All she knew was the soaring intensity of her body's response to him, a surge of pleasure and tightening anticipation that left her breathless and greedy for more.

Brock's big hands drifted to her shoulders, then made a slow journey over her breasts. Through the thin cotton knit of her shirt, her nipples peaked, hard and aching, alive with sensation as he kneaded each heavy mound. Jenna moaned, wanting to feel more of his touch. She caught his hand in hers and guided him up under the loose hem of her top. He didn't require any more direction than that. In less than a second, he'd unfastened the front clasp of her bra and covered her bare flesh with his heated palm.

He teased the diamond-hard bud as he caressed her. "Is that better?" he murmured just below her ear. "Tell me if you like it."

"God...*yes*." It felt so good, she could hardly form words.

Jenna sucked in a hiss of pleasure, tipping her head back as the coil of sensation twisted tighter in her core. He kept touching her, kept kissing her and caressing her, as he slowly removed her shirt. He took equal care with her loosened bra, sliding the thin straps off her shoulders, then down her arms. Suddenly she was standing before him, naked from the waist up. The instinct to cover herself—to hide the scars that riddled her torso from the accident and the one on her abdomen that was a daily reminder of Libby's difficult birth—flared swiftly, but only for an instant.

Only in the time it took for her to glance up and meet Brock's gaze.

"You're beautiful," he said, gently taking her hands in his and drawing them away from her body before she had the chance to feel awkward or embarrassed by his praise or his open observation of her.

She had never felt particularly beautiful. Confident and capable, physically fit and strong. Those were words she understood and could accept. Words that had carried her through most of her thirty-three years of life, even through her marriage. But beautiful? It felt as alien to her as the odd language she'd heard herself speaking on the infirmary video recording yesterday.

Brock, on the other hand, was beautiful. Although that seemed an admittedly odd way to describe the dark force of nature that stood before her now.

Every speck of velvety brown color in his eyes was gone, devoured by the glow of bright amber that warmed her cheeks like an open flame. His pupils had thinned to narrow slivers, and his lean cheeks were now taut and more angular, his flawless dark skin stretched tight across his bones, setting off the astonishing appearance of his long, deadly sharp fangs.

Those searing eyes locked on her, he pulled off his T-shirt and let it fall to the floor beside hers. His chest was incredible, a massive wall of perfectly formed muscle covered in an intricate pattern of pulsing *glyphs*. She couldn't resist touching his smooth skin, just to see if it felt as satiny against her fingertips as it looked to her eyes. It was even softer than she'd guessed, but the sheer, inhuman strength beneath it was unmistakable.

Brock looked every bit as lethal as he had when he'd come to save her in the city, except instead of the cold malice that had rolled off him in waves that night, now he vibrated with something equally aggressive and intense: desire. All of it centered on her.

"You are . . . damn, Jenna," he rasped, tracing the line of her shoulder, then circling the dusky rose tip of her breast. "You have no idea just how lovely you are, do you?"

She didn't answer him, didn't really know how. Instead, she moved closer and brought his mouth down to hers in another scorching kiss. Skin against skin, her breasts crushed against the bulky slabs of his chest, Jenna nearly combusted with need. Her heart was hammering, breath racing, as Brock reached down and unfastened the button and zipper fly of her jeans. She caught her lip with her teeth as he slid his hands between the slack waistband and the skin of her hips, then smoothly eased the denim down over her white bikini panties. He sank to his haunches, following the denim's descent with his hands.

He took care around her healing gunshot wound, cautious not to disturb the bandage that wrapped around her thigh. "Is this all right?" he asked, glancing up at her, his deep voice so rough she hardly recognized it. "If there is pain, I can draw it away."

Jenna shook her head. "It doesn't hurt. Really, it's okay."

His bright amber eyes shuttered with the fall of his lashes as he turned back to his task. Her jeans removed, he sat back on his heels and gazed at her, stroking his hands up and down the length of her legs.

"So, so beautiful," he praised her, then leaned his head in and pressed his lips to the triangle of white cotton between her thighs, the sole bit of clothing that covered her now.

Jenna blew out a shaky sigh as he caught the fabric in his teeth and fangs. With a meaningful look up at her, his hands still caressing her legs, he tugged at the cotton before letting it snap softly back into place against her overheated flesh. He followed it with his mouth, kissing her again, more determinedly now, nudging aside the paltry scrap of material and nuzzling his face deep into the moist cleft of her sex.

His hands clenched her backside as he explored her with lips and tongue and the erotic graze of his teeth against the wet flesh at her core. He eased her out of her panties, then spread her thighs open and suckled her again. He brought one hand between her legs, adding the slick play of his fingers to the already dizzying expertise of his mouth. Jenna trembled, lost to sensation and less than a breath away from flying apart.

"Oh, God," she gasped, quaking as he delved between her drenched folds with the blunt tip of his finger, penetrating her slowly, while his kiss stoked her need ever tighter. She rocked against him, awash in heat. "Oh, my God . . . Brock, don't stop."

He moaned against her wetness, a long purr of blatant male enjoyment that vibrated through her flesh and bone, deep into the heated center of her. Jenna's climax roared up on her like a storm. She shook with the force of it, crying out as the pleasure seized her and flung her skyward. She broke apart, sensation shimmering over her like stardust as she spiraled higher and higher, tremors of pure bliss shuddering through her, one after the other.

She was boneless as she floated back down to reality. Boneless and drained, even though her body was still pulsing and alive with sensation. And Brock was still kissing her. Still stroking her with his fingers, wringing every last quiver from her as she clutched his thick shoulders and panted with pleasurable little aftershocks.

"I think I needed that," she whispered, shuddering as his low chuckle rumbled against her sensitive flesh. He kissed her inner thighs, nipping teasingly, and her legs went a little wobbly beneath her. She tipped forward, draping herself over Brock's broad back. "Oh, my God. I had no idea how much I needed that."

"My pleasure," he rasped. "And I'm not finished with you just yet." He shifted beneath her, bringing his arm around her and settling her over his right shoulder. "Hold onto me."

She had no choice. Before she knew what he intended, he stood up. As in deadlifted all of her weight on one shoulder and rose to his feet like she was nothing but feathers. Jenna held on as he'd told her and couldn't help but admire the sheer power of him as he strode with her into the adjacent bedroom. Clad in just his jeans, his back muscles flexing and bunching beneath his smooth skin with each long stride, a perfect concert of fitness and form.

No doubt about it, he was beautiful.

And her already-electrified body hummed with renewed heat when she realized he was carrying her directly to the big king-size bed.

He pulled aside the coverlet and sheet, then set her down on the edge of the mattress. Jenna watched with growing hunger as he unbuttoned his dark jeans and stepped out of them. He wasn't wearing anything underneath. Elaborate *glyphs* tracked around his trim waist and hips and down onto the sinewy bulk of his thighs. The colors pulsed and mutated, drawing her gaze only briefly from the thick jut of his erection, which stood rigid and immense as he watched her take in the sight of him.

Jenna swallowed on a parched throat as he strode toward her, devastating in his nakedness. The fiery glow of his eyes had grown impossibly brighter, his fangs seeming huge to her now.

He paused at the edge of the bed, scowling when she held his transformed gaze. "Are you afraid of me . . . like this?"

She gave a small shake of her head. "No, I'm not afraid."

"If you're concerned about pregnancy—"

She shook her head again. "My internal injuries in the accident took care of that. I can't get pregnant. Anyway, regardless of that, I understand that Breed and human DNA doesn't mix."

"No," he said. "And as for any other concerns you might have, you're safe with me. There is no sickness or disease among my kind."

Jenna nodded in acknowledgment. "I trust you, Brock."

His scowl lessened but he held himself very still. "If you're not sure—if this isn't what you want, then what I told you before still stands. We can stop anytime." He chuckled low under his breath. "I think it might kill me to stop right now, when you're looking so damn hot in my bed, but I'll do it. God help me, but I'll do it."

She smiled, touched that someone so powerful could have such honor and humility. She pushed back the sheets and made room for him next to her. "I don't want to stop."

His mouth broke into a wide grin. On a growl, he stalked forward and climbed into the bed beside her. At first, they merely touched and caressed, kissing tenderly, learning more about each other's bodies. Brock was patient with her, even though the tension in his body told her he was racked with the need for release. He was kind and caring, treating her like a cherished lover even though they'd both agreed up front that this thing between them could never be more than casual, no strings attached.

It seemed incredible to her that this man she barely knew—this Breed male who should by rights scare her spitless—could instead feel so familiar, so intimate. But Brock was hardly a stranger to her. He'd been at her side through a nightmare ordeal, then again through the days of her recovery here at the compound. And he'd come after her that night she'd been alone and injured in the city, her unlikely, dark savior.

"Why did you do it?" she asked him quietly, her fingers tracing the *dermaglyphs* that swirled down around his shoulder and onto his chest. "Why did you stay with me in Alaska, and then all those days I was in the infirmary?"

He was silent for a moment, his black brows knitted tightly over the fiery glow of his eyes. "I hated seeing what had happened to you. You were an innocent bystander who got caught in the crossfire. You're human. You didn't deserve to be dragged into the middle of our war."

"I'm a big girl. I can handle it," she said, an autopilot response that she didn't truly feel. Especially after the disturbing results of her latest blood work. "What about now . . . what we're doing here, I mean. Is this part of your be-nice-to-the-pitiful-human program, too?"

"No. Hell no." His scowl deepened almost to the point of anger. "You think this is about pity? Is that what it felt like to you?" He rasped out a harsh breath, baring the sharp tips of his fangs as he rolled her onto her back and straddled her. "In case you haven't noticed, I'm pretty goddamned hot for you, lady. Any fucking hotter and I'd be ash."

To prove his point, he gave a none-too-subtle thrust of his hips, seating his shaft between the plush, wet folds of her sex. He pumped a couple of times, sliding the rigid length of his cock back and forth within the slick cleft, teasing her with the hard heat of his arousal. He hooked his arm under her leg and brought it up around his shoulder, turning his face against her thigh and giving the tender skin a sharp nip.

"This is pure necessity, not pity," he said, his voice rough and raw as he entered her, long and slow and deep.

Jenna couldn't form a response, even if she tried. The stunning feel of him filling her up, stretching her deeper with each powerful thrust, was so overwhelming it stole her breath. She clung to him with both hands as he caught her mouth in a bold kiss and rocked over her, his body moving in a fierce, demanding tempo.

Already, the crest of another climax was swiftly rising up on her. She couldn't hold it back. It crashed into her, splintering her senses, sharpening them. She felt the rush of her own blood in her veins, felt the furious pound of Brock's pulse, too, drumming beneath her fingertips and in every nerve ending. Her ears filled with the sound of her breathless shout of release, the slick friction of joined bodies writhing against the sheets. The scents of sex and soap and clean sweat on hot skin intoxicated her. The taste of Brock's searing kiss on her lips only made her crave more of him.

She hungered, in a way she couldn't understand.

She hungered for him, so deeply it seemed to wring her out from the inside.

She wanted to taste him. To taste the power of what he was.

Panting in the wake of her release, she drew back from his mouth. He swore something dark and aggressive under his breath, his strokes growing more intense, veins and tendons popping up in his neck and shoulders like thick cables rising under his skin.

Holding on to him, Jenna let her head fall back for a moment, trying to lose herself in the rhythm of their bodies. Trying not to think about the gnawing ache that was festering in the center of her, the confusing yet irresistible impulse that called her gaze back to his strong neck. Back to the engorged veins that pulsed like war drums in her ears.

She pressed her face into the strong column of his neck and ran her tongue along the pulse point she found there. He groaned, a pleasured sound that only served as fuel for the fire still stoked and burning within her. She ventured a little more, closing her teeth over his skin. He snarled a raw curse, and she bit down tighter, feeling the surge of tension that arrowed through his whole body. He was on the edge now, his arms like granite around her, every thrust of his hips growing more intense.

Jenna clamped down harder on the soft skin caught between her teeth.

She bit down until he was frenzied and wild with passion . . .

Until she tasted the first sweet drop of his blood against her tongue.

CHAPTER
Fourteen

He didn't know what packed the stronger punch—the tight, wet heat of Jenna's sheath gripping his cock as he roared toward release, or her sudden, wholly unexpected nip at his neck.

Together, the two sensations proved cataclysmic.

Brock caught Jenna around her back and pushed her down beneath him as the knot of mounting pressure coiled tighter, hotter, then exploded. Fangs bared and throbbing, he threw his head back on a guttural shout as he came, hard and fast and unrelenting, the most intense climax he'd ever known.

And even as it racked him, his release didn't slake his need for her. Holy hell, not even close. His sex remained rigid inside her, still rampant and thrusting, operating on a will of its own as the earthy, sweet fragrance of Jenna's body mingled with the scent of his own blood.

He reached up to where the sting of her small bite burned. His fingertips came away sticky from the faint rivulet that trickled down onto his chest. "Jesus Christ," he hissed, his voice constricted with surprise and far too much arousal.

"I'm sorry," she murmured, sounding appalled. "I didn't mean to..."

When he glanced down at Jenna, the amber glow of his transformed eyes played over her pretty face and then her mouth. Her kiss-swollen, gorgeous mouth. His blood was there, too, slick and red on her lips.

Everything Breed in him locked onto that dark, glossy stain, wild need flaring in his gut. All the worse when the tip of her pink tongue darted out to sweep the scarlet traces away.

Hunger ratcheted in him like a vise. He was already dangerous with need, and now this other, mounting craving. He reeled back, even though every savage impulse within him bellowed with the desire to take this woman in every way that one of his kind could.

Forcing himself to dial things down before they got any further out of his control, he pulled out of her warmth and swung his legs over the edge of the bed on a ripe curse. The floor was cold beneath his feet, frigid against his enlivened, sweat-sheened skin. When Jenna's hand came to rest lightly on his back, her touch went through him like a flame.

"Brock, are you okay?"

"I gotta go," he said, gruff words that scraped over his tongue.

It was hard as hell to make his body move off the bed when Jenna was so near, naked and beautiful. Touching him with sweet, though unnecessary, concern.

This encounter—the sex he'd so benevolently offered, thinking he had everything so well under control—was supposed to be about her. At least, that's what he'd convinced himself of when he'd kissed her in the war room and realized how long she'd been alone, untouched. But it had been a selfish move on his part.

He'd wanted her, and he'd fully expected that all it would take to get her out of his head—out of his system—was having her in his bed. He'd expected her to be like any other of his pleasantly casual, deliberately uncomplicated dalliances with human women. He couldn't have been more wrong. Instead of dousing his attraction to Jenna, making love with her had only increased his desire for her. He still wanted her, now more fiercely than before.

"I can't stay." The muttered statement was more a reinforcement for himself than an explanation directed at her. Without looking at her, knowing he wouldn't be able to find the strength to leave if he did, he stood up. He reached down to pick up his jeans and hastily put them on. "Sundown is coming soon. I've got patrol orders to review, weapons and munitions to prepare—"

"It's all right, you don't have to give me excuses," she interjected from behind him. "I wasn't going to ask you for a cuddle or anything."

That made him turn around to face her. He was relieved to see there was no judgment or anger in her expression, nor in the steady gaze that locked onto his, but he didn't quite buy the careful set of her jaw. She

probably expected it made her look tough, unflappable—
the cool, practiced confidence that said she would never
back down from any challenge.

If he had just met her, he might have believed that
look. But all he saw in that moment was the fragile, secret
vulnerability that hid behind the take-no-bullshit mask.

"Don't think this was a mistake, Jenna. I don't want
you to regret what happened here."

She shrugged. "What's to regret? It was just sex."

Incredible, mind-blowing sex, he mentally corrected, but
refrained from saying so when just the thought made him
grow even harder. God, he was going to need to find a
very cold shower and fast. Or maybe an ice bath. For a
week straight.

"Yeah." He cleared his throat. "I have to go now.
If your leg bothers you, or if there's anything else you
need . . . anything I can do for you, let me know. All right?"

She nodded, but he could see from the defiant glint of
her eyes and the slight, stubborn rise of her chin that she
would never ask. She might have been reluctant to accept
his help before, but now she'd be damned determined to
refuse anything he might offer.

If he'd wondered whether this encounter had been a
mistake, the answer was staring him full in the face now.

"I'll see you around," he said, feeling just as lame as he
sounded.

He didn't wait for her to tell him not to hold his breath,
or something even more succinct. He turned away from
her and left the bedroom, grabbing his T-shirt on his way
out, and cursing himself as a first-rate asshole as he closed
the door behind him and headed up the empty corridor.

———

With a self-loathing groan, Jenna let herself fall back onto the bed as the door in the other room closed behind Brock. She'd always had a knack for scaring men off, with or without a loaded weapon in her hand, but sending a formidable male like Brock—a vampire, for crissake—into a post-sex bolt out the door ought to win her some kind of prize.

He said he didn't want her to think getting naked with him had been a mistake. Didn't want her to regret it. Yet the expression on his face as he'd looked at her seemed to contradict all of that. And the way he'd hightailed it out of the place didn't leave a lot of room for doubt, either.

"It was just sex," she muttered under her breath. "Get over it."

She didn't know why she should feel stung and embarrassed. If nothing else, she should be grateful for the release of so much pent-up sexual frustration. Obviously, she'd needed it. She couldn't remember ever feeling so heated and out of control as she had been with Brock. As sated as she was, her body still vibrated. All of her senses seemed tuned to a higher frequency than normal. Her skin felt alive, tingling with hypersensitivity, too tight for her body.

And then there was the tangle of her emotions. She lay back, awash in confusion about the still-ripe curiosity that had made her bite Brock—so hard, she'd actually drawn blood. The strange, spicy-sweet taste of him lingered on her tongue, as exotic and enigmatic as the man himself.

She had the fleeting sense that she ought to be appalled at what she'd done—in fact, she had been horrified immediately afterward—but as she lay there now, alone in the bed that belonged to him, some dark, twisted part of her craved even more.

What the hell was she thinking? She must be losing her mind to entertain thoughts like that, let alone to have acted on the impulse.

Or maybe what was driving her was something even worse . . .

"Oh, shit." Jenna sat up, a sudden, sick worry coming over her.

Her blood work and DNA had begun to alter from the implant embedded inside her. What if that wasn't the only thing that was changing about her?

Dread sitting like a cold rock in her gut, she leapt out of the bed and hurried to the bathroom, flipping on all of the lights. Leaning over the marble counter, she peeled back her upper lip and stared into the large mirror.

No fangs.

Thank God.

Nothing staring back at her except her own familiar reflection, her own unremarkable, wholly human set of teeth. She'd never been so glad to see them since the day she first had her braces off at the awkward age of thirteen—a too-tall, too-tough tomboy who'd had to kick a lot of junior high school boys' asses for all the teasing she took about her metal mouth and training bra. A wry, half-hysterical laugh bubbled out of her. She could have saved herself a lot of effort and bruises if she'd been able to flash a pair of razor-sharp fangs at her schoolyard tormentors.

Jenna heaved a long sigh and sagged against the counter. She looked normal, which was a relief, but inside, she was different. She knew that, and she didn't need Gideon's latest test results to tell her that something very peculiar was going on under her skin.

In her bones.

In the blood that seemed to rush like rivers of lava through her veins.

She brought her hand up under the fall of her hair, brushing her fingers over her nape, where the Ancient had made his incision and embedded his piece of hateful biotechnology inside her. It had healed up; she felt no trace of it on the surface of her skin as she had before. But she'd seen the X rays; she knew it was there, burrowing deeper into her nerves and spinal cord. Infiltrating her DNA.

Becoming part of her.

"Oh, God," she murmured, a wave of nausea rolling up on her.

How much more messed up could her life get? She had something this monumental to deal with, and yet she'd gone and gotten naked with Brock. Then again, maybe she'd needed to be with him precisely because of everything else she was dealing with lately. What she didn't need was to complicate an already overcomplicated situation.

She sure as hell didn't need to sit there and worry about what he might think of her now. She didn't need to go there at all, but telling herself that didn't keep the thoughts of him from entering her head.

And as she peeled the bandage from her healing thigh and turned on the shower, she told herself that she didn't need Brock or anyone else to help get her through whatever lay ahead. She'd been alone for a long time. She knew what it was to fight on her own, to pull herself through dark days.

But knowing that didn't keep her from leaning on the memory of Brock's strength—the soothing power of his tender words and his gifted hands. His gently murmured promises that she wasn't alone. That with him, she was safe.

"I don't need him," she whispered into the empty echo of the room. "I don't need anything from anyone."

There was a small quake in her voice, a wobbly note of fear that she despised hearing. She sucked in a sharp breath, blew it out on a curse.

Jenna stepped into the shower and under the warm spray, closing her eyes. She let the steam envelop her fully, let the steady rhythm of the falling water swallow up her soft, shaky sobs.

Brock should not have been surprised to run into one of the other warriors, since nightfall was approaching topside and most of the Order would be heading out soon on patrols of the city. But probably the dead last person he wanted to see as he came out of the shower room, where he'd spent a good hour under a frigid dousing, was Sterling Chase.

The former Enforcement Agent was cleaning his firearms on a table in the weapons room. He looked up from his work when Brock strode through, already dressed in black fatigues and combat boots, ready to get a jump on the night's missions.

"Looks like you and I are partners tonight," Chase drawled. "Lucan's sending Kade and Niko down to Rhode Island. Something about intel Reichen picked up on his recent work in Europe. They're heading out as soon as the sun sets."

Brock grunted. He and Chase, patrol partners? Talk about a bad day heading farther south. "Thanks for the update. I'll try not to accidentally kill you while we're looking for bad guys tonight."

Chase gave him a deadpan look. "Likewise."

"Shit," Brock hissed on a sharp exhale. "Which one of us pissed him off?"

Chase's brows arched under his short-cut, blond crown of hair.

"Lucan," Brock said. "I don't know why the hell he'd team us up, unless he's trying to prove a point to one or both of us."

"Actually, the assignment was my suggestion."

The admission didn't exactly make things better. Brock stilled, suspicion rankling his brow. "You suggested that we partner for patrol."

Chase inclined his head. "That's right. Consider it an olive branch. I was out of line earlier with regard to you and the human. I shouldn't have said what I said."

Brock stared, incredulous. He bore down on him, more than ready to escalate things if he got even so much as a whiff of duplicity out of the arrogant male. "Let me tell you something, Harvard. I don't know what kind of game you think you're playing, but you do not want to fuck with me."

"No game," Chase said, his piercing blue eyes steady. Clear. Honest, to Brock's amazement. "It was beneath me to act the way I did earlier, and I apologize."

Brock backed off, lifting his chin as he considered the surprising sincerity of Chase's words. "All right," he said slowly, cautious that he didn't get too comfortable too soon.

He'd been on enough missions with Sterling Chase. He'd seen him operate, and he knew the male could be a viper—both in armed combat and in wars of words. He was dangerous, and just because he was extending his hand in an apparent truce now didn't mean Brock should be too eager to turn his back to him.

"Okay," he murmured. "Apology accepted, man."

Chase nodded, then went back to cleaning his weapons. "By the way, that cut on your neck is bleeding."

Brock growled a curse as he reached up and ran his fingers over Jenna's little bite mark. There was only the faintest trace of blood there, but even a fraction of that would have been too much to escape the notice of one of the Breed. And under a truce or not, it was just like Chase not to let that notice slide by without comment.

"I'll be ready to roll at sundown," Brock said, his eyes trained on the bent blond head that didn't so much as twitch in response, Chase's attention remaining fixed on the work spread out on the table before him.

Brock pivoted and stalked out to the corridor. He hadn't needed the reminder about what had happened between Jenna and him. She'd been on his mind, occupying the bulk of his thoughts, since the moment he left her in his quarters.

Chase's apology made him realize that he owed one, as well.

He didn't want to leave things the way he had with Jenna. Part of him wondered if he'd been fair in how he'd pursued her, following her after she'd run away from him, fighting back tears. He'd drawn away her grief with his touch, but had doing so also made her more pliable to his own demanding need for her?

It hadn't been his plan to manipulate her into his bed, no matter how badly he'd wanted her. And if he had seduced her, there was no mistaking Jenna's desire once they had gotten started. It didn't take much to relive the feel of her hands on his skin, soft yet demanding. Her mouth had been hot and wet on his, giving and taking, driving him wild. Her body had sheathed him like slick, warm satin, a memory that had him growing hard just to think of it.

And then, when he'd felt the blunt pressure of her human teeth at his throat . . .

Holy hell.

He'd never known anything so hot.

He had never known a woman as hot as Jenna, and he hadn't exactly been living the life of a monk that he lacked the basis for comparison. Human females had long been his preferred type—a pleasant diversion with no threat of attachment. He'd never even been tempted to think past a few nights when it came to his human lovers. Now he wondered if he hadn't been looking at Jenna Darrow in the same light. Deep down, he had to admit that he'd been hoping he could keep her in that neat little compartment.

As of now, he was determined to lock the lid down on his attraction to her and walk away while he had the chance.

But there was still the matter of how he'd left things with her.

Even if she was upset with him, which she had every right to be, he wanted her to know that he was sorry. Not sorry for the sex that had been so hot it was a wonder they hadn't combusted together, but sorry for taking off without manning up to his own weakness afterward. He wanted to set things straight so they could move on.

And what, be friends?

Hell, he wasn't even sure he knew how to do that. He could count his friends on one hand, and none of those friends were human. None of them were females who set him on fire just by being in the same room.

In spite of all that, he found himself standing outside his former quarters, his clenched fist poised to rap on the closed door. He dropped his knuckles against the panel in a light knock. There was no answer.

For a moment, he debated whether he should just turn around and let the whole thing lie. Chalk up the whole episode with Jenna as a lapse in judgment that he was never going to repeat. But before he could decide which would be the bigger offense—walking in uninvited or walking away again—he had opened the door.

The place was dark, not a single light on. He smelled shampoo and dissipating steam emanating from the bathroom as he strode silently through the apartment. He made no sound as he walked into the bedroom, where Jenna lay in his bed sleeping, curled away from him on her side. He drifted over to her, watching for a moment, listening to the slow, quiet rush of her breathing.

The urge to slip in beside her was a strong one, but he held himself in check. Barely.

Her dark hair spread over the pillow in damp, glossy strands. He reached out, let his fingers stray into its softness, careful that his touch didn't disturb her. His apology would have to wait. Maybe she wouldn't even want to hear it.

Yeah, maybe it would be best for both of them if he just backed off from anything personal and kept their interactions on a purely professional level for however long she might remain at the compound. God knew, that sounded like the most reasonable plan. The safest plan for both of them, but especially for her. Getting too close to someone he was assigned to protect meant getting sloppy at what he was trained to do.

He'd been there before, and a vibrant young woman paid the price with her life. He wasn't about to put Jenna in that kind of jeopardy. Sure, she was tough and capable, not the naïve innocent who had put her trust in Brock and died for the mistake. But so long as he was charged with Jenna's well-being—entrusted with her protection—he was going to have to keep her at arm's length. That was one promise he was determined to keep.

Not that she'd likely argue, after the way he'd bungled things between them in this room.

He let the damp, dark tendril fall back into place on the pillow. Without a word, without a sound, he backed away from the bed. He left the apartment as stealthily as he'd entered . . . unaware that in the stillness of the bedroom, Jenna's eyes had opened, her breathing stopped as she listened to him make his almost perfect escape for a second time that night.

CHAPTER
Fifteen

Earth to Jenna. Everything okay with you?"

"Huh? Oh. Yeah, I'm fine." Jenna glanced up at Alex, snapping herself out of the daze that had been hijacking her focus all night. Ever since Brock's unexpected B&E in her room a few hours ago. To say nothing of the incredible sex that had preceded it. "Just lost in my thoughts, I guess."

"That's exactly why I asked," Alex said. "You've been somewhere else since you sat down with me here tonight."

"I'm sorry. It's nothing to worry about. Everything is fine."

Jenna picked up her fork and chased a bite of salmon around her plate. She wasn't hungry, but when Alex had fetched her for a quiet dinner together in her quarters, Jenna couldn't deny that she welcomed her best friend's company. She wanted to pretend, if only for a little while, that things were the same as they'd been in Alaska just a few weeks ago—before she'd known about her brother's corruption and death, before she'd learned about vampires and alien biotechnology and accelerated DNA mutations.

Before she'd compounded all of her problems by getting naked with Brock.

"Hello?" Across the table from her, Alex watched her over the rim of her beer glass. "FYI, in case you're wondering, you're doing it again, Jen. What's going on with you?"

"I suppose you mean other than the obvious," Jenna replied, pushing aside her plate and leaning back in her chair.

She stared at her friend, the most sympathetic, supportive person she knew—the one person, aside from Brock, who'd given her the strength she needed to get through the worst of her life's ordeals. Jenna realized she owed Alex more than the usual don't-worry-about-me façade. Never mind the fact that Alex had the ability to see through any bullshit with her built-in lie detector, courtesy of her Breedmate genetics.

Jenna took a slow breath and let it out on a sigh. "Something happened earlier. Between Brock and me."

"Something...happened?" Alex looked at her in silence for a moment before her brow knit into a frown. "Are you saying..."

"Yeah, that's exactly what I'm saying." Jenna got up from the table and began clearing her place setting. "I was in the war room alone, after everyone had gone to bed.

Brock came in, and we started talking, then we started kissing. Things got really intense, really quickly. I don't think either one of us meant for it to happen."

Alex followed her into the kitchen. "You and Brock... slept together?" she asked. "You had sex in the war room?"

"God, no. We just kissed in there. On the conference table. The sex came later, in his quarters. Or, rather, my quarters." Jenna felt a blush creep into her cheeks. She wasn't used to discussing her intimate life—mainly because she hadn't had one in a very long time. And certainly never anything as out of control as what she and Brock had shared. "Oh, for crissake, don't make me spell out every detail. Say something, Alex."

She stared, somewhat slack-jawed. "I'm, um..."

"Shocked? Disappointed? You can tell me," Jenna said, trying to guess what her friend must think of her, having known how she'd avoided anything resembling a relationship or intimacy in the years since the accident, only to end up in bed with one of the Order's warriors after just a couple of days in his company. "You must think I'm pathetic. God knows I do."

"Jenna, no." Alex took her by the shoulders, forcing Jenna to hold her gaze. "I don't think any of those things at all. I'm surprised... then again, not so much. It was obvious to me that you and Brock had a connection, even before you were brought here to the compound. And Kade mentioned to me a couple of times that Brock was very attracted to you and that he was concerned about you, protective of you."

"Really?" Curiosity fluttered to life inside her against her will. "He talked to Kade about me—when? What did he say?" She suddenly felt like a teenage girl prying for details on a schoolyard crush. "Oh, God—forget it. I don't want to know. It doesn't matter. What happened between us didn't mean anything. In fact, I'd really like to forget about it."

If only it was that easy to put the whole thing out of her mind.

Alex's eyes were soft, her words careful. "Is that what Brock thinks, too? That making love didn't mean anything? That you should try to pretend it didn't happen?"

Jenna thought back to the incredible passion they'd shared and his tender words afterward. He'd told her he didn't want her to regret it. He didn't want her to think it was a mistake. Sweet, caring words that he'd offered just moments before he'd fled from the room and left her sitting alone and confused in the dark.

"We agreed up front that there would be no strings, that it wasn't going to go anywhere between us," she heard herself murmur as she broke from Alex's gaze and pivoted to clear more dishes. She didn't want to think about how good it felt to be in Brock's arms, or the startling hungers he stirred within her. "It was just sex, Alex, and a onetime thing at that. I mean, it's not like I don't have bigger things to worry about, right? I'm not about to make everything worse by getting involved with him— physically or otherwise."

It sounded like a smart and reasonable argument, though whether she was trying to convince her friend or herself, she wasn't totally certain.

Alex drifted out of the kitchen behind her. "I think you already care about him, Jen. I think Brock has come to mean something to you, and it's got you terrified."

Jenna pivoted around, stricken to hear the dead-aim

truth voiced out loud. "I don't want to feel anything for him. I can't, Alex."

"Would it be so bad if you did?"

"Yes," she replied, emphatic. "My life is uncertain enough as it is. How foolish would I be if I let myself fall for him?"

Alex's smile was subtly compassionate. "I think there are worse things you could do. Brock's a good man."

Jenna shook her head. "He's not even totally human, in case either of us is tempted to forget that small fact. Although I probably should be questioning my own humanity, after the way I bit him earlier tonight."

Alex's brows arched. "You bit him?"

Too late to take back her careless blurt, Jenna tapped a finger against the side of her neck. "While we were in bed. I don't know what came over me. I suppose I got swept away in the moment, and I just...bit him. Hard enough to draw blood."

"Oh," Alex replied slowly, studying her now. "And how did that feel to you, biting him?"

Jenna huffed out a short sigh. "Crazy. Impulsive. Like a runaway train. It was embarrassing as hell, if you want to know the truth. Brock seemed to think so, too. He couldn't get away from me fast enough afterward."

"Have you talked to him since then?"

"No, and I hope I don't have to. As I said, it's probably best that he and I both forget the whole thing."

But even as she said it, she couldn't help thinking back to the moment she'd realized he'd returned to the room after she'd showered and gone to bed. She couldn't help remembering how desperate she'd been to hear him speak to her—to say anything—in those quiet couple of minutes that he watched her in the dark, assuming she'd been asleep and didn't know he was there.

And now, after trying to convince herself and Alex, too, that she was in control of the situation with Brock, the memory of their passion put an undeniable quickness in her veins.

"It was a mistake," she murmured. "I'm not going to make it worse by imagining it was anything more than that. All I can do is make a point of not repeating it."

She sounded so sure of herself, she thought for certain Alex would believe her. But when she glanced over at her friend—her best friend, who'd stood beside her through all of her life's triumphs and tragedies—Alex's eyes were gentle with understanding.

"Come on, Jen. Let's finish up these dishes, then we'll go see how Dylan and the others are making out on their investigations."

"We've been sitting here for twenty-five minutes, my man. I don't think your guy is gonna show." Brock turned a look on Chase from the driver's seat of the parked Rover. "How long are we supposed to wait on this asshole?"

Chase stared out at the vacant, snow-covered lot in Dorchester, where their rendezvous with one of his former Enforcement Agency contacts was supposed to have taken place. "Something must have come up. Mathias Rowan is a good man. He never leaves me hanging out to dry. Let's give him another few minutes."

Brock exhaled an impatient grunt and turned up the SUV's heat. He hadn't been excited about partnering with Chase on the night's patrol, but he was even less excited that their work in the city included the prospect of meeting up with a member of the Breed nation's de facto law enforcement organization. The Agency and the Order had a long-held, mutual distrust of each other, both sides in disagreement about the way crime and punishment should work among the Breed.

If the Enforcement Agency had been effective at one time, Brock personally couldn't vouch for it. The organization had long ago become more political than anything else, generally favoring ass-kissing and lip service as a means of handling problems—two things that happened to be missing from the Order's playbook.

"Man, I hate winter," Brock muttered as the flurry of new-falling snow began to come down in earnest. A gust of icy wind buffeted the side of the vehicle, howling like a banshee across the empty lot.

Truth be told, a lot of his foul mood had to do with the way he'd screwed things up with Jenna. He couldn't help wondering how she was doing, what she was thinking. Whether she despised him, which was certainly her right. He was anxious for the night's mission to be over so he could head back to the compound and see for himself that Jenna was okay.

"Your man Rowan better not be dicking us around," he grumbled. "I don't sit in the damn cold freezing my ass off for just anybody—least of all a self-righteous Agency blowhard."

Chase slid him a meaningful look. "Whether you care to believe it or not, there are a few good individuals in the Enforcement Agency. Mathias Rowan is one of them. He's been my eyes and ears on the inside for months now. If we want a fighting chance at routing out Dragos's possible allies in the Agency, we need Rowan on our side."

Brock gave a grim nod and settled back to continue

their wait. Chase was probably right about his old ally. Few in the Enforcement Agency would want to admit there were cracks in their foundation—cracks that had permitted a cancer like Dragos to operate inside the Agency in secret for decades. Dragos had hidden behind an assumed name, accumulating power and intel, recruiting an untold number of like-minded followers willing to kill for him—to die for him, if duty demanded it. Dragos had climbed as high as the director level in the Agency before the Order had unmasked him several months ago and driven him to ground.

Although Dragos was gone from the Agency, the Order was certain he hadn't severed all of his ties. There would be those who still agreed with his dangerous plans. Those who were still allied with him in silent conspiracy, hiding within layer upon layer of bureaucratic bullshit that prevented Brock and the other warriors from going in with guns blazing to flush them out.

One of Chase's main objectives in the months since Dragos turned tail and ran was to start peeling back those layers in the Agency. To get closer to Dragos, the Order would need to get close to his lieutenants without tripping any alarms. One careless move could drive Dragos even deeper into hiding.

The operation was covert in the extreme, made all the more delicate seeing how the Order's best hope of success lay in the hair-trigger, volatile hands of Sterling Chase and his trust in an old friend who was only as loyal as Chase promised him to be.

On the passenger-side dashboard, Chase's cell phone began to vibrate. "That'll be Rowan," he said, grabbing the phone and answering the call. "Yeah. We're waiting. Where are you?"

Brock stared out at the swirling snow through the windshield, listening to Chase's side of a conversation that didn't sound like good news.

"Ah, fuck—anyone dead?" Chase went quiet for a second, then hissed something nasty. At Brock's questioning look, he explained, "Got detoured by another call. Dark-haven kid let things get out of hand at a party. There was a fight, then a feeding on the street outside. One human is dead, another ran off on foot, bleeding bad."

"Jesus," Brock muttered.

The dead human and a feeding taking place on a public street was bad enough. The bigger trouble was the escaped witness. It wasn't hard to imagine the hysteria that a savaged human could cause, running around screaming the word "vampire." To say nothing of what that same bleeding human could incite among Brock's own kind.

The scent of fresh, spilling red cells would be a beacon to every Breed in a two-mile radius. And God forbid there were any Rogues left in the city. One whiff of an open wound would be enough to send the blood-addicted dregs of the Breed population into a feeding frenzy.

Chase's jaw was taut as he went back to Mathias Rowan on the cell. "Tell me your guys have the runner contained." From the harsh grate of the curse that followed, Brock was guessing the answer to that was no. "Goddamn it, Mathias. You know as well as I do that we've got to get that human off the street. If it takes the entire Boston division to track him down, then you do it. Who's down there with you from the Agency?"

Brock watched and listened as the conversation continued, observing a side of Sterling Chase he hardly recognized. The former Agent was cool and commanding, logical and precise. The unpredictable hothead that Brock had grown accustomed to as a member of the Order seemed to take a backseat to the crisp, capable leader sitting beside him in the Rover now.

He'd heard that Chase had been a golden boy with the Agency before he'd joined the Order, though you couldn't have proved that by Brock in the year that he'd been working alongside him. Now he felt a kindling new respect for the former Agent, as well as a gnawing curiosity about the other, darker side of him, which never seemed far from the surface.

"Where are you at, Mathias?" Chase motioned to Brock to put the vehicle in gear as he spoke to his Agency contact. "Tell you what, you let me worry about whether the Order needs to get involved in this. I'm not asking permission, and you and I never had this conversation, got it? Save it for when I get there. We're already heading your way."

Brock turned the Rover onto the street and followed Chase's directions as he cut off Mathias Rowan's audible protests, then stuffed the cell phone back into his coat pocket. They sped deeper into the city, toward the industrial wharfs, where a lot of the younger crowd—humans and Breed alike—met for late-night raves and private, after-hours parties.

It wasn't hard to find the scene of the killing. Two unmarked black sedans were parked at a dockside warehouse. Several Breed males in dark coats and suits stood around a large object lying unmoving in the filthy snow of the lot adjacent to the building.

"That's them," Chase said. "I recognize most of these men from the Agency."

Brock swung the Rover into the area, eyeing the group as all heads pivoted toward the approaching vehicle.

"Yeah, that's them, all right. Useless and confused," Brock drawled, assessing the Agents with a glance. "Which one's Rowan?"

He needn't have asked. No sooner had he said it than one of the group broke away from the others, stalking over at a brisk clip to meet Brock and Chase as they got out of the vehicle. Agent Mathias Rowan was as tall and broad as any one of the warriors, his thick shoulders bulky mounds underneath the heavy fall of his tailored dark wool coat. Light green eyes flashed with intelligence and annoyance as he approached, skin stretching tight across his high cheekbones.

"Understand you Agency boys are having a little trouble tonight," Chase said, pitching his voice loud enough for the rest of the gathered Agents to hear him as well as Rowan. "Thought you might need some help out here."

"Are you fucking nuts?" Rowan growled, low under his breath, for Chase alone. "You've got to know any one of these Agents would just as soon tear your limbs off than have you walking into the middle of their investigation."

"Yeah?" Chase replied, mouth quirked into a cocky grin. "Been a slow night for me so far. Might be interesting to let them try."

"Chase, damn it." Rowan kept his voice low. "I told you not to come."

Chase grunted. "There was a time when I was giving the orders around here and you were the one following them, Mathias."

"Not anymore." Rowan frowned, but there was no animosity in his expression. "We've got three Agents in pursuit of the runner; they'll get him. The building has been cleared of all humans, and any potential witnesses to the incident have been scrubbed of all memory of the entire night. It's handled."

"Well, well...Sterling fucking Chase." The snarled greeting carried on the wintry breeze, across the snow-tossed industrial lot from where a couple of the other men had broken from the pack to amble over.

Chase glanced out, eyes narrowing on the big male in front. "Freyne," he growled, spitting the name like he couldn't stand the taste of it. "I should have known that asshole would be here."

"You're interfering in official Agency business," Agent Rowan said, louder now, intending to be heard by all. He shot Chase a cautioning look, but spoke with the kind of uptight arrogance that seemed to be as standard issue in the Enforcement Agency as their *GQ* suits and polished shoes. "This incident doesn't concern the Order. It's a Darkhaven matter, and we've got the situation under control."

Grinning dangerously at the two approaching new-comers, Chase stepped around his friend with little more than a sidelong glance. Brock followed him, muscles twitching in readiness for battle as he registered the air of menace rolling off the pair of Agents who'd come to confront them.

"Jesus Christ, it is you," said the one called Freyne, his lips curled back in a sneer. "Figured we'd seen the last of you after you popped your Rogue nephew last year."

Brock tensed, caught off guard by the comment and its deliberate cruelty. Outrage spiked in him, yet Chase appeared unsurprised by the heartless reminder. He ignored the jibe, an effort that must have taken incredible control based on the steely clench of his jaw as he brushed past his former colleagues on his way to the scene of the killing.

Brock kept pace with Chase's long strides, cutting through the eddying flurries of snow, past the tinted window of an idling sedan where the Darkhaven kid who'd let his hunger rule him waited inside. Brock felt the weight of the Breed youth's eyes on him as he and Chase passed the car, their images—two heavily armed males in black fatigues and long leather coats, unmistakably members of the Order—reflected in the glass.

On the ground near the building, the snow was stained deep red where the struggle had occurred. The lifeless corpse of the slain human had now been zipped into a body bag and was being loaded into another Agency vehicle parked nearby. The blood was dead and of no temptation or use, but the coppery tang was still strong in the chill air, making Brock's gums tingle with the emergence of his fangs.

Behind them, footsteps crunched in the snow and gravel. Freyne cleared his throat, apparently unable to let things lie. "You know, Chase, I'll be straight with you. No one could blame you for putting the kid down."

"Agent Freyne," Mathias Rowan said, a warning that went unheeded.

"It's not like he didn't have it coming, right, Chase? I mean, shit. The kid was Rogue, and there's only one good way to deal with that. Same way you deal with a rabid dog."

As determined as the other Agent was to taunt, Chase seemed equally determined to tune him out. "Over there," he said to Brock, pointing to indicate a trail of heavy spatters tracking away from the scene.

Brock nodded. He'd already spotted the path the runner

took. And as much as he personally wanted to leap on Agent Freyne and take the smug bastard down a peg or ten, if Chase was able to ignore him, Brock would do his best to do the same. "Looks like our live one ran off toward the docks."

"Yeah," Chase agreed. "Judging by the amount of blood he's spilling, he's too weak to get far. Fatigue will take him down in under a mile."

Brock looked back at Chase. "So, if the area's been swept and no one has found him yet—"

"He's got to be hiding somewhere not far from here," Chase said, finishing the thought.

They were about to head out in pursuit when Freyne's chuckle sounded from behind them. "Putting a bullet in the kid's brain was an act of mercy if you ask me. But you have to wonder if his mother felt the same way . . . seeing how you killed her son right in front of her."

Chase froze at that. Brock glanced at him, saw a muscle ticking dangerously fast in his rigid jaw.

While the rest of the small group moved out of the immediate area, Mathias Rowan stepped in front of his Agent, fury vibrating off every inch of him. "Damn it, Freyne, I said shut the fuck up and that's an order!"

But the son of a bitch just wouldn't stop. He navigated around his superior, putting himself right in Chase's face. "Elise is the one I pity in all of this. That poor, sweet woman. To have lost your brother Quentin in the line of duty all those years ago, then you take her only child before her eyes. I guess it's no surprise she'd look for comfort somewhere—even among the thugs of the Order." Freyne made a vulgar sound in the back of his throat. "Fine-looking female like that could have had her pick of eager males in her bed. Hell, I would have gladly sampled some of that. Surprised you never did."

Chase let out a roar that rattled the ground. In a blur of movement that not even Brock could fully track, Chase launched himself at Freyne. The two big males crashed down to the gravel and snow, Chase pinning the Agent beneath him, pounding his fists into his face.

Freyne fought back, but he was no match for Chase's fury. Observing it up close, Brock wasn't sure anyone could stand up to the feral rage that seemed to pour out of Chase as he landed one punishing blow after another.

None of the other Agents made a move to stop the altercation, least of all Mathias Rowan. He stood back, silent, stoic, the rest of his subordinates seeming to gauge their response on his. They would have let Chase kill Freyne, and whether that killing was deserved or not, Brock couldn't allow the brutal scene to play out to its seemingly foregone conclusion.

He stepped up, put a hand on his fellow warrior's churning shoulder. "Chase, my man. It's enough."

Chase kept hammering, even though Freyne was no longer fighting back. Fangs stretched huge in his mouth, eyes blazing with the amber fire of his rage, Chase seemed unwilling—or unable—to bring the beast in him to heel.

When one of those bloodied fists recoiled to strike another blow, Brock caught it in his hand. He held fast with all his strength, refusing to let the hammer fall again. Chase pivoted a wild look on him. Snarled something raw and nasty.

Brock slowly shook his head. "Come on, Harvard. Let him be now. He's not worth killing, not like this."

Chase glared hard into his eyes, lips curled back off his

fangs. He grunted, animalistic, then swung his head back around to look at the sputtering, bloodied male still pinned beneath him and semiconscious in the muck.

Brock felt the tight fist in his grasp begin to loosen a fraction. "That's it, my man. You're better than this. Better than him."

A cell phone trilled nearby. From his periphery, Brock saw Rowan put the mobile to his ear and pivot away to take the call. Chase was still huffing and dangerous, not yet willing to let Freyne loose.

"They got him," Agent Rowan announced, his calm statement cutting through some of the tension. "Two of my Agents found the runner hiding under a delivery truck down by the wharfs. They've scrubbed his memory of what he witnessed and will drop him near a hospital on the other side of the city."

Brock gave a faint nod of acknowledgment. "You hear that, Chase? It's over. We're done here." He let go of Chase's fist, trusting him not to escalate the situation with Freyne or any of the other Agents still gathered around, watching in anxious silence. "Let him go, Chase. This shit is finished."

"For now," Chase finally muttered, his voice rough and dark. He snuffled, shook off the hand Brock placed on his shoulder. With rage still rolling off him, he delivered one last punishing blow to Freyne's battered face before springing up to his feet. "Next time I see you," he growled, "you're a dead man."

"Come on, Harvard." Brock steered him away from the area, not missing the pointed look that Mathias Rowan leveled on them as they headed back toward the Rover. "So much for diplomatic relations with the Agency, my man."

Chase said nothing. He followed behind a couple of paces, his breath sawing in and out of his lungs, his body throwing off aggression like a nuclear blast.

"I hope we didn't need that bridge back there, because you may have just torched it," Brock said as they reached the vehicle.

Chase didn't answer. Nothing but quiet at Brock's back. Too much quiet, in fact.

He pivoted around. All he found was a lot of empty space where Chase had been standing just a second ago. He was gone, vanished without excuse or explanation, into the snowy night.

CHAPTER
Sixteen

A couple hours after dinner with Alex, Jenna was seated in the Breedmates' war room, at the very conference table where she and Brock had opened a door that likely neither one of them had been prepared to walk through. But she tried not to think about that. She tried not to think about Brock's sensual mouth on hers, or his skilled hands, which had given such intense pleasure even as he drew away her grief and inhibitions.

Instead, she rooted her attention on the discussion taking place between the women of the Order who were gathered in the room to review the status of their mission to locate the captives being held by Dragos. Only Tess was absent from the meeting, the pregnant Breedmate having apparently begged off to rest in her and Dante's quarters while keeping little Mira company, as well.

"She's not feeling ill, is she?" Alex asked. "You don't think the baby might be coming early?"

Savannah gave a mild shake of her head as she rested her elbows on the table. "Tess says she feels great, just a little tired. It's understandable. She's down to just a few weeks now."

There was the faintest hesitation in her voice, then her gaze drifted subtly toward Jenna. A silent curiosity lingered in her eyes. At that moment, Jenna noticed that Savannah's palms were pressed against the table. Her slim black brows lifted slightly, and it was obvious from the partial quirk of her mouth that her Breedmate talent for reading objects with a touch had just told her—no doubt, in vivid detail—of the passionate kiss Jenna and Brock had shared on that very surface.

When embarrassment started to make Jenna look away, Savannah merely smiled in serene amusement and gave her a small nod as if to say she approved.

"You know, Dante's got a pool going on the delivery date," Dylan piped in. "Rio and I have our money on a Christmas baby."

Renata shook her head, the blunt ends of her dark hair swinging around her chin. "New Year's Eve, you wait and see. Dante's son would never miss an excuse for a party."

At the far end of the table, Gabrielle laughed. "Lucan will never admit that he's looking forward to having a baby in the compound, but I have it on good authority that five bucks was placed on December twentieth recently."

"Is there something special about that date?" Jenna

asked, caught up in the excitement and genuinely curious to know.

"It's Lucan's birthday," Elise said, sharing Gabrielle's humor. "And Tegan put a hundred dollars on February fourth, knowing full well it was much too late to be in the running."

"February fourth," Savannah said, nodding with serene understanding.

Elise's smile was tender with memories, bittersweet. "The night that Tegan found me hunting Rogues in Boston and tried to put a stop to it."

Dylan reached out and squeezed the other Breed-mate's hand. "And the rest, as they say, is history."

As the chatter of small, everyday things gave way to more serious talk of pursuing leads and formulating new mission strategies, Jenna felt her respect growing for the smart, determined mates of the Order's warriors. And despite the earlier assurances that Tess's exhaustion was nothing to worry about, she found herself concerned about her, too, feeling as though the fabric of the gathering was missing one of its most vibrant threads.

A thought struck Jenna as she quietly observed, taking in the faces of the other women in the room: Somehow, she had begun to consider all of them her friends. These women mattered to her, and so did their goals. As adamant as she was that she didn't belong in this place, among these people, she realized that she wanted to see them succeed.

She wanted to see the Order defeat Dragos, and there was a part of her—a very determined part—that wanted to have a hand in making that happen.

Jenna eagerly listened as Elise discussed the status of the new sketches she and Claire Reichen had been

working on with Elise's artist contact in the local Darkhaven. "It should only be another couple of days before
we have finished sketches to work with. Claire has been
amazing, making sure every detail is just as she recalls it
from her dreamwalk into Dragos's lab. She's got meticu-
lous notes, and her memory is incredible."

"That's good," Renata said. "We're going to need all
the help we can get. Unfortunately, Dylan and I have run
into a slight snag on Sister Margaret."

"She's living in a home for retired nuns down in
Gloucester," Dylan interjected. "I spoke to the administrator, and told her that my mom and Sister Margaret
used to work together at the women's shelter in New York.
I didn't mention what we were really looking for, of
course. Instead I set it up as a personal call, and asked if it
would be possible to visit with the sister sometime and
chat about her years of volunteer work—maybe remi-
nisce a bit about my mom. The good news is, Sister Margaret loves having company."

"So, what's the snag?" Jenna asked, unable to keep
from jumping on this new intel trail herself.

"Dementia," Renata replied.

Dylan nodded. "Sister Margaret's been suffering from
it for the past couple of years. The house admin said
there's a good chance she might not remember much
about my mom or her work at the shelter."

"But it's still worth a try, right?" Jenna glanced around
at the other women. "I mean, any lead is a good one at
this point. There are lives on the line here, so we have to
make use of everything we can. Whatever it takes to find
those women and bring them home."

More than one head turned with surprise in her direction. If any of the Order's women thought it strange that

she was including herself in their efforts to locate the missing Breedmates, none of them said a word about it.

Savannah's gaze lingered on her the longest, a look of gratitude—of friendship and acceptance—shining in her gentle eyes.

It was that easy acceptance, that sense of kindness and community she'd felt from each of these special women from the first day she awoke, that put a knot of emotion in Jenna's throat now. It overwhelmed her, nearly choking her up to feel even for a second that she could be part of something as tight knit and comfortable as the extraordinary extended family that lived and worked in this place.

"All right. Let's get to work," Dylan said after a moment. "There's a lot to be done."

One by one, they all went back to their tasks, some reviewing open file folders, others taking up positions in front of the war room's many computer workstations. Jenna drifted over to one of the unused PCs and fired up an Internet browser.

She had almost forgotten her message to her friend in the FBI Division Office in Anchorage, but as soon as she accessed the email site, she saw the reply waiting in her in box. She clicked the message and quickly scanned what it said.

"Uh, you guys," she said, feeling a little jolt of excitement and triumph as she read her friend's reply. "You know how you've been trying to get some intel on Terra-Global Partners?"

"Dragos's corporate front," Dylan said, already coming over to see what Jenna had.

Alex and the other women were close behind her. "What's going on, Jen?"

"We're not the only ones interested in TerraGlobal."

Jenna glanced up at the eager faces gathered around her. "An old buddy of mine in Anchorage ran a basic inquiry for me. He got a hit."

Savannah blew out a disbelieving laugh as she read the email message displayed on the monitor. "The FBI has an open investigation on TerraGlobal?"

"According to my friend, it's a relatively new one. It's being headed up by someone in their New York office."

Gabrielle gave Jenna an approving smile. "Nice work. We'd better go inform Lucan of what you've found."

The evening was only half over, but already he considered it a triumphant success.

In the dark of his private helicopter, Dragos smiled with deep satisfaction as his pilot guided the sleek aircraft away from the twinkling winter landscape of the busy capital city below and out over the dark water of the Atlantic, heading north, toward the second of his scheduled appearances tonight. He could hardly wait to arrive, anticipation for still another victory making his blood run faster in his veins.

For some time now, he had been cultivating his most useful allies, gathering his assets in preparation for the war he intended to wage, not only against his own kind—complacent, impotent cowards who deserved to be trampled under his boot—but also against the world at large.

Tonight's private receptions were crucial to his goals, and only the beginning of what would be a staggering offensive strike that he was preparing to deliver on both the Breed and humankind alike. If the Order feared that his grasp extended dangerously deep into the power brokers

206 ⌒⌒⌒ LARA ADRIAN

of the vampire race alone, they were in for a very rude awakening. And soon.

Very soon, he thought, chuckling to himself with eager glee.

"How long before we touch down in Manhattan?" he asked his Minion pilot.

"Fifty-two minutes, Master. We are right on schedule."

Dragos grunted his approval and relaxed into his seat for the remainder of the flight. He might have been tempted to call the evening flawless, if not for one small aggravation that stuck stubbornly in his craw—a bit of annoying news that had reached him earlier in the day.

Evidently some lowly desk jockey working for the Feds in Alaska was sniffing around in his business affairs, making inquiries about TerraGlobal Partners. For that, he blamed the Order. No doubt, it wasn't every day that a mining company—fake or otherwise—went up in a hellish ball of flames, as his little operation in the Alaskan interior had done at the hands of Lucan's warriors.

Now Dragos had the added irritation of having to contend with some public servant gas bag or environmental do-gooder trying to advance a career by going after a villainous corporation for God knew what offense.

Let them dig, he thought, smugly secure that he was free from any potential fallout. There were enough layers between himself and TerraGlobal to keep him insulated from nosy human law enforcement or interfering backwoods politicians. Failing that, he had assets in place who would ensure that his interests were protected. And, in the grander scheme, it didn't matter.

He was untouchable, more so every day.

Before long, he would be unstoppable.

That knowledge kept the edge out of his voice when

his cell phone rang with a call from one of his key lieutenants. "Tell me where the operation stands."

"Everything is in order, sire. My men are embedded in
positions as we discussed and ready to move forward with
the plan for tomorrow at sundown."

"Excellent," Dragos replied. "Inform me when it is
done."

"Of course, sire."

Dragos clapped the phone closed and slipped it back
into his coat pocket. Tonight was a triumphant step
toward attaining the golden future he had designed so
long ago. But tomorrow's move against the Order—the
viper's bite they would never see coming—was going to
be an even sweeter victory.

Dragos let the thought settle over him as he tipped his
head back and closed his eyes, savoring the promise of the
Order's imminent, final defeat.

CHAPTER
Seventeen

Roughly an hour before dawn, Brock arrived back at the compound alone. He hated like hell to leave a patrol partner behind after a mission, but after a night of searching the city for Chase and coming up empty, he didn't see where he had much choice. Wherever Chase had run following his altercation with the Enforcement Agent earlier that night, he clearly didn't want to be found. It wasn't the first time he'd gone AWOL following patrols, but that didn't make his disappearance sit any better with Brock.

Concern for an MIA brother-in-arms hadn't put him in the best of moods as he opened the door to his shared quarters with Hunter and stepped inside the quiet, lightless room. At home in the dark, his vision sharper here than in the light, Brock peeled off his leather coat and draped it on the sofa before continuing on through the living area to the adjacent bunk room.

The place was so dark and silent, he'd assumed his roommate hadn't yet come in himself—until he entered the bedroom and got an immediate eyeful of full-body Gen One *glyphs* tracking the naked male from neck to toe.

"Jesus Christ," Brock muttered, averting his gaze from the unexpected, and totally unwanted, full-frontal glimpse at his roomie. "What the hell, man?"

Hunter stood with his powerful back resting against the far wall, eyes closed. He was as still as a statue, breathing almost imperceptibly, his thickly muscled arms hanging loose at his sides. Although his lids flicked open at Brock's interruption, the immense, unreadable male didn't appear startled or even remotely disturbed. "I was sleeping," he said matter-of-factly. "I am rested now."

"Good," Brock drawled, shaking his head as he gave the naked warrior his back. "How about you put some damn clothes on? I just learned things about you that I really didn't need to know."

"My sleep is more effective without clothing to confine me" came the level reply.

Brock snorted. "Yeah, well, so is mine, but I doubt you'd appreciate looking at my bare ass—or anything else—any more than I want to see yours. Jesus, cover that shit up, will you?"

Shaking his head, Brock unfastened his weapons belt and dropped it onto one of the two undisturbed beds. He thought back to Hunter's lack of response when initially asked about which of the bunks belonged to him and shot a glance over his shoulder at the Gen One, who was stepping into a pair of loose sweatpants.

The Breed male who'd been born and bred to be a killing machine for Dragos. An individual raised in utter solitude, deprived of contact or companionship, except for the supervision of the Minion handler who had been assigned to him.

Suddenly he understood why Hunter hadn't cared less which bed he claimed.

"You always sleep like that?" he asked, gesturing to the place where Hunter had been standing.

The uncanny Gen One gave a vague shrug. "Occasionally on the floor."

"Sure as hell can't be comfortable."

"Comfort serves no purpose. The need for it only implies and fortifies weakness."

Brock absorbed the flat statement, then swore under his breath. "What did Dragos and those other bastards do to you all those years you served them?"

Unblinking golden eyes met his scowl through the darkness. "They made me strong."

Brock nodded solemnly, thinking about the ruthless upbringing and discipline that was all Hunter knew. "Strong enough to take them down."

"Every last one of them," Hunter replied, zero inflection, yet the promise was as sharp as any blade.

"You want revenge for what they did to you?"

Hunter's head slowly pivoted in denial. "Justice," he said, "for what they've done to those unable to fight back."

Brock stood there for a long moment, understanding the cold determination that emanated from the other male. He shared that need for justice, and like Hunter— like any one of the warriors pledged in service to the

Order—he would not rest until Dragos and everyone loyal to his insane mission was eliminated.

"You honor us well," he said, a phrase the Breed reserved for only the closest of kin or the solemnest of events. "The Order is fortunate to have you on our side."

Hunter seemed taken aback, though whether by the praise itself or the bond it implied, Brock couldn't be sure. A flicker of uncertainty shot through the golden gaze, and when Brock reached out to clap his hand against Hunter's shoulder, the Gen One drew away, dodging the contact as though it might burn him.

He didn't explain the flinching reaction, nor did Brock press him to, even though the question begged an answer. "All right, I'm outta here. I need to check in with Gideon about something."

Hunter stared at him. "You're worried about your female?"

"Should I be?" Brock meant to correct the reference about Jenna being his, but he was too busy dealing with the blood that had suddenly gone a bit cold in his veins. "Is she okay? Tell me what's going on. Did anything happen to her while I was out on patrol?"

"I am not aware of any physical issues with the human," Hunter said, maddening in his calm. "I was referring to her inquiry into TerraGlobal."

"TerraGlobal," Brock repeated, dread sitting in his gut. "That's one of Dragos's holdings."

"Correct."

"Jesus Christ," Brock murmured. "You're saying she contacted them somehow?"

Hunter gave a faint shake of his head. "She sent an email to someone she knows in Alaska—a federal agent, who ran a data search for her on TerraGlobal. An FBI unit in New York City responded to the inquiry. They are aware of TerraGlobal, and have agreed to meet with her to discuss their current investigation."

"Holy hell. Tell me you're joking."

There was no humor in the other male's face, not that Brock was surprised at that. "I understand the meeting is already set for later today in the FBI's New York offices. Lucan has arranged to have Renata accompany her."

The more he heard, the more Brock started feeling twitchy and needing to move. He walked back and forth, not even attempting to cover his concern. "Who will Jenna be meeting with in New York? Do we even know if this FBI investigation into TerraGlobal is legit? Good God, what the fuck was she thinking, getting involved in this shit in the first place? You know what—never mind. I'll go ask her that myself."

He was already pacing the room, so it only took a couple of hard strides to carry him out of the apartment and into the corridor outside. With his pulse jackhammering, adrenaline pouring into his veins, he was in no frame of mind to find himself face-to-face with his errant patrol partner.

Chase came stalking up the stretch of hallway at precisely that moment, looking like complete hell. His blue eyes were still shooting sparks of amber, pupils more slits than circles. He was breathing hard, each pull of air dragging through his teeth and fangs. Grime and dried blood caked his face in lurid streaks, still more of it caught in his short blond hair. His clothing was torn in places, stained with God knew what.

He looked and smelled like he'd been through a goddamn war zone.

"Where the fuck have you been?" Brock demanded. "I looked all over Boston for you after you ran off tonight."

Chase glared at him, baring his teeth in a feral sneer, but didn't offer any kind of explanation. He brushed past, letting his shoulder hit Brock and all but daring him to make an issue out of it. If Brock hadn't been so concerned about Jenna and the trouble she'd apparently stirred up, he would have taken the arrogant son of a bitch down.

"Asshole," Brock growled after him as the former Agent swaggered away in stony, secretive silence.

Jenna came up off the sofa in an anxious hop when a hard rap sounded on the door to her quarters. It was early in the morning, just a little after six A.M. according to the clock on the stereo system playing softly across the living room. Not that she'd slept in the handful of hours since she'd spoken with Lucan and Gideon.

And not that she would be able to sleep in the time remaining between now and the important meeting she would be having later that day with the FBI field agent in New York.

Special Agent Phillip Cho had been pleasant enough on the phone when she'd called to speak to him, and she should be grateful that he was available and open to meeting with her about his investigation into TerraGlobal. This was hardly the first time she'd had an audience with the federal end of law enforcement, so she wasn't sure where her jittery nerves were coming from. Of course, she'd never had so much riding on a simple information-gathering meeting before.

She wanted to get this one right, and couldn't help feeling the weight of the world—both hers and the Order's—sitting on her shoulders. She hadn't been a cop for so long, and now she had to put on a command performance in just a few short hours. So, maybe it was only reasonable that she'd feel a bit on edge about the whole thing.

The knock at the door came again, sharper now, more demanding. "Just a second."

She clicked the mute button on the stereo remote, silencing an old Bessie Smith jazz CD that had been queued in the deck when she turned the unit on a while ago to help kill time. She crossed the room and opened the door.

Brock waited in the corridor outside, taking her completely by surprise. He must have just come in recently from his patrol of the city. Dressed head to toe in black combat gear, his fitted crewneck T-shirt clung to his broad chest and shoulders, short sleeves straining around the thick width of his biceps.

She couldn't keep her gaze from wandering the length of him, down past his tight abs, accentuated by the crisp tuck of his shirt into the belted waistband of his black fatigues, which were loose fitting, yet not so much that they masked the trim cut of his hips or the powerful bulk of his thighs. It was far too effortless to recall how well she knew that body. Far too troubling to realize just how much she craved him, even after she'd promised herself she wouldn't travel down that road with him again.

It wasn't until she dragged her gaze back up to his handsome but tense face that she realized he was upset. As in pissed off something fierce.

She frowned up into his stormy gaze. "What's going on?"

"Why don't you tell me." He took a step forward, his big body like a moving wall, forcing her to back into the room ahead of him. "I just heard about your inquiry into TerraGlobal with the goddamned FBI. What the hell were you thinking, Jenna?"

"I was thinking that maybe the Order could use my help," she replied, her own anger spiking at his confrontational tone. "I thought I would tap some of my law enforcement connections to shed some light onto TerraGlobal, since the rest of you had hit a dead end."

"Dragos *is* TerraGlobal," he hissed, still advancing on her, towering over her. His dark brown eyes crackled with tiny flecks of amber light. "Do you have any damn idea how risky it was for you to do that?"

"I didn't risk anything," she said, getting defensive now. Her hackles were rising with every one of his strides that physically edged her farther into the room. She stopped retreating and dug in her heels. "I was totally discreet, and the person I asked to help me is a trusted friend. Do you honestly think I would knowingly put the Order or its missions in jeopardy?"

"The Order?" He scoffed. "I'm talking about you, Jenna. This isn't your battle. You need to steer clear, before you get hurt."

"Excuse me, but I think I can handle myself. I *am* a cop, remember?"

"Used to be," he sternly reminded her, pinning her with a hard look. "And you never went up against anything like Dragos in your line of duty."

"I'm not going up against him now, either," she argued. "All we're talking about is a harmless office meeting with a government field agent. I've been involved in these kinds of territorial pissing contests a hundred times. The

Feds are worried that a local yokel Statie might know more than they do about one of their cases. They want to know what I know, and vice versa. It's not a big deal."

Shouldn't be a big deal, she thought to herself. But those jangly nerves were still clamoring and Brock didn't exactly look convinced, either.

"It could be bigger than you expect, Jenna. We can't be sure of anything when it comes to Dragos and his interests. I don't think you should go." His face was very serious. "I'm going to talk to Lucan. I think it's too dangerous for him to let you do this."

"I don't remember asking what you thought," she said, trying not to let his grim expression and sober tone of voice sway her. He was worried—deeply worried, about her—and part of her responded to that worry with an awareness she wanted to ignore. "I don't remember putting you in charge of what I do or don't do, either. I make my own decisions. You and the Order may think you can keep me on some kind of a leash—or under a damned microscope so long as it suits you—but don't confuse compliance with control. I'm the only one in control of me."

When she couldn't hold his thunderous gaze any longer, she turned away from him and went back over to the sofa, busying herself with picking up the collection of books she'd been thumbing through in her restlessness of the past few hours.

"Christ, you are hardheaded, aren't you, lady?" He blew out a low curse. "That's your biggest problem."

"What the hell does that mean?" She threw a scowl in his direction, surprised to find he had moved up right behind her. Close enough to touch her. Close enough that she felt the heat of him in every awakened nerve ending in her body. She steeled herself against the masculine power that radiated off his big form, hating the fact that she could still be wildly attracted to him even when her blood was simmering in anger.

His stare penetrated, seeming to bore right through her. "It's all about control with you, Jenna. You just can't stand to give it up, can you?"

"You don't know what you're talking about."

"No? I'll bet you were like this from the time you were a little girl." She turned away from him while he was talking, determined not to let him goad her. She grabbed an armful of books and carried them over to the built-in shelves. "I'll bet you've been like this your whole life, haven't you? Everything's got to be on your terms, isn't that right? Never let anyone take the reins, no matter what. You don't budge an inch unless you've got your sweet, stubborn ass planted firmly in the driver's seat."

As much as she wanted to deny it, he was hitting very close to home. She flashed back through the years of her childhood, all the playground fights and daredevil stunts she'd gotten dragged into just to prove that she wasn't afraid. Her time in the police force had been more of the same, though on a grander scale, upgrading from fists to bullets, but still struggling to show she was as good as any man—better, even.

Marriage and motherhood had presented another set of obstacles to master, and that was the one area in which she'd failed miserably. Paused in front of the bookcase, Brock's verbal challenge hanging behind her, she closed her eyes and remembered the argument she and Mitch had the night of the accident. He'd accused her of being stubborn, too. He'd been right, but she hadn't realized that until she'd woken up in the hospital weeks later without her family.

But this was different. Brock wasn't her husband. Just because they'd had a few moments of pleasure together—and despite the attraction that still crackled between them whenever they got near each other—that didn't give him a license to impose himself on her decisions.

"You want to know what I think?" she asked, her movements clipped with irritation as she filed each book back in its rightful place on the shelves. "I think you're the one with the problem. You wouldn't know what to do with a woman who doesn't need you looking after her. A real woman, who can survive just fine on her own and not let you hold yourself responsible if she gets hurt. You'd rather blame yourself for not living up to some imaginary bar you've set—some unattainable measure of honor and worth. If you want to talk about problems, try taking a good look at yourself."

He had gone so quiet and still, Jenna thought he might have walked out of the room. But when she turned around to see if he had left, she found him standing near the sofa, holding the old photograph that she'd first discovered tucked into the pages of one of his books. He was staring at the image of the pretty young woman with the ebony hair and large almond eyes. His jaw was held tight, a tendon ticking hard in his smooth, dark cheek.

"Yeah, maybe you're right about me, Jenna," he said finally, letting the photo drift out of his grasp to the sofa cushion. When he looked over at her, his face was schooled and sober, the consummate warrior. "None of this changes the fact that I *am* responsible for you. Lucan made it my duty to keep you protected while you're in the Order's custody—"

"Custody?" she balked, but he spoke right over her.

"—and that means whether you like it or not, whether

you approve or not, I do have a say in what you do, or who you come in contact with."

She scoffed, outraged. "Like hell you do."

He stalked over to her, barely three long strides before he was standing right up against her, the nearness of him sucking all the air from the room. Glittering heat lit his eyes from deep within. His fierce stare likely should have cowered her, but she was too hot with indignation—and too very much aware of the way her senses reached out to him in longing, despite the anger that made her chin jut upward. When she glared at him, casting inside herself for the tough-as-nails attitude that might have given her the strength to shove him away with harsh words or prickly defiance, she found it had deserted her.

All she could do was hold the breath that had suddenly gone shallow in her lungs. He ran his fingertips along the side of her cheek, such a skating, tender touch. His thumb lingered on her lips, stroking in a lazy pattern as his eyes drank her in for what seemed like forever.

Then he gathered her face in his palms and drew her toward him for a sizzling, and all-too-brief, kiss.

When he released her, she saw the sparks that glimmered in his eyes had now grown to bright, smoldering embers. His chest was firm and warm against hers, his arousal pressing bold and unmistakable against her hip. She staggered backward on her heels, a blaze of desire racing in her veins.

"You can fight me all you want on this, Jenna, I don't fucking care." Although his words were all business, his low voice vibrated through her like the coming of a storm. "You are mine to protect and keep safe, so make no mistake: If you leave the compound, you leave with me."

CHAPTER
Eighteen

Brock made good on his intent to accompany her to the FBI meeting in New York.

Jenna didn't know what he'd said to Lucan to persuade him, but later that morning, instead of Renata driving the Order's black Range Rover through four hours of unfamiliar highway from Boston to Manhattan, it had been Jenna behind the wheel, with GPS on the dashboard and Brock trying to help navigate from the far back of the vehicle. His solar-sensitive Breed skin cells and daytime UV concerns had kept him from even thinking he could sit beside her up front for such a long trip, let alone do the driving.

Although it was probably beyond immature for her to

be amused, Jenna had to admit she took a certain satisfaction in his mandatory banishment to the seat behind her. She hadn't forgotten his accusation about her always needing to be the one in charge, but judging from the impatient driving advice and muttered commentary about the apparent lead in her foot, it was obvious that she wasn't the only one who had a problem surrendering control.

And now, as they sat inside the dark cavern of an underground parking garage across the street from the FBI field office in New York City, Brock was still giving her orders from the backseat.

"Text me as soon as you're past security." At her nod, he went on. "Once you're in your meeting with the agent, text me again. I want periodic text check-ins, no less than fifteen minutes apart or I'm coming in after you."

Jenna huffed out an impatient sigh and shot him a look around the driver's seat. "This isn't a middle school dance. It's a professional office meeting in a very public building. Unless something goes totally off the rails in there, I'll text you when I get into the meeting and when it's over."

She could tell he was scowling behind his wraparound UV-blocking sunglasses. "If you won't take this seriously, then I am going in with you."

"I'm taking it very seriously," she argued. "And as far as you walking into that government building? Please. You're dripping with weapons and covered in head-to-toe black kevlar. You wouldn't make it past the front door security—assuming the daylight didn't fry you first."

"Security wouldn't be an issue. I would be nothing more than a cold breeze at the back of their necks as I passed through."

Jenna barked out a laugh. "Okay, then what? You're going to skulk in the hallway while I meet with Special Agent Cho?"

"I'll do what it takes," he answered, utterly serious. "This information-gathering exercise ultimately belongs to the Order. It's our intel you're going after. And I still don't like the idea of you going in there alone."

She pivoted away from him, stung somehow that he didn't seem to see her as part of the Order, as well. She stared out the window at a flickering yellow light in the cavernous garage. "If you were so concerned I couldn't handle this meeting by myself, maybe you should have let Renata come with me instead."

He leaned forward, stripping off his shades and coming between the seats to take hold of her shoulders. His strong fingers grasped her firmly, his eyes blazing in a mix of deepest brown and fiery amber. But when he spoke, his voice was nothing but velvet. "I am concerned, Jenna. But not as much about the damned meeting as I am about you. Fuck the meeting. There's nothing we can get out of there that's even half as important to me as making sure you're okay. Renata's not here because if anyone's gonna watch your back, it's gonna be me."

She grunted softly, smiling despite her aggravation with him. "You'd better be careful. You're starting to sound an awful lot like a partner to me."

She meant patrol partner, but the remark she'd intended as wry humor now hung between them full of dangerous innuendo. A heavy, unspoken tension filled the cramped space of the vehicle as Brock held her gaze. Finally, he heaved a dark curse and released his hold on her. His cheek pulsed as he stared in lengthening silence.

He sat back, withdrawing from the front of the Rover and settling once more into the shadows behind her.

"Just keep me informed, Jenna. Can you give me that much?"

She let out the breath she'd been holding and reached for the handle on the driver's-side door of the vehicle. "I'll text you from inside."

Without waiting to hear his growled reply, she climbed out of the SUV and headed for the FBI field office across the street.

Special Agent Phillip Cho didn't keep her waiting so much as five minutes in the eighteenth-floor reception area. Jenna had just fired off her text message to Brock when the clean-cut agent in a black suit and conservative tie emerged from his office to greet her. After declining a cup of stale afternoon coffee, she was led past a sea of cubicles to a conference room just off the main office area.

Agent Cho gestured her toward a swivel chair at the oblong table in the center of the room. He closed the door behind him, then took the seat directly across from her. He set a black leather notepad down in front of him and offered her a polite smile. "So, how long have you been retired from law enforcement, Ms. Darrow?"

The question surprised her. Not only for its directness, but for the fact that her FBI friend in Anchorage had offered to keep her civilian status under his hat. Of course, it shouldn't surprise her that Cho would do some homework on her in preparation of their meeting.

Jenna cleared her throat. "Four years ago, I resigned from the AST. Due to reasons of a personal nature."

He nodded sympathetically, and she realized that he'd

already known the answer and her reasons for leaving the Staties.

"I must admit, I was surprised to discover that your inquiry into TerraGlobal wasn't an official investigation," he said. "If I had known, I probably would not have agreed to this meeting. I'm sure you understand that using state or federal resources for personal interests is illegal and can carry severe consequences."

She lifted her shoulder in a faint shrug, not about to let him cow her with threats about procedure and protocol. She'd played that card too many times herself back when she wore a badge and uniform. "Call me inquisitive. We had a mining company in the interior go up in smoke— literally—and no one from the parent corporation has bothered to offer even so much as an apology to the town. There's going to be a hell of a bill attached to the cleanup, and I'm sure the town of Harmony would appreciate knowing where to send it."

Under the stark light of the fluorescent lamps overhead, Cho's unblinking stare put an odd buzz in her veins. "So, your interest in the matter is primarily that of a concerned citizen. Do I understand you correctly, Ms. Darrow?"

"That's right. And the cop in me can't help wondering what kind of management a shadowy outfit like TerraGlobal Partners employs. Nothing but ghosts and phantoms, from what little I've been able to find."

Cho grunted, still holding her in that unsettling stare across the table. "What exactly have you found, Ms. Darrow? I would be very interested to hear more."

Jenna tilted her chin down and gave him a narrowed look. "You expect me to share my intel when you're sitting there giving me nothing in return? Not gonna happen.

You first, Special Agent Cho. What's your interest in TerraGlobal?"

He sat back from the table and steepled his fingers in front of his thin smile. "I'm afraid that's classified information."

His air of dismissal was unmistakable, but she'd be damned if she'd come all this way for the meeting only to be stonewalled by a smug suit who seemed to be enjoying the fact that he was jerking her around. And the more she looked at him, the more his flat expression seemed to make her skin crawl.

Forcing herself to ignore her unease, she attempted a more conciliatory tack. "Listen, I understand. You're obligated to give me the official response. I just hoped that two professionals could help each other out a little bit here."

"Ms. Darrow, I only see one professional at this table. And even if you were still affiliated with law enforcement, I couldn't give you any information about TerraGlobal."

"Come on," she replied, her frustration mounting. "Give me a name. Just one name, an address. Anything."

"When exactly did you leave Alaska, Ms. Darrow?" he asked casually, ignoring her question and cocking his head at an odd angle as he studied her. "Do you have friends out here? Family, perhaps?"

She scoffed and shook her head. "You're not going to give me a damned thing, are you? You only agreed to meet with me because you thought you could wring something useful out of me to further your own interests."

That he didn't reply was telling enough. He opened his leather notebook and began scribbling some notes on the canary paper. Jenna sat there for a moment, staring at him, feeling certain in her bones that the tight-lipped, peculiar federal agent had all of the answers that she and the Order so desperately needed to put them on Dragos's tail.

"All right," she said, figuring it was time to play the only card she had in her hand. "Since you won't give me any names, I'll give you one instead. Gordon Fasso."

Cho's hand stopped moving halfway through what he was writing. It was the only indication that the name meant anything to him at all. When he looked up, his expression was bland, those odd, dullish eyes revealing nothing. "Excuse me?"

"Gordon Fasso," she said, repeating the alias she'd been told Dragos used when he moved in human society. She watched Cho's face, trying to read his reaction in the unblinking, sharklike gaze and coming up empty. "Have you heard the name before?"

"No." He set down his pen and neatly replaced the cap. "Should I have?"

Jenna stared at him, gauging the carefully spoken words and nonchalant way he settled back against his chair. "I would think that if you've done any amount of digging into TerraGlobal, you might have run across that name once or twice."

Cho's mouth flattened into a hard line. "I'm sorry. I don't recall it."

"Are you sure?" She waited through his prolonged silence, keeping her eyes fixed on his dark gaze if only to let him know that she could cling just as stubbornly to their apparent impasse.

The tactic seemed to work. Cho released a slow sigh, then rose up from his seat. "There is another agent in this office who's working the investigation with me. Will you excuse me for a moment while I confer with him about this?"

"Sure I will," Jenna said, relaxing a bit. Maybe now she might actually get somewhere.

After Cho stepped out of the room, she took the opportunity to fire off a quick text to Brock back in the SUV across the street. *Got something. Be down soon.*

No sooner had she sent it, Cho reappeared in the doorway. "Ms. Darrow, will you come with me, please?"

She got up and followed him along a cubicle-lined corridor, past the heads of numerous agents who stared into computer screens or talked quietly into their telephones. Cho kept going, toward a row of back offices on the far end of the floor. He hung a right at the end of the walkway and bypassed the numerous doors with their government-issued nameplates and departmental designations.

Finally, he paused in front of a stairwell door and swiped his clip-on ID badge through the slot on an electronic reader. When the little light turned from red to green, the agent pushed open the steel door and held it for her. "This way, please. The task force is headquartered on another floor."

For an instant, something dark flickered in her subconscious—a silent alarm that seemed to come out of nowhere. She hesitated, her gaze locked onto Cho's unblinking eyes.

He cocked his head, frowning slightly. "Ms. Darrow?"

She looked around, reminding herself that she was in a public office building, among easily a hundred other people working busily in their cubes and offices. There was no reason to feel threatened, she assured herself, as one of those many employees came out of a nearby office. The man was dressed in a dark business suit and tie, clean-cut and professional, just like Cho and the rest of the people in the department.

The man nodded in greeting as he also approached the stairwell. "Special Agent Cho," he said with a polite smile that drifted to Jenna a moment later.

"Good afternoon, Special Agent Green," Cho responded, permitting the other man to walk ahead of them through the open door. "Shall we, Ms. Darrow?"

Jenna shook off her queer niggle of unease and stepped past Cho. He followed immediately behind her. The stairwell door closed with a metallic thud that echoed in the empty enclosure.

And suddenly there was the other man—Green, turning back to hem her in between himself and Cho. His eyes looked eerie now, too. Up close, they were just as dull and emotionless as Cho's had seemed in the interview room.

Adrenaline spiked in Jenna's veins. She opened her mouth, ready to let loose with a scream.

She never got the chance.

Something cold and metallic came up below her ear. She knew it wasn't a gun, even before she heard the electronic crackle of the Taser's power snap to life.

Panic flooded her senses. She tried to jerk out of the debilitating current, but the power of the shock was too great. Fiery pain zapped into her, buzzing like a million bees in her ears. She convulsed under the assault . . . then her limbs dropped out from beneath her.

"Get her legs," she heard Cho tell the other man as he hooked his hands under her armpits. "Bring her to the freight elevator. My car is parked across the street in the garage. We can take the tunnel over there from the basement."

Jenna had no strength to shake them off, no voice to call for help. She felt her body being lifted, carried roughly down a couple of flights of stairs.

Then she lost consciousness completely.

She was taking too damn long.

Brock checked his cell phone and read Jenna's text again. She'd said she'd be down soon, yet she'd sent the message more than fifteen minutes ago. No sign of her yet. No further texts telling him she was delayed.

"Shit," he gritted tightly from the back of the Rover.

He peered out the rear window, toward the open entrance of the underground garage and the blinding glare of the winter afternoon. Jenna was in the building just across the street. Maybe a hundred yards from where he sat, but with broad daylight separating them, she might as well have been a hundred miles away.

He sent her a brief text: *Check in. Where u at?* Then he resumed his impatient wait, all the while keeping his eyes trained on the stream of people entering and exiting the federal building, waiting to see her emerge.

"Come on, Jenna. Get the hell back here."

After another few minutes without a response from her or any sign of her across the street, he couldn't stand sitting idle any longer. He'd worn full-body UV-protective clothing when he left the compound that morning, a precaution that would buy him a little bit of time if he was insane enough to leave the Rover and head across the street like he was thinking. He also had lineage on his side. If he'd been Gen One, he probably would have only about ten minutes tops before the sun began to crisp him, with or without the protective gear.

Brock, being several generations removed from the purest of the Breed bloodlines, could count on roughly half an hour of nonfatal UV exposure time, give or take a few minutes. It wasn't a risk that any of his kind took lightly. Nor did he now, as he opened the back door of the Rover and climbed out.

But something wasn't sitting right about Jenna and this meeting. Although he had nothing but his own instincts to guide him—and the gut-deep dread that he had allowed an innocent woman to walk headlong into potential danger—there was no way in hell Brock could stay put for another second without making sure Jenna was all right.

Even if he had to walk through daylight and an army full of human federal agents to do it.

He pulled on a pair of gloves, then yanked his light-blocking head covering low over his brow. Wraparound UV-proof glasses shaded his already searing retinas as he strode around the sea of parked vehicles, toward the blast of winter sunlight coming from the open maw of the garage entrance.

Bracing himself for the shock of so much furious daylight all around him, he set his sights on the federal building across the street and stepped out of the shelter of the parking garage.

CHAPTER
Nineteen

Consciousness returned in the form of dull pain traveling through her body. Jenna's reflexes came online in a blink, as though a switch had been thrown inside her. The instinct to wake up kicking and screaming was strong, but she tamped it down. Better to pretend she was still laid low from the taser, until she could assess the situation.

She kept her eyes all but closed, lifting her lids only a fraction to avoid tipping off her captors that she'd awakened. She fully intended to fight the sons of bitches, but first she had to get her bearings. Determine where she was and how she might get out of there.

The first part was easy enough. The smell of seat leather and faintly mildewy car mats told her she was in the back of a vehicle, sprawled on her side, her spine resting against the cushioned squab of the wide backseat. Although the engine was running, the car wasn't moving yet. It was dark inside the sedan, nothing but the flicker of a dim yellow light sputtering from outside the tinted glass of the window closest to her head.

Holy shit.

Hope flared inside her, bright and strong. They'd brought her to the parking garage across the street from the federal building.

The garage where Brock was waiting for her, even now.

Had he noticed what had happened to her?

But she dismissed the thought as soon as it occurred to her. If Brock had seen she was in trouble, he'd already be there. She knew that with a certainty that rocked her. He would never let her meet with harm if he could help it. So, he couldn't know that she was there, being held just a few yards away from the Order's black Rover.

For now, unless she could find a way to draw his attention, she was on her own.

Lifting her eyelids another small degree, she saw that her two captors were both seated up front—Cho behind the wheel of the federal fleet Crown Victoria, Green on the passenger side, the business end of his FBI standard-issue Glock 23 pointing over the seat in line with her chest.

"Yes, Master. We have the woman in the vehicle now," Cho said, speaking into a hands-free phone. "No, there were no complications. Of course, Master. I understand, you want her kept alive. I will contact you as soon as we have her secured in the warehouse to await your arrival this evening."

Master? What the hell?

Dread trickled along Jenna's spine as she listened to the robotic obedience in Cho's odd tone of voice. Even without the strangely subservient exchange, she knew that if she permitted these men to take her to another location, she was as good as dead. Maybe worse, if they served the dangerous individual her instincts told her they did.

Cho ended the call and put the car into reverse.

This was her chance—she had to make her move right now.

Jenna shifted carefully on the seat, soundlessly bringing her knees up toward her chest. Ignoring the slight twinge of her healing thigh, she kept coiling her legs by fractions, until her feet were in position near the middle of the split bench seat in front. Once aligned, she didn't hesitate to strike.

She kicked out with both feet, her right slamming into the side of Green's head, her left catching him in the elbow of his weapon arm. Green roared, his chin snapping up as the hand holding the Glock jerked toward the roof of the sedan. Gunfire cracked loudly in the car as a bullet shot through the upholstery and steel above his head.

Amid the chaos of the surprise attack, Cho's foot came down heavy on the gas. The sedan clipped the side of a thick concrete pillar in the row behind them, but Cho recovered quickly. He threw the vehicle into drive and stomped on the pedal again. Rubber squealed as the car lurched into acceleration.

Where the hell was Brock?

Jenna grabbed for the door handle in the backseat. Locked. She kicked at the door on the opposite side, driving her boot heel through the window. Pebbles of safety glass rained down onto her legs and the leather seat. Cold air rushed inside, carrying with it the stench of motor oil and fried food from the deli just around the corner.

Jenna scrambled for the gaping window, but came up short when Green pivoted around and shoved the muzzle of his gun against the side of her head.

"Sit the fuck back and behave, Ms. Darrow," he said pleasantly. "You're not going anywhere until Master says so."

Jenna slowly eased away from the loaded Glock, her gaze rooted on the chilling, emotionally vacant eyes of Special Agent Green.

There was no doubt in her mind now at all. These FBI agents—these beings who looked and acted like men, but somehow weren't—were part of Dragos's organization. Good God, just how far did his reach extend?

The question put a cold knot of fear in her stomach as Cho floored the sedan and sent it peeling out of the garage, then into the busy afternoon traffic outside.

Brock had crossed the sunlit street in mere seconds, using the speed of his Breed genetics to carry him through the afternoon daylight, to the door of the tall federal building. He was just about to enter and make another swift dash, past security, when his keen hearing picked up the muffled *pop* of a gunshot some distance behind.

The parking garage.

He knew it even before he heard the crunch of shredding metal and the shrill squeal of tires spinning on pavement.

Jenna.

Although he had no blood bond with her to alert him

that she was in danger, he felt the certainty of it clawing at his gut. She was no longer in the federal building but back in the garage, across the sunlit street.

Something had gone terribly wrong, and it had everything to do with TerraGlobal—with Dragos.

No sooner had the thought formed, when an unmarked gray Crown Vic burst from the garage exit. As the sedan roared away, he saw two men in the front seat. The passenger was pivoted around to face a single occupant in back.

No, not men—Minions.

And Jenna in the backseat, sitting stock-still, held at gunpoint.

Fury rolled through him like a tidal wave. His sights locked onto the car that held Jenna, he tore past crowds of milling humans on the walkway below the building, moving faster than anyone could track him.

He leapt across the hood of a standing taxi at the curb, then dodged a delivery truck that came up out of nowhere and would have run him down if he hadn't been propelled by his Breed ability and fear for what might happen to Jenna if he didn't reach her in time.

Heart hammering, he raced into the parking garage and jumped into the Rover.

Two seconds later, he was rocketing out into the street, defying the blaze of ultraviolet rays that poured in through the windshield as he sped off in Jenna's direction, praying like hell that he could reach her before Dragos's evil—or the baking afternoon sun—cost him the woman whose life was his to protect.

His woman, he thought fiercely, as he dropped his boot on the gas pedal and took off in pursuit.

CHAPTER
Twenty

Special Agent Green—or whoever, *whatever*, he really was—kept the Glock trained on her with a steady hand as the sedan weaved and lurched through the clotted New York City traffic. Jenna had no idea where they were taking her. She could only guess it was somewhere out of the city as they left the labyrinth of tall skyscrapers behind and headed onto a gothic-looking suspension bridge that spanned the width of a broad river.

Jenna sat back against the seat, jostling back and forth with each bump and acceleration. As the sedan leapt forward to pass a slower-moving vehicle, she was thrown off balance—enough so that she glanced up and caught an unexpected glimpse in the Crown Vic's side mirror.

A black Range Rover was keeping pace with them, just a few cars back.

Jenna's heart squeezed.

Brock. It had to be him.

But at the same moment, she hoped like hell it wasn't. It couldn't be—he would be foolish to risk it. The sun was still a giant ball of fire in the cold westerly sky, at least two hours from setting. Driving in full daylight would be suicide for one of Brock's kind.

And yet, it *was* him.

When the sedan made another sidelong shift in the lane, Jenna checked the mirror again and saw the rigid set of his jaw across the traffic and distance that separated them. Although he wore dark wraparound sunglasses to protect his eyes, the opaque lenses weren't dense enough to mask the ember-bright glow of his eyes.

Brock was behind them, and he was deadly furious.

"Son of a bitch," Green muttered, peering over her head to look through the rear window of the vehicle. "We've got a tail."

"You sure?" Cho asked, taking the opportunity to pass another car as they neared the other end of the bridge.

"I'm sure," Green replied. A note of unease had crept into his otherwise unreadable face. "It's a vampire. One of the warriors."

Cho gunned the vehicle now. "Inform Master that we're almost to the location. Ask him how we should proceed."

Green nodded, and, still holding Jenna under the threat of his Glock, he retrieved a cell phone from his pocket and pressed a single digit. The call rang once over the speaker, then Dragos's voice came on the line.

"Status?"

"We're nearing the Brooklyn cargo docks, Master, as you instructed. But we're not alone." Green spoke in a rush of words, as though he sensed the displeasure that would follow. "There's someone following us on the bridge. He is Breed. A warrior from the Order."

Jenna took no small amount of satisfaction at the violent curse that exploded over the cell phone speaker. As chilled as she was to hear the voice of the Order's hated enemy, it was gratifying to know that he feared the warriors. As well he should.

"Lose him," Dragos growled, pure venom.

"He's right behind us," Cho said, glancing nervously in the rearview mirror as they sped along a road that followed the waterfront toward an industrial area. "He's only one car behind us now and gaining. I don't think we can shake him at this point."

Another snarled oath from Dragos, more savage than before. "All right," he said in a low, even tone. "Then abort. Kill the bitch and get out of there. Dump her corpse off the docks or into the street, I could give a fuck. But don't let that goddamn vampire get near either one of you. Understood?"

Green and Cho exchanged a brief look of acknowledgment. "Yes, Master," Green replied, ending the call.

Cho steered into a sharp left turn off the road and into a parking lot at the water. Large freight trailers and assorted box trucks dotted the ice-spotted, cracked pavement. And nearer to the river's edge were several warehouse buildings, which is where Cho seemed to be heading at breakneck speed.

Green leveled the gun on her, until she was staring down the barrel at the chambered bullet that would soon be unloaded into her head. She felt a surge of power flow

into her veins—something far more intense than adrenaline—as the moment began to play out in slow motion.

Green's finger tightened on the trigger. There was a
soft scrape of responding steel, mechanisms in the firearm
clicking into action as though in the thick fog of a dream.

Jenna heard the bullet begin to explode from the
chamber. She smelled the sharp tang of gunpowder and
smoke. And she saw the quiver of energy rippling in the
air as the weapon fired on her.

She ducked out of its way. She didn't know how she
managed it, nor how it was possible for her to know just
how to dodge the bullet as Green sent it blasting toward
her. She knew only to listen to her instincts, preternatural
as they seemed.

She came up behind Green's seat and wrenched his
arm, snapping the bone in her bare hands. He screamed
in agony. The gun went off again, this time a flailing, wild
shot.

It struck Cho in the side of his skull, killing him instantly.

The sedan veered and rocked, accelerating with the
dead weight of Cho's foot resting on the gas. They hit the
corner of a rusted freight container, knocking the Crown
Vic into a vicious sideways roll across the snow and ice.

Jenna hit the roof of the car as it flipped ass over
teakettle, windows shattering, airbags deploying. Her
whole world tumbled violently, over and over, before finally coming to a jarring halt upside down on the pavement.

Holy bloody hell.

Brock pulled in to the industrial lot and slammed on

the brakes, watching with a mix of horror and rage as the Crown Victoria hit the side of a cargo trailer and pitched into a steel-crushing roll on the frozen pavement.

"Jenna!" he shouted, throwing the Rover into park and vaulting out the door.

The daylight had been a bitch to deal with inside the vehicle; outside it was beyond hellish. He could hardly see through the haze of blinding white light as he raced across ice and cracked asphalt to the overturned sedan. The car's wheels were still spinning, the engine whining, spewing smoke and steam into the frigid air.

As he neared, he heard Jenna grunting, struggling inside. Brock's first instinct was to grab hold of the vehicle and right it, but he couldn't be sure if flipping the car would cause more harm to her, and it was a chance he wasn't willing to take.

"Jenna, I'm here," he said, then reached out and tore the upside-down driver's-side door clean off its hinges. He tossed it to the ground and dropped to his haunches to look into the crushed interior.

Ah, Christ.

Blood and gore were everywhere, the stench of dead red cells combining with the sharp fumes of leaking oil and gasoline to pierce through the sun-scorched fog of his senses. He looked past the corpse of the driver, whose head was blown open by a close-range gunshot wound. All of Brock's focus was trained on Jenna.

The roof of the sedan was buckled and smashed, creating only a small amount of room for her and the other human male, who was struggling to get a grip on her legs. She was fighting him off with one foot while attempting to claw her way out of the nearest window. The human gave up as soon as his flat gaze slid to Brock. Releasing

Jenna's ankle, he ducked back to scramble ass-first through the gaping windshield.

"Minion," Brock snarled, hatred for the soulless mind slave making his blood boil even hotter with fury.

These two men were definitely Dragos's loyal hounds. Bled by him to within an inch of their lives, they would serve Dragos in whatever capacity he required, obedient to their dying breath. Brock wanted to speed the escaping human to that final moment personally. Kill him with his bare hands.

He damn well would, but not until he made sure Jenna was safe.

"Are you okay?" he asked her, stripping off his leather gloves with his teeth and tossing them aside so he could touch her. He smoothed his fingers over her pale, pretty face, then reached down to catch her under the arms. "Come on, let's get you out of here."

She shook her head vigorously. "I'm fine, but my leg is pinned between the seats. Go after him, Brock. That man is working with Dragos!"

"I know," he said. "He's a Minion, and he doesn't matter. But you do. Hold on to me, baby. I'm gonna get you free now."

Something metallic popped outside the car. The loud *ping* echoed sharply, then another one sounded, and still another.

Bullets.

Jenna's eyes found his through the thin smoke and fumes that were closing in on them inside the wrecked vehicle. "He must have another gun on him. He's shooting at us."

Brock didn't answer. He knew the Minion wasn't trying

to hit them through all that metal and machinery. He was firing on the car itself.

Trying to create the spark that would ignite the exposed gas tank.

"Hold on to me," he told her, bracing one hand against her spine as he reached with the other for the crushed seats that had Jenna trapped. With a low growl, he ripped them loose.

"I'm out," she said, already scrabbling free.

Another bullet struck the car. Brock heard an unnatural gasp from outside—a rush of air that preceded the sudden, swelling stench of thick black smoke and the gust of heat that said the Minion had finally hit his mark.

"Come on!" he said, grabbing Jenna's hand.

He pulled her clear of the vehicle, both of them tumbling out to the pavement. A plume of fire erupted from the overturned car as the gas tank exploded, shaking the earth beneath them. The Minion kept firing, bullets zinging dangerously close.

Brock covered Jenna's body with his own as he grabbed for one of the semiautos holstered on his gun belt. He came up onto his knees, ready to shoot—only to realize that his sunglasses had come off in the tumble from the car. Between the wall of heat and roiling smoke, and the searing light of day, his vision was virtually nil.

"Shit," he hissed, wiping a hand across his eyes, straining to see through the agony of his scorched vision. Jenna was moving beneath him now, scrambling out of the shelter of his body. He reached for her, his hand casting out blindly, coming back empty. "Jenna, damn it. Stay down!"

But she didn't stay down. She took the pistol out of his hand and opened fire, a rapid hail of bullets that cracked loudly over the roar of flames and heated metal beside them. Across the lot, the Minion cried out sharply, then went utterly silent.

"Gotcha, you son of a bitch," Jenna said. An instant later, Brock felt her fingers wrap around his. "He's dead. And you're burning up out here. Come on, let's get the hell out of this place."

Brock ran with her, hand in hand across the open lot, toward the Rover. As much as his pride wanted him to argue that he was good to drive, he knew he was too cooked to even attempt it. Jenna didn't give him a chance to protest. She shoved him into the back of the vehicle, then jumped behind the wheel. In the distance, the howl of police sirens sounded, human authorities no doubt responding to the apparent accident near the docks.

"Hang on," Jenna said, throwing the Rover into gear.

She seemed unfazed by the whole thing, cool and collected, the total professional. And damn if he'd ever seen anything so hot in all his years. Brock lay back against the cool leather of the seat, grateful as hell to have her on his side as she stomped on the gas pedal and floored it away from the scene.

CHAPTER
Twenty-one

The drive back to Boston had taken the better part of four hours, but Jenna's heart was still racing—her concern for Brock still fresh and unrelenting—as she swung the Rover through the iron gates of the compound and headed around to the fleet hangar in back of the Order's private estate.

"We're here," she said, parking the vehicle inside the large garage and cutting the engine.

She glanced in the rearview mirror, checking on him for about the thousandth time since they'd set out from New York. He'd been quiet in the backseat of the SUV for most of the trip, despite shifting around in obvious agony as he'd tried to sleep off the effects of his ultraviolet exposure.

She pivoted around in her seat to have a closer look at him. "Are you going to be okay?"

"I'll live." His eyes met hers through the darkness, his broad mouth quirking into more of a grimace than a smile. He tried to sit up, groaning with the effort.

"Stay there. Let me help you."

She crawled into the back with him before he could tell her that he could manage on his own. He looked up at her in a long, meaningful silence, their eyes connecting, holding. All of the air seemed to abandon the space around them. It seemed to leave her lungs, as well, relief and worry colliding inside her as she stared down into Brock's handsome face. The burns that had been livid a few hours ago across his forehead, cheeks, and nose were all but gone now. His dark eyes were still moist and leaking wetness from their edges but no longer bloodshot and swollen.

"Oh, God," she whispered, feeling her emotions break and begin to rush out of her. "I was so scared today, Brock. You have no idea how much."

"You, scared?" He reached up, ran his hand tenderly along the side of her face. His lips curved, and he gave a faint shake of his head. "I saw you in action today. I don't think anything really scares you."

She frowned, reliving the moment when she'd realized he was coming after her in the SUV, sitting behind the wheel in broad daylight. But her worry for him then had grown to something close to terror when, after the car she was in had flipped, Brock was there, as well, willing to walk through lethal UV rays in order to help her. Even now, she was awed and humbled by what he'd done.

"You put your life on the line for me," she whispered,

turning her cheek into the gentle warmth of his palm. "You risked too much, Brock."

He came up off the seat, catching her face in both of his hands. His gaze was solemn, so very earnest. "We were partners today. And if you ask me, I'd say we made a pretty damn good team."

She smiled despite herself. "You had to save my ass... again. As far as partners go, I hate to tell you, but you got the raw end of that deal."

"No. Not even close." Brock's eyes held her with a deep intensity that seemed to reach right into the core of her being. He stroked her cheek, brushed the pad of his thumb over her lips. "And for the record, you were the one who saved my hide. If that Minion didn't take one or both of us out, the sunlight would have finished me off for sure. You saved both of us today, Jenna. Goddamn, you were amazing."

When she parted her lips to deny it, he moved in and kissed her. Jenna melted into him, lost herself in the warm caress of his mouth on hers. The attraction she felt for him hadn't faded a bit since they'd been together in his bed, but now there was something even more powerful behind the swell of heat that flared within her. She cared for him—truly cared—and the realization of what she was feeling took her completely by surprise.

It wasn't supposed to be like this. She wasn't supposed to feel such a strong bond to him, especially not when he had made it clear he didn't want to complicate things with emotion or expectations of a relationship. But when he broke their kiss and looked into her gaze, she could see that he was feeling something more than he'd been prepared for, too. There was something more than desire flickering in the amber light of his absorbing brown eyes.

"When I saw those Minions drive off with you today, Jenna…" The words drifted into silence. He exhaled a soft curse and pulled her close, holding her against him for a long moment. He nuzzled his face into the curve of her neck and shoulder. "When I saw them with you, I thought I'd failed you. I don't know what I would have done if anything had happened to you."

"I'm here," she said, lightly stroking his strong back and caressing his inclined head. "You didn't fail me at all. I'm right here, Brock, because of you."

He kissed her again, deeper this time, an unrushed joining of their mouths. His hands were tender on her, weaving into her hair and moving softly over her shoulders and spine. She felt so sheltered in his arms, so small and feminine against the immensity of his warrior's chest and thickly muscled arms.

And she liked the feeling. She liked the way he made her feel safe and womanly, things she'd never really known before, not even with her husband.

Mitch. Oh, God…

The thought of him made her heart squeeze as though it were caught in a vise. Not because of grief or longing for him, but because Brock was kissing her and holding her—making her feel worthy of his affection—when she hadn't yet told him everything.

He might feel differently if he knew it was her own selfish actions that had caused the accident that killed her husband and child.

"What is it?" Brock asked, no doubt sensing the change that was coming over her now. "What's wrong?"

She withdrew from his embrace, looking away from him, knowing it was too late to pretend everything was all right. Brock was still stroking her tenderly, waiting for her to tell him what was troubling her. "You were right about me," she murmured. "You said I have a problem with needing to be in control, and you were right."

He made a dismissive sound in the back of his throat and lifted her face to meet his. "None of that matters."

"It does," she insisted. "It mattered today, and it mattered four years ago in Alaska, too."

"You're talking about when you lost Mitch and Libby," he said, more statement than question. "You think you are somehow to blame for that?"

"I know I am." A sob crept up the back of her throat, but she choked it back. "It wouldn't have happened if I hadn't insisted we drive home that day."

"Jenna, you can't possibly think—"

"Let me say it," she interrupted. "Please...I want you to know the truth. And I need to speak the words, Brock. I can't hold them in anymore."

He said nothing more, sober as he took her hands between his and let her tell him how her stubbornness—her goddamned need to be in charge of every situation—had cost Mitch and Libby their lives.

"We were in Galena, a city several hours away from where we lived in Harmony. The state troopers had put on a fancy gala there, one of those annual attaboy events where they hand out medals of commendation and take your picture with the governor. I was being recognized for excellence in the department—the first time I'd been singled out for any kind of award. I was convinced it would be good for my career to be seen by so many important people, so I insisted to Mitch that we attend with Libby." She pulled in a fortifying breath and slowly pushed it out. "It was November, and the roads were nearly impassable.

We made it to Galena without too many problems, but on the drive home..."

"It's okay," Brock said, reaching up to sweep aside a loose tendril of her hair. "You all right?"

She gave him a wobbly nod, even though inside she was hardly all right. Her chest was raw with anguish and guilt, her eyes burning with welling tears. "Mitch and I argued the whole time. He thought the roads were too bad for travel. They were, but another storm was on the way, which would only make things worse. I didn't want to wait out the weather because I needed to report in for my shift the next day. So we headed home. Mitch was driving the Blazer. Libby was in her car seat in back. A couple of hours onto the highway, a tractor trailer carrying a full load of timber crossed into our lane. There was no time to react. No time to say I was sorry, or to tell either of them how much I loved them."

"Come here," Brock said, and gathered her close. He held her for a long time, his strength so comforting and warm.

"Mitch accused me of caring about my career more than I did him or Libby," she whispered, her voice broken, the words hard to get out. "He used to say I was too controlling, too stubborn for my own good. But he always gave in, even then."

Brock kissed the top of her head. "You didn't know what would happen, Jenna. You couldn't have known, so don't blame yourself. It was out of your control."

"I just feel so guilty that I survived. Why couldn't it have been me who died, not them?" Tears strangled her now, hot and bitter in her throat. "I never even got a chance to say good-bye. I was medevaced to the hospital in Fairbanks and put in a coma to help my body recover.

When I woke up a month later, I learned they were both gone."

"Jesus," Brock whispered, still holding her in the caring shelter of his embrace. "I'm sorry, Jenna. God, how you must have been hurting."

She swallowed, trying not to lose herself in the agony of those awful days. It helped that Brock was there to hold her now. He was a rock of strength, keeping her grounded and steady.

"When I got out of the hospital, I was so lost. I didn't want to live. I didn't want to accept the fact that I would never see my family again. Alex and my brother, Zach, had taken care of the funerals, since no one knew when I might come out of the coma. By the time I was released from the hospital, Mitch and Libby were already cremated. I've never had the courage to go to the cemetery where they are interred."

"Not in all this time?" he asked gently, his fingers stroking her hair.

She shook her head. "I wasn't ready to see their gravestones so soon after the accident, and every year that passed, I never found the strength to go and tell them good-bye. No one knows that, not even Alex. I've been too ashamed to tell anyone just how weak I really am."

"You're not weak." Brock set her away from him, only enough that he could bend his head down and stare her solemnly in the eyes. "Everyone makes mistakes, Jenna. Everyone has regrets and guilt for things they should have done differently in their lives. Shit happens, and we do the best we can at the time. You can't blame yourself forever."

His words soothed her, but she couldn't accept all that he was saying. She'd seen him grapple too much with his own guilt to know that he was only being kind now.

"You're just telling me this to make me feel better. I know you don't really believe it yourself."

He frowned, a quiet torment passing over his face in the darkness of the Rover.

"What was her name?" Jenna touched his now rigid jaw, seeing the remembered pain in his eyes. "The girl in the old photograph in your quarters—I saw how you looked at her picture last night. You knew her, didn't you?"

A nod, barely discernible. "Her name was Corinne. She's the young Breedmate I was hired to guard back in Detroit."

"That image must be several decades old," Jenna said, recalling the Depression-era clothes and the jazz club where the young woman had been photographed.

Brock understood the question she was asking now, she could see that by the somewhat wry look in his eyes. "It was July 1935. I know, because I'm the one who took the picture."

Jenna nodded, realizing she should be more astonished than she was at the reminder that Brock and his kind were something close to immortal. Right now, and every time he was near her, she thought of him simply as a man. An honorable, extraordinary man who was still hurting from an old wound that had cut him deeply.

"Corinne is the woman you lost?" she asked gently.

His frown deepened. "Yeah."

"And you hold yourself responsible for her death," she prompted carefully, needing to know what he'd been through. She wanted to understand him better. If she could, she wanted to help him bear some of his own guilt and pain. "How did it happen?"

At first, she didn't think he would tell her. He stared

down at their entwined fingers, idly rubbing his thumb over the back of her hand. When he finally spoke, there was a raw edge to his deep voice, as though the pain of losing Corinne was still fresh in his heart.

"Back when I was in Detroit, times were very lean. Not so much for the Breed, but for the human cities we lived in. The leader of a local Darkhaven and his mate had taken in a couple of young homeless girls, Breedmates, to raise as their own children. I was assigned to watch over Corinne. She was a wild child, even as a young girl—full of life, always laughing. As she got older, a teenager, she got even wilder. She resented her father's precautions, thought he was too overbearing. She started making a game of trying to break free from his rules and expectations. She started pushing boundaries, taking awful risks to her personal safety, testing the patience of everyone around her."

Jenna gave him a gentle smile. "I can imagine that didn't go over very well with you."

"To put it mildly," he said, shaking his head. "Corinne was clever, and she tried damned hard to ditch me every chance she got, but she never outfoxed me. Until that last time, the night of her eighteenth birthday."

"What happened?"

"Corinne loved music. At the time, jazz was the big thing. The best Detroit jazz clubs were in an area known as Paradise Valley. I don't think a week went by that she didn't plead with me to take her there. More often than not, I let her have her way. We went to the clubs the night of her birthday, too—no simple thing, given that it was the early twentieth century and she was a white woman alone in the company of a black man." He exhaled a soft, humorless chuckle. "Skin color may be incidental in my world, among the Breed, but that wasn't the case among humankind back then."

"Too often, that's not the case now, either," Jenna said, twining her fingers through his a little tighter and finding nothing but beauty in the contrast of his skin and hers. "Was there trouble at the club that night?"

He gave a faint nod. "There were some looks and whispers. Couple of white men had too much to drink. They came over and said some crude things to Corinne. I told them where they could go. I don't recall who threw the first punch, but things went south from there."

"Did the men know what you were? That you were Breed?"

"Not at first. I knew my rage would give me away, and I knew I had to get out of the club before the whole place saw the changes come over me. The men followed me outside. Corinne would've, too, but I told her to stay in the building, find somewhere to wait for me while I dealt with things." He drew in a ragged breath. "I wasn't gone even ten minutes. When I came back into the club, there was no sign of her anywhere. I turned the place inside out looking for her. I searched every corner of the city and all the area Darkhavens until daybreak. I kept searching every night afterward, even out of the state. But . . . nothing. She had vanished into thin air, just like that."

Jenna could hear the frustration in his voice—the regret—even all these years later. She brought her hand up and gently touched his face, uncertain what to do for him. "I wish I had your gift. I wish I could take away the hurt for you."

He shook his head, then brought her palm to his mouth and pressed a kiss to the center of her hand. "What I feel is anger, at myself. I never should have let her out of my sight, not even for a second. When news reached me that a young woman's brutalized, burned body had been recovered from a city river not far from the clubs, I felt sick with dread. I didn't want to believe it was her. Not even when I saw the corpse with my own eyes . . . what remained of it, after what someone had done to her prior to the three months she'd been left in the water."

Jenna winced, knowing all too well how horrific death could look, particularly to those who cared for the victim. And most especially to a man who had held himself responsible for a crime he had no way of anticipating, let alone preventing.

"She was unrecognizable, except for bits of clothing and a necklace she still wore when she was pulled out of the river. Burning her and cutting off her hands hadn't been enough for whoever killed her. She was also weighted down, making sure she wasn't discovered for a long time after she vanished."

"My God," Jenna whispered. "That kind of brutality and forethought doesn't just happen. Whoever did it did it for a reason."

Brock shrugged. "What reason could there possibly be to kill a defenseless young woman? She was just a kid. A beautiful, wild child who was living every moment. There was something addictive about her energy and her spirit. Corinne didn't give a damn what anyone said or thought, she just chewed through life without apologies. Grabbed hold of every day as though it was all going to end tomorrow. Jesus, little did she know."

Jenna saw the depth of his regret in his carefully schooled expression. "When did you realize you had fallen in love with her?"

His gaze was distant in the dark of the backseat. "I

don't remember how it happened. I made an effort to keep my feelings to myself. I never acted on them, not even when she flirted and teased. It wouldn't have been right. Corinne was too young, for one thing. And her father trusted me to watch over her."

Jenna smiled as she reached out to him, smoothing her hand along his rigid cheek and jaw. "You're an honorable man, Brock. You were then, and you are now."

He shook his head slowly, reflecting for a moment. "I failed. What happened to Corinne—God, what her killers did to her body—was beyond comprehension. It never should have happened. I was supposed to keep her safe. It took me a long time to accept that she was gone—that the charred and desecrated remains had once been the vibrant young woman I'd known since she was a child. I wanted to deny she was dead. Hell, I denied it to myself for a long time, even searched for her across three states, convincing myself she was still out there, that I could save her. It never brought her back."

Jenna watched him, seeing the torment that still lived inside him. "Do you wish you could bring her back?"

"I had been hired to protect her. That was my job, the promise I made every time she stepped out of her father's Darkhaven. I would have traded my life for Corinne's without hesitation."

"And now?" Jenna asked quietly, realizing she was half afraid to hear that he might still love the beautiful ghost from his past.

But when Brock's gaze lifted, his eyes were steady and serious, centered completely on her. His touch was warm and lingering against her face, his mouth so very close to hers. "Wouldn't you rather know how I feel about you?" He stroked his thumb over her lips, the barest skate of contact, and yet she sizzled deep within. "I haven't been able to stop thinking about you, and believe me, I've tried. Getting involved was never in my plans."

"I know," she said. "Allergic to relationships. I remember."

"I've been careful for a long time, Jenna." His voice was thick, a low rasp that vibrated into her bones. "I try very hard not to make mistakes. Especially ones that can't be reversed."

She swallowed, suddenly concerned that his voice had gotten too serious. "You don't owe me anything, if that's what you think."

"That's where you're wrong," he said. "I do owe you something—an apology for what happened between us the other night."

She shook her head in denial. "Brock, don't—"

He caught her chin in his grasp and drew her attention back to his gaze. "I wanted you, Jenna. The way I pursued you into my bed probably wasn't fair. It sure as hell wasn't honorable, using my talent to dull your grief when it might also have drawn away some of your will."

"No." She touched his face, recalling very well how good it had felt to be kissing him, touching him, lying naked with him in his bed. She'd been more than willing to know that kind of pleasure with him, then and now. "It wasn't like that, Brock. And you don't have to explain—"

"Most of all," he said, talking past her denials, "I owe you an apology for suggesting that sex with you would be purely physical, without strings or expectations beyond the moment. I was in the wrong. You deserve more than that, Jenna. You deserve far more than anything I can offer you."

"I didn't ask you for anything more." She caressed the

line of his jaw, then let her fingers drift down the strong column of his neck. "And the desire was mutual, Brock. My will was my own. It still is. And I would do it all over again with you."

His answering growl was purely male as he drew her to him and kissed her deeply. He held her close, his heart-beat thudding powerfully, the heat of his body seeping in through her skin like a balm. When he broke from her mouth, his breath was ragged through his teeth and bright points of his fangs. His dark eyes glittered with brilliant amber sparks. "Christ, Jenna...what I want to do right now is turn this car around and drive off somewhere with you. Just the two of us. Just for a little while, away from everything else."

The idea was more than tempting but made even more irresistible when he leaned in and caught her in a sensual, bone-melting kiss. She wrapped her arms around him and met his tongue with her own, losing herself in the erotic joining of their mouths. He made a low noise in the back of his throat, a rumbling growl that vibrated through her as he drew her deeper into his arms, deeper into his kiss.

Jenna felt the abrading scrape of his fangs against her tongue, felt the hard ridge of his arousal pressing against her hip as he pivoted her around to the long bench seat and covered her with his body.

"Gideon's waiting for us in the tech lab," she managed to whisper as he broke away from her mouth to rain a dizzying trail of kisses along the sensitive skin below her ear. They'd phoned in from the road an hour ago, alerting Gideon and Lucan to the situation they'd encountered in New York and letting them know they were heading back to the compound. "They're expecting us to report in as soon as we arrive."

"Yes," he growled, but he didn't stop kissing her.

He unzipped her coat and slid his hand underneath her shirt. He caressed her breasts over the thin fabric of her bra, teasing her nipples to pebble-hard peaks. She writhed beneath him as he moved atop her, slow thrusts of his pelvis that made her body weep with the need to feel him naked against her. Buried inside her.

"Brock," she gasped, all but lost to the passion he was stoking in her. "Gideon knows we're in here. There's probably a security camera trained on us right now."

"Tinted windows," he rasped, glancing up at her with a sexy grin that bared the gleaming tips of his fangs and made her stomach flip. "Nobody can see a thing. Now stop thinking about Gideon and kiss me."

He didn't have to tell her to stop thinking. His hands and lips erased all thought, except the yearning she had for more of him. He kissed her with demand, pushing his tongue into her mouth like he meant to devour her. His passion was intoxicating and she drank him in, clutching at him, inwardly cursing their inconvenient clothing and the confining interior of the Rover.

She wanted him even more intensely than the first time, her desire fueled by the sweetness of his unnecessary apology and the adrenaline that was still simmering in her veins from all they'd gone through together that day. Murmuring his name around broken, pleasured gasps as his mouth roamed along the side of her neck and his hands caressed the aching swells of her breasts, Jenna knew that if they stayed in the vehicle even one more minute, they would end up naked right there in the backseat. Not that she'd complain. She hardly had the breath to do anything more than moan in pleasure as he slipped his hand between her legs and rocked his palm against her in a masterful rhythm.

"Oh, God," she whispered. "Please, don't stop."

But he did stop—not even a second later. He went still above her, his head snapping up. Then she heard it, too.

The roar of a fast-approaching vehicle outside the fleet hangar. The garage door opened and one of the Order's other black SUVs came flying inside. It screeched to a halt a few spaces away from them, and one of the warriors leapt out of the driver's seat.

"It's Chase," Brock murmured, frowning as he watched out the back window. "Shit. Something's wrong. Stay in here, if you'd rather not let him know we were together just now."

"Forget it. I'm going with you," she said, then pulled herself together and followed him out of the Rover to meet the other Breed male. Sterling Chase was heading for the compound elevator at an urgent clip. He glanced over at Brock and Jenna as they approached. If he guessed at what he'd interrupted, the shrewd blue eyes gave nothing away.

"What's going on?" Brock asked, nothing but business in his deep voice.

Chase was equally grim, hardly slowing down to talk. "You haven't heard?"

Brock gave a curt shake of his head. "We just came in ourselves."

"Got a call from Mathias Rowan a few minutes ago," Chase said. "There's been an abduction at one of the Boston area Darkhavens tonight."

"Oh, my God," Jenna whispered, stricken. "Not another Breedmate?"

Chase shook his head. "A young male, fourteen years old. He also happens to be the grandson of a Gen One elder named Lazaro Archer."

"Gen One," Brock muttered, instincts prickling with alarm. "That can't possibly be a coincidence."

"Doubtful," Chase agreed. "The Enforcement Agency is questioning witnesses, trying to grab any leads they can on where the kid might have been taken, and why. Meanwhile Lazaro Archer and his son, Christophe, the boy's father, are making noise that they want to meet with his abductors personally—whoever they are—to negotiate for his release."

"Ah, Christ. Bad fucking idea," Brock said, sliding a tense look at Jenna as they followed Chase across the garage. "There's only one person I can think of who'd have any cause to snatch a Gen One's family member. It's a trap, Harvard. I smell Dragos all over this."

"So do I. And so does Lucan." Chase paused with them in front of the hangar's elevator and pressed the call button. "He's arranged a meeting with the Gen One and his son here at the compound. Tegan's going to pick them up within the hour."

CHAPTER
Twenty-two

Lucan and Gideon were waiting for them as soon as Brock came off the elevator with Jenna and Chase.

"Hell of a goddamned day," Lucan muttered, taking them in with a glance. "You both all right?"

Brock stole a look at Jenna, who stood calm and steady beside him. She was a little scraped up and bruised, but thankfully she was whole. "Could've been worse."

Lucan raked a hand through his dark hair. "Dragos is getting bolder all the time. Minions in the fucking FBI, for crissake."

"What the hell?" Chase frowned, shooting an incredulous look between Brock and Jenna. "You mean the Fed you met with today—"

"He belonged to Dragos," Brock replied. "He and another of Dragos's mind slaves grabbed her inside the building and took off with her. I pursued the vehicle but wasn't able to catch up to them until they crashed on the other side of the Brooklyn Bridge."

Chase exhaled a low curse. "You two are lucky to be alive."

"Yeah," Brock agreed. "Thanks to Jenna. She took out both Minions, then saved my bacon from going crispy, as well."

"No shit?" Some of the edge left Chase's hard blue gaze as he looked at her. "Not bad for a human. I'm impressed."

She shrugged off the compliment. "I should have known something wasn't right with the agent I met with. I did know, actually. I had a certain . . . sense, I guess you could say. I couldn't quite put my finger on it, but all through the meeting I kept thinking something was odd about him."

"What do you mean?" Gideon asked.

She frowned, considering. "I don't know exactly. It was just something instinctual. His eyes made me uncomfortable, and I kept getting a weird feeling that he wasn't quite . . . normal."

"You knew he wasn't quite human," Brock suggested, as surprised as the rest of the warriors to hear her admission. "You sensed he was a Minion?"

"I suppose I did." She nodded. "But I didn't know to call him that at the time. All I knew was he made my skin crawl the longer I was near him."

Brock didn't miss the silent glance that passed between Gideon and Lucan.

Neither did Jenna. "What is it? Tell me why you're so quiet all of a sudden."

"Human beings don't have the ability to detect Minions," Brock answered. "*Homo sapiens* senses aren't acute enough to pick up on the difference between a mortal and someone whose will belongs to a Breed master."

She arched her brows. "You think this is also related to the implant, don't you? The alien gift that keeps on giving." She huffed out a sharp laugh. "Just how crazy have I become, that this can all just seem par for the course now?"

Brock narrowly resisted the urge to wrap his arm around her. Instead he turned a serious look on Gideon. "Have you found anything more in the blood work results?"

"Nothing significant beyond the anomalies we've already discovered. But I would like to run a few more samples, as well as conduct another stress test and further strength and endurance measurements."

Jenna nodded in agreement. "Whenever you're ready, I'm in. Since it appears there's no way to get rid of the damned thing, I guess I'd better start trying to understand it."

"The tests are going to have to wait a while," Lucan interjected. "I want everyone gathered in the tech lab in ten minutes. A lot of shit went down today, and I need to make sure we're all up to speed before our Darkhaven guests arrive."

The Order's leader slid an approving look toward Jenna, then Brock. "Glad to have you back in one piece. Both of you."

Jenna murmured her thanks, but her expression was pinched with disappointment. "Unfortunately, since the meeting was a setup, we didn't come away with any information on TerraGlobal."

Lucan grunted. "Maybe not, but finding out that Dragos has Minions embedded in human government could prove to be even more valuable to us in the long run. It's sure as hell not good news, but it's something we needed to be aware of."

"He's stepping things up big-time," Gideon added. "Between this discovery today and now the kidnapping of Lazaro Archer's grandson, it's pretty clear that Dragos isn't about to give up."

"And nothing is beneath him," Brock remarked, grave with the possibilities. "That makes him more dangerous than ever. We'd better be prepared for the worst when it comes to this bastard."

Lucan nodded, his gaze sober, reflective. "For now, we'll take it one crisis at a time. Chase, come with me. I want you to ride shotgun with Tegan when he goes topside to collect the Archers. Everyone else, tech lab in ten."

Lazaro Archer was rumored to be close to a thousand years old, but like any other Breed male, outwardly the jet-haired Gen One looked to be no more than thirty. The lines around his stern mouth and the shadows under his dark blue eyes, although pronounced, were just evidence of his distress over the abduction of his young grandson. Those shrewd but weary eyes scanned the faces of everyone who was gathered in the tech lab—the warriors and their mates, and Jenna at Brock's side, as well—all of them watching and waiting as Lucan and Gabrielle escorted the Breed elder and his grim-faced son, Christophe, into the room.

Quick, courteous introductions circled the large conference table, but everyone there understood the meeting was hardly a social call. Brock couldn't remember the last time a Breed civilian was admitted into the compound. Few in the vampire nation even knew where the Order's headquarters were located, let alone stepped inside.

Neither of the Archers looked comfortable being there, either, particularly the abducted boy's father. Brock didn't miss the slightly superior tilt of the younger male's chin as he scanned the tech lab and each of the warriors seated at the table, most of whom were still dressed in night patrol gear, weapons and all. Christophe Archer seemed reluctant, if not resistant, to be offered an empty chair among the heathens of the Order.

Desperate times, Brock thought gravely, inclining his head in greeting as the second-generation Breed civilian in his long cashmere coat and impeccably tailored shirt and pants settled carefully into the seat next to him.

Lucan cleared his throat, his deep voice taking instant command of the room as he glanced at the two newcomers. "First, I want to assure you both that everyone in this room shares your concern for Kellan's safety. As I told you when we spoke earlier, Lazaro, you have the full commitment of the Order in seeing that the boy is found and brought home."

"That all sounds very reassuring," Christophe Archer said from beside Brock, a tense edge to his voice. "The Enforcement Agency has vowed the same thing, and as much as I want to believe it, the fact is we don't even know where to begin searching for my son. Can anyone tell me who would do this? What kind of gutless criminals would break in to our home while we were away and take my boy?"

After speaking again with Mathias Rowan of the Enforcement Agency, Chase had briefed them all on the troubling details of the abduction before the Archers had arrived. Three immense, heavily armed Breed males had apparently invaded the Darkhaven estate where Lazaro and Christophe Archer lived with their families. The elder Archers and their Breedmates had gone to a charity fundraiser that evening, leaving teenage Kellan home alone.

By the sound of it, the kidnapping had been as stealthy as it was precise—all of it hinged on a very specific target. In a span of what could have only been mere minutes, the intruders entered the Darkhaven through a back window, killed two of Christophe's security personnel, then snatched the youth from his upstairs bedroom and drove away with him.

The sole witness to the abduction was a cousin, several years younger than Kellan, who'd hidden in a closet as the invasion took place. Understandably afraid and upset, he could hardly describe the abductors, except to say that they'd been dressed from head to toe in black, with masked faces that obscured everything but their eyes. The boy had also noted that the three males each wore a strange, thick black collar around their necks.

While the Enforcement Agent hadn't fully understood the ramifications of that one crucial detail, every member of the Order did. They had suspected Dragos was at the heart of this, but hearing that a trio of his homegrown assassins—Gen Ones bred and trained to serve him, their loyalty ensured by the lethal UV collars each was forced to wear—had confirmed their suspicions were correct.

"I simply cannot comprehend this kind of madness," Christophe said, leaning his elbows on the table, his features stricken, eyes pleading. "I mean, why? Certainly our race is not so crude as the humans who would grapple and connive over money, so what could anyone possibly have to gain by stealing my only child?"

"No," Lucan replied, the word as grim as his expression. "We do not believe this has anything to do with a potential financial gain."

"Then what could they possibly want with Kellan? What can they gain by taking him away?"

Lucan glanced briefly at Lazaro Archer. "Leverage. The individual who ordered this abduction will, no doubt, issue a demand before too long."

"A demand for what?"

"For me," Lazaro said quietly. When his son's gaze slid to him in question, the Gen One looked at him in frank remorse. "Christophe is not aware of the conversation we had nearly a year ago, Lucan. I never told him about the warning you gave me and the other few remaining Gen Ones that someone was seeking to erase us from existence. He doesn't know about the other killings among our generation."

Christophe Archer's face went a bit pale. "Father, what are you talking about? Who is seeking to harm you?"

"His name is Dragos," Lucan replied. "The Order has been waging a private war with him for some time now. But not before he had the chance to spend several decades—centuries, in fact—building his secret empire. He has already killed several other Gen Ones in the past year alone, and that, unfortunately, is only scratching the surface of his madness. All he knows is power, and the need to claim it. He will stop at nothing to get what he wants, and no life is sacred."

"Jesus Christ. You're telling me this sick bastard is the one who took Kellan?"

Lucan nodded. "I'm sorry."

Christophe vaulted to his feet and began pacing back and forth behind the table. "We have to get him back. Damn it, we have to bring my son home, no matter what it takes."

"We are all agreed on that," Lucan said, speaking for everyone gathered in solemn silence in the tech lab. "But you have to understand that no matter how this unfolds, there will be risks—"

"Damn the risks!" Christophe shouted. "We're talking about my son, my only child. My beloved, innocent boy. Don't tell me about risks, Lucan. I will gladly trade my own life for Kellan."

"As will I," Lazaro put in soberly. "Anything for my kin."

Brock watched the emotional exchange, knowing what it felt like to be helpless in the face of such a loss. But even more than he was moved by the Archers' pain, he was struck by how raw Jenna looked beside him.

Although she held her jaw still, tension bracketed her mouth. Her lips quivered slightly, and her hazel eyes were moist with unshed tears. Whether in sympathy for what the two Breed males were going through or remembrance of her own anguish at having a loved one yanked away so abruptly, he wasn't sure. But the tenderness he saw in her touched him deeply.

Beneath the table, her hand slid over to reach for his. He gathered her slender fingers in his grasp and she glanced to him, smiling faintly as their fingers twined together in silent reassurance. Something deeper passed between them in that moment—an unspoken acknowledgment of the growing bond they shared.

He knew she was strong. He knew she was a courageous, resilient woman who had taken more than her fair share of hits in her lifetime and still came up swinging. But seeing her now, gripped in a moment of quiet vulnerability, made his heart crack just a little.

He loved that she wasn't some delicate flower that wilted under the smallest bit of heat. But he loved this glimpse of softness in her, too.

God, there was so much to love about her.

If not for the slight problem that she hadn't been born a Breedmate, Jenna Darrow was a woman he could easily envision at his side—a true partner, in life and in all things. But she was mortal, and falling for her would inevitably mean losing her. What happened in New York earlier today—seeing her in the hands of Dragos's Minions—had only driven that point home with sharper clarity.

Corinne's death had been a blow he hadn't been prepared for, but he'd managed to go on. Losing Jenna, whether to the age that would eventually take her or by any other means, had somehow become impossible even to imagine.

As he held her hand in his, he knew that he could no longer pretend that she was simply another mission, or that protecting her was merely his duty to the Order. He'd fallen too far and too fast to deny just how much she meant to him.

He was still turning that troubling realization over in his mind as Lucan rose from the table and went to stand near Christophe Archer. Lucan put his hand on the other male's shoulder, his dark brows knitted together in a solemn look. "We won't rest until we find your son and bring him home. You have my word, and you have the word of my brethren here in this room."

At his pledge, Brock and the other warriors also rose from their seats around the table in a show of solidarity. Even Hunter, the Gen One who knew firsthand how ruthless Dragos and his assassins truly were, stood in support of their new mission.

Christophe turned a hard gaze on the Order's leader. "Thank you. There is nothing more I can ask."

"And there is nothing I won't give," Lazaro said, joining his son and Lucan near the back of the room. "The Order has my faith and my full trust. I cannot forgive myself for ignoring your advice a year ago, Lucan. Just look what it's costing me now." He shook his head sadly. "Perhaps I have lived too long, if an evil individual like Dragos can exist among us. Is this what is to become of the Breed? Making war on one another, letting greed and power corrupt us, just like humankind. Perhaps we're not so different from them, after all. For that matter, are we any different from the savage otherworlders who spawned us?"

Lucan's steel gray gaze had never looked more resolute. "I'm counting on it."

Lazaro Archer nodded. "And I am counting on you," he said, sweeping a look over each warrior and the females who now stood with them. "I am counting on all of you."

CHAPTER
Twenty-three

The Order continued the meeting for another couple of hours after Lazaro and Christophe Archer left. Sometime earlier, Jenna and the rest of the women had gone to have their dinner elsewhere in the compound, leaving the warriors to discuss their limited options and tactics for how they might go about searching for the abducted boy.

Although Brock listened and offered suggestions when he had them, his mind—and his heart—was distracted. A lot of his focus had walked out of the room when Jenna left, and since then, he'd been counting down the minutes until he could be with her again. As soon as the meeting in the tech lab broke up, he headed out to the corridor to find her.

Alex was coming out of his quarters, closing the door behind her as he approached. She smiled knowingly when she saw him.

"How is she doing?" he asked.

"A lot better than I would be after what she went through today. She's dead on her feet, but you know Jen. She would never say as much."

"Yeah," he said, returning Alex's smile. "I do know that."

"She's more concerned about you, I think. She told me what you did, Brock. How you came after her, driving into the full light of day."

He shrugged, uncomfortable with the praise. "I had the proper gear. My burns were minimal. They were healed by the time we got back to the compound."

"That's not the point." Alex's mouth curved warmly. Then she abruptly went up on her toes and placed a kiss on his cheek. "Thank you for saving my friend."

When he stood there, unsure how to respond, Alex rolled her eyes. "What are you waiting for? Go on in and see her for yourself."

He waited until Kade's mate had gone before he rapped his knuckles on the door. It took a few moments before Jenna opened it. She was barefoot, dressed in his white terry bathrobe, he was guessing, with little to nothing more beneath it.

"Hi," she said, giving him a welcoming smile that made his blood fire to life in his veins. "I was just about to get in the shower."

Oh, he definitely didn't need that tempting mental image to make his body burn any hotter.

"I wanted to come by and check on you," he murmured, a thick rasp in his voice as he recalled the feminine curves and long, luscious limbs that were hiding under the oversize robe. A robe fastened only by the loosely tied sash around her slender waist. He cleared his throat. "But if you're tired—"

"I'm not." She pivoted away from the door, leaving it open behind her in unspoken invitation.

Brock stepped inside and closed the door behind him.

He hadn't gone there with ideas about seducing her, but he had to admit it seemed like a really stellar idea now that he was close enough to touch her. Close enough to sense that she felt the same way.

Before he could stop himself, he reached out for her hand and brought her back toward him. She didn't resist. Her hazel eyes were wide and welcoming as he cupped his hand around the back of her head and drew her against him. He caught her mouth in a deep, hungered kiss. She sucked his lower lip hard between her teeth, and all of his good intentions, few though they were, went up in flames.

"God, Jenna," he rasped against her mouth. "I can't stay away from you."

Her answer was a throaty moan, the slow feminine purr vibrating through his body and straight into his cock. He was hard as steel, his skin tight and overheated, every nerve ending throbbing in time with the roar of his pulse.

He peeled the loose terry cloth off Jenna's luscious body, revealing her to his thirsting gaze inch by inch, curve by delectable curve. He smoothed his hands over her soft skin, reveling in the velvety feel of her under his rough fingertips. Her breasts filled his palms, a perfect swell of creamy flesh capped with small pink nipples that begged him to taste them. He dipped his head down and lavished her with his tongue, suckling the tight little buds and growling with pleasure as she moaned and sighed above him.

The sweet scent of her arousal slammed into him, making his already emerged fangs punch out of his gums in primal, urgent response. He reached down between her legs, cleaving his fingers into the slick seam of her body. "So soft," he murmured, teasing the petals of her body and reveling in the way she blossomed even fuller under his touch. "So hot and wet. You are so fucking sexy, Jenna."

"Oh, God," she gasped, her fingers digging into his shoulders as he slowly penetrated her with first one finger, then a second. "More," she whispered. "Don't stop."

With a growl, he rocked his palm against her and took her mouth in a hard, possessive kiss, tongue and fingers delving deep, giving and taking until he felt her body quake with the first tremors of release. She let out a sharp, shuddery sigh but he didn't let up until she shattered against him, crying out his name in release.

She was still panting, still holding onto his shoulders as he slowly caressed her sex, and bent to kiss the tight little buds of her nipples.

"You're way overdressed," she murmured, her heavy-lidded eyes dark and demanding, though no more than the hands that were now drifting down his arms and heading on a direct course for the massive bulge below the waistband of his fatigues. She stroked him over the fabric, her unbashful handling of him making his cock surge tighter, fuller, straining to be freed. "Take these off. Now."

"Bossy as ever," he said, grinning as he rushed to comply to her lusty demands.

She laughed, running her hands all over his body as he shucked his clothes. When he was naked, he wrapped his arms around her and pulled her against him until her curves melded with his hard planes and muscles. She was no fragile waif, and he loved that about her. He loved her strength. There was so much he loved about this woman, he realized, standing there skin to skin with her, staring into her eyes.

Oh, yeah . . . he was in big trouble right here.

"You said something about a shower," he murmured, trying to pretend he wasn't falling in love right that very second. Trying to convince himself that he hadn't fallen for her much earlier than this—as early as the moment he'd first seen her, terrorized but unbroken, in the dark of her Alaska cabin.

She smiled up at him, oblivious to the wash of revelation pouring over him. "I did say something about a shower, actually. But it's way over there in the bathroom, and we're out here."

"Easy enough to take care of that." He scooped her up into his arms and used the inhuman speed he'd been born with to carry her into the adjacent bathroom before she could even yelp for him to put her down.

"Oh, my God!" she exclaimed, laughing around the words as he set her feet down on the marble floor. "Neat trick."

"Baby, stick around. I've got plenty more where that came from."

She arched a slim brow. "Is that an invitation?"

"Do you want it to be?"

Instead of shooting back with something teasing or suggestive, she got quiet suddenly. Glanced away for a second. When she looked back up at him, her face was as serious as he'd ever seen it. "I don't know what I want . . . other than more of this. More of you."

Brock lifted her beautiful face on the edge of his hand. "Take all you want."

She brought her arms around the back of his neck and kissed him like she meant to never let go. He held her, mouths joined and needy, as he walked them both into the large shower and turned on the spray. Warm water coursed all around them, drenching them as they continued to touch and stroke and kiss.

Jenna set their pace and he gladly submitted to her, leaning back against the cold marble tile of the shower when she broke away from his mouth and slowly sank down before him. She ran her mouth over his chest and stomach, her tongue following the patterns of his *glyphs* while her wet hands slid up and down his stiff shaft. He nearly lost it when her lips closed around the head of his cock. She sucked him deep, rendering him mindless after just a few moments of her sweet, wet torture.

"Ah, Christ," he hissed, so very close to the edge already. "Come up here now."

He pulled her up against his hard body and kissed her hungrily, thrusting his tongue into the hot sheath of her mouth the way he was dying to be inside her sex. He reached down and parted her legs from behind, spreading the firm, wet mounds of her pretty ass. He hauled her against him and brought his hand around to the slick, hot core of her body.

"I need to be inside you," he growled, hunger ratcheting so tight he felt ready to explode.

Bracing his feet on the floor of the shower, his spine pressed to the wall, he lifted her up onto him. Slowly, hissing with the pure white-hot pleasure of it, he guided her down the full length of his cock.

She moaned, burying her face in his shoulder as he

rocked her in an unhurried tempo, relishing every sigh and gasp of bliss she gave him. She came on a shivery cry, her sheath milking him, tiny pulsations running up and down his shaft.

His own need for release was roaring up on him. He turned her around and splayed her legs in front of him. She leaned forward, palms against the marble wall, water streaming down the valley of her spine and into the crack of her pretty ass. He slid back home, hooking his arm around her waist as he thrust into her, too far gone to take things slowly.

He'd never known sex this intense. He'd never known the depth of need he felt for this woman. The urge to possess slammed into him, just as it had the first time he'd made love with Jenna. The scorching desire to claim her, to mark her as his alone and hold her away from any other male forever, was something he'd never expected to feel.

But it was alive in him now. As he pumped into the soft, wet heat of her body, his gums ached with the hunger to taste her. To bind her to him, regardless of the impossibility of ever truly taking this female—a mortal woman—as his blood-bonded mate.

He snarled with the force of that desire, unable to keep from pressing his mouth to the supple curve of her neck and shoulder as he drove deeper into her with each hard thrust. All the while, the points of his fangs rested against her tender skin. Teasing . . . testing.

"Do it," she whispered. "Oh, God, Brock . . . I want to feel it. I want to feel all of you."

He growled low in his throat, letting the sharp tips sink in a little more, just a breath away from breaking the surface. "It won't mean anything," he rasped harshly, unsure if it was anger or regret that made his voice so raw. His orgasm was coiling tightly, on the verge of exploding. "I just...ah, fuck...I need to taste you, Jenna."

She reached out and put her palm against the back of his head, ready to force him. "Do it."

He bit down, penetrating the soft flesh at the same instant he buried himself to the hilt and spilled deep within her. Jenna's blood was hot on his tongue, a thick, coppery blast of human red cells, but he'd never tasted anything so sweet. He drank from her as she climaxed again, taking care not to hurt her, wanting to give her only pleasure. When she relaxed again, coming down off the crest of her release, he gently stroked his tongue over the twin punctures to seal them.

He turned her around to face him, both of them soaking under the warm deluge of the shower. He had no words, only reverence and wonder for this human female who had somehow stolen his heart. She glanced up at him from under the dark spikes of her lashes, her cheeks pink, mouth still swollen from his kisses.

Brock caressed her jaw, that stubborn, beautiful jaw. She smiled, a sexy curve of her lips, and then suddenly they were kissing all over again. His sex responded instantly, and the fire in his blood stoked back up to a rapid boil. Jenna reached down to touch him, at the same time her tongue slid into his mouth to play along the length of his fangs.

Oh, yeah.

It was going to be a long night.

CHAPTER
Twenty-four

Jenna woke up in Brock's big bed, wrapped within his strong arms.

They'd made love for endless hours: under the water of the shower; against the bedroom wall; on the sofa in the living room . . . she'd lost track of all the places, and all the creative ways they'd found to pleasure each other's bodies.

Now she dragged her eyelids open in a state of blissful contentment as she snuggled further into his embrace, her cheek pressed to his chest, one leg bent and slung over the tops of his thighs. Her shifting stirred a low groan out of him, the deep rumble vibrating through her.

"I didn't mean to wake you," she whispered.

Another groan, something dark and wicked. "I wasn't sleeping."

His biceps flexed as he pulled her closer, then he covered her hand with his and guided her touch down to the part of him that was, without question, very much alert. Jenna's laugh rasped sleepily in her throat. "You know, for an old man, you have amazing stamina."

He gave a faint thrust as she palmed him, his thick shaft growing more rigid, impossibly larger, in her grasp. "You got something against centenarians?"

"A hundred years?" she asked, coming up onto her elbow to look at him. There was so much she didn't know about him. So many things she wanted to learn. "Are you really that old?"

"Somewhere around there. Older, probably, but I stopped counting the years a long time ago." He smiled, just a slight curving of his sensual lips, as he reached out and smoothed some of her hair behind her ear. "Afraid I won't be able to keep up with you?"

She lifted a brow. "Not after last night."

As he chuckled, she leaned down and kissed him. She rose up and straddled him, sighing with pleasure for the way they fit so perfectly together. As she moved lazily atop him, simply relishing the sensation of him filling her once again, she noted the tiny, but healing, bite marks she'd left on his neck during their last bout of lovemaking.

She hadn't been able to resist nipping at him, particularly after he'd drunk from her in the shower. Just the thought of it made her wild with arousal. It made her want to devour him, even now. Instead she bent over him and licked her tongue along the throbbing pulse point at the base of his throat. "Mmm," she moaned against his skin. "You are incredible."

"And you're insatiable," he replied, though it didn't exactly sound like criticism.

"Well, then, consider yourself warned. I seem to have energy to burn, especially where you're involved." She intended it as a joke, but as she said it, she realized just now how much truth there was in that statement. She drew back and stared down at him, astonished by everything she was feeling. "I can't recall how long it's been since I've felt this good. I've never felt more, I don't know . . . more alive, I guess."

His dark brown eyes held her tenderly. "You seem better every day."

"I am." She swallowed, reflecting on all of the changes that had come over her since she'd arrived in the Order's care. She'd never felt more attuned to the world around her, nor more curious and engaged about life. Physically she was still healing, still waiting to see how the ordeal she'd been through in Alaska might impact her moving forward. But inside she felt buoyant and strong.

For the first time in a very long time, inside she felt at peace, hopeful. She felt like it might be possible to fall in love again.

Perhaps she already had.

The realization took her breath away. She stared down at Brock, wondering how she'd let it happen. How could she have opened her heart to him so quickly, so thoroughly? So recklessly . . .

She loved him, and the idea terrified her.

"Hey," he said, reaching up to her. "Are you all right?"

"I'm fine," she whispered. "I've never been better."

His deepening frown seemed to say he didn't quite believe her.

"Come here," he said, and smoothly brought her down around in front of him on the bed, spooning her with his body.

He didn't enter her right away, just nestled his hard erection between her thighs and held her in the warm shelter of his arms. He kissed the back of her shoulder, the very spot he'd taken under his fangs last night. Right now, his mouth was gentle, his breath skating warmly over her skin.

Jenna sighed deeply, so content to simply relax with him. "How long do you think we can stay in bed together before anyone notices we're gone?"

He groaned quietly, then pressed a kiss to her shoulder. "I'm sure it's been noticed. Alex knows I'm here, which means Kade knows I'm here."

"And your roommate," she reminded him.

"Yeah." He exhaled a chuckle. "Hunter doesn't miss a damned thing. I like the guy, but I swear he's a flesh-and-bone machine most of the time."

"I can't imagine what it must have been like for him, the way he was raised," Jenna murmured, unsure how anyone could come out of that kind of environment without some very deep-seated scars. Chilled to think about it, she snuggled deeper into the circle of Brock's warm arms. His body was hot and firm against her backside, some parts significantly more firm than others. She smiled, imagining she could get used to this quite easily. "Speaking of roommates . . ."

He grunted in question, his fingers playing in her hair. "What about them?"

"I was just thinking that it seems kind of silly for you to

give up your quarters, especially now that we're . . ." She let the words drift off, unsure how to categorize their relationship, which was supposed to have been so uncomplicated and casual but had somehow become something so much more.

He dragged his mouth slowly along the curve of her shoulder, then up along the side of her neck. "Are you asking me to move in with you, Jenna?"

She shivered under the moist warmth of his lips and the erotic abrasion of his fangs against her tender skin. "Yeah, I guess I am. I mean, this is your bed, after all. Everything in here is yours."

"What about you?" He gathered her hair and swept it aside, pressing his mouth to her bare nape. "Are you mine, too?"

She closed her eyes, awash in pleasure from his kiss, and pierced with a bright, terrifying joy. "If you want to know the truth, I think a part of me has belonged to you since Alaska."

His answering groan didn't sound the least bit unhappy. He gathered her closer, his tongue playing along the sensitive flesh behind her ear. But then he suddenly went very still.

She hadn't expected the rough curse that followed.

"Jenna," he muttered, alarm edging his words. "Ah, fuck . . ."

A new fear spiked through her, sharp and cold. "What is it?"

It took him a second to answer.

When he did, his voice was low with disbelief. "It's a *glyph*. Holy hell, Jenna . . . you have a *dermaglyph* forming on the back of your neck."

An hour later, Jenna was seated on an examination table in the infirmary, having submitted to a fresh round of blood tests and tissue samples at Gideon's request. She had been shocked to see the small *dermaglyph* that covered the incision location of the Ancient's implant, though perhaps no more shocked than the rest of the compound's residents. Everyone had come to look at the silver dollar–size skin marking hidden underneath the fall of her hair. Though no one had voiced their speculation out loud, Jenna could tell that each of them was concerned for her, if uncertain what this new development might mean to her in the long term.

Now they had all gone from the room except Brock, who stood at her side, grim faced and quiet in his black shirt and dark jeans. Jenna didn't have much to say, either, glancing up anxiously as the Order's resident genius drew one final vial of blood from her arm.

"You're still feeling good, you say?" Gideon prompted, looking at her over the tops of his rimless sky blue shades. "You haven't noticed any other markings on your body? No physical or systemic changes since we last spoke?"

Jenna shook her head. "Nothing."

Gideon slid a glance at Brock before looking back at her. "What about other body functions? Have you noticed any changes in your digestive system? Any changes in your appetite, or lack of interest in food?"

She shrugged. "Nope. I eat like a horse, and always have."

That seemed to relieve him somewhat. "So, no strange cravings when it comes to hunger or thirst?"

A flash of heat washed through her when she lifted her

gaze to Brock. The bite marks she'd left on him were gone now, but she vividly recalled the need that had lived inside her when she'd set her teeth into his flesh during their lovemaking. She had craved him with a thirst she could hardly fathom, let alone explain.

And now she wondered...

"I, um, if you're talking about blood," she murmured, embarrassed by the way her face flamed when Brock's dark eyes stayed rooted on her. "I have had certain... cravings."

Gideon's blond brows rose in surprise an instant before his attention drifted to Brock. "You mean, the two of you—"

"I bit him," Jenna blurted. "Last night, and a few nights ago, too. I couldn't help it."

"Well, fuck me," Gideon said, not even trying to hide his amusement over realizing she and Brock were intimately involved. "And what about you, my man? Have you drunk from her, too?"

"A few hours ago," Brock replied, giving a grim nod but looking anything but repentant when his gaze latched back on to hers. "It was incredible, but I know where you're heading with this, Gideon, and I can tell you that her blood is pure *Homo sapiens* red cells."

"No bloodscent?"

Brock shook his head. "Just coppery hemoglobin. She's human."

"Except in addition to the DNA replications we found in her last sample results and the other things she's mentioned, Jenna now also has a *glyph*." The warrior ran his fingers through the short, disheveled spikes of his golden hair. "There's something else, too."

When he looked at Jenna, there was an anxiety in his expression that she'd never seen before. He appeared unsure of what he intended to say, and for a man who seemed to have answers for every problem imaginable, his uncertainty right now was downright alarming.

"Tell me, Gideon."

Brock came closer and took her hand in his. "Shit, Gideon. What else have you found?"

The other warrior was frowning, mouth pursed in thought. "There is some kind of energy reading that seems to be associated with the implant . . . an emission of some sort."

"What the hell does that mean?" Brock asked, his fingers tightening around hers.

Gideon shrugged. "It's nothing I've been able to capture with any of my equipment, so I can't tell you what it might actually be. It's advanced technology, far more advanced than anything I have here. Probably more advanced than anything we have on this planet. My guess is, this energy emission is integral to the implant itself."

Jenna brought her free hand up to the back of her neck, feeling the slightly raised outline of the *glyph*'s arcs and curves. "Do you think the energy is just an indicator that the implant is active inside me?"

"It could be as simple as that, yes."

She watched him speak, noting that he still wore the same look of caution and gravity. "It *could* be that simple, but you don't think so, right?"

He reached out and lightly touched her shoulder. "We're going to keep looking for the answers, I give you my word."

Brock nodded soberly at his comrade before wrapping his arm protectively around Jenna. "Thanks, my man."

Gideon's smile was brief as he glanced at the both of them. "I'll go run these samples and bring you the results as soon as I have them."

He pivoted to head for the door, at the same time the heavy clip of boot heels approached from the corridor outside. Kade appeared there, his keen silver eyes flashing with urgency.

"Harvard just got a call from Mathias Rowan," he announced abruptly. "The Enforcement Agency has a possible lead on Kellan Archer's location."

"What have we got?" Brock asked, his arm still draped around Jenna's shoulders but his demeanor switching instantly to warrior mode.

"There's another witness, apparently. A human living on the streets out in Quincy claims he saw three big SWAT-looking guys hustle a kid into a construction zone down there late last night."

Brock grunted. "This tip came in from a human? Since when is the Agency using homeless *Homo sapiens* as informants?"

"Don't ask me, man," Kade said, lifting his hands. "Agent by the name of Freyne reported the tip. Harvard says the guy keeps a string of humans on the line who are willing to keep their eyes and ears open around the city in exchange for cash and narcotics."

"For fuck's sake," Brock ground out. "Freyne and a human drug addict are our sources for this lead on the kid?"

Kade shook his head. "Right now, it's all we've got. Lazaro and Christophe Archer have already made arrangements with Mathias Rowan to head down to Quincy tonight with a team of Enforcement Agents to check the location out."

Brock's curse was echoed by Gideon's equally vivid profanity.

"I know," Kade said. "Lucan wants everyone in the tech lab pronto to discuss our options. Sounds like we're gonna be riding shotgun with the Enforcement Agency tonight."

CHAPTER
Twenty-five

There hadn't been a lot of time to prepare for the rendezvous with Mathias Rowan and his team of Enforcement Agents that night. Then again, the entire operation consisted of a tip provided by less than reliable sources and the determination—the desperate hope—of Lazaro Archer and his son that Kellan Archer had, in fact, been brought to the city construction site on the far edge of Quincy.

Neither Brock nor the rest of the Order held out the same hope that the lead would prove fruitful. If Dragos was the instigator of the abduction, and it seemed reasonable to assume as much, then the odds of finding the boy alive, let alone so quickly and neatly after he'd been taken, seemed slim at best.

But none of the warriors said so as they rolled up behind the Enforcement Agency vehicles parked off the street adjacent to the site.

Mathias Rowan was the first to step over and meet them. He cut away from the other six Agents accompanying him and strode toward the Rover as Brock killed the engine and the warriors who'd come along with him climbed out to the frozen pavement. Chase made the introductions, starting with Tegan and Kade, then Brock, who was already familiar with Agent Rowan.

Hunter was part of the Order's operation tonight, as well, but he'd jumped out of the Rover a block before their rendezvous point in order to move in stealth and run a perimeter check of the building and the surrounding area.

The building in question was a ten-story condominium, or would have been, according to the real estate sign out front, if the financing bank hadn't gone belly-up with the recent nosedive of the humans' economy. Half completed for months and showing its neglect, the brick tower was little more than a skeleton of a shelter—empty, unfinished floors and gaping windows. The place looked quiet, desolate enough to be useful as a possible holding location.

"Lazaro Archer and the boy's father are here, as well," Rowan informed the warriors. "They both insisted on coming along, although I have advised them it would be best for everyone involved if they remained in one of the Agency vehicles while we conduct the search."

Tegan inclined his head in agreement. "Your men have not gone near the building?"

"No. We arrived just a moment before you did."

"And you've seen no movement in or out of the building?" Brock asked, glancing over at the dark structure as a flurry of fine snow swirled around them.

"We haven't seen or heard anything," Rowan said. "As far as tips go, I've known a lot better than this."

"Let's go have a look," Tegan said, leading the way.

As they neared the Enforcement Agency vehicles, Brock recognized Freyne among the team of Agents with Rowan. He and two other men leaned against one of the sedans, semiauto pistols holstered and visible under their open winter coats. Brock stared the belligerent Agent down, daring any one of the bunch to make a stupid comment as they approached.

Chase was less subtle. He grinned at his adversary from a couple of nights ago. "Glad to see you back on your feet after I wiped the pavement with your ass the other night. Anytime you want to go again, you let me know."

"Go fuck yourself," Freyne sneered, looking just as ready to escalate things with his former comrade.

The exchange of venom was brief, cut short by the opening of the back door of the Agency vehicle. Lazaro Archer stepped out to the street, his harsh face hard with concern. He nodded to the warriors in solemn greeting. "Christophe and I want to be there for the search of the building," he said, directing his request to Tegan. "You cannot expect us to stand by and wait—"

"That's exactly what I expect." Tegan's voice was firm but not without respect. "We don't know what we might find in there tonight, Lazaro. It could be nothing. But if it's not, then you need to let us handle this."

"My son and I want to help," he argued.

Tegan's jaw was set now. "Then help by letting us do

our job. Stay here. We'll all know soon enough if this lead proves out. Chase, stand guard with Rowan's men until we return. Don't let them out of your sight."

Brock didn't miss the look of irritation on Harvard's face, but the former Agent fell in as he was instructed. With Freyne and the other two sentries standing by, he assisted Lazaro Archer back into the vehicle and closed the door.

He leaned against the car, arms crossed over his chest, and watched as Brock and the rest of the group moved on toward the dark building.

They approached silently, Tegan's signals to split up into two teams understood and accepted by both Brock and Kade and by Rowan and his three Agents. With the Enforcement Agency team heading around to a back stairwell, Tegan, Brock, and Kade entered through the front of the vacant shell, into what would have been a lobby.

Once inside, it became clear that the building was not entirely unoccupied. Booted footsteps shuffled on the concrete floor above their heads. From the same general area, the metal leg of a chair scraped sharply. And then, running undercurrent of the wintry wind that howled through the open window cavities all around them, came the muffled sound of whimpering cries.

Tegan gestured toward a stairwell off the main floor. Brock and Kade followed him, all three climbing up the short flight with weapons at the ready.

As they reached the second floor, Brock's gaze was drawn to a faint light that shone from somewhere near the end of an unfinished apartment. Tegan and Kade saw it, too.

"Humans?" Brock mouthed to his brethren, guessing it might be homeless squatters, since any of his kind could see clearly in the dark and wouldn't have the need for artificial light.

Tegan motioned for them to keep moving and investigate the source of the small glow.

They crept forward in the dark, the three of them branching off to come at the place from all sides. As they neared, Brock caught a fleeting glimpse of three large male figures in head-to-toe black, each holding a semiautomatic weapon. The masked guards loomed over a smaller figure in the center of the wall-less space.

Kellan Archer.

Holy hell, Freyne's tip had been good, after all.

The Breed youth's head hung down over his thin chest, his gingery hair matted and limp, his clothing torn from his captors' apparent rough handling. His hands were fastened behind him, his ankles and torso secured to a metal chair with a couple lengths of chain.

Being Breed, even a teenager, Kellan likely could have broken free of his restraints if he tried. But he stood little chance of escaping three of Dragos's Hunters, each of them armed to the teeth and close enough to fill him with lead.

Tegan glanced at Brock, then Kade, a silent signal for them to move in as one on his go. They had to move in quietly, get into the best position so they could each take on one of the Gen One assassins without trapping Kellan Archer in the crossfire.

But before any of them could take the first step, Brock heard the softest *click* of metal coming from an area deeper in the shadows of the second floor.

Mathias Rowan and his Agents were there. They saw the captured kid, as well.

And in that very next instant, one of the trigger-happy assholes from the Enforcement Agency opened fire.

The eruption of gunfire inside the building carried out to the street below.

"Holy fuck," Sterling Chase snarled, his head snapping up at the sudden blast of noise. "Jesus motherfucking Christ—they must have found the kid!"

Freyne watched the former Enforcement Agent react in a state of near panic as the gunfire continued. Chase drew his weapon and threw a wild look at the building across the construction site. Sterling Chase, the Breed male who'd had a golden career with the Agency not so long ago, but had thrown it all away to join up with the Order.

Idiot.

He could have allied himself with a much more powerful organization, as Freyne himself had done just a few months past.

"I'm going in," Chase said, cocking the black 9mm pistol and already moving away from the Agency vehicle on the street. "You and your men stay put, Freyne. Don't turn your backs from this post for so much as a goddamned second, understood?"

Freyne gave an agreeable nod, trying hard to curb his eager smile. This was exactly the opportunity he'd wanted. In fact, he'd been counting on things playing out precisely as they were now.

"Keep the Archers secured in the vehicle," Chase called as his boots chewed up the snow-covered asphalt, taking him toward the chaos of weapons fire still ringing out in the skeletal tower up ahead. "Don't take your eyes off them, no matter what."

"You got it," Freyne muttered under his breath once the former Agent was well out of earshot.

Next to him in the street, the backseat passenger window slid down. Christophe Archer peered out from inside the sedan, his normally proud face drawn taut with worry. "What's happening?" He flinched at the racket echoing into the darkness. "Good God—who's shooting in there? Have they found my son?"

Archer made a move as though he intended to get out of the vehicle. Freyne stepped up, blocking the door.

"Relax," he told the nervous father. As he spoke, he smoothly drew his semiautomatic out of its holster. A barely discernible flick of his eyes commanded the other two Agents with him on the opposite side of the car to follow suit. "We've got everything under control."

CHAPTER
Twenty-six

The entire second floor of the gutted apartment building was a chaos of flying bullets and coarse shouts from both the Order and Mathias Rowan and his men. The three immense guards in the room with Kellan Archer returned fire, shooting wildly into the shadows, taking out two of Rowan's Agents within moments of the surprise confrontation.

The third went down with a howl of pain, his kneecap shot out from beneath him just before another round silenced him for good. The relentless fire continued, Brock narrowly dodging a bullet that whisked past his head.

In the confusion and scuffle, the fat pillar candle being used for light in the room with Kellan was kicked over. It rolled underfoot of his captors, its small flame fizzling out on the floor and plunging the place into darkness. The slim light extinguished, Brock hardly noticed its absence, nor did any of his companions. Dragos's men, however, seemed momentarily disoriented in the dark.

Brock took out one of them with a dead-aim shot to the head. Tegan nailed another not even a second later. While the last remaining assassin showered the air with round after round from his automatic rifle, Brock moved in from the side. He dived low, scrambling for the chair where Kellan Archer sat, now frantically struggling to break loose of his restraints.

The warriors and Rowan closed in on the third black-clad assassin, every weapon trained on him in tandem. There was a frenzied hail of gunfire as the target was swiftly obliterated and fell to the floor in a savaged, blood-ied heap.

Brock grabbed Kellan Archer's narrow shoulders, calming the boy's terrified screams. "It's okay, kid. You're safe now."

The sudden, unexpected whiff of hemoglobin from somewhere nearby took him aback.

What the fuck?

His fangs tore from his gums, instinctive physiological response, as his Breed senses detected the presence of fresh-spilling blood. He threw an abrupt look at Tegan and the others and saw that they, too, had picked up on the scent of coppery red cells.

"Humans," Tegan muttered, his transformed amber eyes narrowed on the three dead guards lying in bloodied pools on the floor nearby.

"No collars," Brock added, realizing only now that below their black head coverings, Kellan's captors did not wear the UV-rigged obedience devices of Dragos's true Hunters. "Holy shit. These aren't the Gen One assassins who abducted the boy."

Kade and Mathias Rowan both came over at the same time. They stooped down to remove the masks of the felled men. Kade lifted the closed eyelids of one of them and hissed a curse. "They're Minions."

"Minions meant to make us think they were Gen One assassins," Brock added, removing the last of Kellan Archer's restraints and helping him to his feet. "This was some kind of setup."

"Yeah," Kade said. "But for what purpose?"

"Jesus Christ." Chase stood behind the group, having just arrived that very moment. His eyes threw off a blaze of amber, pupils narrowed down to thin, feral-looking slits, his fangs huge behind the curl of his upper lip. He stared, attention rooted to the bleeding humans. "What the hell happened in here?"

Tegan rounded on him. "Where are the Archers?"

"They're outside," he replied, his voice gravelly. It seemed to take some effort for him to wrench his focus back to Tegan. "I left them back there with Freyne and his men when I heard the gunfire up here."

A look of sudden dread washed over Tegan's normally impassive face. "Holy fuck, Harvard. I told you not to let them out of your sight."

Hunter made no sound at all as he returned from his perimeter check of the construction site. He raced back, having heard the racket of weapons fire pouring out of the apartment building, but at the moment he was more interested in the single gunshot that rang out near the Enforcement Agency vehicles in the street.

Through the snow flurries that swirled through the dark night air, he spotted the agent called Freyne holding a smoking pistol in front of the open backseat window of the Agency's black sedan. In that same instant, Freyne's companions opened fire on the car, as well, shooting from all sides.

Hunter sprang into a vaulting leap, traveling the several yards that separated him from the scene in barely the blink of an eye. He came down on Freyne. As he took the vampire to the ground, he glimpsed the gore of an exploded skull fouling the interior of the sedan. The stench of gunpowder and death filled the air as the other two Agents continued their assault on the vehicle's occupants.

Freyne roared beneath Hunter, flailing, trying to throw him off. Hunter clasped his hands on either side of the vampire's head and gave a sharp, efficient twist. The struggle ceased. Freyne dropped lifeless to the curb, his sightless eyes staring at an unnatural angle over his shoulder.

At the same moment, a rumble shook the car. A howl vibrated the ground, and then the door on the other side blew off its hinges. It sailed several feet before crashing down on the pavement.

Lazaro Archer erupted from within, his coat and face splattered with blood and bits of bone and brain matter.

He launched himself at one of the traitorous Enforcement Agents, catching the other male's throat under the sharp daggers of his enormous fangs. As the pair flew to the ground in a deadly embrace, Hunter jumped over the hood of the sedan and grabbed the last of the assailants, disabling the Agent as easily as he had Freyne.

He cast an apathetic eye on Lazaro Archer and the Breed male whose throat now gaped open, spurting blood from a vicious, lethal bite. Archer wasn't finished, even though the Agent pinned beneath him was surely as good as dead. He was savage in his fury, lost to a pain on which Hunter—raised devoid of emotional attachments—could only speculate.

Hunter stood and glanced into the vehicle, where Lazaro's son lay slumped and lifeless on the floor of the backseat, killed by the bullet Freyne had fired point blank into the side of his head.

Tegan's dread inside the building hadn't been misplaced. In fact, what awaited the group as they rushed outside with young Kellan Archer was even worse than they could have imagined.

Death was ripe in the street where the Enforcement Agency vehicles were parked. One of them—the one that had held Lazaro and Christophe Archer—was riddled with bullet holes and shattered windows. On closer look, Brock could see that the opposite side of the sedan was torn wide open, the entire backseat door ripped off its hinges.

There had been an ambush of the car's occupants, a cowardly attack from outside the vehicle. No question who had perpetrated it...nor how it had ended. Freyne and the other two Agents lay broken and blood-soaked, lifeless on the pavement. Hunter stood over them, impassive, his keen golden eyes scanning the surrounding area for new trouble and ready to take on any threat single-handed.

And seated just inside the sedan, his head and torso

bent over a lifeless form sprawled across his lap, was Lazaro Archer. Even at this distance, Brock could see blood and bits of tissue flecked on the Breed elder's dark coat and caught in his hair. The huge Gen One was weeping quietly, grief-stricken over the loss of his son.

"Jesus," Chase whispered from next to Brock. "Oh, Jesus Christ . . . no."

"Freyne," Brock snarled. "That bastard must have been working with Dragos."

Chase shook his head, scrubbed a hand over the top of his scalp in obvious misery. When he spoke, his voice was airless, flat with shock. "I shouldn't have left them with him. I heard the gunfire inside the building, and I thought . . . ah, fuck. It doesn't matter what I thought. Goddamn it, I should have known Freyne was not to be trusted."

Probably so, Brock thought, though neither he nor the rest of the group voiced any blame aloud. Chase's anguish was written all over his face. He didn't need anyone else to tear into him over the lapse in judgment that had cost Christophe Archer his life tonight. The typically cocky Harvard seemed to pale a bit, disappearing into himself as he wheeled away from the carnage and walked deeper into the shadows of the vacant construction lot.

As for Brock and the others, a grave silence had settled over the living in the face of so much bloodshed and death. Lazaro Archer's grandson had been rescued from his captors, but the price had been steep. Lazaro's son lay horribly slain in his arms just a few yards away.

While the group absorbed the weight of the night's grim turn of events, young Kellan Archer suddenly roused from his own state of shock. He came around from behind Brock, apparently just then noticing Lazaro seated in the sedan up ahead.

"Grandfather!" he shouted, tears choking his youthful voice. He pulled out of Brock's grasp. Then, limping, he started to break into a weak run. "Grandfather! Is Papa with you, too?"

"Hold the boy," Hunter called out evenly. "Do not let him near."

Brock caught Kellan by the arm and wheeled him around in the opposite direction, shielding him from the carnage with his body.

"I want to see my grandfather!" the boy cried. "I want to see my family!"

"Soon," Brock said. "Just be strong right now, my man. You're gonna be with your family very soon. We've got to take care of some things first, all right?"

Kellan's struggles lessened, but he kept trying to get another look around Brock. Kept trying to see what it was they were hiding from him inside the shot-up sedan on the street.

"Come and wait over here with me," Kade said as he moved in and corralled the youth, draping his arm around the thin shoulders as he guided the boy farther up the curb, away from the bloodshed at the other end of the street.

After Kellan was safely out of earshot, Mathias Rowan muttered a quiet curse. "I had no idea that Freyne or the others with him were corrupt, I swear it. My God, I can't believe what happened here tonight. All of my men, Christophe Archer . . . all dead." He grabbed for his cell phone. "I have to call this in."

Before he could touch the first key, Tegan clamped his hand around the Agent's wrist and gave a sober shake of his head. "I need you to keep this as quiet as you can. Can you delay your report while the Order looks deeper into the abduction and the ambush?"

Rowan inclined his head in agreement. "I can delay it for a few hours, but anything more could prove difficult. Some of these Agents had families. There will be questions."

"Understood," Tegan replied. His grasp on the Agent's wrist didn't let up, and Brock knew the Gen One's talent for reading a person with a touch would tell him if Rowan was truly an ally to the Order or not. After a moment, Tegan gave a faint nod. "I know you've been Chase's contact on the inside of the Agency for a while now, Mathias. The Order greatly appreciates your help. But no one is to be trusted now, not even your best Agents."

Mathias Rowan inclined his head in agreement, his gaze solemn as he took in the destruction then glanced back to Tegan and Brock. "If this is an example of what Dragos is capable of, then he is my enemy, too. Tell me what the Order needs, and I will do whatever I can to help you bring this son of a bitch down."

"Right now, we need time and silence," Tegan replied. "I don't believe Dragos is finished with Lazaro Archer and his family, so their protection is paramount. I'm sure Lucan will agree that the rescue tonight seemed too easy, despite the casualties. Something doesn't sit right about any of this."

Brock nodded, having had the same feeling when they'd discovered Kellan's captors were Minions and not the trio of Gen One assassins who'd been witnessed abducting the boy. "The kidnapping was a ruse. Dragos has something more up his sleeve."

Tegan's look was grim. "That's what my gut is telling me, too."

"I pray you're both wrong," Rowan said, his sober gaze drifting over to the sedan where Lazaro Archer still held his dead son. "These past few hours have been bloody enough."

"We should vacate the building and the street and clear out of here," Tegan said. "It's too risky to let either of the Archers stay out in the open any longer."

"I'll get started on the evidence cleanup," Brock offered.

As soon as he turned to walk toward the apartment building, Rowan was right beside him. "Let me help you, please."

They strode across the construction site, but hadn't even gotten halfway there when Rowan's cell phone trilled with an incoming call. He held it out in front of him, as though to ask Tegan's permission to take the call. The Gen One warrior nodded.

Rowan put the phone to his ear, and Brock watched in a state of mounting alarm as the Enforcement Agent's face blanched. "There must be some mistake," he murmured. "The whole Darkhaven . . . Good Christ."

Brock motioned to Tegan, feeling ice begin to settle in his gut as Rowan said a few more words of disbelief, then woodenly disconnected the call.

"What's going on?" Tegan demanded, having jogged over on Brock's signal. "What the hell just happened?"

"Lazaro Archer's Darkhaven," Rowan murmured. "It burned to the ground tonight. There was an apparent gas leak and a massive explosion. There were no survivors."

No one said a word for a very long while. A light flurry of snow swirled under the wintry starlight, the only movement in a night gone suddenly cold and dark as a grave.

And then, across the way, young Kellan Archer buried

his face in his hands and began to cry. Great, racking sobs of raw anguish. The boy knew what he'd lost tonight. He felt it. And when he glanced up with tear-filled eyes that flashed with furious amber sparks, Brock saw the rage that was already smoldering in the young male's heart.

As of tonight, the boy he'd been was gone. Like his grandfather, who sat several yards away, covered in his own son's blood, Kellan Archer would never forget—or forgive—the death and sorrow dealt so treacherously tonight.

"Let's get this place swept and get the fuck out of here," Tegan said finally. "I'll put the boy and his grandfather in the Rover. They are now under the protection of the Order."

CHAPTER
Twenty-seven

Lazaro Archer stoically refused the Order's offer to take him past the remains of his Darkhaven for a final good-bye. He'd had no wish to see the rubble of his life, which had claimed nearly a dozen innocent people, including his beloved Breedmate of several long centuries. Although the official report out of the Enforcement Agency had attributed the blaze to a gas leak, everyone in the Order—and Lazaro himself—understood the incident for what it truly was. A wholesale slaughter, carried out at Dragos's command.

Archer's grief had to be profound, but by the time he arrived at the compound he was the picture of emotional control. Showered now, his gore-caked clothing thrown away and replaced by a set of fresh black fatigues from the Order's supply room, Lazaro Archer seemed transformed, a darker, more formidable version of the civilian Breed elder who'd stood in the tech lab just a night before, desperate to find his grandson. Somber, subdued, he appeared determined to rally his entire focus around the health and welfare of his grandson and sole surviving heir.

"Kellan says he doesn't remember much about the abduction itself," Lazaro murmured as he and Lucan observed the boy through the window in his infirmary recovery room. The youth was cleaned up and resting, at the moment being kept company by little Mira, who'd taken it upon herself to read to him at his bedside. "He says he woke up in that rat-infested building, freezing cold, held at gunpoint. The beatings didn't start until he was conscious. He said the bastards told him they wanted him to scream and suffer."

Lucan's jaw tensed as he listened to the abuse the youth had subjected to. "He's safe now, Lazaro. You both are. The Order will see to that."

The other Gen One nodded. "I appreciate all you're doing for us. Like most civilians, I know the Order values its privacy, particularly when it comes to your headquarters. I realize it cannot be easy for you to permit outsiders into the compound."

Lucan raised a brow in acknowledgment. He could think of only a few rare instances, beginning with Sterling Chase and Tegan's mate, Elise, more than a year ago, followed most recently by Jenna Darrow. For more than a century before them, there had been no exceptions.

As much as Lucan disliked having his hand forced, he wasn't such a coldly rigid leader that he would turn his

back on someone in need. A long time ago, perhaps—
before he'd met and fallen in love with Gabrielle. Before
he'd come to know what it was like to have family and a
heart that beat out of devotion to another.

He put his hand on the Gen One's broad shoulder.
"You needed a safe house, you and the boy both. You'll
find no more secure shelter than this compound."

As for any concerns Lucan might have had about en-
trusting the compound's location to Archer or his young
grandson, Tegan had assured him that both males were
free of duplicity. Not that Lucan had suspected either one
of being anything less than honorable.

Still, he was careful not to place his trust blindly. He
had to be careful. Every time he looked around lately, he
felt the weight of so many lives resting on his shoulders. It
was a responsibility he took seriously, all too aware that if
Dragos wanted to strike at the heart of the Order, he
would do so at this very location.

It was a thought he didn't like to dwell on but one he
couldn't afford to ignore.

He didn't think he could bear it if the Order—his
family—was dealt a blow as staggering as the one that had
come down on Lazaro Archer tonight. All the Gen One
civilian had left after a thousand years of living was the
battered young boy in the infirmary bed and the bullet-
ravaged body of the son that Tegan and the rest of
tonight's team had brought back with them to the compound.

Lucan cleared his throat. "If you would like to hold funeral rites for Christophe in the morning, we will make
the necessary preparations."

Lazaro gave a somber nod. "Thank you. For everything, Lucan."

"Accommodations here at the compound are limited, but we can rearrange a few things to make space for you and Kellan in one of the bunk rooms. You're welcome to stay for as long as needed."

Archer held up his hand in polite dismissal. "That's more than generous; however, I have personal holdings elsewhere. There are other places that my grandson and I can go."

"Yes," Lucan replied, "but until we can be certain that you and Kellan are not in imminent danger from Dragos, I'm not comfortable releasing you from the Order's protection."

"Dragos," Archer said, his face hardening with restrained fury. "I recall that name from the Old Times. Dragos and his progeny were forever corrupt. Devious, conniving. Morally decayed. Good Christ, I'd thought the entire line had died out long ago."

Lucan grunted. "A second-generation son remains, hidden for decades behind multiple aliases but not dead. Not yet. And there is more, Lazaro. Things you don't know. Things the civilian population would not wish to know about Dragos and his machinations."

Grim, ageless eyes held his stare. "Tell me. I want to understand. I *need* to understand."

"Come," Lucan said. "Let's walk."

He guided Archer away from his grandson's infirmary room and along the quiet corridor outside. The two Gen Ones strode in silence for a short distance while Lucan considered where to start with the facts they knew about Dragos. At the beginning, he finally decided.

"The seeds of this war with Dragos were sown centuries ago," he said, as he and Archer progressed up the white marble hallway. "You must remember the violence of those times, Lazaro. You lived through it the same as I did, when the Ancients ran unchecked, driven by their thirst for blood and the thrill of the hunt. They were our fathers, but they had to be stopped."

Archer nodded gravely. "I do remember how it was then. As a boy, I can't tell you how often I witnessed my own sire's savagery. It seemed to escalate over time, growing more feral and uncontrolled, particularly after he'd return from the gatherings."

Lucan cocked his head. "The gatherings?"

"Yes," Archer replied. "I don't know where he and the other Ancients met, but he would be gone for weeks or months at a time. I always knew when he was back in the area because then the killings in the human villages around us would begin again. I was relieved when he finally left for good."

Lucan frowned. "My father never mentioned gatherings, but I know he roamed for long periods. I know he hunted. When he killed my mother in a fit of Bloodlust, I knew it was time to put an end to all of the savagery."

"I remember hearing what happened to your mother," Archer replied. "And I remember your call to arms to all Gen One sons to band with you in war against our alien fathers. I didn't think it possible that you would succeed."

"Not many did," Lucan recalled, but he wasn't bitter, not then or now. "Eight of us went up against the handful of surviving Ancients. We thought we'd killed the last of them, but we had traitors in our ranks—my brother, Marek, as it turned out, and the Gen One father of Dragos, as well. They plotted in secret and built a hidden mountain crypt to house the last of the Ancients. They'd claimed he was dead but kept him protected in hibernation for centuries. He was later removed from the crypt, and survived under Dragos's control until only recently. Dragos kept him drugged and starved in a private laboratory. We don't know the extent of Dragos's madness, but we are sure of one thing: Over some decades, he's used the Ancient to breed a small army of Gen Ones. These offspring now serve Dragos as his personal, homegrown assassins."

"Good God," Archer murmured, visibly stricken. "I can hardly believe all of this is true."

Lucan might have felt the same at one point, but he had lived it. He thought back on everything that had occurred in the past year plus. All the betrayals and revelations, the explosive secrets and unexpected tragedies that had stabbed deep into the fabric of the Order and its members.

And the fight wasn't over. Not even close.

"So far, Dragos has managed to elude us, but we're getting closer to him every day. We've driven him to ground by destroying what was likely his primary location. He lost another key piece when the Ancient escaped some of his men in Alaska. We tracked the creature down and took him out. But a lot of the damage has already been done," Lucan added. "We don't know how many Gen One assassins Dragos managed to create or where they might be. We intend to find them, however. And we have one working with us now. He joined the Order not long ago, after freeing himself from Dragos's bonds."

Archer's face drew into a cautious look. "Do you think that's wise? Placing your trust in anyone who's been so closely linked to Dragos?"

Lucan inclined his head. "I had the same reservations at first, but Hunter has proven more than worthy of the Order's trust. You've met him yourself, Lazaro. He was there tonight with you, and helped to kill Christophe's assassins."

The Gen One exhaled a quiet curse. "That warrior saved my life. No one could have acted swiftly enough to save my son, but if not for Hunter, I would not be here, either."

"He is an honorable male," Lucan said. "But he was bred and raised to be a killing machine. Based on the descriptions we received of Kellan's abductors, we're all but certain that it was three of Dragos's Hunters who took him from your home."

"I thought I heard some of the warriors tonight say that the captors who were killed inside the building earlier were humans—Minions."

Lucan nodded. "They were. For some reason, they'd been made to look like the same individuals who took Kellan, but the Minions were part of some larger scheme. As was the attack on your Darkhaven, I have no doubt."

"But why?" Archer murmured. "What did he hope to gain by taking nearly all of my family and reducing my home to ash?"

"We don't have that answer yet, but we won't rest until we do." Lucan paused in the corridor, crossing his arms over his chest. "Dragos has given us a hell of a lot to deal with lately, and my gut tells me we're only seeing the beginning of what he's capable of. We've recently discovered that he's got Minions embedded in at least one human government agency, as well. No doubt, there's more bad news where that came from."

Archer cursed, low under his breath. "To think all of this has been taking place right under our noses. Lucan, I don't know what to say, other than I regret not giving you my support sooner. You can't know how sorry I am for that."

Lucan shook his head. "It's not necessary. The fight belongs to the Order."

Lazaro Archer's expression was grim with purpose. "As of now, the fight is mine, as well. I am in, Lucan. In whatever means that I can serve you and your warriors, if you'll accept my offer—belated as it is—then I am in."

Dragos's black limousine pulled up to the ice-crusted curb where his lieutenant waited, huffing and shivering under a streetlamp in his dark cashmere coat and low-brimmed hat.

As the Minion driver braked to a stop, Dragos's man came over to the back passenger door and climbed inside the vehicle. He pulled off his hat and gloves, pivoting to face Dragos beside him in the backseat.

"The Order was tipped off about the building where the boy was being held, sire. They showed up tonight just as we'd anticipated, along with Lazaro Archer and his son and a unit from the Enforcement Agency. The Minions who'd been guarding the boy were killed within moments of the confrontation."

"Hardly a surprise," Dragos said with a mild shrug. "And Agent Freyne?"

"Dead, sire. He and his men were killed by one of the warriors as they were attempting to carry out their mission. Christophe Archer was eliminated, but his father still lives."

Dragos grunted. If one of the Archers had to survive the assassination he'd arranged, he would have much preferred Lazaro dead over his society-bred son. Be that as it may, the multipronged assault he'd orchestrated tonight had still been a success. He had watched from a safe distance, secure in his limousine, as Lazaro Archer's Darkhaven exploded into the winter night like a Roman candle.

It had been glorious.

A total annihilation.

And now he had the Order precisely where he wanted them—confused and scattered.

His Breed lieutenant went on, ticking off the rest of the evening's outcome. "The fire at the Darkhaven claimed all lives within, and I have reports that Lazaro Archer has not been seen or heard from in the hours since. Although I've not had confirmation, I suspect that both the Gen One and the boy are in the Order's custody as we speak."

"Very well," Dragos replied. "As Lazaro Archer is still breathing, I'd hardly call this a flawless execution of my orders. But then, if I expect perfection, I should have to do everything myself."

His lieutenant had the gall to look affronted. "All due respect, sire, but had I known the Order now counts one of your Hunters among them, I might have taken extra precautions concerning Freyne's role in the mission tonight."

Dragos had lived long enough that surprises rarely had the power to take him aback. But this news flash—this disturbing bit of intelligence—actually made his pulse knock a bit against his sternum. Rage filled his skull, a cold fury that practically had him spitting the curse that leapt to his tongue.

"You didn't know?" asked his lieutenant, crowding against the door in an effort to put as much distance as possible between them.

"A Hunter," Dragos replied, amber sparks flashing in the darkened cabin of the limo. "Are you certain this is true?"

His man nodded soberly. "I had surveillance cameras trained on the construction site from more than one location nearby. The way he moved, the sheer size of him, and the precision of his kills . . . sire, there could be no mistaking the warrior for anything but one of your Hunters."

And there was only one of his specially bred, ruthlessly trained killers who had managed to connive his way out of Dragos's control and make his escape. That he had allied himself with the Order was a shock, plain and simple.

Dragos had assumed the Hunter had escaped the bonds of his obedience collar and fled into obscurity, a stray dog, lost without its master. On some level, he'd assumed the fugitive assassin had ended up dead or Rogue by now.

But not this.

And no, he reflected now, not this particular Hunter.

He had been different from the start. Chillingly efficient. Coldly intelligent. Relentlessly disciplined, yet far from submissive. That was a lesson he'd never been able to learn, no matter how mercilessly it had been drilled into him.

Dragos should have had the son of a bitch put down, but he'd also been the best assassin in his personal Gen One army to date.

And now he'd apparently sided with Lucan and the warriors in this mounting war.

Dragos growled with outrage at the mere idea.

"Get out of my sight," he snarled to his lieutenant. "Await my orders to begin the next phase of the plan."

The other Breed male scrambled out of the car without

another word, slamming the door behind him and hurrying off in the opposite direction of the street.

"Drive," Dragos barked to the Minion behind the wheel.

As the limo sped off into the hustle of Boston's evening traffic, he straightened the lapels of his Italian silk tuxedo and smoothed his hand over his meticulously styled hair. In the dim glow of the highway lights, he withdrew an embossed invitation from out of his jacket pocket and read the address of the political fund-raiser he had just attended downtown.

A small droplet of human blood stained the lower corner of the ivory paper, still fresh enough to smear under the press of his thumb.

Dragos chuckled under his breath, recalling how pleased the group of city officials had been with the generosity of his donation.

How stunned they had been just a few minutes later, when they realized what each of them would be surrendering to him in exchange.

Now he leaned back and closed his eyes, letting the hum of the road lull him as he savored the buzz of power still swimming in his veins.

CHAPTER
Twenty-eight

Jenna had never seen Brock so quiet.

He and the other warriors had returned a short time ago, accompanied by Lazaro Archer and his grandson. The relief surrounding the boy's rescue was severely dampened by the cost at which it had come. While arrangements were made to accommodate the new arrivals at the compound and get them cleaned up and settled, Brock and the other warriors on tonight's mission had dispersed to their own quarters.

Brock had hardly uttered a word since he'd returned. He'd been covered in blood and grime, his face drawn taut with tension and not a little horror for what he and his brethren had witnessed during the recovery of the boy.

Jenna had walked with him back to the room they now shared and had since been sitting on the edge of the bed alone, staring at the closed bathroom door while he ran the shower on the other side.

She didn't know if he'd welcome company or preferred his solitude, but after hearing about what had occurred on his patrol, she found she couldn't sit idle when he might be hurting on the other side of the closed door.

She walked over and tested the latch. It wasn't locked, so she cracked it open and peered inside.

Brock was naked under the steaming spray, his *glyph*-covered back toward the door, hands fisted and pressed against the shower wall in front of him. Although she didn't see any wounds on him, the water ran in red trails down his dark skin before swirling into the drain at his feet.

"May I come in?" she asked softly.

He didn't reply, but he didn't tell her to leave him alone, either. She entered, shutting the door behind her. She didn't need to ask him if he was all right. Despite that he seemed physically unharmed, every thick muscle in his broad back was bunched with tension. His arms were trembling, his head bent low against his chest.

"An entire family was blown to bits tonight," he murmured, his voice rough and raw with restrained emotion. "That kid's life is never gonna be the same."

"I know," she whispered, drawing nearer.

He lifted his face into the hot cascade of water, then slicked a hand over the top of his head. "I tell you, there are times when I don't think I can handle all of the goddamned pain and death."

"That's what makes you human," she said, then laughed quietly to herself at how easy it was to think of him as a man—her man—despite all the things that made him something more than that.

Hell, it was getting hard to think of herself as being purely human anymore. She was morphing into something she didn't quite understand—more and more every day—but she was growing less afraid of the changes taking place within her. They were making her stronger, giving her a renewed sense of purpose . . . a rebirth.

She found herself looking forward to the chance to have a different life. A new life, perhaps right here in this place. Perhaps with Brock at her side.

After the last time she'd been in his arms, she realized she was less afraid of the feelings she had for him, too.

It was that lack of fear that prompted her to take off her top and step out of her loose yoga pants. Her bra and panties went next, discarded on the floor as she walked into the shower with Brock and wrapped her arms around his strong back.

He tensed at the contact, drawing in a sharp breath. But then his arms came down over hers and he held her there, his big hands warm and soothing as he caressed her. "I'm filthy from the mission, Jenna."

"I don't care," she said, pressing a trail of kisses to the smooth, muscled arch of his spine. His *dermaglyphs* pulsed with deepening color. "Let me take care of you for a change."

She pulled her arms from around him and took the bar of soap from the shower shelf. He stayed unmoving as she filled her hands with lather, then began to gently smooth the suds over his immense shoulders and bulky biceps. She washed his strong back, then slowly let her hands drift down, past his tight waist, to the sides of his lean hips.

She felt the powerful twitch of his body as she reached around to the front of him, her soap-slicked hands skirting the edge of his groin. He was erect even before she got there, moaning as she splayed her fingers around the base of his cock, teasing but not yet touching. She brought her hands around and gathered more lather, then crouched down behind him to wash the lengths of his legs.

He shuddered as she dragged her soapy fingers back up his thighs, pressing her body flush against him as she rose, slippery from the suds that still lingered on his skin. She wrapped one arm around the front of his waist, her other hand reaching down to stroke his hard shaft. He growled a dark curse as she caressed him, his sex swelling even greater in her grasp.

She found a rhythm that seemed to please him, and she worked it mercilessly, delighting in the feel of his body's response to her touch. With a low moan, he leaned forward to brace one elbow against the shower wall in front of him. "Ah, fuck, Jenna . . . I love your hands on me."

She smiled at his praise, losing herself in his pleasure as she stroked him harder, more intensely. He grunted, his sex kicking in the tight hold of her pistoning fist. Then, before she could make him lose all control, he hissed a raw curse from between his gritted teeth and fangs.

He flipped around to face her. His erect cock rose up past his navel, hard as steel but hot as a flame when he dragged her against him, his big hands firm on her upper arms, his hold possessive and fierce. His handsome face was drawn in sharper angles in the throes of his passion, his eyes as bright as glowing coals, his fangs stark white and enormous, deadly sharp.

Jenna licked her lips, her throat suddenly gone dry with need.

He knew what she wanted. She could read his understanding as surely as he'd read the hungered look in her
own eyes.

He lifted her off her feet, guiding her legs around his
waist as he carried her out of the bathroom and toward
the big bed in the other room. Their bodies were wet, still
slick in places from errant suds as they flopped onto the
mattress together in an intimate tangle.

He kept her thighs wrapped around him as he rolled
onto his back, settling her on top of him. He thrust inside
her, filling her up so perfectly. She tipped her head back
and exhaled a slow, pleasured sigh as he seated himself to
the hilt beneath her.

"You're so beautiful," he murmured, his touch roaming all over her sensitive flesh.

She opened her eyes and stared down at him. "I want
to be beautiful to you. That's how you make me feel." She
held his unwavering amber-flecked gaze, forcing herself
to not shy away from the emotion that was swamping her.
She felt safe with him. Safe enough to tell him what was in
her heart. "I feel happy, Brock, for the first time in a very
long time. Because of you, I'm feeling so many things..."

"Jenna," he murmured, frowning now, his expression
turning very serious.

She forged on, having already stepped past the edge
of this cliff and determined to take it all the way down.
"I know you said you don't like complications or long-
term relationships. I know you said you don't want to get
involved—"

"I *am* involved," he said, running his hands down her
sides, resting them on her hips where their bodies were intimately joined. He rocked into her slowly. "It doesn't get
more involved than this. God, I never planned on you,

Jenna. I thought I was playing it safe, but you've changed everything." His touch was light as he caressed her cheek and jawline. "I don't have the answers when it comes to you . . . to us . . . and what we have together."

She swallowed, shaking her head in mute denial.

"I didn't want to fall in love," she whispered. "I didn't think I could ever again."

He held her in a tender gaze. "And I told myself I wouldn't."

Jenna parted her lips, uncertain what she meant to say. An instant later, it didn't matter. Brock drew her down to him and kissed her, wrapping her in his arms. His mouth pressed hers, his tongue pushing past her lips and driving her mad with the need for more. She ground against his hips, heat flaring brighter in her core and flowing out to her every nerve ending.

She rose up, panting now, unable to keep from moving on him as her need swelled to a fever pitch.

"You're in control, baby," he said, his voice thick and raspy. "Take whatever you want."

She eyed his throat, watching the vein that pulsed so strongly at the side of his neck. Hunger kicked deep inside her, startling her with its ferocity. She pulled her gaze away and met the glittering heat of his transformed eyes.

"Anything," he said, looking more than eager for her to have her way with him.

She rocked on him, savoring the feel of their joined bodies, and half dizzy from arousal already. Her orgasm roared up on her quickly. She tried to stave it off, but sensation flooded her as she rode the heat and power of Brock's sex.

He watched her with avid interest, his lips pulled back off his fangs, the ropelike tendons in his neck strung tight as he arched his shoulders up off the bed. Jenna couldn't keep her eyes from the frantic beat of his pulse. It echoed in her bones, in her own veins. In the impatient rhythm of her body as she shuddered with the sudden detonation of her release.

"Yeah," he groaned, splaying his hands at her back and not letting her draw away when the hunger bore down on her like a tidal wave. "Let it go, Jenna. Anything you want."

With a snarled cry she couldn't hold back, she buried her face in the side of his neck and bit down hard. Blood surged into her mouth, hot and thick and spicy-sweet.

Brock hissed a rough curse that sounded anything but sorry. His body shook as he drove deeper inside her, every hard thrust increasing her pleasure, driving her hunger to even greater heights. He shouted as his orgasm racked him, his strong pulse drumming against the tip of her tongue as Jenna closed her lips around his open vein and began to drink.

CHAPTER
Twenty-nine

Two days had passed since the attack on Lazaro Archer's family and the rescue mission that saved young Kellan. The boy was recovering physically from his capture and mistreatment, but Jenna knew as well as anyone that his emotional scars—the reality of all he'd lost in one hellish moment—would be with him long after the cuts and bruises had healed. She only hoped he'd find a means of coping with them in less time and self-defeating agony than it had taken her to deal with her own.

She wished the same for his Gen One grandfather, too, although Lazaro Archer hardly seemed the kind to need anyone's sympathy. Once the funeral ceremony for his son, Christophe, had taken place at the compound,

Lazaro had refused to so much as speak of that violent night. In the time since, he'd devoted himself to working closely with the Order. The Gen One civilian now appeared as determined as any of the warriors to see Dragos and his entire operation destroyed.

Jenna knew that feeling. It was maddening to think that evil like Dragos was loose in the world. He was stepping up his operation, which meant the Order could not afford to let any opportunity to gain an upper hand slip away. After what he'd been willing to do to Lazaro Archer and his family, Jenna couldn't help worrying even more about the group of Breedmates known to be kept under his control.

At least on that front, there was a glimmer of hope. Dylan had gotten a call that morning from the administrator at Sister Margaret Howland's retirement home in Gloucester. The elderly nun had been told about Dylan's request for a visit, and she was excited for a little company and conversation.

Jenna had been first to volunteer when Dylan announced the afternoon excursion. Renata and Alex had also offered to ride along, everyone eager to see if Claire Reichen's sketches of the captive Breedmates would bear fruit.

Now, as the four women drove into Gloucester in a black Rover from the Order's fleet, all they had to hope for was a few moments of mental clarity from the aging sister.

Even Lucan had agreed that if they could get just so much as one female's name, it would make the entire mission worthwhile.

Brock hadn't been thrilled about the prospect of Jenna leaving the compound, particularly so soon after the violence perpetrated on Lazaro Archer and his kin. He worried, as always, and where it used to rankle, now his concern warmed her.

He cared about her, and she had to admit, it felt very good to know that she had someone guarding her back. More than that, she believed Brock was a man who would guard her heart every bit as carefully as he did her safety and well-being.

She hoped he would, because over the past few days— and incredible nights—she had laid her heart openly in his hands.

"Here we are," Dylan said from the front passenger seat of the Rover as Renata turned into the retirement home driveway. "The administrator told me that Sister Margaret takes her afternoon tea around this time in the library. She said we could just go on in."

"There it is." Alex pointed toward a bronze sign sticking out of a snowbank in front of a modest little clapboard cottage.

Renata parked in the half-empty lot and killed the engine. "Here goes nothing, eh? Jenna, will you grab that leather tote bag from the back?"

She pivoted to pull the collection of file folders and notepads out of the cargo area, then climbed out of the vehicle with her friends.

As Jenna came around the front of the Rover, Dylan took the tote bag from her and held it against her chest. Pursing her lips, she blew out a heavy sigh.

Alex paused next to her. "What's wrong?"

"All my research the past few months is coming down to this moment. If this turns out to be a dead end, you guys, then I don't have a clue where to begin to looking next."

"Relax," Renata said, taking Dylan's shoulders in a sisterly hold. "You've been busting your ass on this investigation. We wouldn't even be this far without you. You and Claire both."

Dylan nodded, although not quite buoyed by the pep talk. "We just really need a decent lead. I don't think I could handle it if we end up back at square one."

"If we have to start all over," Jenna said, "then we just work harder. Together."

Renata smiled, her pale green eyes twinkling as she buttoned up her leather duster to conceal the blades and gun belt that studded her fatigues-clad hips. "Come on. Let's go have tea with the nice old ladies."

Jenna thought it wise to zip up her own coat, too, since Brock insisted she carry a weapon whenever she left the compound. It felt strange to wear a firearm again, but it was a different kind of strange from the way she'd felt back in Alaska.

Everything about her felt different now.

She was different, and she liked the person she was becoming.

More important, she was learning to forgive the person she'd been in Alaska.

She'd left a part of herself back in Harmony, a part she could never get back, but as she stepped into the warm cottage library with Renata and Dylan and Alex, she couldn't imagine returning to the woman she'd been before. She had friends here now, and important work that needed to be done.

Best of all, she had Brock.

It was that thought that made her smile a little brighter as Dylan brought them over to a frail elderly woman who sat quietly on a rose-patterned sofa near the library's fireplace. Cloudy blue eyes blinked a couple of times from beneath a fluffy crown of white curly hair. Jenna could still see the kind expression of the nun in the shelter photograph in the lined face that peered up at the Order's women.

"Sister Margaret?" Dylan said, holding out her hand. "I'm Sharon Alexander's daughter, Dylan. And these are my friends."

"Oh, my goodness," exclaimed the sweet old nun. "They told me I was having company for tea today. Please, sit down, girls. I so rarely have guests."

Dylan took a seat on the sofa next to the sister. Jenna and Alex sat on either side of the coffee table, in a pair of worn wingback chairs. Renata positioned herself with her back to a wall, her eyes on the door—a trained warrior, ever on guard.

Never mind that the only people in the room besides the four of them and Sister Margaret were a couple of cotton-topped ladies hobbling behind metal walkers and wearing emergency call necklaces along with their rosary beads.

Jenna listened idly as Dylan attempted a bit of small talk with Sister Margaret, then delved into the purpose of their visit. She pulled out a handful of sketches, trying desperately to jump-start the aging nun's failing memory. It didn't appear to be going very well.

"Are you sure you don't remember any of these girls being clients of the shelter?" Dylan slid a couple more sketches in front of the old woman. The sister peered at the hand-rendered faces, but there was no glint of recognition in the kind blue eyes. "Please try, Sister Margaret. Anything you recall could be very helpful to us."

"I am sorry, my dear. I'm afraid my memory isn't what

it used to be." She picked up her teacup and took a sip. "But then, I never was any good with names and faces. God saw fit to give me enough other blessings, I suppose."

Jenna watched Dylan deflate as she reluctantly began to gather up her materials. "That's all right, Sister Margaret. I appreciate that you were willing to see us."

"Oh, my word," the sister blurted, putting her cup back down on the saucer. "What a terrible hostess I am! I forgot to make you girls some tea."

Dylan reached for her tote bag. "It's not necessary. We shouldn't take up any more of your time."

"Nonsense. You came for tea."

As she got up from the sofa and shuffled into the cottage's little kitchenette, Dylan sent an apologetic look at Jenna and the others. As the sister rummaged around in the other room, putting on the water and rattling cups, Dylan swept up all of the sketches and photographs. She stuffed everything back in the tote bag and placed it next to her on the floor.

After a few minutes, Sister Margaret's reedy voice filtered out to them. "Was Sister Grace able to help you at all, dear?"

Dylan glanced up, frowning. "Sister Grace?"

"Yes. Sister Grace Gilhooley. She and I volunteered at the shelter together. We both were part of the same convent here in Boston."

"Holy shit," Dylan mouthed silently, excitement glittering in her eyes. She got up off the sofa and walked into the kitchenette. "I would love to talk to Sister Grace. You don't happen to know how we can find her, do you?"

Sister Margaret nodded proudly. "Why, of course, I do. She lives not even five minutes from here, along the coast.

Her father was a sea captain. Or a fisherman. Well, I don't quite recall, to tell you the truth."

"That's okay," Dylan said. "Can you give us her phone number or address, so we can contact her?"

"I'll do better than that, dear. I'll call her myself and let her know you'd like to ask her about some of those shelter girls." Behind Sister Margaret, the teakettle began to whistle. She smiled, as pleasant as a sweet little granny. "First, we're going to have that cup of tea together."

They'd gulped their tea as quickly as they could without seeming completely rude.

Even so, it had taken more than twenty minutes to get away from sweet Sister Margaret Mary Howland. Fortunately, her offer to phone Sister Grace had proven useful.

The other retired nun was apparently in better health than her friend, living without assistance, and, from the one-sided conversation Jenna and the others had been privy to, it sounded like Sister Grace Gilhooley was willing and able to provide whatever information they needed about her work in the New York shelter.

"Nice place," Jenna remarked as Renata wheeled the Rover along a stretch of shoreline road that led to a cheery yellow Victorian secluded on a jutting peninsula of rocky land.

The big house sat on about two acres of land, a postage stamp compared to home sites in Alaska, but clearly a luxury setting here on the coast of Cape Cod. With snow filling the yard and clinging to the rocks, the steel blue ocean sprawling out to the horizon, the bright canary Victorian looked as wholesome and inviting as a spot of warm sunshine in the midst of so much cold and winter.

"I hope we have better luck here," Alex said from beside Jenna in the backseat, peering out at the impressive estate as they followed the white picket fence in front, then turned into the narrow driveway.

As Renata parked the Rover near the house, Dylan pivoted around from next to her up front. "If she can't help identify some of the missing women from the New York shelter, maybe she'll be able to tell us the names of the Breedmates in the two new sketches Claire Reichen has given us."

Jenna got out of the back with Alex, both of them coming around to the front of the Rover, where Renata and Dylan now stood. "I didn't realize we had new sketches."

"Elise picked them up from her Darkhaven friend yesterday."

Dylan handed Jenna a manila file folder as they walked toward the gingerbread-style veranda and front porch of the house. Jenna opened the folder as she followed her companions up the creaky wooden steps to the front door. She glanced inside at the artist's renderings, which were based on Claire's recollections of faces she saw some months ago, when her talent for dreamwalking had given her unexpected access to one of Dragos's hidden labs.

Dylan rang the doorbell. "Cross your fingers. Hell, say a prayer while you're at it."

A housekeeper appeared a moment later and politely informed them that they were expected. Meanwhile, Jenna studied the two sketches a bit closer...and her heart dropped like a stone into her stomach.

An image of a young woman with sleek dark hair and

almond-shaped eyes stared back at her. The delicate face was familiar, even in the pencil drawing that didn't quite capture the full impact of her exotic beauty.

Corinne.

Brock's Corinne.

Could it really be her? If so, how? He had been so certain she was dead. He'd told Jenna he'd seen the Breedmate's body after she had been recovered from the river. Then again, he'd also mentioned that it had been months since she'd vanished before her remains had been found, and that all they had to identify her was her clothing and the necklace she'd been wearing when she disappeared.

Oh, God . . . could she actually be alive? Had she somehow ended up in Dragos's hands and been held captive by him for all this time?

Jenna was too astonished to speak, too numb to do anything more than follow her friends into the house after the housekeeper invited them inside. One part of her was squeezed tight with the hope that a young woman presumed to be dead might, in fact, be alive.

Yet another part of her was gripped with a dark, shameful fear—the fear that this new knowledge might cost her the man she loved.

She had to tell Brock as soon as possible. It was the right thing to do—he had to know the truth. He had to see the sketch for himself and determine if Jenna's suspicions might be correct.

"Please, make yourselves comfortable. I'll go tell Sister Grace that you're here," said the pleasant little woman as she left Jenna and the others alone in the front parlor.

"Alex," she murmured, giving a little tug of her coat sleeve. "I need to call the compound."

Alex frowned. "What's wrong?"

"This sketch," she said, glancing at it once more and feeling utterly certain now that Claire Reichen had seen Corinne during her dreamwalk into Dragos's lair. "I recognize this woman's face. I've seen it before."

"What?" Alex replied, taking the folder to look at it herself. "Jen, are you sure?"

Renata and Dylan moved closer, as well, all three of Jenna's companions huddling around her in the quiet front room of the house. She pointed to the delicate face of the dark-haired young woman in the sketch. "I think I know who this Breedmate is."

"By all means, dear," said a cool, female voice. "Do tell."

Jenna's gaze snapped up and clashed across the room with a pair of calm gray eyes that stared back at her from a lined, outwardly kind-looking face. With her long silver hair caught in a loose chignon, Sister Grace Gilhooley's pale blue floral housedress and white cardigan made her seem like something out of a Norman Rockwell painting.

But it was those eyes that gave her away.

Those dullish eyes, and the prickling of Jenna's new senses, which lit up like a Christmas tree as soon as the woman entered the room.

Jenna held the sharklike stare, realizing in an instant just what the good sister was.

"Holy shit," she said, recalling the same peculiar look in the eyes of the FBI men who'd tried to kill her and Brock in New York just days before. Jenna glanced over at Renata. "She's a fucking Minion."

CHAPTER
Thirty

"That's about the tenth time you've checked that thing since we came down here." Brock smirked at Dante as the warrior—the anxious, expectant father—broke away from the group in the weapons room to look at his PDA. "Damn, my man, you're about as jumpy as a cat."

"Tess is napping in our quarters," Dante replied. "If she needs anything, I told her to text me."

Apparently finding no messages since his last look about five minutes ago, he set the device back down on the table and returned to the firing range where Brock, Kade, Rio, and Niko waited to resume their target practice.

As Dante swaggered back to his place among his brethren, Niko peered at him with mock intensity, getting

up close and staring at his face before finally giving an ex-
aggerated shrug. "I'll be damned. Nothing there, after all."

"What?" Dante asked, his black brows crunched into a
scowl. "What the hell are you doing?"

Niko grinned, baring his twin dimples. "Just looking for
a nose ring or something. Figured Tess might have had
one installed on you to go along with that short leash she's
got you attached to."

"Piss off," Dante said around a deep chuckle. He
pointed a finger in Niko's direction. "I'm gonna remind
you of this when Renata's the one who's eight and a half
months pregnant and it's your turn to worry."

"No need to wait on that," Kade put in. "Renata's already got him trained to jump on command. Probably got
him on a leash of her own, too."

"Yeah?" Niko reached for his belt and made a show of
starting to unbuckle it. "Give me a second and I'll show
you."

Brock shook his head at his brethren, not quite feeling
part of the jokes and lighthearted smack-talk about
Breedmates and babies soon to be on the way. He couldn't
help thinking about Jenna, and about how he might find
a way to make a future for them together.

She wasn't a Breedmate, and that troubled him. Not
because of the fact they would never have offspring together. Not even because of the absence of a blood bond,
which would connect them to each other inexorably for as
long as both of them lived.

He didn't need a blood link to strengthen what he felt
for her. She was his mate already, in all the ways that mattered. He loved her, and although he wasn't sure what
their future would look like, he couldn't begin to imagine
living it without her.

He looked to the other warriors in the weapons room with him, and knew that he would die for Jenna if it came down to that—the same as any other blood-bonded Breed male.

As his gaze traveled past Kade and Niko and Dante, he realized that Rio had gone quiet in the past few minutes. The scarred, Spanish-born warrior leaned against the nearby wall, staring at nothing in particular as he idly rubbed his fist in a small circle at the center of his chest.

"You all right, Rio?"

He glanced over at Brock and gave him a vague shrug. His fist kept circling, directly over his heart. "What time is it?"

Brock checked the clock at the other end of the facility. "Almost three-thirty."

"The women ought to be calling in any minute now," Kade said. His gaze seemed preoccupied, as well, his silver eyes glinting with a note of unease.

Niko set down his weapon and grabbed his cell phone. "I'm going to call Renata. Something doesn't feel right to me all of a sudden."

"Yeah," Kade agreed. "You don't think anything is wrong, do you?"

Although Brock wasn't liking the suddenly serious vibe that was coming over his brethren, he assured himself that everything was fine. The day trip Jenna and the other females were on was just a quick drive to the Cape. A visit to a seventy-year-old nun, for crissake.

Jenna had a weapon on her, and so did Renata, and both of them knew how to handle themselves. There was no reason at all to be concerned.

Dante walked over, frowning darkly, while Niko waited

in prolonged silence for his mate to pick up his call. "Any answer?"

"No," Niko replied quietly.

"Madre de Dios," Rio blurted as he pushed away from the wall. "Something has Dylan frightened. I can feel her fear in my veins."

Brock registered the alarm traveling through each of his brethren now. "The both of you, too?" he asked, shooting a grim look at Kade and Niko.

"My pulse just kicked into overdrive," Kade said. "Ah, shit. Something bad is going down with Alex and the others."

"It won't be dark for another hour, minimum," Dante reminded them, sober with the warning.

"We don't have that long," Niko said. "We've got to go after them now."

With Dante looking on, Brock fell in alongside his three fellow warriors, feeling lost and adrift, dependent on their instincts to help guide him toward whatever threat was now facing Jenna and the other males' Breedmates.

Holy hell. Jenna was in danger and he'd had no clue.

She could be dying that very moment, and he wouldn't know until he was standing over her body.

The realization was as cold as death itself, reaching into his chest and seizing his heart in an icy fist.

"Let's go," he barked to his brethren.

Together the four of them raced out of the weapons room, gathering their guns and gear as they went.

At the same instant, Jenna and Renata both had their pistols drawn and leveled on the smiling nun—the Minion, whose dead eyes looked through them as though they weren't there.

As though they were nothing, meant nothing.

Which to this woman, Jenna knew without question, they weren't, and didn't.

Behind Sister Grace, two bulky men now stood. They'd been lurking in the shadows of the hallway at her back, summoned forward even before Jenna and Renata had raised their guns to shoot. The men's eyes held the same cold stare as the nun's. Each of them held a large pistol—one aimed at Renata, the other leveled on Jenna.

The standoff played out in wary silence for a long moment, time that she used to calculate possible ways of disabling one or both of the men without putting either Alex or Dylan in harm's way in the process. But damn, it didn't seem viable. Even if she hoped to use the implant-enhanced speed her reflexes seemed to have now, the risk to her friends was too great to chance it.

And then, more bad news.

From somewhere to her left, another male Minion stepped up and rested the cold nose of a revolver against her head.

The nun smiled her false smile. "I'm going to have to ask you girls to put down your weapons now."

Renata didn't budge. Neither did Jenna, despite the metallic *click* of turning gears as the Minion at her side chambered a round.

"How long have you been working for Dragos?" Renata asked the female mind slave. "He's your Master, am I right?"

Sister Grace blinked, unfazed. "One more time, dear. Put down your weapon. The rug you're standing on has been in my family for more than two hundred years. It would be a pity to ruin it by having Arthur or Patrick here blast a fucking hole in your chest."

Jenna's own chest constricted with fear at the thought of any of her friends being hurt by these Minion assholes. She waited in tense, terrified silence, watching as Renata's lean arm muscles lost some of their tautness. Jenna thought she was about to comply, but the subtle, sidelong glance Renata gave her seemed to indicate otherwise.

Jenna acknowledged that look with a barely discernible shift of her own gaze. There would be only one chance to make her move. A split second to either make it work or lose everything in an instant.

Renata exhaled a resigned-sounding sigh.

She started to lower her gun . . .

As she did so, Jenna seized on every bit of speed she could summon from the tendons and sinews of her human limbs. She pivoted with blinding swiftness and snapped the wrist of the Minion holding her at gunpoint. He screamed in pain, throwing the whole room into a state of chaos.

In what seemed like slow motion to Jenna but probably played out in fractions of seconds, she leveled her pistol on the fallen Minion and put two bullets in his head. Renata meanwhile had shot one of the others behind the nun. As the second Minion spurted a bloody fountain from his chest and dropped to the floor, Sister Grace turned to dash for the hallway.

Jenna was on her before she could take even two steps.

She leapt over the Minion, heading her off in an instant. She thrust her hands out at the woman and shoved her backward, sending the gray-haired monster airborne. She crashed down onto the parlor floor as Renata plugged the last of the male Minions and left the body twitching and bleeding on Sister Grace's heirloom rug.

Jenna stalked over to the scrabbling Minion nun and hauled her up onto the delicate silk-covered settee near the window. "Start talking, bitch. How long have you been serving Dragos? Did you already belong to him when you were working in his shelter?"

The Minion grinned through bloodstained teeth and shook her head. "You won't get anything out of me. You don't scare me. Death doesn't scare me."

As she spoke, a pair of heavy footsteps thundered up from somewhere below the house. Two more Minions, racing up from the cellar. The door off the hallway crashed open as they stormed out. Renata swung around and nailed each one dead center in the head, stopping them in their tracks.

Dylan let out a little whoop of triumph as the house went silent once again.

And then . . . the faintest sounds of voices coming from the cellar deep below.

Female voices.

More than a dozen different voices, all of them screaming and shouting, calling out to whoever could hear them.

"Holy shit," Alex murmured.

Dylan's eyes went wide. "You don't think—"

"Let's go find out," Renata said. She turned to Jenna. "Will you be all right up here?"

Jenna nodded. "Yeah, I'm good. I can hold her until you get back. Just go."

In the momentary inattention, Sister Grace fidgeted on the little sofa, digging around in her sweater pocket. Jenna looked back at her, just in time to see her stuff something small into her mouth. She swallowed quickly, gulping the object down. The tendons in her throat constricted. Her mouth started spewing thick white foam.

"Oh, shit!" Jenna cried. "She's poisoning herself!"

"She's dead. Forget the bitch," Renata said. "Down here with us, Jenna!"

She turned away from the Minion, letting the convulsing body fall to the floor. Together she and the other women raced down the old stone steps that led into the dimly lit, enormous cellar, which looked to be carved out of the craggy rocks of the peninsula itself.

Deeper and deeper they went, the cries for help growing louder.

"We hear you!" Dylan called back to the terrified women. "It's okay, we've found you!"

Jenna was not prepared for what awaited them as the cellar widened out ahead of them. Hollowed into the stone was a large cell, covered by an iron grid. Inside were upward of twenty women—filthy, unkempt, dressed in tattered laboratory gowns. Some of them were heavy with child. Others were waif thin and wan. They looked like the worst prisoners of war, neglected and forgotten, most of their faces drawn and expressionless.

They stared at their rescuers, some of them mute, some weeping quietly, while others sobbed openly in great, chest-racking heaves.

"Oh, Jesus," someone whispered, maybe even Jenna herself.

"Let's get them out of here," Renata said, her voice wooden. "Look for a key somewhere that fits this goddamned grate."

Dylan and Alex began searching the dark space. Jenna walked toward the far corner, peering into the deep shadows that seemed to continue on forever into the cavelike hollows of the old cellar. In her peripheral vision, she caught the slight hand movements of one of the captives. She was trying to get Jenna's attention, gesturing covertly toward the lightless tunnel that stretched farther into the darkness of the place.

Trying to warn her.

Jenna heard the nearly imperceptible scuff of a footstep coming out of the dark. She turned her head—just in time to see a flash of metal, a rushing movement. Then she felt the sudden body slam of another Minion, barreling out at her and knocking her nearly off her feet.

"Jenna!" Alex shouted. "Renata, help her!"

The gun blast echoed like cannon fire in the enclosed cellar. The captive females screamed and shrank back away from the sound.

"It's all right," Jenna called out. "He's dead. Everything's going to be fine."

She shoved the lifeless heap off her and crawled out from beneath him. Something metallic jangled as the Minion rolled onto his back and expelled his last breath.

"I think I found the key," she said, bending over him to remove the ring of several keys from his pants pocket.

She ran over to the cell and began searching for the one that would fit the padlock on the grate. The Minion's blood soaked her coat and palms, but she didn't care. All that mattered was getting the captive Breedmates out of this place.

The lock sprang loose on the second try.

"Oh, thank God," Dylan gasped. "Come on, everyone. You're safe now."

Jenna swung open the large iron grid and watched with a sense of pride and relief as the first few captives began to shuffle out of their prison. One by one, woman by woman, the group of them stepped away, finally free.

CHAPTER
Thirty-one

The warriors had been only a few miles away from the location when Rio got a frantic cell phone call from Dylan, telling him everything that had happened. Even though they had been clued in, even though they knew that she and Alex and Renata and Jenna had somehow—miraculously—found and freed the captive females Dragos had imprisoned for so many years, Brock and his brethren seated in the Order's SUV had not been prepared for the sight that greeted them as they roared up the shoreline road and saw the big yellow house on the rocks.

The sun had just begun to dip below the opposite horizon, casting its last, long shadows across the snow-covered yard of the tall Victorian. And in that yard, filing out of the front door wrapped in blankets, antique quilts, and crocheted afghans, were easily a dozen bedraggled, haggard young women.

Breedmates.

Several were already in the Rover parked in the driveway. Still others were being escorted out of the house by Alex and Dylan.

"Jesus Christ," Brock whispered, awed by the enormity of what had occurred.

Renata was standing near the Rover, helping some of the former captives into the backseat.

Where the hell was Jenna?

Brock scanned the entire area in a quick glance, his heart climbing up his chest. God, what if she was hurt? Dylan surely would have said something if there'd been casualties, but that didn't keep the rock from forming in the pit of his stomach. If anything had happened to her...

"Hang on," Niko said, as he pulled in to the driveway, then steered the big SUV right up onto the lawn.

Brock leapt out even before the vehicle had come to a full stop.

He had to see his woman. Had to feel her warm and safe in his arms.

He ran across the frozen yard, his boots chewing up the distance in mere seconds.

Alex looked up at him as he tore toward her.

"Where is she?" he demanded. "Where's Jenna? Did anything happen to her?"

"She's fine, Brock." Alex gestured toward the open front door of the house, where the bloodied corpse of at least one Minion lay visible and motionless inside. "Jenna's making sure the rest of the women get out safely from the cellar where they were being held."

He sagged at the news that she was okay, unable to hide his relief. "I have to see her."

Alex gave him a warm smile as she led one of the shivering, wan Breedmates toward the pair of waiting vehicles. He stepped forward and was about to vault up onto the veranda porch.

"Brock?"

The small, feminine voice—so unexpected, so distantly familiar—stopped him dead in his tracks. Something clicked in his brain. A spark of disbelief.

A grinding jolt of recognition.

"Brock . . . is it really you?"

Slowly, he pivoted around to face a diminutive, dark-haired female who was paused in the driveway, just off the steps of the porch. He hadn't noticed her when he'd passed her a moment ago. Good Christ, he wasn't sure he would have recognized her if she'd come right up to him in the street.

But he knew her voice.

Beneath the grime of her captivity and the neglect that had made her cheeks sallow, her alabaster skin marred with dirt and scratches, he realized that he did, in fact, know her face, as well.

"Oh, my God." He felt winded, as if someone had kicked all the air out of his lungs. "Corinne?"

"It *is* you," she whispered. "I never thought I'd see you again."

Her face crumpled, and then she was sobbing. She ran to him, throwing her thin arms around his waist and weeping hard into his chest.

He held her, unsure what to do.

Unsure what to even think.

"You were dead," he murmured. "You vanished without

a trace, and then they pulled your body from the river. I saw it. You were *dead*, Corinne."

"No." She vigorously shook her head, still sobbing, her small body heaving with soul-racking gasps. "They took me away."

Fury flared in him, burning through the shock and disbelief. "Who took you?"

She hiccuped, drawing in a shaky breath. "I don't know. They took me away and they kept me prisoner all this time. They did . . . things to me. They did horrible things, Brock."

She buried herself in his embrace, clinging to him like she never wanted to let go. Brock held her, struck stupid by all he was hearing.

He didn't know what to tell her. He had no idea how what she was saying could possibly be true.

But it was.

She was alive.

After many long years—decade after decade of blaming himself for her death—Corinne was suddenly living and breathing, wrapped in his arms.

Jenna climbed the cellar stairs behind the last of the captives. She could hardly believe it was over, that she and Renata, Dylan, and Alex had actually located the women and managed to set them free.

Her heart was still pounding hard in her chest, her pulse still racing with adrenaline and a profound sense of accomplishment—of relief, that the ordeal for these nearly twenty helpless women was finally ended. She guided her last charge around the slain Minions in the parlor and led her outside to the veranda. Dusk was gathering now, washing over the crowded yard in placid shades of blue.

Jenna breathed in the crisp, twilight air as she stepped onto the porch behind the shuffling Breedmate. She glanced over toward the driveway, where Renata and Niko were helping some of the females into the Rover. Rio and Dylan, Kade and Alex were busy on the snowy front lawn, walking still more released women into another of the Order's SUVs.

But it was the sight of Brock that made her freeze in place where she stood.

Her feet simply stopped moving, her heart cracking open as she saw him locked in a tender embrace with a petite, dark-haired female.

Jenna didn't need to see her face to know that it would match the sketch Claire had provided. Or that the fragile beauty wrapped so gently in Brock's strong arms was the same young woman in the photograph he'd kept with him all the years after he'd thought her dead.

Corinne.

By some miracle of fate, Brock's past love had been returned to him. Jenna choked back her bittersweet sob, realizing that he'd just been granted the impossible: the gift of love resurrected.

As much as it tore at her own heart to witness it, she couldn't help but be moved by their tender reunion.

And she couldn't bear to interrupt it, no matter how desperately she yearned to be the one in his sheltering arms at that moment.

Steeling herself, she took a quiet step off the porch and headed past them to continue the evacuation of the other freed captives.

CHAPTER
Thirty-two

Brock glanced up and saw Jenna walking away from him, toward the ongoing activity in the driveway.

She was safe.

Thank God.

His heart leapt in his chest, jolting with such relief to see her, he thought it might burst out of his rib cage.

"Jenna!"

She pivoted slowly toward him and the relief he'd felt a moment ago drained into his heels. Her face was stricken and pale. The front of her coat was torn in places and stained a garish, deep scarlet.

"Oh, Jesus." He broke away from Corinne and raced over to where Jenna had now paused. Grabbing her by the shoulders, he took her in from head to toe, his Breed senses overwhelmed at the presence of so much coppery spilled blood. "Ah, Christ...Jenna, what happened to you?"

Her face pinched a bit as she shook her head and drew away from him. "I'm okay. The blood isn't mine. One of the Minions came at me in the cellar. I shot him."

Brock hissed, racked with worry even though she was standing in front of him now, assuring him that she wasn't harmed. "When I heard something had gone wrong here—" His voice choked off on a dark curse. "Jenna, I was so damned scared that you might be hurt."

She shook her head, her hazel eyes seeming sad but steady. "I'm fine."

"And Corinne," he blurted, glancing across the way to where she still stood, looking small and forlorn, a dim shadow of the vibrant girl who'd vanished from Detroit all those decades ago. "She's alive, Jenna. She was being held here with the others."

Jenna nodded. "I know."

"You do?" He stared at her, confused now.

"One of the new sketches Claire Reichen had provided," she explained. "I only saw it as we arrived here, but I recognized Corinne's face from the picture you have of her back in your quarters."

"I can't believe it," he murmured, still stunned as hell by all he'd just heard. "She told me someone took her that night. She doesn't know who. I have no idea whose body I saw, or why it was staged to look like hers. My God... I'm not sure what to think about the whole thing now."

Jenna listened to him ramble on, her expression patient and understanding. Far calmer than he was. True to form, she stayed in rock-steady control, the cool professional, even though she'd just been through a hell of an ordeal herself.

Emotion swamped him, his respect for her immeasurable in that moment.

As was his love for her.

"Do you realize what you've accomplished here?" he asked her, reaching out to smooth his fingers along her blood-splattered cheek. "My God, Jenna. I couldn't be more proud of you."

He kissed her and pulled her against him, ready to tell her right there and then how grateful he was to have her in his life. He wanted to shout his love for her, but the depth of his feelings had devoured his voice.

Then all too soon, Jenna withdrew from his arms, both of them alerted to the sound of footsteps approaching from nearby. Brock turned to face Nikolai and Renata. Dylan walked past them to retrieve Corinne and gently led her to the open passenger-side door of the Rover in the driveway.

Niko awkwardly cleared his throat. "Sorry to interrupt, man, but we need to get moving. The Rover is almost full, and Rio's called the compound for a couple more vehicles to pick up the rest of the females. Chase and Hunter are already en route with additional transport."

Brock nodded. "They're going to need shelter somewhere."

"Andreas and Claire have offered to open their house in Newport for all of the captives," Renata replied. "Rio's going to drive the other SUV down there now."

"Right," Niko added. "Kade and I will stay here with Renata and Alex to clean up the scene and wait for Chase and Hunter to arrive with an extra vehicle for the remaining women and one for our return to the compound."

"We need someone to drive the Rover to Newport," Renata said.

Brock was ready to volunteer, but he could hardly stand the thought of being taken away from Jenna, even for a few hours to make the run.

Torn, he glanced at her.

"Go on," she said softly.

He wanted to drag her into his arms and never let her go again. "Will you be all right until I get back?"

"Yes. I'm going to be fine, Brock." Her smile was somehow sorrowful. Her hands trembled as she reached out to take light hold of his. She kissed him, a fleeting graze of her lips across his. "You don't have to worry about me now. Do what you need to do."

"We have to get rolling," Niko pressed. "This place needs to be cleared before any curious humans start sniffing around."

Brock reluctantly agreed, stepping back from Jenna. She gave him a faint nod as he drew away another step.

He turned and strode toward the waiting Rover. As he got behind the wheel and started backing out to follow Rio in the other vehicle, part of him couldn't help feeling as though the chaste kiss Jenna had given him was something more than good-bye.

It took Jenna and the others better than an hour to dispatch the dead Minions and clear the big old house of all traces of the battle that had occurred there. Hunter and Chase had since come and gone with the last of the rescued captives, leaving one of the Order's SUVs for the cleanup team to drive back to the compound.

Jenna had worked in heavy silence, feeling tired and

exhausted—emotionally drained—as she helped Alex roll up one of the bloodstained rugs and carry it out to the back of the Order's vehicle.

She couldn't stop thinking about Brock. Couldn't stop dreading that she'd made a terrible mistake in letting him go to Newport with Corinne.

She wanted desperately to call him and urge him to come back.

But as much as she wanted to claim him for herself, she couldn't be that unfair to him.

He had been granted a miracle tonight, and she would never dream of trying to take that away from him.

How often had she prayed for a second chance with Mitch and Libby after she'd lost them? How often had she wished their deaths had just been a cosmic mistake that could somehow be righted? How many times had she hoped beyond all hope for some impossible twist of fate that would bring back the love she'd lost?

She wondered now if she would still be able to make those prayers and wishes. She knew she couldn't. To do so would be to negate all she felt for Brock, something that seemed even more impossible to her than a miraculous reversal of death.

But at the same time, she couldn't ask Brock to make that kind of choice.

Even if it shattered her heart to let him go.

A wave of sadness rushed over her with the thought. She grabbed for the side of the Rover, her legs all but swept out from beneath her.

Alex was at her side in an instant. "Jen, are you okay?"

She nodded weakly, feeling suddenly more than empty inside. Her head spun, vision beginning to blur.

"Jenna?" Alex moved in front of her and sucked in a sharp breath. "Oh, my God. Jenna, you're wounded."

Dazed, she glanced down to where Alex was now unfastening her bloodstained coat. As the thick wool parted, she saw the terrible truth of what had her friend's face turning white as a sheet.

Jenna's mind flashed back to the Minion who'd crashed into her from out of the shadows in the cellar. She recalled the glint of something metallic in his hand. A knife, she guessed now, staring at the slick red blood that soaked her shirt and ran all the way down the side of her leg, dripping a dark pool in the snow beneath her feet.

"Kade, hurry!" Alex shouted, panic climbing into her voice. "Renata, Niko—somebody, please. Jenna's been hurt!"

As the others rushed out of the house in response, Jenna's world began to fade around her. She heard her friends speaking anxiously around her, but she couldn't keep her eyes open. Couldn't keep her legs from crumpling beneath her.

She let go of the vehicle and the heavy darkness pulled her under.

CHAPTER
Thirty-three

Andreas and Claire Reichen's house in Newport was a hive of anxious activity as the rescued Breedmates arrived that evening and began to settle into the large estate on Narragansett Bay. Brock and Rio had been the first to get there. Hunter and Chase had arrived moments ago with the rest of the former captives and were in the process of bringing them inside.

"Unbelievable," Reichen said, standing with Brock in the second-floor hallway of the seaside mansion. The German vampire and his New England–born Breedmate had been living in the house for only a few months, the newly mated couple having relocated to the States after surviving their own ordeal at the hands of Dragos and his dangerous allies. "Claire's been haunted all this time by what she glimpsed during her dreamwalk through Dragos's laboratory, but to actually see these women now, alive and out of danger after all this time...Christ, it's overwhelming."

Brock nodded, still in disbelief himself. "It was good of you and Claire to take them in."

"We wouldn't have it any other way."

Both males turned as Claire came out of a bedroom carrying an armload of folded towels. Petite and beautiful, the dark-haired female had a glow about her as she strode into the hallway and met the approving gaze of her mate.

"I've been praying this day would come for a long time," she said, her deep brown eyes shifting from Reichen to Brock. "I almost didn't dare hope that we might actually succeed."

"The work you and the rest of the Order's women have done is beyond admirable," he replied, certain that he would never forget the image of Jenna and the others guiding the freed captives out of the cheery-looking house that had been their most recent prison.

God, Jenna, he thought. She'd been on his mind the entire time. The only place he wanted to be right now was with her—to feel her safe and warm in his arms.

She'd been the reason he'd driven in silence from Gloucester to Rhode Island, tormented by the fact that Corinne had been dozing in the passenger seat beside him—impossibly alive, after so many years—yet every fiber of his being felt pulled inextricably back toward Boston.

Back to Jenna.

But he couldn't just walk away from Corinne. He owed

her more than that. Because of him, because of his carelessness in protecting her, she'd been yanked away from everything she knew, forced to endure unspeakable torture at Dragos's hands. Because of him, her life had been shattered.

How could he simply ignore all of that and go back to the happiness he'd found with Jenna?

As if conjured by the weight of his dark thoughts alone, he felt Corinne's presence behind him.

Reichen and Claire said nothing as they both glanced past him, then turned to walk away together, leaving him alone to face the ghost of his past failures.

She was bathed and dressed in clean clothing. But God, she was still so small and fragile. The long-sleeved fleece top and yoga pants hung loosely off her tiny frame. Her cheeks were pale and gaunt. Dark circles rose beneath her once-sparkling, almond-shaped eyes.

With her raven hair pulled back in a long ponytail, he could see that she had aged since he'd last seen her at eighteen. Although the passage of years would put her in her nineties now, Corinne looked closer to thirty. Only the regular ingestion of Breed blood would have preserved her youth, and Brock was appalled to imagine the circumstances of how those feedings might have occurred while she was in Dragos's terrible labs.

"Jesus, Corinne," he murmured, moving toward her when she remained frozen and silent a few feet away from him in the upstairs hall. "I don't even know where to begin."

Small nicks and scars blemished the face that had been so flawless in his memory. Her eyes were still exotic, still bold enough that they didn't flinch—not even under his stricken scrutiny—but there was an edge to her gaze now.

Gone was the playful imp, the sweet innocent. In her place stood a quiet, calculating survivor.

He reached out to touch her, but she backed away with a small shake of her head. He let his hand drop, fist hanging at his side. "Ah, Christ, Corinne. Can you ever forgive me?"

Her slim brows knitted slightly. "No . . ."

Her softly voiced denial blasted him deeply. He deserved it, he knew, and he could hardly say a word in his own defense. He'd failed her. Perhaps more than if she had died all those years ago. Death would have been better than what she'd likely endured while imprisoned by a sick bastard like Dragos.

"I am sorry," he murmured, determined to get the words out even though she was mutely shaking her head, her frown deepening. "I know my apology doesn't mean anything now. It doesn't change a damned thing for you, Corinne . . . but I want you to know that a day hasn't gone by that I didn't think about you and wish that I had been there. I wish I could have traded places with you, my life instead of yours—"

"No," she said, her voice stronger than before. "No, Brock. Is that what you thought? That I blamed you for what happened to me?"

He stared, astounded by the lack of anger in her eyes. "You have every right to blame me. I was supposed to protect you."

Her dark gaze went a little sad now. "You did. No matter how impossible I was, you always kept me safe."

"Not that night," he reminded her grimly.

"That night, I don't know what happened," she murmured. "I don't know who took me, but there was nothing you could do, Brock. You were never to blame. I never wanted you to think that."

"I looked everywhere for you, Corinne. For weeks, months...years after they pulled the body from the river—your body, I thought—I kept looking for you." He sucked in a sharp breath. "I never should have let you out of my sight that night, not even for a second. I failed—"

"No," she said, shaking her head slowly, her face devoid of any recrimination, utterly forgiving. "You never failed me. You sent me back inside the club that night because you thought I would be safer there. How could you have known I would be taken? You always did everything right for me, Brock."

He shook his head, astonished by her absolution, humbled by the resolve in her voice. She didn't blame him, and some of the leaden guilt he'd been carrying for so long simply broke away.

In the wash of relief that poured over him, he thought of Jenna, and the life he wanted to begin with her.

"You are involved with someone," Corinne said, studying him in his silence. "The woman who helped save all of us today."

He nodded, pride swelling inside him despite the dull ache of regret that still held him when he looked at the young girl—now the frail, serious woman—that Corinne had become during her years of imprisonment with Dragos.

"You're in love?" she asked.

He couldn't deny it, not even for her. "Yeah, I am. Her name is Jenna."

Corinne smiled sadly. "She's a lucky woman. I am pleased that you're happy, Brock."

Overwhelmed with gratitude and hope, he couldn't

help himself from reaching out to Corinne and pulling her into a tight embrace. She was stiff in his arms at first, her small body flinching as if the contact startled her. But then she loosened slightly, her hands coming to rest lightly on his back.

He let go after a moment and drew away from her. "What about you? Will you be all right, Corinne?"

She gave him a weak smile as she lifted one frail shoulder. "All I need now is to go home." Something empty and raw, something that seemed to bleed inside her like an open wound, shadowed her gaze. "All I need now is to be with my family."

Dragos's lieutenant trembled as he broke the day's bad news.

All of the females Dragos had collected over the past several decades for his private laboratory—the ones who'd survived his prolonged experimentations and breeding requirements, that is—had been discovered and released by the Order.

Even worse, it had been the Order's women, not Lucan or his warriors, who made the discovery earlier that day. The Minion nun who'd served him, first as a shelter worker who had assisted him in locating Breedmates for his cause, then, more recently, as the warden of his little prison by the sea, had failed to protect his interests. The useless cow was dead, but not before she'd cost him the roughly twenty females in her care.

And now the Order had managed to chip away at another brick in the bedrock of his operation.

First, they took his autonomy, ending his years of unchecked power as a director within the Enforcement

Agency. Then they took his secret lab, raiding his headquarters and forcing him to ground. Next, they killed the
Ancient, although Dragos likely would have put the creature down sooner than later himself.

And now this.

Standing just inside the vestibule of Dragos's hotel
suite in Boston, his lieutenant fidgeted with his hat, wringing it in front of him like a wet rag. "I don't know how
they managed to find the captives' location, sire. Perhaps
they'd been watching the house for some reason. Perhaps
it was pure luck that brought them there and they—"

Dragos's furious roar silenced the prattle instantly. He
vaulted off the silk sofa, his arm sweeping out in front of
him to lash out at a crystal vase of orchids that sat on a
delicate pedestal nearby. The piece exploded against the
wall and shattered, spraying glass and water and bits of
flowers in all directions.

His lieutenant gasped in fright and leapt backward,
hitting his spine against the closed door. His eyes were
nearly popping out of his head, his face stricken with ball-
shriveling fear. His expression turned even more dread-
filled as Dragos bore down on him, seething with rage.

In those terrified, widening eyes, he saw his lieutenant's
remembrance of a threat Dragos had made in this very
hotel room just a week before.

"Sire, please," he whispered. "The Minion failed you
today, not me. I am only responsible for the message, not
the mistake."

Dragos didn't care about any of that. His anger was
too far gone to be reined in now. With an animal war cry
meant more for Lucan and his warriors than the insignifi-
cant pawn who stood quivering before him now, he reeled
his fist back and punched it hard into the vampire's chest.

He smashed through clothing, skin, and bone like a hammer and plucked out the frantically beating organ caged inside.

The dead lieutenant collapsed at his feet. Dragos glanced down at him, his closed fist blood-soaked and raining a scarlet cascade onto the corpse and the white carpet around it.

Dragos tossed the vampire's heart like so much trash, then tipped his head back and bellowed, his fury vibrating the air around him like a roll of thunder.

"Dispose of this rubbish," he snarled to the pair of assassins who looked on in silence from the other side of the hotel suite.

He stalked into the bathroom to scrub the offending gore from his hands, calming himself with the knowledge that although the Order had managed to deliver yet another strike against him today, he still had the upper hand. A pity they didn't realize it yet.

Very soon, they would.

He had the Order squarely in his sights now.

And he was more than ready to pull the trigger.

CHAPTER
Thirty-four

When Jenna woke up, she was staring at the ceiling of the compound infirmary. She blinked slowly, waiting to feel the searing pain of the knife wound in her side. Instead, she felt a warm touch skating tenderly along her arm.

"Hey" came the deep, velvet voice that she'd been hearing in her sleep. "I've been waiting for you to open those pretty eyes."

Brock.

She turned her head on the pillow and was struck to see him seated next to her by the bed. He looked so handsome, so caring and strong. His dark brown gaze drank her in, his sensual mouth curving with just the barest traces of a smile.

"They called me in Newport and told me about your injury," he said, then exhaled a soft curse. "I saw the blood on you outside the Minion's house, but I didn't know it was yours, Jenna. I couldn't get back here fast enough to make sure you were okay."

She smiled up at him, her heart soaring to be near him again, even while she was afraid to be happy, uncertain whether or not he'd returned only to help her heal.

"How are you feeling, Jenna?"

"Okay," she replied, and realized just then that she actually felt very good physically. She sat up a bit and moved aside the sheet and blanket that covered her. The ugly gash that should have been below her rib cage was nothing more than a small scab, the wound that had been bleeding so profusely now all but gone. "How long have I been out?"

"A few hours." Brock's expression softened as he looked at her. "You've surprised us all, particularly Gideon. He's still trying to figure out what's going on with your physiology, but it appears your body is learning to heal itself. Adaptive regeneration, I think he called it. He says he wants to run more tests, try to determine if the regeneration might also impact the aging of your cells over time. He seems to think there's a decent chance that's going to be the case."

Jenna shook her head, astonished. Also wryly amused. "You know, I'm starting to think it might be kind of fun being a cyborg."

"It doesn't matter to me what you are," he replied soberly. "I'm just glad to see you're doing well."

In the silence that stretched out between them, Jenna

fidgeted with the edge of the sheet. "How are the other women—the Breedmates we rescued?"

"They're all settling in at Reichen's place. Gonna be a long road for a lot of them, but they're alive and Dragos can't touch them ever again."

"That's good," she replied quietly. "And Corinne?"

Brock's face grew solemn. "She's been through hell and back. She wants to go home to her family in Detroit. She says there are things she needs to take care of back there, in her past, before she can think about her future."

"Oh," Jenna said.

She understood how Corinne felt. She'd been thinking about her own past a lot, as well, and about the things she'd left unfinished back in Alaska. Things she had been too cowardly to face before but now felt ready to confront as soon as she was able.

Since the rescue today, she'd been thinking about her future, too. It was impossible to picture without Brock in the equation, especially now that she was looking up into his handsome face, feeling the warmth and comfort of his dark gaze and his gentle touch.

"Corinne has asked me to take her back home," he said, words that tore at her heart.

She bit back the selfish reply that might have implored him not to go. Instead she nodded, then blurted out the things she knew he'd need to hear.

Things that would relieve him of any guilt about what they'd shared together or the tender promises he'd made her in the time before he knew his past love would be delivered back into his arms.

"Brock, I want to thank you for helping me the way you have. You've saved my life—more than once—and you've been the kindest, most tender and giving man I've ever known."

He frowned, parting his lips as if to say something, but she talked over him.

"I want you to know that I'm grateful for the friendship you've given me. Most of all, I'm grateful for the way you've shown me that I can be happy again. I didn't think I ever would be, not really. And I never thought I'd be able to fall in love again—"

"Jenna," he said, his voice stern, his dark scowl deepening.

"I know you have to go with Corinne. I know I can't give you any of the things that she can, as a Breedmate. We could never have children, or a blood bond. There's a good chance we won't have anything close to the time you'll be able to share with her." He shook his head, muttered a low curse, but she couldn't stop until she'd said it all. "I want you to go with her. I want you to have your second chance—"

"Stop talking, Jenna."

"I want you to be happy," she said, ignoring his quiet demand. "I want you to have everything you deserve in a mate, even if that means without me."

He finally silenced her with a hard kiss, putting his hand on the back of her neck and bringing her up against him. He drew back, holding her gaze in a passionate, possessive stare.

"Stop telling me what I need to do." He kissed her again, softer now, his mouth covering hers, tongue demanding entrance. She felt his need, and the emotion that seemed to say he never wanted to let her go. When he finally released her, his dark eyes were glittering with amber sparks. "For one damned second, Jenna, let someone else be in charge."

She stared at him, hardly daring to hope she knew where he was heading.

"I'm in love with you," he whispered fiercely. "I love you, and I could give a damn if you're human, cyborg, alien, or some mixed-up combination of all three. I love you, Jenna. I want you to be mine. You *are* mine, damn it. Whether we only have a handful of decades together or something closer to forever. You are mine, Jenna."

She sucked in a ragged breath, overcome with joy and relief. "Oh, Brock. I love you so much. I thought I'd lost you today."

"Never," he said, staring deeply into her eyes. "You and me, we're partners. Partners in everything now. I'm always gonna have your back, Jenna."

She laughed around a sob, and gave him a shaky nod. "You'll always have my heart."

"Always," he said, then pulled her into his arms for a deep, never-ending kiss.

Epilogue

Jenna's boots crunched in the moonlit snow as she stepped onto a patch of pristine, hallowed ground just outside the tiny village of Harmony, Alaska.

It had been a couple of days since she'd awakened in the compound infirmary, fully healed from the stab wound she'd received during the rescue of the captive Breedmates.

Only a couple of days since she and Brock had promised to spend their future together as lovers, mates ... partners.

"Are you sure you're ready to do this?" he asked her, wrapping his strong arm around her shoulders.

She knew he hated the cold of this place, yet he'd been the one to suggest the trip north. He'd been patient and understanding, and she knew he would stand out here with her forever if he thought she needed the extra time. His breath steamed in the frigid night air, his handsome face solemn, yet reassuring within the deep hood of his parka.

"I'm ready," she said, turning a misty glance onto the small cemetery that stretched out sleepily before her. Twining her gloved fingers through his, she walked with him toward the far corner of the plot, to where a pair of tall granite markers stood side by side in their thick blanket of snow.

She'd been prepared for the wave of emotion that swamped her as she and Brock approached Mitch and Libby's graves for the first time, but it still took her breath away. Her heart clenched, her throat constricted, and for a moment, she wasn't sure that she'd have the strength to see this through, after all.

"I'm scared," she whispered.

Brock squeezed her hand, his deep voice gentle. "You can do it. I'm gonna be right here next to you the whole time."

She looked up into his steady, dark eyes, feeling his love enfold her, lending her his strength. She nodded, then continued walking, her wet gaze rooted on the etched lettering that made everything seem so irrefutable.

So very raw and real.

The tears started falling the moment she stepped onto the ground in front of the headstones. She let go of Brock's hand and moved closer, knowing she had to make it through this part on her own.

"Hi, Mitch," she murmured quietly, kneeling down into the snow. She placed one of the two red roses she'd brought with her at the base of his marker. The other one—fastened with a pink ribbon to a small, stuffed teddy bear—she laid carefully near the smaller gravestone. "Hello, sweetpea."

For a long moment, she remained there, listening to the wind as it blew through the boreal pines, her eyes closed on her tears as she remembered happy times with her husband and daughter.

"Oh, God," she whispered, choked with emotion. "I'm so sorry. I miss you both so much."

She couldn't hold back the pain. It poured out of her in great, ugly sobs—all the pent-up anguish and guilt that she'd been holding locked inside her since the night of the accident.

She'd never been able to feel this purge before. She'd been too afraid. Too angry with herself to give into the grief and finally let it go.

But she couldn't stop it now. She felt Brock's steady presence behind her—her lifeline, her safe haven in the midst of the storm. She felt stronger now, safe.

She felt loved.

Even more miraculous to her, she felt worthy of being loved.

With a few more murmured words of good-bye, she touched each of the gravestones, then slowly rose to her feet.

Brock was right there, his open arms waiting to catch her in a tender embrace. His kiss was sweet and soothing. He looked down into her eyes, his fingers light and gentle as he swept away her tears. "Are you all right?"

She nodded, feeling lighter despite the lump that still rose in her throat. She felt ready to begin a new chapter in her life. Ready to start her future with the extraordinary

Breed male she loved with all the mending pieces of her heart.

Gazing into Brock's warm eyes, she reached out for him, slipping her hand into his. "I'm ready to go home now."

Thirsty for more?

Don't miss the next novel in Lara's
hot and thrilling
Midnight Breed series

Deeper Than Midnight

BY
LARA ADRIAN

Coming soon from Dell Books

The club was private, very much off the beaten path, and for damned good reason. Located at the far end of a narrow, ice-encrusted back alley of Boston's Chinatown district, the place catered to an exclusive, if discriminating, crowd. The only humans permitted inside the old brick building were the stable of attractive young women—and a few pretty men—kept on hand to satisfy the late-night clientele's every craving.

Concealed within the shadows of an arched vestibule at street level, the unmarked metal door gave no indication of what lay behind it, not that any local or tourist in their right mind would pause to wonder. The thick slab of steel was shielded by a tall iron grate. Outside the entrance, a big guard loomed like a gargoyle in a knit skullcap and black leather.

The male was Breed, as were the pair of warriors who emerged from the gloom of the alleyway. At the sound of their combat boots crunching in the snow and frozen filth of the pavement, the guard on watch lifted his head. Under a thick, bulbous nose, thin lips curled away from crooked teeth and the sharp tips of the vampire's fangs. Eyes narrowed at the uninvited newcomers, he exhaled a low snarl, his warm breath steaming from his nostrils to plume into the brittle December night air.

Hunter registered a current of tension in his patrol partner's movements as the two of them approached the vampire on guard. Sterling Chase had been twitchy ever since they'd left the Order's compound for tonight's mission. Now, he walked at an aggressive pace, taking the lead, his fingers flexing and contracting where they rested none-too-subtly on the large-caliber semiautomatic pistol holstered on his weapons belt.

The guard took a step forward, too, putting himself directly in their path. Large thighs spread, boots planted wide in warning on the pitted pavement as the vampire's big head lowered. The eyes that had been narrowed on them before in question now went tighter with recognition as they hit and settled on Chase. "You gotta be kidding me. What the hell do you want out here on Enforcement Agency turf, *warrior?*"

"Taggart," Chase said, more growl than greeting, "I see your career has been in no danger of improving since I quit the Agency. Reduced to playing doorman for the local sip-and-strip, eh? What's next for you—security detail at the shopping mall?"

The agent pursed his lips around a ripe curse. "Takes

some kind of balls to show your face, especially around here."

Chase's answering chuckle was neither threatened nor amused. "Try looking in a mirror sometime, then let's talk about who's got balls showing his face in public."

"This place belongs to the Enforcement Agency," the guard said, crossing beefy arms over a barrel chest. A barrel chest sporting the broad leather strap of a weapons holster, with still more hardware bristling around his waist. "The Order's got no business here."

"Yeah?" Chase grunted. "Tell that to Lucan Thorne. He's the one who will have your ass if you don't move it out of our way. Assuming the two of us standing here cooling our heels for no good reason don't decide to remove you ourselves."

Agent Taggart's mouth had clamped shut at the mention of Lucan, the Order's leader and one of the longest-lived, most formidable elders of the Breed nation. Now, the wary gaze strayed from Chase to Hunter, who lingered behind his fellow warrior in measured silence. Hunter had no quarrel with Taggart, but he had already calculated no less than five different ways to disable him—to kill him swiftly and surely, right where he stood—should the need arise.

It was what Hunter had been trained to do. Born and bred to be a weapon wielded by the merciless hand of the Order's chief adversary, he was long accustomed to viewing the world in logical, unemotional terms.

He no longer served the villain called Dragos, but his deadly skills remained at the core of who, and what, he was. Hunter was lethal—unfailingly so—and in that instantaneous connection of his gaze and Taggart's, he saw that grim understanding reflected in the other male's eyes.

Agent Taggart blinked, then took a step back, removing himself from Hunter's stare and clearing the path to the door of the club.

"I thought you might be willing to reconsider," Chase said, as he and Hunter strode to the iron grate and entered the Enforcement Agency establishment.

The door must have been soundproof. Inside the dark club, loud music thumped in time with multicolored, spinning lights that lit a central stage made of mirrored glass. The only dancers were a trio of half-naked humans gyrating together in front of an audience of leering, hot-eyed vampires seated in booths and tables on the floor below the stage.

Hunter watched the long-haired blond in the center wind herself around a metal pole that climbed up from the floor of the stage to the ceiling. Swiveling her hips, she lifted one of her enormous, unnaturally round breasts up to meet her snakelike tongue. As she toyed with the pierced nipple, the other dancers, a tattooed woman with spiked purple hair and a dark-eyed young man who barely fit inside the shiny red vinyl pouch slung around his hips, moved to opposite sides of the mirrored stage and began their own solo routines.

The club reeked of stale perfume and sweat, but the musty tang couldn't mask the trace scent of fresh human blood. Hunter followed the olfactory trail with his gaze. It led to a far corner booth, where a vampire in the standard-issue Enforcement Agency dark suit and white shirt fed judiciously from the pale throat of a naked, moaning woman sprawled across his lap. Still more Breed males drank from other human blood Hosts, while some in the vampire-run establishment seemed intent on satisfying more carnal needs.

Beside him near the door, Chase had gone as still as stone. A low, rumbling growl leaked from the back of his throat. Hunter spared the feeding and on-stage spectacle inside the place little more than an assessing glance, but Chase's gaze was fixed and hungry, as openly riveted as any of the other Breed males gathered there. Perhaps more so.

Hunter was far more interested in the handful of heads that were now turning their way within the crowd of Enforcement Agents. Their arrival had been noticed, and the simmering looks from every pair of eyes that landed on them now said the situation could get ugly very quickly.

No sooner had he registered the possibility than one of the glaring vampires reclining on a nearby sofa got up to confront them. The male was large, as were his two companions who rose to join him as he cut a clean path through the crowd. All three were visibly armed beneath their finely cut, dark suits.

"Well, well. Look what the cat dragged in," drawled the agent in the lead, a trace of the South in his slowly measured words and in his refined, almost delicate, features. "How many decades of service with the Agency, yet you never would have deigned to join any of us in a place like this."

Chase's mouth curved, barely concealing his elongated fangs. "You sound disappointed, Murdock. This shit was never my speed."

"No, you always held yourself above temptation," the vampire replied, his gaze as shrewd as his answering smile. "So careful. So rigidly disciplined, even in your appetites. But things change. People change, don't they,

Chase? If you see something you like in here, you need only say so. For old times' sake, if nothing else, hmm?"

"We've come for information about an agent named Freyne," Hunter interjected when Chase's reply seemed to take longer than necessary. "As soon as we have what we need, we'll leave."

"Is that so?" Murdock considered him with a curious tilt of his head. Hunter saw the vampire's gaze drift subtly away from his face to note the *dermaglyphs* that tracked up the sides of his neck and around his nape. It took only a moment for the male to discern that Hunter's elaborate pattern of skin markings indicated he was Gen One, a rarity among the Breed.

Hunter was nothing close to the ages of his fellow Gen One warriors, Lucan or Tegan, however, sired by one of the race's Ancients, his blood was every bit as pure. Like his Gen One brethren, his strength and power was roughly that of ten later-generation vampires. It was his rearing as one of Dragos's personal army of assassins—a secret upbringing known by the Order alone—that made him far more lethal than Murdock and these couple dozen agents in the club combined.

Chase seemed to snap out of his distraction at last. "What can you tell us about Freyne?"

Murdock shrugged. "He's dead. But then, I expect you already know that. Freyne and his unit were all killed last week while on a mission to retrieve a kidnapped Dark-haven youth." He gave a slow shake of his head. "Quite the pity. Not only did the Agency lose several good men, but their mission objective proved less than satisfactory as well."

"Less than satisfactory," Chase scoffed. "Yeah, you

could say that. From what the Order understands, the mission to rescue Kellan Archer was fucked six ways from Sunday. The boy, his father, and grandfather—hell, the entire goddamned Archer family—all of them wiped out in a single night."

Hunter said nothing, letting Chase bait the hook how he saw fit. Most of what he charged was true. The night of the rescue attempt had been a blood-soaked one that had ended with too much death, the worst of it being dealt to the members of Kellan Archer's family.

But contrary to Chase's assertion, there had been survivors. Two, to be exact. Both of them had been secreted away from the carnage of that night and were now safe in the protective custody of the Order at their private compound.

"I won't disagree that things could have ended better, for both the Agency and the civilians who lost their lives as well. Mistakes, although regrettable, do happen. Unfortunately, we may never be certain where to place the blame for last week's tragedy."

Chase chuckled under his breath. "Don't be so sure. I know you and Freyne went way back. Hell, I know half the men in this club traded favors with him on a regular basis. Freyne was an asshole, but he knew how to recognize opportunity when he saw it. His biggest problem was his mouth. If he was mixed up in something that can be tied back to the kidnapping of Kellan Archer or the attack that left the Archer's Darkhaven in rubble—and just for argument's sake, let's say I'm goddamned sure Freyne was involved—then the odds are good he told someone about it. I'm willing to bet he bragged to at least one loser sitting in this shithole of a club."

Murdock's expression had been tightening with every second that Chase spoke, his eyes beginning to transform in fury, dark irises sparking with amber light for every decibel that Chase's voice rose into the crowd.

Now half the room had paused to stare in their direction. Several males got up from their seats, human blood Hosts and half-drugged lap dancers pushed roughly aside as a growing horde of offended agents began to converge on Chase and Hunter.

Chase didn't wait for the mob to attack.

With a raw snarl, he leapt into the knot of vampires, nothing but a flash of swinging fists and gnashing teeth and fangs.

Hunter had no choice but to join the fray. He waded into the violent throng, his sole focus on his partner and the intent to pull him out of this in one piece. He threw off every comer with hardly any effort, disturbed by the feral way Chase was fighting. His face was drawn taut and wild as he landed blow after blow on the crush of bodies pressing in on him from all sides. His fangs were huge, filling his mouth. His eyes burned like coals in his skull.

"Chase!" Hunter shouted, cursing as a fountain of Breed blood shot airborne—his patrol partner's or another male's, he couldn't be sure.

Nor did he have much chance to figure it out.

A blur of movement on the other side of the club caught Hunter's eye. He swung his gaze toward it and found Murdock staring back at him, a cell phone pressed to his ear.

An unmistakable panic bled into his features as their gazes locked over the brawling crowd. His guilt was obvious now, written in the whitening tension around his mouth and in the beads of perspiration that sprang up on his brow to glisten in the swirling lights of the empty stage. The agent spoke swiftly into his phone now, his feet carrying him in an anxious rush toward the back of the place.

In the fraction of a second it took for Hunter to toss aside a charging agent, Murdock had vanished from sight.

"Son of a bitch." Hunter vaulted past the fracas, forced to abandon Chase to pursue what he knew to be the very lead they'd been hoping to find tonight.

He broke into a run, relying on his Gen One speed to carry him into the back of the club and through a door that was still ajar, swinging onto the narrow brick corridor where Murdock had fled. There was no sign of him either left or right in the alleyway, but the sharp echo of running footsteps on an adjacent side street carried on the frigid breeze.

Hunter took off after him, rounding the corner just as a big black sedan screeched to a halt at the curb. The back door was thrown open from the inside. Murdock jumped in, slammed it tight behind him as the car's engine roared to life once more.

Hunter was already plowing toward it when the tires smoked on the ice and asphalt, then, with a leap of screaming metal and machinery, the vehicle swung into the street and sped off like a demon into the night.

Hunter wasted not so much as an instant. Leaping for the side of the nearest brick building, he grabbed hold of a rusted fire escape and all but catapulted himself up onto the roof. He ran, combat boots chewing up asphalt tiles as he hoofed it from one rooftop to another, keeping a visual track on the fleeing vehicle dodging late-night traffic on the street below.

When the car gunned it around a corner onto a dark bit of empty straightaway, Hunter launched himself into the air. He came down onto the roof of the sedan with a bone-jarring crash. The pain of impact registered, but for less than a moment. He held on, feeling only calm determination as the driver tried to shake him off with a side-to-side sawing motion of the wheels.

The car jerked and swerved, but Hunter stayed put. Splayed spread-eagle on the roof, the fingers of one hand digging into the top rim of the windshield, he swung his other hand down and freed his 9mm from its holster at the small of his back. The driver tried another round of zigzags on the street, narrowly missing a parked delivery truck in his attempt to shake off his unwanted passenger.

Semiauto gripped in his hand, Hunter heaved himself into a catlike flip off the roof and onto the hood of the speeding sedan. Lying flat, he took aim on the driver, finger coolly poised on the trigger, ready to blow away the bastard behind the wheel so he could get his hands on Murdock and wring the traitorous bastard of all his secrets.

The moment slowed, and there was an instant—just the barest flicker of time—when surprise took him aback.

The driver wore a thick black collar around his neck. His head was shaved bald, most of his scalp covered with a tangled network of *dermaglyphs*.

He was one of Dragos's assassins.

A Hunter, like him.

A Gen One, born and raised to kill, like him.

Hunter's surprise was swiftly eclipsed by duty. He was more than willing to eradicate the male. It had been his pledge to the Order when he joined them—his personal vow to wipe out every last one of Dragos's homegrown killing machines.

Before Dragos had the chance to unleash the full measure of his evil on the world.

The tendons in Hunter''s finger contracted in the split-second it took for him to realign the business end of his Beretta with the center of the assassin's forehead. He started to squeeze the trigger, then felt the car clamp up tight beneath him as the driver drove the brake pedal into the floor.

Rubber and metal smoking in protest, the sedan stopped short.

Hunter's body kept moving, sailing through the air and landing several hundred feet ahead on the cold pavement. He rolled out of the tumble and was on his feet like nothing happened, pistol raised and firing round after round into the unmoving car.

He saw Murdock slide out of the backseat and dash for his escape into a shadowed back alley, but there was no time to deal with him before the Gen One was out of the car as well, the barrel of a large-caliber pistol locked and loaded, trained squarely on Hunter. They faced off, the assassin's weapon raised to kill, eyes cold with the same emotionless determination that centered Hunter in his stance on the iced-up patch of asphalt.

Bullets exploded from the two guns at the same time.

Hunter dodged out of harm's way in what felt to him like calculated slow motion. He knew his opponent would have done the same as Hunter's round sped toward him. Another hail of gunfire erupted, a rain of bullets this time as both vampires unloaded their magazines on each other. Neither of them took anything more than a superficial hit.

They were too evenly matched, trained in the same methods. They were both hard to kill, and prepared to take the fight to their final breath.

In a blur of motion and lethal intent, the pair of them ditched their empty firearms and took their battle hand-to-hand.

Hunter deflected the rapid-fire upper torso blows that the assassin led with as he roared up on him. There was a kick that might have connected with his jaw if not for a sharp tilt of his head, then another strike aimed at his groin, but diverted when Hunter grabbed the assassin's boot and twisted him into a midair spin.

The assassin regained his footing with little trouble, coming right back for more. He threw a punch and Hunter grabbed his fist, crushing bones as he tightened his grip then came around to use his body as a lever while he wrenched the outstretched arm backward at the elbow. The joint broke with a sharp crack, yet the assassin merely grunted, the only indication he gave of the certain pain he was feeling. The damaged arm hung useless at his side as he pivoted to throw another punch at Hunter's face. The blow connected, tearing the skin just above his right eye and hitting so hard, Hunter's vision filled with stars. He shook off the momentary daze, just in time to intercept a second assault—fist and foot coming at him in the same instant.

Back and forth it went, both males breathing hard from the exertion, both bleeding from various places where the other had managed to get the upper hand. Neither would ask for mercy, no matter how long or bloody their combat became.

Mercy was a concept foreign to them, the flipside of

pity. Two things that had been beaten out of their lexicon from the time they were boys.

The only thing worse than mercy or pity was failure, and as Hunter took hold of his opponent's broken arm and drove the big male down to the ground with his knee planted in the middle of the assassin's spine, he saw the acknowledgment of imminent failure flicker like a dark flame in the Gen One's cold eyes.

He had lost this battle.

He knew it, just as Hunter knew it when a clear shot at the thick black collar around the assassin's neck presented itself to him in that next instant.

Hunter reached out with his free hand to grab one of the discarded pistols from its place on the pavement. He flipped it around in his hand, wielding the metal butt like a hammer, then brought it down on the collar that ringed the assassin's neck.

Again, and harder now, a blow that put a dent in the impenetrable material that housed a diabolical device. A device crafted by Dragos and his laboratory for a single purpose: to ensure the loyalty and obedience of the deadly army he'd bred to serve him.

Hunter heard a small hum as the tampered casing triggered the coming detonation. Dragos's assassin reached up with his good hand—whether to ascertain the threat or to attempt to stop it, Hunter would never be sure.

He rolled away . . . just as the ultraviolet rays were released from within the collar.

There was a flash of searing light—there and gone in an instant—as the lethal beam severed the assassin's head in one clean motion.

As the street was plunged back into darkness, Hunter stared at the smoldering corpse of the male who had been like him in so many ways. A brother, though there was no kinship among any of the killers in Dragos's personal army.

He felt no remorse for the dead before him, only a vague sense of satisfaction that there was one less assassin to carry out Dragos's twisted schemes.

He would not rest until there were none.